Newton Neighbors

By
Suzy Duffy

TWCS
PUBLISHING HOUSE

First published by The Writer's Coffee Shop, 2013

The Writer's Coffee Shop
(Australia)   PO Box 447 Cherrybrook NSW 2126
(USA)   PO Box 2116 Waxahachie TX 75168

Paperback ISBN- 978-1-61213-163-4

E-book ISBN- 978-1-61213-164-1

A CIP catalogue record for this book is available from the US Congress Library.

Cover image and design by: © QuartSoft, Tatyana Shevchenko

www.thewriterscoffeeshop.com/sduffy

Chapter One
Sitting Pretty

"Hubba-hubba!" Rick said, making Maria smile.

She still knew how to work her charms—hands on hips, subtle breath in through parted lips to elevate bust, chin raised, head tilted. She could do it all in a microsecond but make it look natural.

Tonight she was wearing a brand new, figure hugging scarlet-red dress with a plunging neckline. "You like?" She pouted for extra effect.

Rick crossed the room in three strides. "Baby, you're still my weapon of mass seduction." His voice had dropped an octave already. Blood was on the move. *Damn.*

Maria pushed against his chest as he wrapped his arms around her, because she knew where this was going. "Ricky, I was looking for your approval, not sex. Look, Cody's downstairs, the sitter's due here any moment, and we don't have time."

"Oh, come on." He kissed her neck and nuzzled into her long, wavy hair, but she pushed him away.

"What if your son walks in?"

"We can lock the door?"

Maria tried to laugh it off, knowing it was her fault for giving him the come-on.

"No! You grab a bottle of wine for the party and I'll check on the baby." She walked away without giving him a chance to argue. Everything she had said was correct—they didn't have time for sex—but that wasn't why she'd pushed him away. The truth was she had a secret. If Ricky thought she was a weapon of mass seduction, it was because Maria had upgraded her ammunition.

It looked like a gymnast's leotard, but it was made by NASA and the ad had promised to reduce her waist by at least two inches. The fact it took fifteen minutes to squeeze into and she had no idea how long before she might asphyxiate was academic. Maria was thrilled with the result. She looked like her old self, with curves hauled back into the right position, and that was all that mattered. But there was no way she was showing it to Ricky. The plan was to wear it to the party, look amazing, and then when they got home, she would peel it off in the bathroom before he ever saw. Easy but spontaneous seductions were not part of the agenda.

Alice's room was across the hall from hers, and the door was already ajar. Maria tiptoed in her room because her little girl was a light sleeper. *Who knew two children could be so different?* she thought, admiring her perfect little girl. With her eyes closed and gorgeous little body so still, it was hard to believe she was such a fussy baby. Alice was difficult to keep happy. She seemed to be either whining or crying all the time. Maria had brought her to three different doctors, but they had each said the same thing—Alice was a healthy little ten-month-old.

Cody was ten years old now, but Maria still remembered how mellow he had been as a baby. All she had to do was look at him and he smiled. No matter what she tried with Alice, the baby cried. It had been a very tough ten months, but none of that mattered tonight. Alice was asleep, and Maria and Ricky were going out for a good night with friends.

"Maria?" Ricky called her from downstairs. Alice stirred and Maria froze.

"Shhh, honey, shhh. Don't wake up." She rested her hand on the baby's stomach to try to lull her back to sleep. "Good girl."

"Maria!" he shouted even louder. This time she ran out of the room and closed the baby's door quietly.

Maria bent over the banister rail and whisper-shouted to her husband. "Ricky, keep it down. You know Alice is asleep."

He walked to the bottom step of the stairs. "Damn. I'm sorry. Look, do you want to call the sitter? She's real late."

The dreaded sound of a baby starting to cry filled the landing.

"Now look what you've done!" Maria glared at her husband, kicked off her stilettos, and went back into Alice's room. She knew she would be pacing the nursery floor for the next hour. It was no place for three-inch heels.

Rick was annoyed with himself for shouting up the stairs and even more so that the sitter was late. What kind of first impression was that? Then the doorbell rang.

His son and the dog sprinted to answer it.

"Cody, you wanna get that?"

Rick was joking, because there was really no way to outrun the ten-year-old. Cody was going through the first-to-be-everywhere phase. To add to the chaos, the Labrador started another of her barking frenzies.

"Quiet, Orga!" Rick yelled at the dog, but it didn't do any good. He could still hear Alice wailing, and her protests were getting louder not softer. The ruckus downstairs would only unsettle her more.

Damn. He headed for the kitchen to grab a bottle of something to bring to the party. The sooner they got out the better. They needed a break.

Cody had been sulking around the house all afternoon, telling everybody who would listen that he was too old for a sitter. He claimed some of his friends didn't even have sitters anymore, but when Rick had talked it over with him, it turned out it was the ones with older sisters. Cody had eventually decided if any of his friends found out, he'd say his mom got the sitter for his little sister. Rick agreed that was a great idea.

Rick decided to bring a bottle of champagne to the party because it was a birthday celebration and it might earn him some brownie points with Maria. Then he headed back to the hall to meet the new sitter.

The first thing Rick saw was Cody smiling and the sitter laughing at something his son had said. She was gorgeous. Long blond hair, big eyes, striking features. Rick had met many sitters over the ten years of his son's life. They had been a normal mix of pretty, plain, fun, dull, but this one was a real beauty. She could have been modelling instead of watching kids.

He pushed the notion out of his mind. "Hi," he said, his voice a little too jovial. *Take it down a notch.* "I see you've met Cody already."

The dog was still barking.

"Orga, be quiet." The hound started sniffing the newcomer instead. He moved the champagne bottle to his left hand so he could shake with his right. "I'm Rick, Cody's dad."

"Hullo, I'm Jessica Armstrong." Her smile was timid, cute. "And I've met Cody and Orga."

Rick felt uncomfortable and his face was hot. Was he blushing? He wondered if that was even physically possible. Wasn't there an age limit on blushing? The last time he'd glowed this hot, he was in the fourth grade and Judi Schillawaski had—without any warning—kissed him.

This girl was more beautiful than Judi Schillawaski.

"Maria's upstairs with Alice. She just woke up." Rick winced when the baby let out another wail. "You might need to play with her for a while. Alice, I mean. You might have to play with Alice, the baby, not Maria, my wife."

Just stop talking, you idiot!

Jessica laughed. "I'm the eldest of five and love babies, so really, I'm happy to play with Alice." She glanced at Cody who was surreptitiously studying her. "And I love playing with big boys, too," she said.

Now it was Cody's turn to blush. He turned away. If it hadn't been for his own discomfort, Rick might have felt sorry for the boy. He had clearly spotted that the new sitter was a beauty. The kid was growing up.

Orga started barking again.

"Cody, will you put that damn dog out in the backyard? I'm sorry,

Jessica. She gets excited, but she'll calm down in a few minutes. It's just because you're new."

"Not a problem. Honest, I love dogs, too."

With the boy gone, they were alone, and Rick felt his body tense. What in the hell was his problem? He was usually good with meeting new people. This one was different.

"Let me show you around," he said, but the words felt awkward. Until this evening, the sitters had been little more than kids themselves. He'd never felt wrong-footed or goofy like he did now. *Get a grip*, he chastised himself, and then he gave best his corporate smile. "I'm thinking that's an English accent?"

"Yes. I'm English, from a town called Dorking, in Surrey. It's just south of London."

"Yeah? My wife, Maria, is from Puerto Rico." *Why did I say that? Act normal, you ass!* "What are you doing in Newton?"

"I'm over here for a year. Studying at Wiswall College."

"Oh, that's cool. It's just down the road."

"Yes, it is. I'm so sorry I was a little late this evening. I got lost, but I assure you, Mr. Sanchez, it won't happen again. That is, if you want me back."

"Please, call me Rick."

Jessica had enormous dark blue eyes which seemed bigger now that she looked anxious. He got the urge to reach out, but that would have been ridiculous. Inappropriate. Against the law?

He laughed louder than he meant to. "No problem about being late. We're pretty relaxed in this house. If you keep the kids content, Maria and I will be more than happy." They walked into the living room.

"Oh, an Xbox." Jessica grinned at Cody, who was back from putting the dog out. "How good are you on this thing? Because I have to warn you, I'm an ace." She winked at the ten-year-old. Cody's eyes lit up, and he lunged for the controls.

"You've just secured a place in my son's heart, Jessica. Xbox is his life. If you're as good as him, he'll never want another sitter."

She sat down next to Cody and took the other controller. Then she glanced at Rick. "Call me Jessie."

He nodded. There was a time when something like this—seeing an incredibly good-looking woman—would have fired him up. Rick would have had all the witty one-liners, all the charm he required, but time had softened him. Eleven years of marriage, two kids, and the fact he spent more time at the country club than the nightclub all meant he'd lost his edge. How could he have let that happen?

Rick watched the two of them settle onto the sofa. Seeing the gorgeous young sitter with the game controller was a reminder that he was ancient in comparison. She had more in common with Cody than with him.

Lucky kid.

Rick and Maria were heading out to yet another fortieth party, but the stunning blonde on his living room sofa made him think it would be a lot more fun to stay in than head out.

Would you get a grip? You could almost be her dad—almost.

Maria was at her wit's end. How could he have shouted up the stairs like that? Was he absolutely brain-dead? With an hour's sleep, Alice was sufficiently rested for a big-time tantrum.

She tried to soothe her back to sleep but that didn't work. So Maria scooped up her daughter and paced the floor in the darkened nursery. Alice was a strong-willed baby, however. She wouldn't stop until Maria switched on the bedroom light. For a moment it looked like that worked. Then the doorbell rang and Orga started barking, and the child knew something was going on downstairs. Alice wailed even louder, huge sobs racking her little body.

Then it happened.

Maria wasn't quick enough, and Alice off-loaded her full nighttime bottle of milk—now semi-curdled—over Maria's cleavage and new dress. The warm, wet liquid soaked through the cocktail dress and secret underwear onto her skin. It appeared even NASA technology was no protection against baby puke.

Maria called down the stairs for help, but everyone was out of earshot. Eventually she gave up, stomped back into the nursery, and peeled off both Alice's clothing and her own. She gave herself and the baby a quick wipe down with a damp cloth and then got Alice into a new pink onesie. The baby cried the entire time, and Maria wondered why her husband didn't bother to come up and help. He was always better at soothing their little girl. Maria had a dark suspicion her daughter simply preferred Ricky to her. Even Cody seemed to have a way with his little sister. Sometimes when she cried and Maria couldn't stop it, her ten-year-old boy would take over and soothe Alice with ease.

Maria was tempted to cancel the night. It was Ricky's fault. If he hadn't shouted, Alice would still be asleep. She took the little screamer into her bedroom and let the baby bawl on her bed for a minute while she wiped herself down again. Maria tried to sniff her own skin and didn't smell any baby puke, so she threw on her old black party dress, scooped up the still-screaming Alice, and headed down the stairs.

Naturally enough, as soon as Alice saw they were going down to where all the action was, she stopped crying. It was so damn frustrating. Maria prayed the new sitter would be good with babies. Stopping in the kitchen, she picked up a fresh bottle of formula and then followed the sounds of laughter into the living room. Cody was yelling death threats already, so she knew he was playing his precious Xbox, and Rick was shouting encouragement at the seventy-two-inch flat screen. The level of excitement in the room was at a fever pitch.

"Hi," Maria said as she walked in the room. Then she saw her sitter. *Wow*, she thought. In all the years she'd been hiring sitters, she'd never had such a pretty one. Maria stopped and looked at Cody sitting right beside her on the sofa and Rick hovering next to them. Her men sure seemed to like the new girl. She scowled. Was that why her husband hadn't heard her?

Jessie hit the pause button on her controller as soon as Cody jumped to the next level in his game, and then she jumped to her feet. "Hullo there," she said, but her focus was on Alice not Maria. The baby looked mildly interested as the sitter slowly approached.

"Maria, this is Jessica—Jessie—our new sitter," Rick said. "She's from England and she's the eldest of five. She likes dogs, too."

This much information annoyed her. "Didn't you hear me calling you?"

Rick looked blank. "No. It must have been when I was walking Jessie around the house. You okay? You've changed your dress."

"Alice vomited all over me."

"Poor you. How awful," Jessie said. "Do you think the baby is sick?"

Maria appreciated the sympathy but said, "No, I don't think so. She was settled for the night, but *somebody* shouted up the stairs and woke her." She glared at her husband. "Alice here was crying so hard she made herself sick. She does that sometimes."

Jessie stood next to mother and baby and stroked Alice's tiny fingers. She talked in a gentle, higher pitched voice—cooing and gurgling at the baby. It worked. Alice started to gurgle back.

"May I?" She gestured to Maria, putting her hands out to take the baby. Maria wasn't so sure.

"She's in a foul mood this evening." But even as Maria said it, she could feel Alice's body shift. The baby leaned toward Jessie, wanting to get into the new girl's arms.

Maria felt a tiny stab of jealousy but suppressed it and let the sitter take her daughter. It was a seamless handover. Alice looked highly amused by the ridiculous noises the newcomer was making.

"I think I'll let you ladies talk," Rick said and left the room.

Jessie sat beside Cody and bounced Alice gently on her lap, which gave Maria a chance to sit and really study the new girl. Her long blond hair was scooped in a loose clasp, but a few spiral tendrils had escaped and fell around her face in soft waves. Her skin was very fair, and she wore almost no makeup, perhaps just a little pink on her cheeks. Or was that natural? There was a glow to her skin—*the glow of youth*, Maria thought, starting to feel frumpy and a million years old.

Jessie spoke to Cody. "Will you help me with your little sister? You'll be able to tell me where I go to change her nappy and show me where her crib is?"

Cody dropped his remote on the sofa and began gently banging the leg of the table with his foot. Maria knew what he was doing—it was just enough to show that he was fed up but not so much that she would get mad. Her boy was obviously upset that he'd lost his Xbox partner thanks to his sister's intrusion.

"I don't know what a nappy is," he grumbled, clearly not wanting to cooperate.

"Oh, I'm sorry. I think I mean diaper," Jessie said. "Look, as soon as she's down, I'll challenge you to a rematch and we'll play for the whole night. What do you think?"

Cody glanced up at her, grinned, and then ran out of the room. Maria was impressed because she knew how hard it was to keep two children happy. Not bad for a girl who had been in the house twenty minutes—if that.

"Alice started on formula last month, so here's one." She put the bottle on the table next to them. "And there's more in the fridge if you need it, but I don't think you will."

"Would you like me to heat the bottle before I give it to her?" Jessie asked.

"No, she's used to it cold," Maria said. The girl knew a thing or two about babies, she realized. "So you have little brothers and sisters?"

Jessie nodded but continued playing with Alice. "There are four more at home—two boys and two girls, all younger than me. In fact the youngest is only eight, so he's younger than Cody. His name is Tristan."

"And you're British?"

She nodded again. "I'm studying here for a year."

"What's your major?"

"Psychology. I'm doing my master's."

"Wonderful. You can help me figure out what makes my two tick. What aspect of psychology are you doing your master's in?"

Jessie's eyes brightened. "Emotion regulation and interpersonal competence in romantic relationships."

"Oh." Maria felt awkward now. "Anything else?" She was joking, but it seemed Jessie thought she meant it.

"Well," she said, "I also have an interest in the role of the family environment on a person's emotional development."

Cody picked that precise moment to skip back into the room balancing the toaster on his head. "Mom, can Todd and I go toasting later?"

Maria glanced at the sitter. "You came to the right house if you want crazy family environments." She rolled her eyes. "Cody get that toaster off your head!" She wondered if Jessie could see through her and her happy family façade.

"What's toasting?" Jessie asked Cody.

"You don't know what toasting is?" Cody's tone was condescending. "It's ghosting but with burnt toast."

She smiled, all the time stroking Alice's little back. "Okay, you'll have to tell me what ghosting is."

"Don't tell me you don't know what ghosting is? Everybody has that." He plonked the toaster on the coffee table.

Jessie shook her head. "I don't think we have it in the UK."

"Cody, you're making a huge mess. Crumbs everywhere. Put that thing back in the kitchen." Maria stood up and put her hands on her hips in annoyance.

He picked up the toaster, balanced it back on top of his head, and made for the door. "No ghosting? Jeez," he said.

Maria watched her boy leave the room and then sat back down. "You could as easily have said you didn't have electricity. He wasn't impressed. Ghosting is a Halloween thing. It's kind of a nice idea. The kids put a note on a friend's doorstep telling them they've been ghosted, and they leave a little bag of candy."

The boy bounced back into the room, without the toaster this time. "It has to be anonymous," he said.

"Oh, Cody. Good job! That was one of your list words from school this week. Well used." Maria meant it as a compliment, but then she saw her son flush and realized too late that she had embarrassed him in front of the pretty new sitter.

"So you don't write your name on the note?" Jessie asked. Maria studied the younger girl. Was she oblivious to Maria's mistake or smoothing things over? She couldn't tell, and that unsettled her even more.

Cody moved on. "No way, and you have to do it when it gets dark. You put the note and the candy on their doorstep without anybody seeing you. Then you ring their doorbell and run as fast as you can. If you do it right, you can hide and watch them open the door to get the candy. It's cool."

Maria sighed. "Yes, we've had a lot of visits this year, but the problem is Orga gets overexcited and now she's barking at everybody."

"Okay, I'll keep an eye out for that."

Then Cody jumped up. "But I want to do toasting with Todd—not ghosting."

The sitter smiled at his enthusiasm. "Now what's that?"

"Well, you see everybody expects candy when they're ghosted, so it's sick to give them burnt toast instead and see how mad they get when they open their bags."

"It's not very nice." Maria pretended to look stern, but she wasn't annoyed at all. In fact, she was relieved to see Alice was still content. The baby seemed very happy with Jessie. It was amazing how fast she'd calmed down. Jessie seemed to have Cody and Ricky's talent for keeping the baby happy. What was their secret?

"Aw, Mom." In a heartbeat, Cody was back to looking miserable. "Can I just do Mitch Jackson's house? He did us last night."

"Mitch is a boy who lives a few houses down the road at number thirteen. He's a seventh grader, so he's a little older than Cody," she told Jessie.

"He's a bit mean to Cody sometimes."

The sitter gave an understanding nod.

Maria looked at her son. "Tell you what—if Todd's mom says it's all right, I'm okay with both of you toasting Mitch Jackson. But nobody else. Promise?"

Cody punched the air with his hand. "Score!" he yelled, frightening Alice a little, but Jessie was on it and upped her cooing for a moment.

"Just Mitch, right?"

"Yeah, yeah. I have to call Todd." He ran out of the room again. "Adios!" he yelled as he disappeared down the hall.

"Is your little brother as energetic as he is?" Maria asked.

"Tristan? He sure is." Jessie smiled. "And the others are worse."

"Are they away from home, too?"

The girl shook her head. "No. I'm the first. The next one down is doing her A levels this year, so she'll head to college next autumn."

"That's tough on your parents. Education is expensive."

"It's not as bad in the UK as it is here, and I'm on a scholarship. My mum couldn't afford to pay Wiswall fees. My dad is deceased."

"Oh, I'm sorry."

Jessie shrugged.

Rick reappeared at the door to the living room.

"Ready to go, honey?" He looked at Maria. She nodded and stood.

"Well, you seem more than capable of handling things here. I've left both our numbers next to the phone in the kitchen, although I know you have mine already. I'll have my cell with me all night, and we should be home around midnight. All right?"

The sitter stood up and shifted Alice to her hip with the fluency and ease of a young mom.

"That's fine. I do have your number, but I'll save Rick's in my phone, too, so we're doubly covered. Have a good night."

"Don't come out to the door with us. It'll upset the baby," Maria said, although she didn't think her daughter looked too sad anymore.

Rick reached over and stroked her arm. "Are you aware Cody is on the phone calling Todd? I overheard him asking his partner-in-crime to come over so they can toast Mitch Jackson together."

Maria rolled her eyes. "You know what, if it amuses him and makes Jessie's job a little easier, I say go for it."

Jessie was studying Alice and playing with her tiny hand. "I think we're okay coming out to the door with you."

It irked Maria that the girl was overriding her authority, and what's more, she seemed so damn capable with Alice. She knew that was crazy, because it was great to have a good sitter. Maria and Rick got their coats from the closet while Jessie focused on keeping Alice happy.

"By the way," Maria said, "I turned on the house alarm but left the front door off the system. That way the boys can come and go, and you'll be able to answer it if you get ghosted."

Jessie nodded. "Have a smashing night," she said.

Maria smiled. "Your British accent's really cute."

Jessie looked a little embarrassed. "I do feel a bit conspicuous. I keep using words I assumed were normal over here, but they're not."

"Gimme an example," Rick said.

"Oh, let me think. *Fortnight* caused some confusion when I started school."

"I know what a fortnight is," he said, looking proud. "It's fourteen nights —two weeks. So Wednesday fortnight would be the Wednesday two weeks from next. Am I right?"

Jessie smiled and nodded. "My roommate didn't know what I was talking about."

"American English and English English—they're not the same language, are they?" Rick asked.

She shook her head. "Definitely not, but we get by."

Maria kissed Alice on the cheek and shouted a good-bye to her son, who was more interested in his phone call than seeing his parents off. "See you around midnight."

Rick took Maria by the arm when they were walking to their car. "She seems cool."

"She's very pretty."

"A pretty sitter, sitting pretty with our precious little babies." Rick had a habit of making up marketing jingles on the spot because it was part of his job, but Maria was in no mood for them just then.

Maria looked at her husband. It was getting dark, but she could still see his face. "She's very beautiful, isn't she?"

"Is she? I hadn't noticed."

She elbowed her husband. "Rick, you would have to be blind not to notice."

Chapter Two
Blind Ambition

"Michael, you should've seen our new sitter." It was almost the first thing Rick said to his best friend when he got him alone. Maria and Rick had been late arriving at the party because of all the fuss with Alice, and by the time they'd arrived, the party was in full swing. Maria had gone in search of the hostess to give her the champagne, while Rick made a beeline for Michael. He found him at the bar, so they each grabbed a bottle of beer and moved away to talk in private.

Michael studied his friend's face. "Tell me all about her. Is she nice?"

"Nice doesn't even start to cover it, man. She's an eleven out of ten. No, scratch that. She's twenty out of ten—plus she's good with the kids."

Michael laughed. "You were doing well till you mentioned the bit about being good with the kids. If she's that hot, who cares?"

Rick shrugged and grinned. "What can I say? I'm a broken man. But I have to tell you, I haven't seen a girl that gorgeous in years." Then he stood a little taller. "Don't get me wrong. I know she's a kid and I'm married, but still, I know beauty when I see it—and she's British."

"Ah, a European import? Sweet." Michael looked like he was studying his beer bottle label. "Tell me—would you?"

"Would I what?"

"You know—would you?" He nodded toward the door of the room as if that explained what he was saying, but Rick already knew.

"Nah, relax." He tried to sound convincing while remaining blasé. "Too much hassle. Not worth the risk. Besides, I love Maria."

Michael laughed again. "I can see it in your eyes, friend. Beautiful women make the most moderate men morons."

"What is that? A quote from Shakespeare?"

"No. Me." He draped an arm around Rick's shoulders and whispered, "Can I recommend a cold shower and getting a new sitter?"

"Did I mention she's great with the kids?"

Michael shook his head and pulled his arm back. "Lose her, bro. Get her the hell away from you. One of two things is gonna happen. One, she'll drive you crazy with desire, or two, you'll do something you're sure to regret—or three, you'll do one and two. I'm telling you, get her out of *su casa.*"

Rick said nothing and took a large swig of beer. Michael seemed to understand the situation pretty well. "This sort of thing ever happen to you?"

"What? Having a hot sitter? Cathi wouldn't let me. She has more sense."

"Well, tonight was just her first night. We got her from a sitter website. Her credentials were great. I just didn't realize her body—that is, the rest of her was so great, too," Rick said. "I couldn't exactly fire her as soon as I saw her."

Michael raised a hand in defeat. "Okay. Whatever you say."

Rick began to grind his teeth in annoyance. "All right, I'm going to get another beer. Do you want one?"

"Sure. Thanks. That way we can get drunk and pretend there isn't a twenty out of ten sitting in your house giving Cody all of her attention instead of you."

Rick threw him a dirty look as if to say *enough* and went to get the beers. The problem was everything Michael had said was true.

"I love your dress," Cathi said when Maria eventually caught up with her. "Did you get that in Boston?"

"You know this old dress, but thanks, *chica.* I need you to boost my spirits."

Cathi wrapped her arm around her old friend. "Maria? Honey, what's wrong? Your dress might be nice, but you look miserable. What happened? Is it Alice again?"

Maria was relieved to get a supporting shoulder to cry on. "Yes. I swear, Cathi, that child hates me. I did have a new dress for tonight, but she vomited all over me and my new miracle underwear."

Cathi squeezed her friend a little firmer. "How many times do I have to tell you? You don't need it! Your figure is fabulous, and you know that this just a phase with Alice. She'll come through the other side. Is she not sleeping? Could she be teething?"

Maria pulled away and looked at her friend. "Oh, I never thought of that. It's like I've forgotten all about babies. Cody never gave me a moment's trouble. No, I managed to get Alice to sleep. I really worked hard this evening to get organized. I gave her a bath, read to her. I took it real slow so she'd settle well, and it all worked. She was out cold until my idiot of a husband yelled up the stairs at me and woke her just minutes before we were walking out the door. When she wakes like that, she's impossible to get back to sleep."

A passing waiter carried a large silver tray of glasses full of pink punch. Cathi grabbed a fresh one for herself and Maria.

"Here, you need this. You poor doll. We forget how much work babies are, but remember, they do grow up pretty fast."

Maria took a large gulp of punch and continued. "You're the best, Cathi, but I haven't told you the worst part yet. The most beautiful girl in the world walked into my home just as I was being puked on and Alice was screaming her head off. You should have seen her. She's so beautiful. Damn near perfect. And she's young and great with kids and she's over here to do a master's in psychology. So she's smart on top of being beautiful. God, I feel sick." She gulped down the rest of the punch in her glass.

"Over here from where?"

"Oh yeah, she has a real sophisticated accent, as well. She's British. She was even teaching Rick words before we left. Rick—my husband—not Cody. That said, I think Cody has his first crush, too."

"It's not Cody I'd worry about. Come on, let's get you a refill, girl. I think you need it. What did you say she was doing with Rick?"

The women headed over to the punchbowl and took another glass of the raspberry-colored liquid for Maria.

"Oh, I was there for that. It wasn't suspicious or underhanded. It was more annoying than anything. They were just talking about the difference between American English and English English, and next thing I knew she was telling him new words like *fortnight*." Maria tried to speak in an upper class English voice, which made Cathi laugh.

"Your Puerto Rican accent is too thick. That's the funniest attempt at an English accent I've ever heard." Then Cathi tried to put on an English voice, too. "Is she rather posh?"

"Nah, I don't think so. She seemed pretty normal, eldest of five. Her dad is dead. It's just—oh, I don't know. To see both my men acting dopey around her . . . that's some power. It's a pain in the ass, if you want to know the truth. I mean do these women, these—what would you call them— swans? Do they know the power they have over normal men?"

"Don't forget she's smart, too."

"Yeah."

"And good with kids."

"Okay, don't rub it in."

But Cathi wouldn't stop. "So you're saying this girl literally has it all, beauty and intelligence. She's thoughtful, caring, and even has a sense of humor. You know we have a better word to describe these women. Just take the first letter from each word to abbreviate it—*B* for beauty, *I* for intelligence, *T* for thoughtfulness, *C* for caring, and *H* for humor. Now let me think . . ."

Maria figured it out and laughed. "Thanks, *chica*."

Cathi took a sip of her punch. "Look, honey, for a start there aren't many of them around—thank the Lord—and second, are you sure you aren't blowing this a little out of proportion? I mean, you're gorgeous. I've always told you that. I still see men checking out your curves. That Puerto Rican va va voom is really impossible to beat. It's downright sexy."

Maria shook her head vigorously. "Wait till you see her. She looks like a cross between Taylor Swift and a Victoria's Secret model."

"Ew, Taylor Swift? The girl who was voted sexiest woman alive last month?" Cathi put her arm around her friend's waist again. "Okay, if she freaks you out this much, just don't use her again after tonight."

"But you should have seen her with Alice. I thought we were going to have a problem being able to leave tonight. Alice just wouldn't settle with me—nothing new there—but this kid, Jessie, she just took my little girl in her arms, my baby, and Alice cheered up right away. It's damn annoying. Go figure."

Cathi laughed. "If she hadn't managed that, you would have missed the party."

"I know. It makes no sense." Maria swirled her red drink and studied the miniature tornado she'd created.

"Ah, that's where you're wrong. It all makes perfect sense. First off, she's pretty and you think Rick noticed, so you feel threatened as a wife and woman. Second, even Cody spotted how cute she was, and now you feel bad because at some subconscious level you know your darling little boy is getting older and will one day leave you for another woman. And third, even Alice was happy with this new woman. I figure that threatened you most of all, because being a mother is what you're all about. It's how you define yourself. You were really sideswiped."

Maria stared at her friend openmouthed. She didn't know how to respond, but she knew there was no need—her friend was on a roll.

"In theory this woman could replace you. That's gotta be tough to absorb."

"Seriously? You got all that just from what I said?"

Cathi nodded and raised her empty glass. "Well, something very similar was on *Dr. Phil* yesterday."

Maria laughed. The party was getting busier and the music louder. "What happened at the end of the show?"

Cathi, never one for subtlety, sighed. "The couple broke up. That's quite unusual for *Dr. Phil*."

"Twenty minutes in the company of a pretty new sitter and you think Rick and I are heading for divorce?"

"Sorry, I didn't mean you guys. I was talking about the people on the show. No way. You guys are cool. All you have to do is seduce Rick tonight. Remind him how good you are. You're a red-blooded woman with a terrific body. Let him at it."

Maria slapped her forehead. "Cathi, I just stopped nursing Alice. I still have all my baby weight. I'm not as hot as I was a couple of years ago."

"Neither is he. Come on, girl. We're all aging, but remember, youth is no replacement for experience. You may be a little softer around the edges, but you've given him two amazing kids and he loves you."

"Thanks, Cathi. I need a refill." Maria sighed, noticing she'd drunk her swirling tornado.

"Now that's a great idea. Afterward, we can come up with lots of X-rated ideas for how you're gonna spice up your love life when you get Rick home later tonight."

Maria groaned. "I'm done with X-rated sex. You know Alice is a *Fifty Shades* baby."

"I think half the babies born last year were *Fifty Shades* babies. You don't have to make a baby. Just play with Rick. If you blow his mind, he won't be able to think about your pretty little sitter. Trust me."

The women headed back to the punch bowl and put Jessie right out of their minds.

"Tell me, have you had any luck with your old neighbor, Noreen Palmer?"

Maria gave a helpless shrug. "I don't know how to get through to that woman," she said. "It's easy enough to bump into her because she's out walking her dog so much. I just grab Orga and head out. I've already had three conversations about this with her in the last two weeks. She knows I'm up to something."

Cathi looked eager. "What did you say to her?"

Maria saw two seats by the window and headed for them. When they got settled, she continued. "The first time, I asked if she was finding the house a little big now since the kids are all gone. Of course, I didn't just blurt it out. I kinda worked up to it. Anyway, she didn't seem to think so. I told her I thought I knew somebody who might want to buy her house for a fair price. She looked a little interested, but then she changed the subject again. Then yesterday I asked her if she'd thought any more about my friend who was interested in her house, and she looked at me like it was the first she'd heard about it."

Cathi huffed in frustration. "Is she getting confused in her old age? Does she know I want to make her an offer?"

"Oh, I think so. I more or less said that, but she just laughed and waved her hands. I don't think she's interested, Cathi. What more can I do?"

"Try harder." Her friend looked exasperated.

"You know, hers isn't the only house with a view of the water. You could get a realtor to approach all the homes overlooking Crystal Lake. Maybe somebody else would think of selling."

"I like her house best, and you'd be surprised how few do sell in a year. There are lots of houses in the neighborhood but not right on the lake. They seem to change hands privately, which is where you come in. You're right there. You live on Newton's most desirable street. I know you can find me a way in," Cathi said, pleading.

"You know we found our house by pure chance. We were just out walking and saw the for sale sign. I'm sure that could happen to you."

Cathi shook her head, looking impatient. "That was a decade ago. Things have changed, Maria. You and I have to think outside the box. The trick is for me to hear about a house first and make an offer, which I get accepted before it goes on the open market."

Maria wasn't convinced. Of course she would love it if Cathi lived closer. They were best friends, after all. Their husbands had been working at the same marketing company for about nine years, and the four of them had become very close. But did it have to be right next door?

Plus, Maria *liked* Mrs. Palmer. She was a widow who lived alone. The woman was a little absentminded now in her old age, but the kids adored her—even Alice. She was a soft little woman in the Angela Lansbury mold. One time, Cody had even asked his mom if Mrs. Palmer was the woman from *Murder, She Wrote*. Maria had really laughed at that.

A decade earlier, when she and Rick had bought number seven, Crystal Lake, the house had been in bad condition. Back in those days, they had been just starting out, so what they'd lacked in finances they'd made up for in energy. Ricky had done a lot of the renovations himself. Maria hadn't been able to do too much—she'd been pregnant with Cody—but as soon as he was born, it had been a different story.

Most of Newton's new moms cocooned themselves in a love-bubble of soft pink or blue. They breastfed their newborns, took gentle walks around the lake, and did multiple mommy-toddler mornings. Maria was cut from a different cloth.

Cody had dozed happily while she'd painted the nursery sky blue. She'd nursed him in the Lowes plumbing department and changed his diapers at Home Depot. She had been up ladders, down at the DIY stores, and around that house like a woman possessed.

Maria had laughed when Mrs. Palmer urged her to slow down. She'd said she would stop when the house was finished. Noreen was a treasure in those early years. The older woman had helped with the newborn Cody, and she'd given Maria lots of old furniture, including all her old baby stuff that had been stored for years in the loft of number nine.

Mrs. Palmer had been a bit like a mother figure to Maria over the last decade, but Maria could see her next-door neighbor was aging. She was beginning to slow down. Maria thought maybe their roles were reversing now. Perhaps it was her turn to start helping the older lady.

Instead, her best friend Cathi had notions of getting her hands on number nine, Crystal Lake. She wanted to renovate the house and then live in it herself. When Maria had told her friend the next-door neighbor had been living in the house for fifty years, Cathi had become even more determined. She'd made a powerful argument that Mrs. Palmer was sure to make a financial killing and end up being a very rich woman. She could head to Florida and kick her heels up in the sun. Newton was too cold in the winter for the elderly.

That's what Cathi said, but Maria knew Mrs. Palmer never headed south in the colder months. She stayed in her home at Crystal Lake. Noreen was a hardy woman and walked her dog once the roads were cleared of snow. She wrapped up warm and got out in the winter weather. She wasn't one of the snowbirds who left at the first sign of frost.

Noreen was a Newton woman through and through. Cathi didn't seem to appreciate that. Half a century in one house was an amazing achievement, and her roots were deep. Having had the conversations with her neighbor, Maria seriously doubted Cathi would manage to get her hands on the property.

"What about the other side of the lake?" she said, but Cathi shook her head.

"Believe me, I've done the research. The houses on your road look over the lake to the west, so you guys get sunsets over the water. It has to be on your road and your side of the street. And you know I can only afford one that needs renovation. Numbers five and three have been renovated in the last few years, so they'd be crazy money if they ever went up for sale, and the other three on the waterfront seem settled. I can't get any info on them." Cathi looked very serious as she spoke. "The even numbered houses don't interest me because they don't back onto the lake. They're on the wrong side of the road. No, I think it has to be Noreen Palmer's house. We just have to find a way to convince her to sell."

Maria had already knocked back two glasses of punch, and she was a beginning to feel a little calmer, maybe even good. Looking at Cathi's intensity, she began to giggle. "You know, you're taking all of this very seriously. Does it really matter? It's just a house."

Cathi didn't look amused. "It's not just a house, Maria. It's a home. It's a statement of where you're at in life. It says how rich and successful you are. It tells the world what your values are—big house, big family, big success. You know all that."

Maria frowned. "*Chica*, if you ask me, big houses mean big bills and lots of cleaning. Our house isn't so big. I think you're crazy. You don't even have a big family—unless you have something to tell me?"

Cathi blew out a jet of air—something she often did when she was impatient. "Are you insane? There's no way I'm going back there! My baby days are behind me."

"Okay, you have Katie and Stacy. You'd get by in a two bedroom if you wanted. Mrs. Palmer's house has six bedrooms. It's huge—too big. She had a bunch of kids, and you know her son, Greg, lives just across the road. She's not going to want to move away from her grandson, Todd. He's Cody's friend. Why would you want that much space?"

Cathi's eyes lit up. It was obvious she'd given the question a lot of thought. "I want one room for each of my girls. I want a study for myself, and I'd like to convert another of the bedrooms into a huge bathroom off the master suite. Didn't you say she doesn't have en suite bathrooms?"

"No. The house was built long before such things were deemed necessary."

Cathi smiled. "It's begging to be renovated, and I'm just the woman to do it." She raised her glass.

Maria clinked and smiled—on the outside, anyway. She didn't like to see her elderly neighbor forced into something she might not want to do. That said, she knew Cathi very well. Once her friend set her mind on something, she was rarely beaten. If Cathi wanted number nine, she'd find a way to get her hands on it. Mrs. Palmer wouldn't stand a chance.

"Can you imagine the parties we could have? We could do joint celebrations and open up the two backyards. What fun would that be?"

Maria smiled. "It'd be fantastic in the summertime. We can have boats on the lake. Crystal Lake Lane is amazing in July."

"Oh, I was thinking nighttime parties. If I could get a swimming pool in the backyard, it would be the best ever."

"Why do you need a pool with the lake right beside us?" Maria wondered if her friend was going a bit too far. "What does Michael think about all this?"

Cathi glanced at her friend. "We don't need to tell him until we're a little further along in our plans."

"Okay, now I'm curious. How much further?"

Cathi laughed. "I guess we'd have to tell him before the furniture removal guys arrive."

Maria sighed. "He is a very tolerant man, *chica*. Ricky would kill me if I bought a house without telling him. I don't even know if I could do it legally. You have such blind ambition."

Cathi looked affronted. "It's not blind. I have a very clear vision of where I'm going and how I'm getting there. I am simply determined to own a house on Crystal Lake." Their husbands were approaching them. Cathi gave a dazzling loyal-wife smile and whispered to Maria, "Don't say anything in front of the boys yet—not until I have everything under control."

Chapter Three
No Need for Alarm

Back at Crystal Lake, Jessie was happy she had everything under control. When she first met Maria, the woman had implied Alice would be a handful. It sure hadn't turned out that way. Jessie thought the little girl was a cutie and an easy baby to care for. With just a few cuddles and one peekaboo game, Alice had been ready for a diaper change and a full bottle of milk before settling back into her crib. She'd fallen asleep before the Incy Wincy Spider was anywhere near the top of the garden spout.

Now the house was quiet. Orga was back inside and seemed to be calmer, and Cody was still out with this friend, so it looked like Jessie was going to have an easy night. With the house so peaceful, she realized there was a good chance she could get some homework done. She headed to the kitchen to find the teapot. Maria had told her to make herself at home, and she always liked a cup of tea next to her while she studied. While she waited for the water to boil, she found the note with their cell phone numbers and added Rick to her contacts. Just then she heard the front door slam followed by the thundering feet of Cody and Todd as they came bounding into the room.

"Did Mitch Jackson toast us again, Jessie?" He stood legs apart, fists clenched, ready for war.

She wanted to laugh at his anxious little face but knew better. For him, this was serious business. "Not only have we not been toasted, we haven't even been ghosted. I was rather looking forward to that," she said. "Now tell me—where would I find a mug?"

Cody went to the cupboard above the dishwasher. "We just toasted him, but I have a feeling he saw us. We're waiting for a counterattack." He took out a coffee mug and put it on the counter beside her just as the doorbell rang.

The boys tore off, and she followed them in time to witness Todd racing for the road to see if he could catch who had rung and run.

Meanwhile, Cody was checking out the contents of the little brown bag on their doorstep. He slapped his forehead in anguish. "Aw, man, I told you he saw us," he said, showing her the burnt toast in the bag.

Jessie felt his pain. Clearly this was war. Todd returned looking deflated.

"Come in," she said, getting into the spirit of things. "He could be watching us at this very minute, and you guys don't want to be seen like this. We have to talk strategies."

She could see that was music to the boys' ears.

"You could be an ally for our side," Todd said.

Soon the three of them were standing around the island in the kitchen. Jessie reckoned the smooth marble countertop was the perfect place to lay out a large sheet of paper and draw a map of the neighboring houses. The boys got her paper, sharpies, and a ruler while she got herself the mug of tea. Then they watched transfixed as she began to sketch a rough map of the street. Jessie knew there was a lake behind them, but since she hadn't seen it yet, the boys took her into the dining room to look out over the back of the house.

That was the first time Jessie saw Crystal Lake. It was dark out, but that didn't matter. The view was hypnotic. She'd walked through the dining room with Rick earlier on her tour of the first floor of the house, but somehow she'd missed the incredible view outside.

The backyard of the Sanchez house stretched back about seventy feet, and beyond that was a low cut hedge. Without a doubt, the shrubs were cut back to see the lake because it was so pretty. The night was still and so the water was, too. It looked like a sheet of black glass spreading out across . . . she didn't know how far, but she could see the homes on the other side, the buttermilk-yellow light of their little windows mirrored on the water. Jessie wondered if, across the lake, the Sanchez house looked as appealing to them as those buildings did to her. The night sky was clear, and the moon reflected on the lake like a picture in a children's story book.

Funny it's called Crystal Lake, she mused. *It looks so dark—like jade or ebony—but not something bright and illuminating like crystal.* She thought of her mother's precious crystal vase collection at home. Wedding presents from years ago. She should phone her mother soon.

"We're not allowed to go down to the lake at night." Cody cut into her thoughts.

Jessie swung around. "I should think not. It could be very dangerous. Are you okay in the back garden if you stay away from the water?"

He nodded.

"Righty ho, men. Let's plan your attack strategy," she said in her best British army voice and marched back into the kitchen.

"Check," Todd said.

"I know what can help us." Cody rushed out of the room.

Todd and Jessie only had to wait a moment before he reappeared with the iPad. "Google Maps," he said with satisfaction.

"Gotta hand it to you, kid—you're a good cadet." She laughed, and with the aid of the tablet, she had a pretty good map of Crystal Lake Lane done in minutes.

The young men settled down to talk tactics. It didn't take them long to decide to go behind Mrs. Palmer's, the house next to them. She wouldn't mind. Then they'd cut across the front of number eleven, and finally they could swing around behind Mitch's house—number thirteen.

"Approaching from the rear gives you the element of surprise," Jessie said. "But nowhere near the lake. Deal?"

The boys high-fived each other and cheered. Cody was in charge of making a fresh batch of toast.

"It has to be really black this time. The burnter the better." Todd was insistent.

Jessie left them to it, and taking her mug of half-drunk tea, she went back to the dining room window. The view of the lake was calling her. She could see the attraction of the neighborhood. There was no question a house like this would be expensive, but it was worth it, in her estimation. The peaceful feeling it evoked in her was enchanting, hypnotic, magical.

There were no lakes around Dorking, where she lived in the UK, so if she wanted a sea view, she had to head to the English coast. It had never occurred to her when she'd arrived in Newton, Massachusetts, that she'd get a lake view. If she lived in this house, Jessie knew she'd spend hours just gazing at the water. *Would that be a terrible waste of time or a life well-spent?*

The smooth surface of the water had a calming effect on her. Surely that was a good thing. Jessie put her mug down on the table and folded her arms. Just to stand there and watch the water was cathartic. Why was that? Was it primal or psychological? What was the appeal? It was worth discussing with one of her professors.

In a heartbeat, all hell broke loose, and the peace was shattered by a deafening screech. The volume was absurd. Jessie ran to the boys and found them in a cloud of burnt-toast smoke. Cody looked guilty and panicked in equal measure.

"What the heck?" she yelled, but shouting was useless over the noise. "Must be the fire alarm, with all the smoke in here!"

It was much louder than it needed to be, and she was pretty sure the damage being done to their eardrums was worse than any smoke damage to the beautiful cream-colored kitchen. The black toast had popped out of the toaster, and there was no real danger to the children or the house.

"You guys, get out into the front garden and take Orga with you. Don't move from there. I'll get Alice." She yelled as much as she could, but she used hand signals, too. The boys nodded and ran out the front door with the dog.

Jessie took the stairs two at a time, but even at that speed, by the time she got to the baby, Alice was crying. She couldn't hear the baby over the noise of the fire alarm, but she could see Alice's tiny fists closed tight and her little chest heaving with sobs. Jessie scooped her up and grabbed a blanket from the crib.

Bounding down the stairs, between one shrill from the alarm and the next, she heard the house phone ringing. Perhaps it was Maria. She knew some alarm systems were connected to the house owner's cell phone. Maria would tell her what to do. As Jessie fled the house, she snatched the portable telephone and then swept out the door with Alice in one arm.

The boys were standing in the front garden with Orga cowering beside them, and they'd been joined by Mitch Jackson. Jessie knew from the boys' perspective this was way cooler than toasting. She felt a little better now that they were all safe and out of the house, but the noise was still very upsetting.

She answered the ringing phone in her hand. "Hullo."

"Good evening, ma'am. This is the fire department. Your alarm has been activated. Can you apprise me of the situation?"

Jessie was a little intimidated by the efficiency of the woman on the other end. Her voice sounded officious—almost aggressive.

"Um, yes. It was the family toaster," she said. "No harm done. I just don't know how to switch the alarm off."

"A toaster? Is that what you said?"

"Yes, just a toaster. It's fine, really. In fact there's no fire. It's all just smoke."

She heard the woman talking to somebody else. There was a crackle on the line, and it was difficult to focus with Alice crying in her arms and the blaring noise just twenty feet away. Jessie tried to listen to the phone conversation.

"Confirming, Unit One. It's a domestic toaster at Crystal Lake." Then she sounded like she was talking to Jessie again.

"Ma'am, is everybody out of the building?"

"Yes, yes. Everything's okay, honest. I don't know how to switch off the alarm. That's the main problem here."

"You need the fire alarm code for that, ma'am. Without the code, the alarm will keep ringing. There's a unit on its way to assist."

"A unit of what?" Jessie asked. Back in England, they measured alcohol in units. Maybe she was sending around a gin and tonic. That would be nice. The only other thing she knew measured in units was blood, which she didn't think was really necessary.

"Look, I'm just the sitter. I have a ten-year-old and the baby with me. If I just go in and get the ruddy toaster, I can bring it out here. That might shut the stupid alarm off."

The lady on the phone interrupted. "Did you say you have an infant with you, ma'am?"

"Yes, but she's out here in the garden with me."

The lady was talking to somebody else again. "Unit Two, there are two, repeat two, children at the scene. A ten-year-old and an infant. The sitter is outside in the front yard."

"A second unit? Are we talking double G and Ts?" She gave a nervous laugh. The truth was beginning to dawn, however. Her mystery phone woman was probably talking to fire engines.

Jessie became anxious. "Look, we don't need any help. I just need the alarm to be switched off. It might switch itself off if I get the toaster out." She felt more panicky now. The appalling noise of the house alarm was very jarring, and Alice was still crying.

"Do not reenter the building, ma'am. I repeat, do not reenter the building." Then the voice down the phone spoke to the others. "Unit One, step on it. We have a potentially escalating situation at Crystal Lake."

Jessie cut in. "I can hear you, and I'm not an escalating situation!" she shouted. "Just switch off the damn alarm, and I'll calm down."

"You need to have the code for that, ma'am." There was no emotion in the dispatcher's voice, no panic, and this unnerved Jessie even more.

"Look, you keep repeating the fact I need a dumb code, which I clearly don't have, because if I did, the ruddy alarm wouldn't still be screeching. Can you understand me?" Jessie knew she shouldn't yell, and she wanted to sound in control, but it was too late. "I don't have the code. I'm the minder."

Then she thought about her cell phone. She should phone Maria and get the code herself. She would switch the mad noise off and everybody could get back to normal.

That was when the enormous red fire engine truck arrived. A police car escorted it—lights flashing on both vehicles and sirens shrilling in perfect disharmony. The already earsplitting noise level in the neighborhood doubled. Jessie took Cody by the hand, and with Alice still screaming in her arms, they all backed away as a herd of hardy firefighters took over.

Jessie watched in disbelief as two men started unrolling the enormous water hose from their truck. Two others ran into the house and opened all the windows, and two more sectioned off a part of the front yard with hi-vis tape. It reminded her of *CSI*, because the taped area was usually the place where the dead body was buried. *Hopefully not today,* she thought—although she did love *CSI*.

Expecting one of her heroes from the television show to appear any second, she watched two more men, clad in canary-yellow moon suits, walk through the yard and enter the house. They had the full-inferno fire-protection kit on—the oversized yellow hood with fireproof glass to cover the face, enormous heat-resistant coats, matching trousers, and finally those big boots they could walk across the sun in. After a few moments, they came out carrying the tiny toaster between them. The little machine had long since given up smoking and completely cooled down, but it looked like they were taking no chances.

Despite the seriousness of the situation and the obvious cost of the exercise, Jessie was amused. From behind, the men in yellow looked a little like *Sesame Street* Big Birds. She wanted to laugh but didn't.

It would have been so much better if there was a decent house fire for them to fight. Then at least the big yellow birds would have had something good to chirp about. Maybe the baby had similar thoughts, because it was around that time that she gave up crying and decided to watch the theatrics.

Another fire engine arrived, adding to the cacophonous cocktail. But after a few hand gestures between them, the fire officers from Unit Two didn't disembark. A gaggle of neighbors had begun to converge next to the enormous red engine and the police car. As the danger levels subsided, Jessie felt her face burn with embarrassment. Was all of this excitement her fault? Had she miscommunicated the size of the emergency? And would somebody ever switch off that darn house alarm?

Cody pulled Jessie's sleeve. "The lady on the phone is still talking to you," he said. Jessie had let her hand drop, but she still held the receiver and, it appeared, the emergency dispatcher.

"Hullo," she said, feeling a little dazed.

"Unit One has informed me they have the situation contained, ma'am. Are you in a position to switch off the fire alarm yet?"

Jessie shook her head. "I still don't know the code. I could phone the family, but my mobile—I mean my cell phone—is in the house."

"One moment please." She stopped talking to Jessie again. "Unit One, she's just the sitter. Can you get her into the house to get her cell so she can call the parents to get the code?"

Jessie heard a man reply through the crackle. "That's affirmative. I'll do that now."

Then she saw one of the firefighters walking over to her. Everything had happened so fast she didn't know what he had done to assist the containing of the situation, but at least he wasn't one of the big yellow birds. This guy was in a navy T-shirt and pants. He was maybe a little older than her and was smiling. He didn't look worried.

"Hi, I'm Dan Walker, and you are?" He reached his hand out to shake hers.

"Jessica, or Jessie, the minder." She went to shake his hand, but the phone was in it and Alice was keeping her left arm busy.

"Hi, Jessica or Jessie."

"I'm Jessie."

He winked and took the phone from her. "Cindy, that you? Yeah. We're clear here. Yeah." He listened to her say something and said "yeah" a few more times before hanging up.

"Okay, Jessie, you can call the parents now." He handed her back the phone.

"I don't know their cell numbers off the top of my head."

"I do," Cody said, looking delighted to be able to help a real firefighter.

He said the number of his father's cell first, but it went to voice mail.

Jessie left a message, and then they tried Maria's. The same thing happened. Dan shook his head in disbelief.

"There's no accounting for some folks," he said with a shrug.

"My, my, what's all this about?" An elderly lady approached the little group.

"Hi, Mrs. Palmer," Cody said. "Our toaster went all smoky and it set off the house alarm, and now we have two fire engines and one patrol car. Cool, huh?"

"Very," she said. Then she looked from Jessie to the firefighter. "I'm Noreen Palmer from next door. Can I help?"

Jessie nodded at the older woman but was more interested in the firefighter's help. "Can we go back into the house? I'd love to check my cell phone just to see if I have the same contact numbers as the ones Cody here gave us and also to see if they've maybe called me."

"I can take you back in, but it's real noisy in there." Then he looked at Noreen. "You live next door?"

"Yes. What can I do?"

"Well, could you maybe hold the baby for a moment while I take this young lady in to get her phone?"

"I'd be delighted. Or better yet, I can take Cody and Alice to my house." She pointed to the building just next door. "It's so noisy out here and much quieter inside. Cody knows my kitchen well, as do Todd and Mitch. Alice has been in there with her mom plenty of times, too. We can have cookies and milk, and you can join us in a few minutes if that works for you."

"Shouldn't we get Todd and Mitch back to their parents?" Jessie asked.

"I'm Todd's grandma. I'll phone his mother now, and I see Mitch's dad standing over there. They live two doors down from me."

Jessie looked behind her. Where a few curious people had stood a short while ago, now the entire neighborhood had poured out to have a look. "Oh," she said and gave a weak wave. She even got a few waves back.

"Let me take Alice, and then you go into the house and get your phone with this nice fireman. Cody, you take Orga with us."

Jessie wondered if this lady was perhaps a little too elderly to take charge of Alice, but what choice did she have? The baby seemed happy to go with her, and it would only be for a few minutes.

"Thank you so much. What did you say your name was?"

"Noreen."

"Thanks, Noreen. I really do need the help."

Then Jessie headed into the blaring house with Dan the fireman to find her phone. He checked the alarm system while she moved back outside with her cell, but there were no new messages. Then she tried both parents with the numbers in her phone but had the same luck as before. She left them each a second voice mail, and then she was all out of ideas.

She went to look for Dan inside but the shrill of the alarm was too loud and they both headed back outside. That's when Cody reappeared, waving a piece of paper over his head. "Mrs. Palmer thought you might want this. It's the fire alarm code. Mom gave it to her once."

Dan grabbed the note and was back in the house playing with the key panel on the wall in seconds. Jessie and Cody were only steps behind. She watched him press the buttons and couldn't help noticing the tattoo on his muscular forearm. It was a falcon with outstretched wings swooping down, like it was about to attack. Jessie gave an involuntary shiver. His entire body looked strong. All in all, Dan seemed to be in good shape. As he tapped the last digit of the code into the keypad, the shrilling fire alarm subsided. Almost immediately, it started back up again.

"What now?" he yelled in exasperation and read the small LED panel above the keys.

Jessie read it, too. "I don't believe this. Intruder alert?" She remembered the firefighters opening every window in the house. The phone began to ring again. Jessie ran back outside with Cody just as she'd done a little earlier and answered it.

"Hello, ma'am. This is Newton Emergency Services. We have notification of an intruder alert in your home. Can you appraise me of the situation?"

"It's okay," she shouted into the phone. "It was a fire—well, not a fire, just smoke, but all the windows were opened. The house alarm was on at the time, so we've tripped that. Can you switch it off?"

"No, ma'am, you have to do that. Do you have the intruder alarm cancellation code?"

"No, I don't!" she wailed. "I'm just the minder."

"Very well, ma'am. Sit tight. I'm going to send a unit over."

Jessie looked at Dan. "Here we go again," she said, looking miserable.

But he smiled at her with a twinkle in his eye. "Yep," he said. "Here we go again."

Chapter Four
A New Flame?

"Never again," Jessie mumbled to herself as she waved off Rick's car. If he glanced in his rearview mirror, he would see her smiling even though she was anything but happy. Jessie was shattered and glad to be heading for bed. She pushed open the glass door to her dormitory building and was hit by a blast of welcome warm air.

"Who knew so much could go so wrong in just one night?" she said to herself as she pressed the elevator button.

A group of students walked past the open doors. "Elevator's busted," someone said.

"Just great." Jessie groaned as she considered the daunting prospect of climbing four flights of stairs with her huge bag of books.

"You can come with us?" A boy from the group winked at her, but she forced a smile and waved him off. There weren't supposed to be men in the building, but it was crazy late on a Saturday night and not her problem.

Feeling utterly shattered, Jessie hauled her bag over her shoulder and headed for the stairwell. Even though she was twenty-three, it was her first time living away from home. She'd commuted to university in England, because living there would've cost more money and Jessie's family didn't have much of that.

Things were different in America. She'd earned an academic scholarship to Wiswall, and part of that package was accommodation on campus. Before coming to the States, Jessie hadn't realized how many different types of rooms there would be, and because hers was free, she'd taken what she was given. The first shock, however, was she had been placed in an all-girl building. It never occurred to her they'd be segregated from the boys. Okay, separate bathrooms and bedrooms were a good idea, but buildings? What did American guys do that was so naughty they had to be kept in another building?

A bigger shock had been the discovery she was in an alcohol-free community. Jessie was in college, damn it, and she was already one degree down and doing a master's. She was of age and deserved a drink if she wanted one. At first, Wiswall had seemed more like an old Victorian boarding school than a huge, progressive American college. Her alcoholic concerns had dissolved, however, in the first few weeks when she got invited to some of the wildest parties of her life. And even the absence of men in the building had its advantages.

For a start, her roomie was the best buddy ever. Ely Briskin came from South Carolina. Like Jessie, she was studying psychology. But unlike Jessie she was rich—very rich. Even though they were the same age, Ely was just starting her degree.

"Welcome," her new roommate had said as Jessie entered the dorm room for the first time. "I'm Ely. Well, actually I'm Elyse, but I hate that, so call me Ely." She spoke without getting off the bed she was lying on.

Jessie had just flown in from London to Boston and caught a taxi to the college, so she was exhausted. She had two enormous pieces of luggage and was beginning to feel the strain of jet lag combined with leaving her mother for the first time.

"This bed mine?" Jessie asked.

Ely shrugged and nodded, so she fell onto it without any bedding or even a pillow and closed her eyes.

"Come a long way?" Ely asked. "Got any help with your stuff?"

"London and no. I'm alone. Name's Jessica, but you can call me Jessie."

This made Ely sit up. "London, England? You're British? Hey, that's cool. I didn't know you were going to be foreign. I like that. It makes us more sophisticated—international." She got up and pulled Jessie's second suitcase into the room.

The noise made Jessie open her eyes. "Oh, thanks, but don't worry. I'll do it. I just needed a minute to catch my breath."

"I'm not doing it for you, sunshine. I'm doing it for me, so we can close this dang door and share a quick drink to celebrate your arrival."

That was when Jessie discovered they were in a dry, all-girl dormitory. She didn't mind too much, especially as Ely was determined to flaunt the rules from the get-go.

Ely Briskin was like nobody Jessie had ever met before. Her broad Southern drawl made her sound so laid-back and chilled out, except when she got excited. Then she raised the pitch of her voice so much it sounded almost comical, but Jessie soon discovered Ely was not to be underestimated. She explained to Jessie that she had taken the scenic route to Wiswall College. Jessie learned her roommate had flunked out of three colleges already. That was why she was a little older than the average freshman. Ely said she didn't like socializing with the younger girls, so she was very happy to be with Jessie and able to hang with the postgrad set.

Ely's dark brown hair was long and straight, and she kept it tied back in a ponytail. Her style was casual, but whether she wore jeans or dresses, she always had her leather cowboy boots on. They were the same color as her hair and suited her Southern accent and self-contained attitude.

Ely said her parents had coerced her into coming to college up north because they thought her horizons were too narrow. She loved the South and thought Northerners were stiff and serious. "The partyin's a case in point," Ely said on their first night together. "Not enough of it goin' on up here. What's with that? We only got one life—we gotta live it." She spoke with conviction.

Jessie hadn't met anyone from South Carolina before, and she loved the singsong way they spoke. Ely reminded her of an older version of Miley Cyrus before she cut and colored her hair, but she didn't say it, thinking it would sound gauche.

"What is this we're drinking?" she asked on that very first night together. Jessie took a sip of the clear liquid Ely had given her.

"Moonshine. Good shit, huh?"

Somehow Jessie managed to get her bed made up, but her clothes remained unpacked because four cups of Ely's home brew combined with one transatlantic flight was enough to induce an eight-hour coma.

It was a good lesson for Jessie. Ely was a fun girl, and it looked like she would be a terrific roommate, but Jessie needed to watch how much she partied with her new friend. Her body was just not designed to ingest moonshine. She was more of a glass-of-wine type of girl, but most of all she was there to study. If her master's was good enough, she knew she'd land herself a great job and that would help out a lot at home.

The weeks after that first night zoomed by, and Jessie was soon well settled. She wasn't surprised when Ely found a boyfriend on the football team. He was from North Carolina. "A whole state away from home," Ely had said, to prove she was broadening her horizons. Jessie loved Josh from the moment she met him. He was basically a male version of Ely—bigger, of course—with the same dark brown hair and adorable Southern drawl. He had cowboy boots, too.

"You're perfect together," Jessie said one night.

"He has a friend." Ely sang this, then hugged herself and started making kissing noises.

Jessie laughed. "Ely, you have the subtlety of a snowplow! I'm here to study and then I'm going home."

"Well hell, Jessie, that don't mean you can't have no fun along the way, sunshine." Then she used her mantra. "We only got one life."

When she finally climbed the four flights of stairs, Jessie was relieved that Ely was home now. She needed to vent.

"Thank God you're here. You would not believe what happened to me tonight," she said, shaking off her coat.

"That good?" Ely tapped her tablet screen to pause the movie she was watching. "Tell me all about your first night babysitting." She was lying on her bed, propped up by a mountain of Carolina cotton-covered pillows. "Are American kids that different from British ones? Did you get real brats? You know, it ain't called Snootin' Newton for nothing. They're all little trust fund babies around here." She waved her arms in the air like she was swatting flies.

Jessie plonked down onto her bed. "So are you, or have you forgotten?"

"Yeah, but I'm nice," Ely said, drawing out the word *nice* like it had three syllables. She did that a lot, and Jessie loved it.

"Yes, Ely. You're lovely. So were the kids tonight, but I managed to get emergency services out to the house—not once but twice." She covered her face with her hands, and Ely sat up to pay better attention.

"What did you do, sunshine? What happened?"

Jessie filled her in on everything, and by the end of the story, Ely announced they both deserved a drink—Jessie because of the night she had been through, and herself because her roommate shouldn't drink alone.

Jessie didn't have a particularly big appetite for drinking, but she knew Ely's case was a little different. Her roomie liked to party a little too much, which was why her parents had chosen New England. Ely found the nightlife in Miami, Austin, and Atlanta a lot more fun than college life in those three cities, and she'd failed with spectacular success out of all three universities. Her parents were giving her one last chance by sending her to the calmer waters and more studious environment of Wiswall. They had placed her in an all-girl, no alcohol environment in hopes she might, at last, settle down.

Two months into their academic year, there was no sign of that happening. In fact, quite the opposite. Ely had discovered a business enterprise supplying alcohol to all the younger girls in their dorm, and she'd even managed to do a deal with one of the night security men. Now he did the shopping for her in return for a large financial kickback. Jessie wasn't worried about her friend. There was little chance of her getting her degree, but there was every chance of her starting up and running a very successful business.

Tonight, Ely gave her a glass of white wine, and she was glad for it.

Jessie continued. "So, at last, Maria phoned me in a blind panic."

"Darn sure. What did she say about not being on her cell all night?" Ely asked, acting indignant for her friend.

Jessie shook her head and sighed. "She said it was on silent and she didn't realize until she checked it at the very end of the night. To be fair, she was in a right state when she called me, but all the fuss was over by then."

"What about the dad's phone?"

Jessie looked up. "Rick's?"

"You call him Rick?" Ely was incredibly perceptive—she claimed she spoke body language fluently. "Was he hot?"

Jessie laughed. "You're irrepressible, Ely! I have to say he was a very good-looking guy, but he's old. Oh, and hullo, he's married, too. But yes, he was quite hot—for an old guy."

"No way." Ely was on her feet and refilling their glasses.

"Way." She almost regretted saying it, because now Ely would want her to pursue him.

"This is the first time you've even expressed an interest in a man."

Jessie took a large drink of wine. "Look, he's attractive—for an older guy —but he's married, and Maria is beautiful. She's from Puerto Rico, and she's got that whole sexy thing going on. She has an amazing figure, and I didn't see it, but I'm guessing she has a wild temper, too. They both have gorgeous tanned skin—a very good-looking family, in fact. Rick has a strong American accent. Maria's Puerto Rican accent is exquisite—and did I mention she's beautiful? There's no way I want to flirt with her husband."

"Exquisite? You say she talks nice, and here you are using words like *exquisite* in normal conversation?" Ely rolled her eyes. "Nobody talks as pretty as you do, darlin'."

Jessie put her glass on the floor, sat back on her bed, and hugged her knees. "Oh no, Maria is very beautiful."

"She can't be as hot as you."

Jessie shook her head in earnest. "She darn well is. To be honest, she reminded me of JLo. That's how hot she was. Anyway, Rick might be handsome, but he's too old and he's married."

"You gotta live, sunshine."

"I am living. I love this course I'm doing. I'm learning tons, and then I'm going back to England. To home, my mum. It's a good life."

But Ely disagreed. "You can't leave the States. Not now. I like you too much."

"Aw, Ely, you doll! You have no idea how nice it is to hear you say that. All I need is one good friend, and that's you."

"You better believe it, and that's why you can't leave the US now!"

"We can stay friends even when I move back to England."

"Well, tell me, did they at least give you extra money after leaving you in the lurch like that?"

Jessie smiled. "Oh yeah. I got a hundred bucks. Can you believe it? Not bad for a Saturday night."

Ely sat back down on her bed and smiled at her friend. "Nice! Want to go shopping in Boston tomorrow?"

"Ely, you're impossible. No. I'm saving my money. I'm not going to blow it as soon as I get it. Anyway, aren't you going horseback riding with Josh tomorrow?"

Jessie had learned the one thing her roommate missed most about home was her horses—much more than she missed her parents. Josh was crazy about them, too, so they spent most of their weekends at a stable they'd found on the outskirts of Newton.

"He's in New York for the weekend. I'm all yours," Ely said with a smile as broad as Texas.

It made Jessie laugh. "Having missed this evening, I planned on studying all day tomorrow."

Ely put the glass down on her bedside table and clapped her hands together. "You ever gonna learn, sunshine?"

Jessie shook her head. "Probably not."

Ely went back to her movie, and Jessie summoned enough energy to take a shower and wash her hair. Even though she was tired, she felt like she smelt of smoke. She knew it was maybe in her mind, but still, she wanted to wash it all away before she fell into bed.

As she shampooed, she thought about the evening and how it had unfurled. The Sanchez family had been so nice. Cody was a great kid, and Alice was a delight to care for. She hadn't been exaggerating when she told her roommate Rick was a great-looking guy, but he was almost old enough to be her dad—if she had a dad. When he drove her home, it was pretty obvious he didn't see her as a woman. In his eyes, she was still a student—and that was a good thing. Jessie stood under the shower and looked up into the jet stream. The water washed away her shampoo, and her mind flowed back to earlier that night.

The old lady from next door had been a blessing. Mrs. Palmer was a bit of a grandmother type, but she had been so kind to Jessie and the kids—a terrific woman to have as a neighbor. Maria Sanchez was lucky. It was Mrs. Palmer who gave Cody first the codes for the fire alarm, and then a little while later she suggested using the same numbers for the intruder alarm. It worked, bless her.

Jessie got all the windows and doors shut and then the fire brigade cleared off. She tried both parents' cell phones again. When she got their voice mails for the third time, she headed over to Mrs. Palmer's. The woman had a cup of Earl Grey tea ready and the children content watching *Dumbo*. She explained to Jessie she had a full library of DVDs for when her grandchildren visited. It gave her more time to talk to her own kids if the grandchildren were occupied. She was a wise granny. Todd's dad, Greg Palmer, was there by then, too.

They barely got a chance to talk, because eventually Maria did check in. She was frantic when she phoned Jessie's cell to get an update on the situation. Jessie tried to calm her and said everything was okay. She said she was at Noreen Palmer's and would be heading back with the two kids to the Sanchez home as soon as the movie was over, but Maria couldn't be reassured. She was already in the car and on her way home.

Rick and Maria arrived before Dumbo had even learned to fly. They swooped into Mrs. Palmer's kitchen on a wave of panic. The older woman tried to de-stress them with tea, but little Alice, who had nodded off again, woke up when she heard her mother's anxious voice. For a short time, hysteria was restored. The Sanchez family all shouted when they got excited—it was mayhem, but Jessie and Mrs. Palmer worked together and managed to get the movie off, the Sanchez family back into their own house, and the children bedded down. Maria was effusive in her thanks and apologies to Jessie. She wrote down the code for the alarms and gave them to the sitter.

All a little late, Jessie thought, but maybe they would ask her to babysit again. That would be good.

The more money she made, the better. Jessie was broke. Her mother had very little money, and there were four children still at home. This scholarship was Jessie's key to future success. She was determined to make a go of her life, and she was on the right path. She turned the water pressure up to wash out the conditioner, and when her hair was squeaky clean, Jessie stepped out of the shower.

She thought about Ely. The girl was extremely perceptive and understood Rick was cute just by the way she'd said his name. Wow.

Jessie patted herself down with a towel. If she had mentioned Dan, the fireman, by name, she knew she would have giggled, blushed, or maybe even stuttered. That would have been a dead giveaway for Ely. At least when she spoke about Rick she could hide behind the fact he was old and married. If Ely thought for one moment Jessie had come across a guy who was real attractive and their age—and a firefighter no less—she'd have been out lighting fires all over campus just to get the guy to show up.

Dan was cute. He was nice, too, but most of all, he had a charm Jessie found very appealing.

Covering herself in moisturizer, Jessie thought about how she didn't have a boyfriend waiting for her back at home in England. There had been a guy in her first year, but she'd found him messing around behind her back. Since then she had stayed single. There were lots of dates but no relationships. Most guys she met were too immature.

Of course, all the ones in her psychology classes were obsessed with trying to analyze her. It was a common flaw with psych students. They felt the need to analyze the world. She had no desire to be psychologically dissected by a boyfriend—or by anybody, for that matter. But Dan was different. He was a real live hero. She doubted analyzing her was high on his agenda. He gave Jessie a pretty good idea of where his interest lay.

Jessie rubbed on more cream. She didn't know for sure, but Dan looked like he was in his late twenties. He wasn't particularly tall, just a little more so than she—perhaps five foot ten or eleven. Not tall by American standards, but she didn't mind. That navy T-shirt he had worn had been tight across his chest for all the right reasons. She could tell he was solid muscle underneath. And that falcon tattoo . . . "He must work out," she whispered to herself as she got into her pj's.

She liked his dark brown hair and long fringe that fell over his forehead, almost blocking one of his eyes. She couldn't remember which one now, but he sure had a roguish look. His eyebrows were heavy, set over brooding, darker eyes. Jessie didn't know what color they were yet, but she knew mischief when she saw it. The slight stubble on his chin and around his mouth was very butch. It was a nice mouth, too. They were nice lips, curved up slightly—like he was smiling. Maybe he was just a happy guy.

Earlier, when he had fiddled with the keypad for the house alarm, she couldn't have helped but notice how pumped his biceps were, too. He had a lot of muscle. *What a good model he would make for those raunchy firefighter calendars,* she thought and tried to remember back to their full conversation.

"I didn't realize how much I loved the silence until it was gone," Jessie had said, smiling at him when the second alarm finally stopped.

"Now," he said without missing a beat. "I think I should take your phone number, you know, just in case there are any follow-up questions we might need to ask you."

At first she wasn't sure. "I'm not in trouble for this, am I?"

He laughed, the sound deep and warm. "Nah. This is all pretty standard stuff. It's just, if I have any questions, like perhaps if you might like to go out for a drink sometime."

She smirked. "Are you hitting on me?" He gave her a guilty-as-charged grin, but it faded fast when a senior officer walked in to see what was going on.

"Did you get the code?" the man asked.

Jessie nodded, a little spooked by his military style.

"Very good." Then he looked at Dan. "Walker, no messing about, you hear? Let's move out," he said and left as quick he had entered.

Dan pulled his cell phone out. "Quick, your number."

Jessie slipped into her oversized dressing gown. "Ring, ring, ring," she whispered while standing in the bathroom. She didn't want Ely to hear about Dan—not yet. If he called her and they dated, good, but if he didn't, she wouldn't want Ely feeling sorry for her. He was very cool, a swashbuckler, running into burning buildings and liberating smoking toasters. She smiled at her reflection. No, that wasn't fair. Firefighters were heroes. They often found themselves in extreme, dangerous situations. Literally saving people's lives, making the difference between life and death. It took a certain kind of man to be willing to run into a burning building. She had found a guy who couldn't be further removed from her psychologist suitors if she had tried. They were all thinkers and talkers. Dan was a doer.

If he phoned, what, she wondered with a shiver of anticipation, would he do to her?

Chapter Five
Maria's Little Secret

"What am I going to do?" Maria asked her little girl.

Alice was strapped into her high chair, finger painting with a great big globule of yogurt. Maria had tried to spoon-feed it into the baby, but it appeared Alice didn't like peach flavor, so she spit it out very effectively. While it was no fun for her to eat, it looked like it was great fun to play with. At least she wasn't screaming. That was a small mercy. The one time Alice seemed content with her company was at mealtimes.

"You're lucky," Maria said to her daughter. "You have no worries yet."

It had only been four days since the fire incident, and Maria was still in shock. There were a few things that bothered her about that night. For years now, really since she had gotten pregnant with Alice, she'd been watching her figure slip. At first it had been in the name of a healthy pregnancy. She'd forgiven herself because her daughter was young. Eventually she'd stopped thinking about it and just accepted her new shape in the name of motherhood. It had nothing to do with the fact that she liked a glass of wine most nights now. It was easy enough to settle for the middle-aged suburban housewife look because she was a busy mother of two and a good mom, but now she questioned her good mom title.

Would a good mom go out and leave a brand new sitter alone without the alarm codes or even a number to contact her? Would a good mom have gotten so caught up on how pretty the sitter was? What did that matter, as long as she was good with the kids? Would a good mom let herself get so out of shape? Maria began to wonder if she was doing anything right. Raising Alice seemed to be a lot harder than bringing up Cody.

"Everyone tells me the weight gain is normal at this time of life." She gently wiped the edges of her daughter's mouth with the rim of the baby spoon. "To be expected, even."

She'd heard it a million times, but it didn't help. "Getting old and getting fat—ha, what fun it is looking at reality. At least there's always the chance I might lose the weight, but there is no way on God's good earth I can turn back the clock. I've got to face up to getting older, and those sitters are only going to get prettier, Alice."

These issues had been bubbling under the surface for months, but the night Jessie arrived had crystallized everything for Maria.

She had seen the way Ricky looked at the new girl. It had been subtle, difficult to pinpoint, but very real nonetheless. He had stood a little taller, more alert, and held himself like he had when he'd been courting her. Ricky was attracted to Jessie.

Maria had teased him about it in a lighthearted way, and of course, he'd denied it. He hid behind the surprise of "toast-gate," as they now referred to it. But Maria knew that look. She'd seen it a million times on her husband's face—when they'd first met, first dated, first made love—but she hadn't seen it in a long time. They had slipped into a mediocre marriage. Funny, she had filled out and softened around the edges, but he hadn't.

Rick's drug of choice was adrenaline. He was a runner, but in the last few years he had taken even that up a notch and now did marathons. He'd done the Boston one first and then the New York and Chicago Marathons. More recently, Rick had run Dallas, and last night he mentioned the London City Marathon. Ricky had never thought of doing a marathon outside the States before. If he was going to, there were literally hundreds of options, and all of a sudden he wanted to do the London Marathon. London, Jessie's hometown.

Maria had asked if it was because of her. She'd tried to make it sound like a joke, but he got mad and had told her to stop raving about the sitter and let it go. He had accused her of being delusional.

Was it all in her head? Was she going nuts over nothing? Maybe it was a natural male reaction to a pretty woman. She had experienced that enough herself when she was younger. It was frustrating, though. He could still flirt, but she couldn't.

She was past her best. The whole darn reason her figure was ruined was because of his kids, and now he got to look at other woman while she—

Alice picked that precise moment to splash the little puddle of yogurt hard with the palm of her hand. It splattered up in all directions, and one particularly large dollop landed in Maria's eye. The timing was sublime. This—this was what Maria got, while Rick got marathons and flirtations with younger women.

Bad enough she'd lost her figure and was aging faster than she could say "corrective surgery," but now she was proving to be a bad mother, too? She had missed all of Jessie's phone calls. For Maria, that was unforgivable. What sort of woman goes out and drops her purse on the floor without thinking to check her messages until it's just about time to go home? A bad mother. That was who.

Maria had been a mom for over a decade. She was proud of her title and had thought she was a good one, but not anymore. What if it had been more serious? What if a child had been hit by a car and needed a kidney or a blood transfusion—not that her blood had been in any state to be transfused after all the fruit punch she'd drunk. But what kind of a mom would be so irresponsible? Only a cruddy one.

Maria got a paper towel and wiped her eye clean. Then she noticed her sweater had a peach-colored splat, too. Rubbing at it just made it worse. What did it matter? Maria deserved to look and feel awful.

Alice began to whine, causing Maria to jump. If she didn't get something tasty for the baby fast, her daughter would head straight into a major meltdown. She got the box of crackers from the cupboard and gave one of those to her daughter instead. Alice parked the tantrum when she saw the food she loved. Maria sat heavily into the seat beside her and ate a cracker, too.

"So you see, Alice, I'm old, fat, and don't get me started on being stupid." She tried to remember what that smarty-pants was studying. "Emotion regulation and blah, blah, blah romantic relationships. I don't even know what that means," she said with exasperation. "Do people regulate their emotions? For real? I sure don't."

It was impossible for Maria not to compare the woman she was today with the girl who had graduated from the University of Vermont a short fifteen years earlier. That was where she had met Rick, and she smiled at the memory. He used to say Maria was his *treasure*. It was pure chance they had both ended up at the beautiful lakeside campus.

For Maria it had been right down to the wire. She had been nervous about traveling so far from her beloved Puerto Rico. Missing the weather was one thing—Maria was a sunshine kind of girl—but she had known the culture would be very different, too, and the distance vast. Traveling home hadn't been easy or cheap. All of that had been incidental, though. At the very last minute, in the name of exploration and bravery, she had opted for Vermont over Fort Myers in Florida. That had been her other option and the one preferred by her parents. Back then, she'd decided it was time to spread her wings, so she had gone to Vermont to study business administration. As luck would have it, so had Ricky.

His full name was Ricardo. That was what his late mother had called him, but he made sure everybody called him Rick—everybody except Maria. She used the pet name Ricky. She was the only one who could do that.

When they had first met at a party, she had given him the cold shoulder. But she'd liked him right away. Who wouldn't? He was a good-looking guy, his Puerto Rican ancestry visible, even though she had soon learned that he'd been born in the US. Rick had tanned skin and dark eyes. He reminded her of Johnny Depp—small frame, extremely self-assured, eyes that penetrated. Even after all these years, he still had the thin physique and dark complexion. Ricky hadn't aged as much as she had—running held back the years for him. Things had been different when they first met. Way back then she hadn't shown that she liked him, not at first. Maria knew how to handle herself around men, and the last thing a woman should do was show interest.

"The more a man has to chase a woman, the more he wants her," she said to her little girl. "That's what my mother taught me, and in time I'll explain it all to you."

Alice gurgled in agreement.

That night fifteen years ago, the rule had served her well. She had ignored Ricky to start with, and he had fought for her attention. Finally, he'd made a concerted effort to get her to talk with him and then to dance, but she hadn't made it easy.

"A man has to work for you, *cariño*," she told Alice with enthusiasm. "You have to be a great prize for him to win. He has to be proud to win you, hungry to win you."

Alice farted. Maria slumped. That life was such a distant memory now. When was the last time Ricky had looked at her the way he looked at Jessie? Years, for sure.

Way back then, Maria had her choice of men. With her long dark hair and sassy curves, she had never been short of boyfriends. If there was one thing she would have liked to change about herself it was her height. She was only five-foot-four, but then again, that meant she could always wear heels and her legs looked great.

Her eyes were a deep, dark brown, which were regular enough in Puerto Rico but highly prized in Vermont. She had a wide mouth and perfect teeth, without the help of an orthodontist. Her friends used to call her 'Jenny from the Block' because she looked a lot like Jennifer Lopez. But Maria, although flattered, had laughed it off. "I would rather have her bank account than her body," she would say. But still, it was a heck of a compliment.

Those days were gone now. Jennifer Lopez had produced twins and still looked like a sex siren, whereas Maria looked like she'd swallowed JLo! Losing her youth and her looks was bad enough for Maria, but if she had Ricky's undying love, it would still be okay. Now she was beginning to wonder if that was conditional, too.

Was it her body he'd fallen in love with and not her personality? Was he really going to stick around if he was beginning to look at the sitters that way already? What would their marriage be like in five years if they'd reached this point in just a decade?

When she'd left home, Maria assumed she would go to college in Vermont, work for a while in New York, perhaps, and then head back to Puerto Rico. It had never been in her plan to leave the tropical island forever, but life had other plans. Ricky Sanchez had stepped into her world.

His grandmother and his mother, both now deceased, had been Puerto Rican. Ricky spoke fluent Spanish, but more important than any of that, he simply got her. Maria used to tease him that he was marrying his mother, because both she and her mother-in-law came from the same little island in the Caribbean, but he insisted that there were plenty of differences between the women. Ricky had been so romantic back in college. He had written her notes and left them under her pillow or next to the bathroom sink. She would find them in her folders or even in the fridge. In those letters he swore his undying love. Ricky wrote with such passion—how could she not fall in love?

Then there was the sex. It had been amazing in those early days. Ricky hadn't been able to get enough of her. They'd been like rabbits, morning, noon, and night. It was a miracle she had scraped through her degree, they'd spent so much lecture time in bed together. But somehow both of them had left college with degrees, and she'd also gained an engagement ring. The rest—she took another cracker—was history.

Ricky had gotten a terrific job in a large marketing firm in Boston and worked his way up to head of his department in Internet marketing. She had paid little attention to his work at that stage, although she did know he'd secured a generous share option in the company during his last bout of employment contract negotiations. This meant as the company grew so did their nest egg, but it also meant he was tied to the company for the foreseeable future. Michael, Ricky's best friend, worked there, too. Cathi's husband wasn't quite as senior, but the men liked working together. She knew from listening to her husband that his work life was fun. Lucky him.

Maria cleaned Alice's face, unstrapped her out of the high chair and let her down on the kitchen floor. The baby couldn't walk yet, but she was a fast little crawler. Maria had tried to encourage her onto her feet, but Alice would give one of her piercing screams, pull herself back down onto her backside, and then speed crawl away. Today Maria was in no mood to fight, so she let the girl do what she wanted. It was dangerous to let Alice out of her eyesight for even a minute, because she could head for the front door, or worse—the back. It would be difficult but not impossible for her to get to the lake if she was determined. Maria needed to speak to Ricky about enclosing the backyard for the baby's safety. There hadn't been the money to do it when Cody had been small, but now she felt the need.

It was Cathi who had told her to put up a fence. "You wouldn't believe how many domestic accidents there are each year in the United States—just with babies crawling into danger, Maria. I'm telling you, don't leave it to chance."

Maria believed her. Cathi was a great mom with two little girls, Stacy and Katie, nine and ten years old. Michael called the three women in his life *his girls*. He doted on them and with good reason.

Cathi was the consummate corporate wife. She ran an oh-so-smooth house. The children were always immaculately dressed and had perfect manners. Maria knew their grades were excellent, and both excelled at ice hockey and tennis. Meanwhile, Cody was always filthy, and despite her trying to buy his clothes to coordinate, they never did. She even bought ensembles so he could wear them together, but Cody wouldn't do that.

Nothing he wore ever matched. The more expensive the outfit, the quicker it seemed to get ripped, trashed, or lost. If she didn't know better, Maria would have thought he was doing it on purpose.

Alice was a different matter. Anything she wore only lasted a nanosecond before it got filthy with food, but at least she'd wear whatever Maria put on her, and dressing a little girl was pure heaven. Her entire wardrobe was full of cerise pinks and raspberry reds. Like her parents, Alice had saucer-size, dark brown eyes, but her hair was still baby fluff. Maria knew soon enough it would be as dark as her own, but for the time being, Alice's hair was a light fluffy brown. Maria's mother took huge pleasure in buying little dresses that had matching headbands and shoes. Thousands of photographs had already been taken of her little girl. These days, the dresses weren't very practical, because Alice wanted to crawl everywhere and her knees kept catching in the folds of her skirts. Maria knew she should start to buy her daughter leggings soon, but she was delaying it because she liked the girlie stuff so much. Maybe as soon as Alice started to walk she could get her back into dresses. The leggings could be just for the crawling stage.

Maria thought about Cathi's perfect children and wanted Alice to follow in their footsteps. Cody was so different. He rarely obeyed her. Both she and Ricky had enormous Latin spirit, and it looked like Cody did, too. He was a little wild, but that was what gave life such excitement and passion. She didn't want him to lose that—ever. Ricky still had it. He ran with passion, worked with passion. The only place the passion seemed to be petering out was in the bedroom.

It wasn't like they'd stopped having sex—it just happened so rarely these days. Even after Cody was born, she had been happy to get romantic two or maybe three times a week. The older he'd gotten, the more nervous Maria had become that Cody might walk in on them. Then when she got pregnant with Alice, she was so tired. Since her little girl had arrived, she seemed permanently exhausted. If they made love twice a month it was an achievement. He still kissed her in the morning, but it was all so rushed. They didn't seem to hug for no reason anymore. When had that crept into their lives?

Could she get back to the way they once had been? Maybe that was where she should be focusing her energies. Instead of worrying about nonexistent affairs between Ricky and Jessie, perhaps she should be scheming up ways to get her husband's attention back on her.

Alice had reached the back door and was trying to pull herself up to a standing position, but Maria knew Cody would barge in from school through that same door pretty soon. She went over to the baby and pulled her back to the leg of the table. It was no surprise when Alice ramped up to a full-scale tantrum.

"Suck it up," Maria said, knowing there was no way she could soothe her child. She went back to wiping down the countertop. Perhaps she should join a gym. After all, Alice was turning one two days before Christmas. But why wait that long? If she got cracking now, maybe she would even be in great shape for her baby's first birthday. Not to mention her own fortieth birthday was looming on the horizon later that spring. How cool would that be?

She knew Cathi was a good person for fitness advice—she went to the gym almost every day—but Maria wouldn't share this decision with her friend. She wouldn't even tell Ricky. She would do this by herself, and then her magnificent new figure could be a surprise. She wondered how much she could improve in two months.

But what would she do with Alice while she went to the gym? Maria knew her baby would go crazy if she tried to drop her off at one of those baby daycares they had in some gyms. It would be better to get a sitter to come take care of the baby at home.

Maria thought about Jessie. She really was an amazing babysitter, and Alice loved her. The last few girls she'd hired had been disasters, more interested in texting, tweeting, or doing whatever the latest craze was. They had all spent their time with their noses in their cell phones and not focusing on her precious children. Jessie was so much better than that.

Maria remembered what Cathi had said about keeping pretty women away from her husband. Yes, Ricky seemed to have noticed how pretty Jessie was, but if it was to be just a few mornings a week when he wasn't even around, what harm could it do? In fact, in a perverse sort of way it might motivate Maria. Seeing Jessie, her beautiful, young competition, would push Maria to work out even harder.

Alice had reached the back door again. "You're going to get hurt." The baby looked at her and cooed. "When Cody comes in, he'll smash that door open and you with it if you stand there."

Maria picked her up and put her out of harm's way. Orga began to bark outside, which meant Cody was close. Alice started to wail, annoyed at being taken away from the back door again. So Maria gave her another cracker and took one for herself, as well.

"Okay," she said to Alice. "Soon, I'll get organized and Operation: Transformation can begin, but it has to be our little secret."

Chapter Six
A Sectional Seduction

Crystal Lake was the worst kept secret in Newton. Cathi fumed as she tapped the Hello Kitty mouse next to her computer with more force than was necessary. Her platinum-blond bob was swept back from her face with a wide, white headband. She wore a fitted, winter-pink cowl neck sweater with a pair of Not Your Daughter's Jeans. Cathi always gave a lot of thought to how she looked, and this morning was no different. Today, like every day, she was the picture of a perfect Newton wife—on the outside. On the inside, however, she was a churning mass of frustration.

"Fudge and double fudge," she said with suppressed fury. Her strict Catholic education might have taught her to curb the use of bad language, but it had done nothing to restrain her ambitions in life, and Cathi was certainly ambitious. Her daughters were in the best private school within a twenty-mile radius. She was married to Michael, an amazing man with a glamorous job in marketing, and Cathi knew he was still an attractive man. Tall and thin, he was soft-spoken but smart. He would never be the life and soul of the party, but he was strong and dependable. She was the go-getter in the house. Cathi was head of the New to Newton Society, an organization that dedicated itself to the successful integration of new families in the area. And of course, she had a perfect house. The problem was after eight years in the same home, she felt it was time to trade up.

Cathi had been indulging in her latest obsession—property trawling. It was an addictive pastime, and she liked to do it often because local real estate websites uploaded new properties any time during the day. She was even able to narrow her search so she would be shown just the houses within a three-mile radius of her target—Crystal Lake Lane. Cathi could quote her price per square foot just by knowing their proximity to Newton town center and how close they were to the commuter train, the T.

Public transport into Boston meant sellers could hike the price up for commuters. Thankfully, that didn't bother her. Cathi drove everywhere, and so did Michael. His job downtown in Post Office Square came with a parking space, so they rarely used the T. Much more important than trains, transport, and town to Cathi was the water. The lake. Ever since she'd been a little girl, she'd wanted a house on the water, and now, quite suddenly and with no warning, one had popped up for sale. She couldn't believe it.

Having just shut down the website, she reopened it again. "Recession, my foot," she grumbled. Fifi, their shih tzu, sat on the floor next to her swivel chair and watched Cathi with tiny adoring eyes.

She clicked the newest listing on the property page and reread the house description.

Newton's best kept secret, it promised.

"Not anymore," she said and read a little more.

Number sixteen, Crystal Lake is tucked away on Crystal Lake Lane, a cul-de-sac of the most desirable detached residences. Many of these magnificent family homes have direct access to the ever popular Crystal Lake. This waterfront home comes to the market in pristine condition.

"Etcetera, etcetera, etcetera," Cathi said to the dog.

She didn't need to go over it again. It was painful enough to read it once. What galled her was the price tag. Some developer had moved in and renovated number sixteen. It was the last house on the dead-end street, on the right-hand side. Cathi didn't drive past it on her way to Maria's, so she'd missed the amount of work that must have been done. Now in immaculate condition, the property was for sale for crazy money.

"I'd have to win the lottery." She drummed her fingers. "How could they be asking for that much? They don't even have access to the water." There was a small lane down the side of number fifteen, so in theory they did—or at least the blurb said they did—but the views couldn't be nearly as good as Maria's. What kind of value did that put on her friend's house? How had Maria managed to get a house there before the last boom?

She cast an embittered eye around her own study. The entire room had been fitted with English mahogany bookshelves to give it an old-world-library feel. Cathi had filled it with silver framed photographs of her girls and volumes of everyone from Emily Bronte to Danielle Steel. Ironic now that all the works were available on her e-reader, but still she liked the feel of the room.

An interior decorator had done the entire project for Cathi when Stacy, her younger daughter, had turned five. That had been four years ago already. Where had the time gone? Back then, Cathi had decided the children were done being messy, which meant she could think about a more adult environment. She was thankful the girls were out of the sticky finger stage, but sad that their girlie world still reigned supreme, her hot pink mouse being a good example. How was she ever going to finish the house in a regal and gentrified fashion while all this junk kept arriving?

Birthday parties were the worst. After one of those, there was a tsunami of pink plastic and multicolored trash in the house. It all came in the guise of new presents, but Cathi knew most of it would end up in the town dump or, at best, on their charity pile. Every few months, she dropped off items for charity due to the amount of junk her family accumulated.

At least the girls were through the Happy Meal stage. Nobody had told her about that difficulty when she'd been pregnant or when the girls had been small. It was bad enough they ate that stuff at all, but what made it worse were the little bits of pink garbage the girls called toys that hung around the house for weeks after until Cathi managed to dispose of it.

She'd always aspired to living a life straight out of *Coastal Living*. Her first mistake was not living on the coast, but several articles had convinced her not to stop living the dream because she lacked that small detail. She could still decorate her house in a manner the magazine suggested. Cathi had the good sense to avoid the *beach this way* sign because it would look a little stupid in landlocked Newton, but she could certainly use sailor's stripes on her sofa cushions and shells in the bathroom. Even the master bedroom hadn't escaped. It was home to an oversized, antique captain's storage trunk at the foot of their bed.

Her regular subscriptions had taught her everything was in the details. Cathi spent hours considering colors, such as the merits of aqua over ecru and bamboo over basket. She knew two or three misplaced shams made the difference between a breezy bedroom and a hurricane hit. Cathi also knew she had good taste, because she'd spent years developing it under the tutelage of every interior magazine she could get her hands on. Still, that hadn't stopped her from hiring the best professional help she could find when she had done her big makeover a few years back.

She clicked her mouse again, closed the laptop down, and picked up Fifi. Her day had just gotten a whole lot worse. Cathi left the library and headed for her galley kitchen. She switched on her shiny new chrome coffee maker, and it started to gurgle reassuringly.

Things would feel better after a nice warm drink. Leaving the machine to do its job, she carried Fifi with her into her living room, where she flopped down onto her pastel blue sofa and let the dog settle next to her. She loved this room since the redecoration. It wasn't a big room, but the interior designer had shown her how to use a sectional couch fitted in the corner to maximize her sedentary space. Her ottoman doubled as extra seating and storage—how clever was that? The entire ground floor of the house had been redecorated at the same time so that each room complemented the next. The colors flowed from one room to the next. For example, the creams in the library sofa matched the cushions in the living room. The pastel blue sectional was the same color as the paint she'd used in the girls' desert island den. Their toy boxes in that room were made of the same mahogany as her library shelves. It was meant to be inconspicuous, but even an amateur would see how the entire house worked together.

It was supposed to be subliminal, tasteful—very Cathi. Moneywise, she'd spent more than she planned, but she couldn't stop halfway through such a project. Once she had committed, it would have been insanity to quit—a false economy. Michael had been mutinous when he'd seen the bills coming in, but by then it was too late. He'd also thought they were getting the entire house redone for that price, when in fact it had just been the downstairs. That had been a sticky point. A few months after the job had been finished, and even Michael had agreed it looked terrific, he'd asked when work was to commence on the upstairs.

Sitting in her sectional, Cathi remembered the argument well.

She had tried to act surprised. "You want me to get that done, too?"

"Well, isn't that what your designer has been paid for? I mean, she's only halfway through the makeover."

"I thought you were unhappy with the cost. I didn't go ahead with upstairs." Cathi forced a smile.

"I was unhappy with the cost." Michael frowned. "No, correction—I *am* unhappy with the cost. We could have bought a holiday home with the money you've pumped into this one. I assumed the bill I was looking at was for the entire house, Cathi."

She knew Michael was beginning to feel yet another penny drop, following the thousands that had already dropped from their account.

She couldn't really stall him anymore. It was better to come clean, and it was too late anyway. "No, we just contracted her for the downstairs. That's what we paid for. If you want me to get her to do upstairs, I'm sure I can ask her for a more competitive quote, especially with the recession."

Michael was on his feet. "What? You're telling me all that money— almost a year's salary—went on a few cushions and shams?"

"The paint was organic," Cathi said, but she knew Michael was on the edge of a major meltdown. There was only one way to defuse him when he got this mad, and she knew what to do. The girls were at camp, so the house was empty. Cathi got up and wrapped her arms around his neck. She kissed his cheeks and then his lips. "I'm sorry, I'm sorry, I'm sorry," she said between each kiss. Then she dropped her hand, and pretty fast, his ire turned to desire.

"If you think you can talk your way out of this one . . ." he said while he kissed her back. She could feel his anger subside as his passion flared. That was the day they christened their sectional.

Cathi heard the coffee percolator click and headed back into the kitchen. Her plan had been to redesign the house then sell it. Even back then she was determined to trade up. She had parked the idea for a while after the redecoration—in part because it was so nice, but mainly because Michael had still been upset about her financial extravagance. She knew if she had suggested selling, he would have turned her down. A lot of time had passed since then. She thought perhaps now the time was right for a move. They would turn a good profit on the house after all she'd done to it.

Was there any way in heaven she could get the money together to buy number sixteen Crystal Lake? If she could pull it off, she'd never ask for anything again. It was already renovated, so they wouldn't have to spend any more. How could she convince Michael? Where in the world would she find that kind of money?

Armed with her coffee, Cathi walked around the ground floor of her home. It was such a great house, close to good schools and downtown Newton. The first thing she decided to do was call a realtor and get an appraisal. Then at least she could calculate how much she needed. Perhaps if she put it on the market, she could see what sort of demand was out there. If she was lucky, maybe she'd get two parties involved and start a bidding war. That way she'd make a good profit to carry forward.

"But what about Michael?" she asked Fifi, who was walking alongside her. Cathi took a sip of her coffee and thought about their last property discussion. She would bring the matter up on an evening when both the girls were out at slumber parties and when he had a glass of wine in his hand. She'd see to it that she looked great and had her hair blown out. But most of all—Cathi smiled—she would be sure she asked when Michael was sitting on the sectional.

Chapter Seven
The First Date

"I'm sitting on my bed, in my room, in *America*! You know, I still can't believe I'm here," Jessie said when she was talking to her mother on the phone. "I mean *college in America*—me? I never thought it would happen for real."

Her mother laughed through the telephone line. "Every time we speak, you say that. I never doubted it. You're a great girl, but if you've one fault, it's you don't realize just how good you are."

"Mom."

"Did you just call me 'Mom'?"

"Sorry, Mother."

"Sweetheart, from your first semester in college back here in dear old England, your dean of faculty told you a master's was a good idea because you're so smart and driven."

"Okay, I hear you." Jessie tried to stop Elizabeth Armstrong's high praise, but it was too late.

"Not only that, but you know how much I appreciate you at home, too. Life hasn't been easy since Dad died, but when I had to work, you always stepped in and minded the younger ones and cleaned."

"Mum, you're embarrassing me."

"You even ironed. Now, don't get me wrong, your siblings are a big help to me, too, and little Tristan is getting bigger by the day, but believe me when I say we miss you."

"Oh, Mum, I miss you guys, too. Tristan most of all."

" 'You guys'? Are you talking American now?"

Jessie laughed. "Hardly. It's been a little over two months since I landed here."

"The year will be over before you even realize you're there, pet. Now go and enjoy yourself. Just don't fall in love. It would break my heart if you stayed in the States with some American man."

"Mum, as if. Although . . ." She didn't know whether to tell her or not. Part of her knew her mother would worry, but then again, they had never kept secrets. Maybe it was a bad idea to start now.

"Jessica?" Elizabeth must have already heard the hesitation in her voice. "Have you something to tell me?"

"Well . . ." She wove a strand of her hair through her fingers. "Um, so I met this guy last week. He's a fireman."

"Ooh, isn't that dangerous?"

"Not the night I met him. Believe me, Mum, it's not all raging fires and heroic rescues. These guys have a lot of humdrum to deal with, too."

"You mean like cats up trees?"

"Yes, and burnt toast."

Elizabeth laughed. "They wouldn't come out for something as daft as that, would they?"

Jessie flicked her hair away and coughed to clear her throat. "Anyway, his name is Dan and he's asked me out."

"So you haven't been on the date yet?"

"No, he's collecting me any minute now. I just wanted to tell you."

"Thanks, luv. Just don't let it get serious. You know that wouldn't be wise."

Jessie was quick to reply. "Oh, I don't have any intention of falling in love, Mum. It's just a date. He seems like a nice guy."

She made sure to sound convincing so her mother accepted it. "Well, you deserve a little fun time, too, dear. It's just so important to remember I need you back at the end of the year. You won't lose sight of that, will you?"

"I swear, Mum. I'll keep my head screwed on. I'm here to study, and then I'm coming home to London. I'll get a great job and earn enough money so you can stop working and everybody can go to good colleges. That's my plan. Nothing and no one is going to make that change."

"Good girl." Elizabeth Armstrong sounded content. "Have a good time with this Dan chap," she said, and soon after, they finished their call.

Jessie checked her reflection again. She'd spent too much time getting ready, and Ely had understood pretty fast that she was going on a date. For a change, the girl went easy on her, because she'd admitted that it had taken Dan a whole week to phone her.

Either he wasn't interested, or he was playing it cool. Neither was an attractive option. When he had, at last, phoned her, Jessie played it cool, too. She had pretended she didn't remember him. He'd laughed it off and reintroduced himself. They had talked for a while, and then he'd asked her out. After a little stalling, she had accepted. The truth was she so wanted to go out with him. He was damn good-looking, and she remembered how brave he'd looked walking into the house with her. Never mind there was no fire—he had a swagger about him and a confidence that said if there *had* been a fire, he would have been able to handle it.

As it was, he had managed the fire and intruder alarms with marvelous finesse. Yes, he was all man, and she would have been crazy not to accept a date with him, but her guard was up. If she thought he was cute and manly, chances were lots of girls thought the same. This was another reason she had no intention of getting serious with him—he might have had loads of girlfriends, and that was why he'd taken so long to call her.

Her cell phone buzzed. No name came up with the number, so she was pretty sure it was Dan. When he'd last called, she had ignored the urge to save his number. If he wanted her, he would call. She wasn't going to have his number in her phone's memory. That way she couldn't accidently butt dial him or maybe even send him a text about how gorgeous he was after half a bottle of wine.

Jessie answered the phone. "Hullo."

"So which building is yours?" he asked without even introducing himself. He was so damn self-assured.

"I'll come down." There was no way she was letting him inside her room. Nor did she want him to know she lived in an all-girl house—how juvenile was that?

On the night of the fire, Jessie's hair had been clipped up. This afternoon, she let it hang down her back, long and loose. Her light blond curls danced around her shoulders and down her back over a navy blue puff jacket. Under that, she had a pair of faded denim jeans and trainers. She hoped he would approve.

Jessie trotted out of the building but stopped short when she got outside and looked around. There was no sign of Dan. She took her phone out and considered the possibility of redialing the number that had just called her, but then a guy in a biker jacket and helmet walked toward her. He waved, and she looked back over her shoulder. When he took off the motorcycle helmet and smiled, she realized it was Dan.

"Hi," she said. "I didn't recognize you with that thing on."

He shrugged and crossed the distance to her.

"Hi, yourself. You look great." He leaned over to kiss her on the cheek, like it was the most natural thing in the world.

"You have a bike," she said, glancing at his helmet and then mentally kicking herself for stating the obvious.

Dan held the enormous headgear under his arm and nodded. "Yep. You like bikes?" He grinned.

She bit her lip. "I don't know. I've never been on one. I expect they're very exciting but quite scary, too."

He laughed. "You got it, girl. Are you ready to be excited?"

Jessie went straight for scared. "I don't know if I have the right clothes, and I don't own a helmet."

"It's okay." He took her arm and guided her to the biggest motorcycle parked in the lot. "I have a second helmet for you, and I promise I won't drive too fast."

Up close, the machine looked even more intimidating. It was huge. He put the extra helmet on her head and clipped the toggle underneath. Jessie felt like a little girl getting dressed by her father. It was a long time since she'd experienced that.

Dan clipped his own helmet on and mounted the bike. When he kicked the pedal to fire up the mighty engine, she shrieked. He looked back as if to say "get on," so she threw her leg over. It took a lot more effort than she thought it would. Then she settled on the padded seat and lodged her feet onto the pedals on either side.

She was acutely aware of how snugly her legs were wrapped around his body. At a loss for what to do with her hands, she placed them on her knees. Again, Dan looked back at her. Talking was almost impossible with the muffled helmets and noise of the engine, so he took both her hands and wrapped them around his waist, tight.

"You're gonna need to hold on," he yelled as the bike began to move forward.

Jessie was pretty sure it would have been very exciting if she dared to open her eyes. She never thought of herself as a coward before, but seeing the road rush by—just inches under her feet—terrified her. She knew if Dan crashed, they were both dead or worse. *Imagine if I break my neck and have to be hospitalized for life*, she thought in a panic. Here she was, over in America to get a qualification so she could help out at home, and she was taking chances that could result in her being in a wheelchair for the rest of her life. Some help she would be to her family then.

"You okay?" Dan bellowed over his shoulder. They were driving out Route 9, away from the city and out of Newton.

"Yeah," she yelled back without much conviction. Was he trying to scare her? That would be a bit tacky. She reckoned he must have felt her fear, because he slowed down. At the new speed, Jessie began to look around and tried to relax. It was a clear blue-sky afternoon, and Route 9 wasn't congested. He turned off the larger road and drove for another few miles. They came to a gate that was closed to motorists, but with a little careful maneuvering he was able to get the motorbike through a pedestrian access and onto the private road. They drove for about another mile before arriving at what looked like a beautiful deserted beach on a private lake.

He cut the engine and glanced back over his shoulder to gesture she could dismount, which Jessie was more than happy to do. Her legs felt wobbly, but she managed to unclip the helmet strap and pull it off.

"Enjoy that?" he asked, pulling off his own helmet—again with that amazing smile.

It was impossible not to smile back at him, so she did and nodded, too. Just like the last time she'd seen him, he had slight stubble peppering his chin. His hair was a bit messed up after the helmet, but he combed it through with his fingers, and she caught a glimpse of his tattoo again.

"What did it feel like?" he pressed her for a reaction.

Jessie was a little tongue-tied. The truth was she'd been terrified and thought she was crazy to be on the back of a bike. She thought he was even crazier to own one, but it was exciting, too. "Exhilarating," she finally said.

He looked at her and laughed. "Exhilarating?" He said it like it was a new word to him. "I like that. I guess it's a good start to a date—exhilarating."

"This place is pretty." Jessie looked out over the water. "Where are we?"

"I wanted to take you here because it's kinda special to me. It's called Morses Pond."

"That's no pond," she said with a laugh. "It's a bloody lake."

"You think?"

"Oh, what do I know? Everything seems bigger in the States."

He raised his eyebrow and gave her a predatory grin. "Everything?"

Jessie felt herself blushing. Was he asking what she thought he was asking? Just as fast as his wolfish grin appeared, it faded again. "During the summer it's real busy with a boardwalk and lifeguards, but now it's all shut up for the winter. It'll be frozen over in a few more months. I spent all my summers here when I was young, and I love it."

Dan went over to the lifeguard hut which was boarded up for the winter with a *no trespassing* sign nailed on the door. He started to scour the ground until he found a few pebbles. She watched him move to the water's edge where he stopped and focused on the lake. He furrowed his brows in concentration, arched his right arm back, and snapped it forward so fast she could barely follow it, but she saw the little pebble skip along the water's surface easy enough.

"Wow, five, six, seven—that's great!" she said.

"Eight, nine, ten." He kept counting as the pebble seemed to defy gravity and bounce on top of the water until it slipped down into the inky blue.

She walked over to him. "I've never seen a pebble go so far before. How'd you do that?"

He shrugged. "I've done fifteen, but it depends on the stone, the water, the wind. Too many variables." He looked at the sky as if the weather was to blame for his lower than average score.

"Well, I'm impressed. Show me how you did it."

He glanced at her with a look of mild surprise. "You never learned to skip stones?"

She shook her head. "Come on, share your secrets."

He laughed. "I'd rather teach you how to skip pebbles!"

They searched for stones, and Dan explained how they bounced better if the pebbles were disk shape and smooth, but they were difficult to find. After a while, they had a small bundle and the lesson began.

He stood behind her and took her right hand in his. "You need to focus on the surface of the water. Don't think about the stone." Dan placed a pebble in the palm of her right hand, but she couldn't concentrate on the lake. How could she think about that with the warmth of his body pushing against hers? She smelled his aftershave, and when he leaned forward, his chest pressed into her back. Jessie felt him pull her arm back, but they weren't working together and he almost knocked her over when he tried to throw her arm forward too fast.

The little stone arched in the air and sank into the water with a satisfying plop.

"That was probably the worst skip I've ever seen," he said.

"It's harder than it looks."

"Let's try again." He bent down and took another pebble from their stash. This time she really tried to listen to him and work with his body, and the result was better. The second stone bounced once before it sank.

"Success," she shouted and glanced over her shoulder at him. He smiled back. They were so close. It would have been easy for him to kiss her, but he looked away at the ground as if he were scouring for more pebbles. His reaction frustrated Jessie, so she focused on her stone bouncing.

The third one sank like a brick.

"The secret is all in the wrist action," he said. "Watch me do it." He stood back from her, giving her the perfect excuse to study his form as he again stood, legs apart, leaning back a little. He stared hard at the water, his face solemn. He looked even cuter with his serious face on and his lips slightly open. She had been watching his mouth so intently that she missed the actual throw. The stone bounced along the water's surface again, but it sank too fast.

"That one wasn't so good." He scowled.

"Bad stone, I say."

She was over the terror of the bike ride, and he looked like he was enjoying himself, too.

"So tell me, Jessie, what do you think you'll do after your year at college here?"

"I'm going home. I have to. My family's in England," she said. They both sat down on the beach and looked out on the water. "What about you? You settled in New England?"

He looked out over the water and nodded. "This is where I grew up. I wouldn't want to be anywhere else."

This is good, she thought. They were laying out the parameters of their relationship straight away. Sometimes it was a pain being a psychology major. But it was good to know, just the same. Wasn't it better to be open and honest from the start?

"Hungry?" he asked.

"Yes." She braced herself for the fact they were going to have to drive to get to any restaurant—Morses Pond was deserted.

Dan jumped to his feet. "Stay here. I'll be right back," he said and jogged back to the motorcycle.

She hadn't seen the storage space on the bike and was surprised when he arrived back to her with a promising looking brown paper bag.

"Dan, a picnic? How clever are you?" Even though it was November and back in England it would have been impossible to eat out, in Massachusetts it was hit and miss. Some days it was so cold Jessie needed gloves, but the next day she could be in jeans and a T-shirt. Today was a little cool for the T-shirt, but she was more than happy to sit out with Dan to eat and chat.

"Who says romance is dead?" He smiled as he opened the bag and pulled out two sandwiches, potato chips, and two cans of soda.

"This is perfect," Jessie said, and she meant it. At first she'd been a bit surprised when he suggested collecting her midafternoon. She was used to first dates being an evening affair. They usually involved dinner, wine, and some guy trying to get as much action as he could. This was different. Dan, it seemed, was different.

"I'm guessing the beach is man-made." She stroked the sand they were sitting on.

He nodded because he had a mouth full of bread and turkey.

"In England, where I live, it's quite a distance from the sea, but we've nothing like this. There's a town pool, but it has to be indoors. Dorking is too cold—even in the summer."

"Hey, wait for the cold. Believe me, New England winters are big."

"So I've been told. I'm looking forward to the snow. We don't get much of that in the UK."

"Well, you should have enough here to last you a lifetime. But the skiing is great."

"You ski?"

"As much as I can. You?"

She shook her head. "Lots of the kids did back in college in London, but there was never enough money in our house for that."

"I'll take you this winter if you like," he said.

"Are you a bit of a speed junkie?"

"Fast bikes, fast snow, fast women." He laughed and looked at her sideways so she knew he was joking.

"I'm into slow bikes, slow snow, and even slower men," she said in a small voice. He furrowed his brow.

"I should have picked you up on my bicycle? Might have taken a bit longer to get here." He reached over and stroked her cheek, and the mood between them changed. Their eyes met. "I can go slow, Jessie," he said, and her stomach flipped.

Was he going to kiss her? It felt right—natural. But then, just as fast, he looked away and stood up.

"Did you hear that?" he said. "Sounded like thunder to me. Don't think you'd like to ride in the rain. That would kinda spoil the day. I should get you home before the storm hits."

Jessie blinked, coming out of the daydream she was in. There she was, thinking about kissing him, and now he was talking about driving her home. Did that mean the date was over—already?

Dan had their lunch things in the paper bag in seconds. He was just as quick putting Jessie's helmet back on her head, and he drove fast taking her home. Again she hung on tight, but she wasn't so scared this time. Jessie adapted fast. That's what all her tutors had said about her. She knew she could change to suit a new set of circumstances, which was good, because this wasn't like any date she'd been on before. Dan hadn't even made a move on her. How frustrating.

There was no way she was going to sleep with him yet, but she'd been looking forward to a bit of romance. Every guy she'd ever dated had made a move on her on the first date. Why hadn't he?

She tried to hide her disappointment when he got her back to the dorm. It was only five o'clock. Jessie had assumed the date would last for the entire afternoon when he'd suggested a three o'clock pickup.

"Looks like it's not going to rain after all," she said, trying to sound more chipper than she felt and also hinting at the fact they could stay out longer if he wanted. Dan didn't take the hint. He took his helmet off but didn't dismount from the motorcycle.

"Oh yeah," he said, glancing skyward. "Look, I enjoyed this afternoon. Maybe we can do it again sometime."

Sometime? she thought. *When is sometime?* But her face remained the picture of calm. "That would be nice. You have my number." She forced a smile but turned to leave fast. "Bye, Dan. Thanks," she called from over her shoulder, but he was already putting his helmet on.

Jessie walked into her block and pushed the door closed with her back. She shook her head in confused misery and groaned. "He hates me."

Chapter Eight
Falling in Love

"He loves you," Ely announced when her roommate walked into their dorm moments later and grumbled about Dan's apparent lack of interest. Josh was there, too. He was having what Jessie reckoned was a post-sex cigarette along with a bottle of beer. He was dressed, but his hair was wet and slicked back, so she was pretty sure he just got out of the shower. As usual, Ely lay on her bed while Josh sat on the floor next to her with his head resting beside his girlfriend's hand so she could stroke him.

"You'll get us evicted one of these days." Jessie glared at him and pointed to his cigarette. "You know how much I hate those things." She opened the bedroom window next to her desk to clear the smoke. "And no, Ely, I don't think Dan loves me. He didn't seem to be that interested in the date from the start. But his motorbike was nice."

"He has a bike? What kind is it?" Now Josh was sitting upright and listening to the girl talk.

Jessie shrugged and sat down on the chair next to her desk. "It was big and black, but there was a bit of red on the top. I think I saw the Bugatti name on it. Is that good?"

He groaned and reached for his crotch in ecstasy, so Ely thumped him. "Hey, I thought I was the only thing that had that effect on you."

Josh winked at his girlfriend and smiled. "Still. I'd like to get me a bike."

Ely shook her long dark hair with the vehemence of a five-year-old. "Not while you're with me, you don't. You know they call them organ donor machines, right?"

"Huh?"

"The people who drive motorcycles end up being organ donors real fast —as in dead real fast."

Jessie nodded. "It was terrifying to see the ground whizz by so close to me and at that speed. I know it must be dangerous, but I have to admit it was bloody exciting."

"They're way cheaper than cars." Josh nodded in approval, but Ely wrung her hands together.

"So are bicycles, and you don't see me rushing out to buy one of those." Then she gave him a smirk that made Jessie feel uncomfortable. "No, Josh, you have a car. It might be a wreck, but it's good enough for what we need."

Jessie guessed they did more than drive in the old banger. Suddenly she needed to get out of the room.

"I think I'll head over to the library," she said, grabbing her pile of notes and her laptop. "I need to catch up on some work."

"Don't go," Ely said.

"I have to. I feel like a spare wheel around you two lovebirds."

Ely laughed. "What's wrong with being a spare wheel? Ever heard of a tricycle? Best bikes ever made!"

"Outside of the Bugatti," Josh mumbled, and his girlfriend smacked the top of his head.

"I'm serious. You can't go anywhere." Ely got off her bed and stood in the middle of the bedroom between Josh and Jessie. "I have to tell you about my new business plan. It's so cool. It's going to make me a million bucks."

Jessie was surprised. She knew her roomie was a natural business woman. Ely was already making a tidy profit on bootleg Bollinger and prohibition pinot grigio, but she hadn't been talking about any other business ideas.

"What you talkin' about, baby?" It seemed to be news to her boyfriend, too.

Josh was so laid-back Jessie wondered if he and her friend would really make it as a couple. Ely was a party girl, but she was also, in her own way, very ambitious. The problem was her parents were pointing her in the wrong direction. The Southern belle was not cut out for college life. She was too much of a free a spirit. Whoever thought she should do psychology was so misguided.

Jessie knew Ely had already received a few warnings from various teachers for nonattendance, and the sole reason her homework was up to scratch was because Jessie did most of it. She thought Ely shouldn't be in college at all, but she kept these thoughts to herself. Ely's parents ran a very successful hair product company. Briskin Hair Care was one of the biggest brand names in the country. Not only did they sell in the States, they were available in the UK, too. Jessie hadn't made the connection between her roommate and the hair care giant until Ely told her about it. At the time, she'd seemed embarrassed to admit her parents' success.

"It's hardly something to be ashamed about," Jessie had said, suppressing the envy. She'd already had a pretty good idea Ely's family was wealthy, but to own Briskin Hair Care? That put them in a whole new league of wealth. They were as big as L'Oreal.

"Now, I know you're going to think I'm crazy, but hear me out. This could really work, and if it does, it'll change the way we shop forever." Her eyes were bright, and she was on fire with her idea in a way Jessie had never seen.

"Okay." Ely got off the bed to make a proper presentation. She wore dark blue denim jeans tucked into her perennial cowboy boots and a blue-gray checkered shirt hung loose. Ready to begin, she stood with her legs slightly apart, her hands on her hips, and looked at her little audience. Then she took a deep breath. "Do you remember when we were kids? We used to get our water from the faucet, but now everybody drinks bottled water."

She looked from Jessie to Josh, waiting for agreement, so they both smiled and nodded. "Well, every now and then something comes along we *think* we don't need, but then we think, 'Hey, why haven't I been using this all my life?' Okay, I have one of those products."

Josh took Ely's place on the bed, fluffed up her pillows, and lay down. "Where you going with this, babe? You're being a bit vague."

"Honey, I know you have a low boredom threshold, but stay with me for a little longer. Please try to engage! I'm talking about shampoos. I know it's the family business, but I can really add something new and exciting."

Inside Jessie winced. Everybody knew the shampoo market was overstocked with a zillion products.

"There ain't nothing you can add to that business that your daddy hasn't thought of already, darlin'."

"Well," she said, looking coquettish. "There was a time when we just had shampoo, and then along came conditioner. Size of the market was doubled over night." Her Southern drawl became more pronounced as her conviction grew. "Between the three of us, I can tell y'all the size of my daddy's business doubled back then. Next we developed a product range for all the different hair types, and I gotta tell you, the market exploded again." She began to pace the floor as she talked. "For the past five years, give or take, there have been no real leaps forward. Sure, we're always tweakin' and addin' new things, but there hasn't really been anything big, anything new, in a long time. Well, I have an idea, and believe me, it's big."

She stopped walking and turned toward Josh and Jessie, who were both listening and intrigued. "I see this product being launched through the medium of television, so I'm just gonna go ahead and sing the commercial I see hitting your screens in the not too distant future." She scanned the room. "Wait a minute. I need to hold something, like it's my new product." Her eyes fell on her wide paddle hairbrush and she grabbed it. "Okay, pretend this is a bottle of my new shampoo." She held it up and gave a huge smile. Josh and Jessie nodded and tried to stay patient.

She took a big breath, composed herself, and held the hairbrush upright in front of her with two hands. Pretending it was a bottle of her new shampoo, Ely launched into her little singsong rhyme.

"Straight hair, curly hair, dry hair, colored hair.

Blond hair, black hair, blue-gray-green hair.
Dead head, bed head, stick it in the air head.
Any hair left? I hear you wonder.
Yes, you bet—the hair Down Under!"

Then, with one hand, she pointed to her crotch. After a second of disbelief, both Josh and Jessie started to laugh, but Ely continued to sing.

"Every kinda hair needs its own kind of care,
This ain't no different just 'cause it's there."

Both Josh and Jessie were howling with laughter. Then Ely stopped singing and switched to what she obviously thought was a television announcer's voice.

"Down Under is the new shampoo for you.

There's Bruce for the boys and Sheila for the girls.

'Specially made for those delicate curls."

Josh rolled off the bed, unable to contain himself, and Jessie was wiping her eyes because she was crying with laughter.

"Well, what do you think? It's great, right?"

"Oh, it's great all right." Jessie laughed, still trying to compose herself.

Josh looked like he wanted to speak but was still cracking up. "Down under hair is not delicate."

"That's 'cause you're not using the right shampoo. Don't y'all see? That's what's so cool about this new product. One of the primary purchasing forces in any market is fear. If I scare the market enough into realizing they've been using the wrong shampoo on their nether regions since forever, they'll buy it by the truckload. Fear is a great sales tool." Then she stopped for breath. "Of course, humor is, too. That's why I came up with my little song and dance."

Jessie spoke next. "Ely, you don't seriously think this is going to work, do you? TV stations wouldn't let that ad on the screens."

"Yes they would, and even if they didn't, I could make a music video and have it go viral, then sell it on the Internet. What about the name Down Under? You don't think I'll upset the Australians?"

"Oh, I don't know." Josh couldn't stop laughing. "They might be bummed!"

He howled again, and Jessie joined in. "Won't be long before the market bottoms out," she said.

Ely wasn't impressed. "Go on, laugh all you like. People did the same when bottled water came out first, and now it's a billion dollar industry."

"I'm sorry, Ely, it's just the whole concept . . . well, it's nuts." Jessie tried to calm herself down, but when Josh heard her say *nuts*, he started laughing again.

"Cleanest nuts in South Carolina, mind you. Anyway, you'll have to take a haircut on the pricing structure," he said.

"Ha-ha," Ely said, sounding sad. "I thought you two would have more foresight."

"Nah, just foreskin." Josh couldn't seem to stop himself.

"Yeah? Well, many a genius was ridiculed in the beginning, so stick it. I think it's a great idea, and I know it can make me money."

"It might." Jessie crossed the room and put her arm around Ely's shoulders. "If you get people to take it seriously."

"Ely." Josh coughed and sat up on the bed. "I'm with Jessie. Maybe you could make a go of it. Who knows? One day, the company could even go pubic. Sorry, I mean public."

Ely had heard enough. "Okay, forget I ever mentioned it. You know, I don't need your approval. I can do this by myself." She threw the hairbrush at the floor and ran out of the room. Jessie looked to Josh, who was still recovering.

"One of us has to go after her. You or me?"

Josh rose to his feet slowly. "Relax. You women . . . so darn dramatic. I'll go get her. God, it was funny, though. What's she gonna do next? Armpit hair shampoo?" He shook his head in bewilderment and then loped out the door after his girlfriend.

It was only when she was alone that Jessie noticed her cell phone was flashing. She'd received a text from Maria Sanchez. "She wants me three mornings a week!" Jessie squealed out loud even though she was now alone. That money would help offset her living expenses. She thought about her class timetable. It was doable, depending on the mornings Maria wanted. It might mean a little rearranging of homework, but most of her classes were in the afternoons, so she could do it.

"When do you want me to start?" she said aloud as she typed the words into her phone.

It only took a few minutes to get Maria's reply.

How about Monday?

Ely hadn't got very far by the time Josh caught up with her. She was walking slow along the path toward the campus exit. In truth, she had no idea where she wanted to go, and she was hoping either he or Jessie would come after her.

"Sugar, wait up," he called. She turned and watched him jog toward her. All those hours of practice for football made him supremely fit. Damn, he was sexy.

"Honey, I'm sorry," he said before he'd even reached her. He stretched his arms out toward her. "Come here, Ely."

She didn't move, but at least she'd stopped walking away. He finally caught up and wrapped his arms around her. "We shouldn't have laughed at you like that. We ain't got vision like you do. Sorry, babe."

Ely didn't speak but was happy to be hugged. Like his legs, his arms went on forever. Those fabulous long arms had carried her into the shower just a few short hours ago. Josh's hands had reached parts of her no shampoo would ever go. How was it possible to stay mad with him when as he was apologizing and so sincere? He cupped her chin in his hand and tilted her face upward.

"Forgive me?"

"I do." She granted him a half smile. "But you can't go laughing at new business ideas, especially in these tough economic times. How in the world we ever gonna make progress if we don't dream big?"

"Babe, you know you're way ahead of me on this stuff. You're more mature, smarter, more ambitious, and that's why I'm crazy about you. Even if you have some harebrained ideas."

She looked at him with a warning glare.

"You dream big, darlin', and I'll support you," he said.

She looked stern. "You sure about that?"

"I'm certain," he said, and kissed the top of her head and took her hand. Josh stood a good six inches taller than Ely, which was a pretty unusual feeling for her because she was a tall girl, taking after her father in stature. They walked along hand in hand, not heading anywhere in particular. The weather was pleasant for November in New England. It was good to be outside.

"Why don't you come meet my parents over Thanksgiving?" Josh said suddenly.

Ely stopped walking and looked at him in surprise. "You want me to meet your folks?"

He studied the sidewalk for a moment like he was making up his mind. Then he produced a wide smile. "Yeah, why not? It'll be fun. They'll love you."

It was the first time either one of them had mentioned the L-word. Okay, he hadn't said *he* loved her but rather his parents would. Ely started to feel unsure, something that didn't happen to her very often. She hadn't thought about bringing Josh home to meet her parents yet. It was way too soon for that, wasn't it?

"Gee, Josh." Ely started to walk again so she could look at the ground and not him, because this was too intense.

"Thanksgiving—it's a big time of year in my home," she said. "I've never been away for it before. My little brother, John Jr., will be back from the west coast and my two aunts, too. Marybeth—she's the one that never got married, and Aunt Mona—she's married to Uncle John, with the teenage girls. I think I told you about my cousins, Becky and Kaitlin." Ely was talking too fast—ranting—so Josh had to talk faster to cut in.

"It's okay if you don't wanna come. All you have to do is say it." He sounded hurt.

"It's not that I don't wanna. It's . . ." She thought about rambling on again but then decided against it. Better to be honest. "I'm not ready for

Thanksgiving with you just yet, Josh. I'm sorry. You know I like you a lot, and Lord knows, I love the way you can scrub me down." She laughed, and he smiled. "I sure think you enjoyed our soap-on-a-rope adventure today." He nodded and Ely continued. "Oh yes, but let's just take things easy, all right?" She looked up at him with worry in her deep brown eyes.

"You know what?" he said. "I don't think I want to take things easy. I want to take them fast. In fact, I wanna take them to the next level. I want you in my life, Ely, and there's no doubt about it." He took her hand and pulled her back so she had to stop walking and face him. "I love you, Ely Briskin," he said.

She blinked. "You what?"

"You heard me. I love you. What do you have to say about that?" It sounded like a challenge.

"Josh, oh God. This is, I mean . . . well . . . ." She stared up into his face. "Are you sure about this? I'm two years older than you, don't forget."

He picked her up and swung her around. "I don't care, baby. I love you, and that's a fact. Now, you ready to tell me you love me, too? Because you know you do."

Ely laughed but pushed against his shoulders to be put back down on the sidewalk. "Put me down, you jackass," she said and laughed. "Put me down."

He did.

"Well?" he asked.

"Well . . ." she said.

"I could tickle it out of you."

"No, don't do that."

"Then tell me you love me, baby."

"Josh . . . I want to say it, honestly I do, but it can't just be a reaction to what you're sayin'. Can you give me a little more time?"

"What do you need time for? I think you pretty much know every square inch of me at this point."

"I do, darlin'." She smiled. "And that's a lot of fun-filled inches, but it's just—well, it's a big step. I think I'm falling, but I really do need a little more time."

He rolled his eyes. "You're not gonna tell me you love me, are you?"

She gave him a guilty smile.

Josh swung his arm over her shoulder, and they started to walk along the sidewalk again. He gazed up at the cloudy sky. "Well, so what if it takes you longer to fall in love with me? I'm only twenty-one to your twenty-three." He hugged her shoulder tighter. "Time is the one thing I got plenty of, Ely Briskin. So if you want time, take as long as you like."

Chapter Nine
Hot to Trot

"This won't take long." Maria was a little anxious about her Monday morning run. Jessie had just arrived to babysit Alice.

"Take as long as you like. We're going to play lots of fun games while you're gone." Jessie smiled. "It's nice to be back here, and Maria, I have to say you look fabulous."

"What? In my sweats? I don't think so." She laughed, but Jessie was insistent.

"Last time I saw you, your hair was down and it was pretty, but pulled back tight like you have it now—well, it shows off your amazing bone structure. You're beautiful."

Maria was flattered. She knew her big eyes were overshadowed somewhat when she wore her hair blown out, but today, with a long ponytail—yes, her eyes were a lot more pronounced. However, so were her ever-growing butt and waist.

"I wish I could go for a long run—you know maybe an hour or so—but I'm not healthy enough. If I last thirty minutes, it'll be a miracle."

"You told me this is your first run since you had Alice? Well then, you've got to take it easy or you'll do yourself harm. You have to start back slow and build it up over time."

"I know." Maria sighed. "I never really had to exercise before. This is all new to me. By the way, I haven't mentioned this to anybody, so I'd like to keep it private until I'm a little healthier. Okay?"

Jessie nodded. "No problem." Then she focused on the baby.

Maria was glad Alice looked like she remembered Jessie. The baby seemed happy to stay with her while Maria headed out for her run. But it only took a few minutes of jogging for her to discover how out of shape she'd become.

She was just past the turn onto Crystal Lake Lane when she had to stop. Her chest screamed for air, her stomach had a stitch, and she just couldn't keep going—already. Maria considered herself a pretty determined woman and she believed in mind over matter, but her matter overruled her mind today. It seemed like her legs had a mind of their own, too. And they had decided against running, so she walked. She tried to keep a brisk pace because then she was getting some sort of exercise, but it was damn demoralizing.

Maria spent so much time in the car, it was difficult not to run over the occasional jogger or Newton runner. They were endemic in the area. Having watched them in action for so many years, she had sort of thought she could join their ranks without too much effort. She couldn't have been more wrong. Running was torture. After a few minutes of walking, Maria tried to upgrade to a jog again. She lasted even less time. It was humiliating to have to slow down after only a few hundred yards—not that anyone was watching her anyway.

How did all those marathon moms make it look so easy? This was worse than waxing, but it was the only way Maria knew she could rescue her old figure from the layers of baby fat and white-wine binges of the last decade. As she lumbered on, she fumed about letting herself go in the first place. What had she been thinking? No cocktail or carbohydrate was worth this torture.

That said, Maria was thrilled when she looked up from her uncooperative feet and saw she had lapped half the lake. She was well into her planned route for the morning. Even more surprising was her husband's red sports car whizzing by.

As usual, he was on his cell and wrapped up in the business world. Maria almost waved to him before she remembered her Operation: Transformation was a secret. Everybody would ask her how she did it, and of course, she would lie. Maria was already fantasizing about how she would accept the Christmas compliments with a shrug, explaining the baby calories had simply melted away by themselves. Wasn't that how everybody did it? Nobody would admit to the hell she was putting herself through.

She watched Rick turn on his left blinker. Where was he going at this time of the morning? Home? Not possible. He never came home during the day. Unless . . .

"Stop it," she said. Rick didn't even know Jessie was going to be there this morning. But then again . . .

"Stop!" she said. Rick thought Jessie was cute. Darn it, even *she* thought Jessie was cute. Cody and Alice loved her, too. So everybody loved Jessie, but that didn't mean her husband was rushing home to see her.

Maria finally gave up all pretense of running and settled for a brisk walk. Her mind moved faster than her feet as she whizzed back through the years and remembered her time at college with Rick. When she'd had a late start and he an early one, he would come to her after his first class to have his wild way with her just as she woke up. Rick was always more of a morning man. He loved sex before breakfast. In those days, he really had loved sex all the time. The memory made her sad. Those years had raced by so fast. Rick still took care of her needs, but he sure wasn't rushing back from his morning meetings to have his way with her, wild or otherwise. So where was he going?

Rick was more surprised than anyone to meet the sitter in his house. "Oh, Jessie, hi. I didn't realize you'd be here this morning."

Alice bounced up and down on Jessie's lap when she saw him. "Dada."

"Hullo, Mr. Sanchez. Yes, I'm in for a few hours so Maria can, um, get out."

"Oh, okay. Funny she didn't mention it." He was good at reading people and felt the girl was holding something back. "Did she say where she was going?"

Jessie shook her head with a little too much conviction. "No, she's just gone out." Alice strained to get out of Jessie's arms and into Rick's.

"Wow, who's a daddy's girl?" Jessie worked to keep hold of the baby.

"Dada," Alice repeated, clearly wanting his attention.

It worked this time, and he crossed the room, taking his baby girl for a moment. "Hello, little princess. Are you being good for Jessie?" He kissed her soft cheek.

Then he smiled at Jessie. "Are you over the shock of your last babysitting adventure in this house?"

"What? Oh yes, what an experience that was, Mr. Sanchez." She grimaced.

He looked down at the pretty girl who was sitting at his kitchen table. "Please call me Ricky. I feel so old when you call me Mr. Sanchez. That's my dad."

"Oh, sorry—Ricky."

It jarred in his ear. "Did I say Ricky? Uh, I meant Rick. You better call me Rick. That's what everybody calls me." He looked guilty. "Well, Maria calls me Ricky, but she's the only one."

Jessie looked embarrassed and gave a mute nod. He handed the baby back to her, but Alice protested.

"Sorry, baby, Daddy has to go to work." He patted his daughter on the head and then looked at Jessie. She was one good-looking woman—no girl. "College life good here?" he asked, lingering more than was necessary.

She smiled.

What a smile.

"I love it. I have a crazy roommate from South Carolina, and life is always fun with her around."

"No big American football player stolen your heart yet?"

Jessie blushed. Her eyes hit the floor, and she shook her head.

"Ah," Rick said. "That's a surprise. You're such a"—what could he say? —"lovely girl." *What am I doing here? Get out of here, Rick boy.*

"Well, I have to go," he said with a sudden urgency, and headed for the kitchen door. He didn't mean to turn back, but he couldn't help himself.

"It's good to see you again, Jessie." He tried to make it sound casual.

"Great to be here," she said. Her smile was broad and open. She had no idea what he was thinking. Rick nodded and left. He went to the study and grabbed the file he'd come home for.

I'm an idiot! She sees me as an old guy, not a possible—what? Boyfriend? Is that what you're thinking here, Rick?

He remembered what his friend Michael had said. Thinking about her would only drive him nuts. It looked like he was right, because his was not rational thinking. Rick knew he had to stay away from Jessie. And he had to get out of the house fast.

Maria thought it quite possible she wasn't going to make it home. How could she have become so unhealthy? In fairness, she'd never been a runner. Beach volleyball—while she perfected her deep tan—was more her style.

She sat down on the garden wall of number two, Crystal Lake, just to catch her breath before she went back to her house. It was remarkable Rick didn't see her sitting there as he drove out of the neighborhood, but he was on the phone again and he looked stressed. So he had been home. Doing what? He never came home during his work day. She would have to ask him later. Maria didn't notice the car coming in the other direction until it slowed down and the window lowered.

"Hey, missy. I didn't know you'd taken up running," Cathi said in her normal chipper voice. Right now it annoyed Maria.

"I haven't. I was just out for a walk." The lie came easy.

"Funny, you look flushed—like you were running." Cathi reached over and opened her passenger door. "Come on, hop in. I need you to look at a house with me."

"Ah, Cathi, I'm all hot and sticky. I'm so not in the mood for house hunting." In truth, Maria wasn't in the mood for anything, but Cathi was her usual unsympathetic self.

"Get in," she said, and her voice brokered no room for argument. "It's one of your neighbors—number sixteen. You should know what it looks like inside, because it'll give you an idea of what yours is worth."

With obvious reluctance, Maria got into the car, but her mood changed real fast when Cathi told her the asking price for the house. "That's far too much. These houses are nice, but they're not in Beverly Hills," she said.

"I keep telling you that you live on one of the most desirable streets in one of the most desirable areas of Boston. Now do you believe me?"

Maria looked out the window of Cathi's car and saw her house as they drove by. Jessie had wrapped Alice up in her little coat and was just bringing her outside to play. She was a great babysitter. What a pain she was so pretty.

"It's the last one on the right." Cathi was focused on her newest target.

"Why are we even looking? I don't mean to be rude, but our husbands work together, and I have to say, I don't really think we're in the multimillion dollar house bracket, are we?"

Cathi laughed at her friend's practical streak. "Didn't I tell you, Maria Belen Sanchez, where there's a will, there is a way. First let's have a look at it. We may not even like it."

"Hi there, Mrs. Palmer," Jessie said when she saw Maria's next-door neighbor walking past with her bulldog on his leash. "Out for a bit of fresh air?"

"Yes, we are. Hello, Alice." She tapped her forehead with her fingers. "I'm sorry, but I've forgotten your name."

"I'm Jessie, the one you helped the night the fire brigades arrived here. Remember?"

Noreen chuckled. "Indeed I do. I might forget the odd name, but I wouldn't forget a night like that in a hurry. I haven't gotten that fuddled yet. What excitement it was. It was just your name I'd misplaced." She smiled at Jessie. "How are you, dear?"

"Very good, thanks. I'm minding Alice a few mornings a week now, so Mrs. Sanchez can get some things done. She seems to like being outside." Jessie looked at the little girl, who was sitting upright in her stroller and gurgling happily at Mrs. Palmer's dog.

"Rusty, get down," the older lady commanded when the dog started to sniff around the baby.

"You call him Rusty? How nice. I left Orga in the house. I didn't want to have the baby out and the dog on the leash at the same time. The last thing I need is another emergency."

Noreen laughed again. "Oh, you're okay on Crystal Lake Lane. It's a cul-de-sac, so the dogs are safe wandering about. Orga and Rusty are great friends."

"How did you come up with the name Rusty?"

Noreen looked at the dog. "We've always had bulldogs because my husband was English. We started with one called Churchill, then Charlie. The list goes on, but this is Rusty because he's a mix of rust and white, so it seemed like a good idea. I also thought if one of us has to be rusty, I would rather it was him and not me. I'm rather forgetful, you see."

Jessie saw.

"Did you tell me the other night you were living here?"

It saddened Jessie a little. She'd talked quite a bit with the older woman about the fact she was English. Noreen had told her she was American-born, but her late husband had been British. They'd moved to Crystal Lake fifty years ago. "I'm English," Jessie said now, knowing what was going to come next.

Noreen's face lit up. "You're English. You know, so was my late husband, Joe."

That's when Jessie realized just how forgetful Mrs. Palmer really was. How very sad. She was such a nice woman, so sweet and kind, but it seemed she was beginning to lose touch with reality.

Noreen cut into her thoughts. "Are you married?"

"No, not yet."

The older woman looked surprised. "But why ever not? You're such a pretty thing. I'll bet they're lining up for you. You're not too fussy are you? That's not wise."

"No, it's not that." She thought about Dan and the fact he hadn't phoned her in the two days since their date. "It's just I never really seem to meet the right guys."

"Well, you know what they say . . ." Mrs. Palmer looked conspiratorial. "If you can't find Mr. Right, you may as well play around with Mr. Wrong."

Of all the things she could have said, that was the least expected. Jessie burst out laughing. "Mrs. Palmer, you wild woman. Who'd have thought?"

Noreen smiled. "I know my mind is slipping, but it's nice to still make people laugh. You're a lovely girl, and you're even prettier when you smile."

Jessie blushed.

"What were we talking about again? I really must focus more. Either that or start taking those darn tablets my son, Greg, gave me. Joe, my late husband, wasn't half as bossy as Greg is." She looked at Jessie as if this explained everything. "Tell me, angel," she said. Jessie guessed that the endearment was Noreen covering for the fact she had forgotten her name already. "Would you and Alice like to come in for a glass of milk and a cookie?"

The baby didn't have many words yet, but she knew the word cookie, and so did Rusty. Suddenly Alice was clapping, and Rusty was yapping about the idea of a treat. It made Jessie smile.

"That sounds perfect. Let me just leave a note in Maria's kitchen so if she comes back she doesn't worry. Then we'll be right over."

"Bring Orga," Noreen said. "Did you know *orga* is the Irish word for gold? Now how did I remember that nugget?"

Maria hadn't wanted to see number sixteen, Crystal Lake Lane, but she was glad she had. "That house is probably the nicest I've ever seen in my life." She was gushing as they walked out and said good-bye to the realtor.

Cathi, it seemed, thought likewise. "I can't believe the views. I thought you'd have to live on the lake to get that, but oh, the master bedroom—it was heaven," she said.

"What about the kitchen?" Maria sighed. "I've never seen so much white marble. It was so light and modern."

"I know. I always thought I wanted a traditional kitchen," Cathi said, thinking about her own galley-style one. "But seeing that, I'll have to do a total rethink."

Maria had cheered up since Cathi forced her to get into the car. Seeing the new house had taken her mind off her own bad mood. "Do you want to come back to my place for coffee?"

"That sounds great. Thanks. Where is Alice anyway?"

"I left her with the sitter. Do you remember Jessie? I got her back. She was just so good with the kids."

Cathi frowned. "I thought she was too pretty and you were never going to use her again."

"I know, but what the heck? I trust Ricky, and Jessie is so damn capable."

The other woman shook her blond bob. "You're putting temptation in your husband's path," she said. "Look, I trust Rick as much as I trust Michael, but I think you're putting a great big doughnut right in front of Rick while he's on a diet. *You're* his diet. Don't flaunt what he's not allowed to have in his face."

Maria looked at her own rather extended waistline. If anybody was at the doughnuts, it was her, but maybe Cathi was right. Her plan had been to keep Jessie and Rick apart, but judging by his movements this morning, that wasn't working. Even if she got her figure back, she still wouldn't be able to compete with Jessie's incredible beauty—or worse, her youth.

"Okay, I hear you. It's just so difficult to get a good sitter, but I'll go back to the website and get a different one."

"Good girl," Cathi said. "Wise decision—and over coffee at your place, you can help me to figure out how the heck I'm going to get my hands on Noreen Palmer's house."

Chapter Ten
Naughty Neighbors

"Hello, Mrs. Palmer, are you here?" Maria's voice was more jovial than she felt, but when Cathi spotted the note from Jessie on the kitchen table, there was no stopping her.

She squeezed Maria's arm so hard it hurt. "This is far too good an opportunity to miss." Cathi was insistent, but Maria backed away and reread the note.

> *Mrs. Palmer has invited Alice and me in for milk and cookies.*
> *We're just next door if you're looking for us.*
> *Jessie*

"Come on." Cathi pulled at Maria's sleeve. "Look, you told me yourself you're not getting anywhere with her. Maybe if I meet her, I can convince the old bat. We can pretend we're just stopping by to pick up Alice. Once we're in the door, leave the rest to me. I'll have the chance to talk with her, and if I'm very lucky, I'll even get to have a look around house."

Maria scrunched up her nose. "Cathi, I don't think she wants to sell." She was beginning to feel her friend was going too far. There was another house for sale on the road now. If she were that desperate, she could buy number sixteen and saddle herself with a gazillion-year mortgage. Kicking out poor Mrs. Palmer wasn't the answer.

"Look, she's going to have to move soon enough, if what you say is true about her beginning to lose her marbles. I'm not kicking her out on the street—I'm just giving her a little nudge, and I'll pay her a good price. Just not as good as the one across the road. I mean, they're developers—it's highway robbery."

"But she's happy there."

"No she's not. She just *thinks* she's happy. That house is way too big for a woman her age, and she's living alone. I'm sure it was a great place to raise kids. That's what I want to do. She needs to think about the rest of her life. We all need to look forward, not back."

And so, despite Maria's reluctance, they headed over to Noreen Palmer's house.

"We're in the front room," Noreen called when she heard the voices. "Maria, is that you?" The old lady made her way through the even older house to greet her next-door neighbor at the back door. "Oh, and you have a friend." She smiled when she saw them.

"I hope we're not intruding." Maria was worried, but Noreen shook her head.

"It's lovely to see you. The girls are having milk and cookies. Perhaps I could make you ladies a cup of coffee or maybe even tea?"

"We don't want to be a bother."

"Tea would be perfect," Cathi said. "Can I help you?"

And with that, Maria watched her friend set to work.

"You sit down and let me help," Cathi said. "I'll find the milk."

Noreen looked amused to have such an organizer in her kitchen, and she did as instructed while watching Cathi take control in her new surroundings.

"Now, where's the fridge? Ah yes, there it is. Wow, this is such a big fridge. It seems too large for one. Do you live alone, Mrs. Palmer? Not too lonely, I hope."

Maria couldn't listen anymore. She headed into the living room to say hi to Jessie and Alice.

"How did it go?" she asked Jessie.

"Not a problem. This little girl is a real dote. She's a pleasure to mind, to be honest."

"Oh, I forgot your money. It's back at my house."

Jessie shook her head. "Don't worry about it. I can get it from you later in the week. You did say you wanted me the day after tomorrow, didn't you?" she asked with a smile as wide as Crystal Lake.

Maria stalled. Had she said that? She had. Well, she couldn't fire her now. She would get her to babysit this week and then let her go after she had paid her.

"Okay, that's fine." Maria nodded and scooped up her little girl. "Thanks for today. It was great to get out. You can take off now if you like."

"I just want to say good-bye to Mrs. Palmer and thank her. She's such a nice woman."

"She is, isn't she?" Maria felt even guiltier for the way she knew her friend was treating her neighbor. They walked back into the kitchen where Cathi was putting the finishing touches on a tray laden with a large pot of tea, a jug of milk, cookies, and linen napkins. Cathi was in top gear.

"This house is really too big for just you. I mean, it must be hard rattling about in it, all alone. I have to say I'd be nervous with all the burglaries that have happened. You need better security, but then a new alarm system would cost you thousands."

Maria squeezed her lips tight to stop from speaking. The police had been quite clear when they told her Crystal Lake Lane was safer than most because it wasn't a through road. Thieves didn't like places that were hard to get out of. Cathi stopped ranting when she saw the others.

"I wanted to say good-bye and thanks a million for the cookies, Mrs. Palmer," Jessie said.

"You're so welcome dear," Noreen said. "It was very nice to see you again. Come back soon."

"I will."

"Hi there." Cathi cut in the conversation as she was so good at doing. "I'm Cathi Grant," she said, standing tall and sizing up Maria's babysitter for the first time.

"Hullo, I'm Jessie Armstrong." She shook Cathi's hand.

Maria watched them with interest. The two women stood about the same height, but Cathi's blond bob was poker straight. It was cut with laser-like precision to hang a half an inch above her shoulders. Meanwhile, Jessie's hair fell loose and careless, curls dancing down her back in a haphazard way. Both were the same shade of blond and both had terrific figures, but Maria could see the twenty year chasm that separated them made a world of difference. Jessie seemed relaxed and at peace with the world, while Cathi looked severe and suspicious.

Maria wondered if it was the years that made Cathi so wary and Jessie so innocent, or was it their personalities? Cathi hadn't gotten to this point in her life by being an open and honest woman. She was tough and got what she wanted most of the time. Michael, her husband, was a case in point. He'd been engaged to another woman when Cathi met him, but she had worked her magic, weaved her plan, and wore down her opponent until she got her prize. *It's just as well she's my friend*, Maria thought. Cathi was a great comrade, but she would make a vicious adversary.

"Leaving?" Cathi asked Jessie, eager to focus on her real prey—Noreen.

"I am. Thanks again, Mrs. Palmer." Jessie went over and kissed the older woman on her soft, sunken cheek. "See you soon," the young girl said in a half whisper and left.

"I love your home," Cathi gushed before the back door had even closed behind Jessie. "It must have been a terrific place to bring up children. I have two little girls. I'll show you their photos. Where should I take this tray?" She was already heading out of the kitchen and toward the front room.

Maria looked at her next-door neighbor when Cathi had walked on ahead. "Are you sure we're not imposing?"

"Not at all." Noreen chuckled. "I'm quite enjoying this," she said and glanced sideways at Maria. For a moment, the younger woman saw a clarity in her neighbor's eyes she hadn't seen for a long time. Did Noreen know what Cathi was up to? Not possible. Cathi hadn't said anything about her neighborly intentions yet, and Maria hadn't told Mrs. Palmer the name of the woman who was interested in buying. No, there was no way she could have made the connection.

Cathi didn't seem to need to ask permission. She looked very comfortable playing the part of hostess in Noreen Palmer's house. Meanwhile, Maria felt awkward. But Noreen looked mildly amused.

"Milk?" Cathi asked.

Noreen nodded. "Just a splash."

"Maria?"

"Um, you know, I think I'll just get myself a glass of water. I need to rehydrate. I was out running. It was meant to be my big secret get-skinny project but—well, it's a bit obvious what I was up to," Maria said and headed back out to the kitchen with Alice.

"Can I get it for you, angel?" Noreen spoke from the sofa.

"No, no, you stay where you are," Maria said. "I'll just get a glass of tap water."

"Speaking of water . . ." Cathi was back on the attack without missing a beat. "I'm surprised your drawing room is here at the front of the house and not the back. Your views of Crystal Lake must be as good as Maria's. Seems a shame not to enjoy them." She handed a steaming mug to Noreen.

Maria escaped to the kitchen for a moment. "This is wrong," she said to the baby on her hip. "Cathi is going to railroad Noreen into something. I can't just stand by and let that happen."

Alice gurgled in approval, so Maria headed back to the hall as quickly as she could to eavesdrop on their conversation.

"I must say, you make good tea. Joe used to fuss over me like this," Noreen said, sounding sentimental. "Now, what were you saying? Oh yes, the views. You know, I've lived here for so many years that I've chopped and changed the rooms on more occasions than I can remember. I use this room more now because it's smaller and easier to heat. The television is in here, and I like to watch the news most nights. The lake is pretty, but I don't want to stare at it every night. Beautiful as it is, fifty years is a long time to watch one mass of water." She chuckled. "I can watch the comings and goings on the street from this room, too. It's amazing what you can pick up about your neighbors just by sitting here and looking out now and again."

Maria walked back into the room with Alice just in time to see a brief flicker of panic on Cathi's face, but it disappeared fast.

Noreen turned her attention to her neighbor and changed the subject. "Good for you getting out this morning, Maria. How far did you go?"

Maria sat back down and cuddled her daughter on her knees. "Not far, Noreen. I'm so out of shape. I lapped the lake. I wanted to run, but I walked most of it."

"Well, you have a wonderful sitter in that young English girl. She's so friendly, and she did a very responsible job that night with the firefighters."

Alice lunged forward when she saw the cookies on the tray.

"Do you have fire alarms?" Cathi asked Noreen. "I'm sure these old wooden houses would burn up fast."

"Oh yes. Greg, my son, lives across the road. He keeps an eye on me. He grew up in this house, and he checks in at least once a day. I keep trying to tell him he should move his family in here and I'd take that house. This one's so much bigger."

Cathi let out small noise that sounded more feline than female. It made both Noreen and Maria glanced at her.

"Are you all right, dear? Did you choke on your cookie?" the older woman asked.

Cathi was quick to recompose. "Yes, yes, fine." Maria knew she was putting on her best Stepford Wife voice. "Really, I'm good. Please, would you show me your views of the lake? I just love water vistas."

Maria was not happy. She was seeing a whole new—and very insincere—side of her friend. She never would have guessed just how two-faced Cathi could be, and felt really bad for bringing her into Noreen's life. Mrs. Palmer was so sweet and trusting of people—would Cathi worm her way in and talk Noreen right out of her house?

"I'd love to show you the view," Noreen said to Cathi. "It's looking so beautiful now with all the trees changing color around the shoreline. I find it breathtaking even after all these years."

Maria gave Alice a cookie and followed the other two women into the living room at the back of number nine. The first thing to hit her was the temperature of the room. It was freezing but huge, about twenty-five feet long.

"This is amazing." Cathi sighed, twirling around like Cinderella in the ballroom. "The parties you must have had in here."

Mrs. Palmer gave a soft nod. "We bought this house in 1963, and yes, those early years before the children . . . well, they were pretty wild. The parties in the sixties were just crazy."

"You lived here in the sixties?" Maria had never done the math.

"You bet." Noreen laughed. Her eyes seemed clearer. They walked over to the double doors that led out to the deck overlooking the yard and the lake beyond.

"Joe worked for WSLZ-TV. It was an affiliated television station here in Boston. Back then, television was so glamorous. Joe was quite the local celebrity." Noreen smiled. "In those early years of TV, anything seemed possible."

"Of course. That was the time of the Kennedys and Neil Armstrong landing on the moon," Cathi said, looking a little serious, but Noreen shook her head.

"I'm talking about the contraceptive pill and the Beatles, to be honest. For us, life was one long party. Joe was always interviewing rock stars and fashion models. He had a way with people, you see, and everybody loved him."

"Who did he meet that we'd know?" Maria asked, fascinated to hear about the old days. Cathi seemed enraptured, as well.

"Oh, he met them all, but he became friends with a select few and they'd come to stay with us when they were in Boston."

"They were in this house?" Cathi looked like she could hardly contain herself. "Rock stars from the sixties? Who?"

Noreen looked like she was having difficulty opening the latch on the back door. Of course, her hands would be weak, Maria realized. Her own arms were full with Alice, so she looked at her friend. "Cathi, can you help Noreen?"

Cathi's eyes seemed saucer-size with excitement. She had to snap out of her rock-star-hostess daydream to see the problem Noreen was having with the door. "Oh, here, let me do this," she said in a brisk tone. She turned the old iron key in the latch and the double doors to the outside deck clicked open. Noreen nodded, and then she walked out onto the balcony overlooking the lake.

"Joe always had a bit of a thing for Brigitte Bardot. She was one of his first interviews, and in all honesty, I think she had a soft spot for him, too. She stayed here often."

Cathi looked like she had lost the ability to speak, and she just mouthed the name.

"OMG. What an icon. She actually stayed here?" Maria asked.

Noreen nodded again, looking happy to reminisce. "And she brought the rock star Mick Wolf with her once. He's much smaller in real life than you'd expect, but my word, did he party hard. They were very naughty."

Cathi sat down on a nearby bench, such was the weight of that name.

But Maria was enraptured. "How naughty was naughty?"

"I remember Joe saying there was more crystal meth in the house than Crystal Lake outside."

Maria hugged her baby. "Jeez, the wildest party I've been to in Newton involved an ice sculpture luge and a few joints."

Noreen sighed. "My son, Greg, says the same thing. I think we were a lot naughtier than the Newton neighbors of today." She gazed out over the lake and then turned to see where Cathi had gone. She was still sitting down. It seemed like she was trying to take in the incredible history of the house.

"Mick Wolf and Brigitte Bardot," Cathi whispered. "What an amazing house."

"This is the view you wanted to see," Noreen said to her now. Cathi roused herself and came over to the railings where the other women stood. It was just as glorious as Mrs. Palmer had promised. The well-tended yard was a gentle slope down to Crystal Lake. The trees along the sides and on the far side of the water had changed to a kaleidoscope of reds, oranges, yellows, and golds. On top of that, the low autumn sun hit the gently moving water, making it shimmer and sparkle.

"I think I'm going to cry," Cathi said. "I love this house. I just love this house."

"Oh." Noreen looked a little surprised. "Would you be interested in buying it?" she asked. Maria and Cathi snapped to attention.

"Gosh, this is all a bit sudden," Cathi said.

That annoyed Maria. She knew how her friend's mind worked. Cathi wouldn't have planned on going straight for the deal that day. She would much rather soften Noreen Palmer up with a few more cookies, chats, and the photos of her girls, or she would have liked to bring a pie.

Cathi continued. "I want to say—yes. I'd love to buy this house, Noreen —especially as you seem to have a mind to sell it."

Noreen smiled. "No, not at all. I'm in no rush. You just said you loved it, but perhaps I misunderstood." She shrugged.

"How much?" Cathi asked a little too fast. She put her hands down and clasped the deck railing, like she needed the support.

"Oh, that's the exact spot where Mick Wolf stood and the exact way he held the railings when he asked me the very same question." Noreen grinned.

"He tried to buy this house?" Cathi asked, sounding breathless. Maria thought her friend's knees might buckle at the news.

"No, angel, he was trying to convince Joe to sell *me*. I think Mick was going through an older women phase, because if memory serves, both Brigitte and I were a good few years older than him. Funny he asked Joe and didn't do the haggling straight with me.

"I suppose things were very different back then. We didn't have the equality you girls have these days. If Mick Wolf were here today, I am sure he wouldn't ask your husband's permission to buy you. He'd buy you direct —if you were for sale in the first place—which of course I wasn't.

"But I have a vague recollection he thought we should all pretend to be bread rolls and smear ourselves in peanut butter." Then she gave a little sigh. "Funny the things you remember. It sounds dumb now, but it seemed very reasonable that night."

"Ooh!" Maria laughed. "Gross. Wouldn't you have ruined your clothes?"

"No, pet, we'd been swimming. We were well past the clothing stage."

"Skinny dipping in the lake?" Maria squealed out loud. "We've often talked about it but never dared to do it."

"How much would you want for the house?" Cathi asked Noreen. Maria knew she was trying to bring the house sale conversation back because they had wandered off the subject again. Cathi was now massaging the Wolf-stroked wooden railing.

Mrs. Palmer blinked. "Oh, yes. Well, let me see—the one for sale across the road is six thousand square feet on a quarter acre plot with indirect lake views, and we all know what it's listed for. This house is also six thousand square feet, but we're on a larger half-acre plot, and of course, we have direct access to the lake. I think I'd consider any offers five hundred thousand above their asking price." She stopped and looked at Cathi with a small smile. Then she wrapped her arms around herself. "You know, I feel a chill in the air. Shall we go back inside? It wouldn't do for Alice to get cold." She reached over to stroke the baby's cheek and managed a quick wink at Maria at the same time.

Maria didn't speak but watched the scene unfold with amazement. The old lady's mind was as clear as the water in Crystal Lake. She knew the chill Noreen felt had more to do with her friend's icy glare than any change in the weather. For Cathi's part, Maria knew it was one of those rare times she wouldn't be able to find a response. What was there to say? Maria knew Cathi would claim Noreen was being delusional. For that kind of money, Mick Wolf would have to be thrown into the deal as the live-in landscaper. Then perhaps the price tag would make sense. But in the real world, nothing was worth that kind of money. That was what Cathi would say.

Maria watched her friend try to compose herself.

"Ah, Mrs. Palmer, I don't think that price is reasonable," she said as they came inside.

"Don't you?" The old lady closed up the doors to the deck and guided them back into the front room where their tea waited.

"Number sixteen is in mint condition. This house would need a total refurbishment."

Noreen settled herself onto her sofa and looked around the room. "Do you think? Funny, I think it's fine just the way it is. Now, can I give you a refill?"

Cathi didn't sit down again. Instead she glanced at her watch. "You know what? I have to get to the school. I have a meeting with Katie's teacher soon. It was so nice to meet you, Mrs. Palmer, but I really have to leave now."

Cathi was out the door so fast, neither Noreen nor Maria got a chance to say good-bye. They watched the void created as she swept out of the room, which was punctuated by the slam of the back door behind her. Then both women burst into laughter. Even Alice joined in. Rusty and Orga settled on the carpet, looking just as glad to see the back of her.

"I am so sorry about that, Noreen," Maria said.

"No problem. I quite enjoyed it, as a matter of fact. I assume that is the woman you've been talking about when you said you had a friend who wanted to buy the house?"

Maria gave a guilty nod. "She came on a bit strong, didn't she?"

"Have you told her about our ever more frequent flooding problems?"

"Yes. It doesn't seem to bother her, or maybe she just doesn't get how bad it is."

"Silly girl."

"I'm the silly one, letting her into your house like that. I'm sorry, Noreen. I was so nervous she'd try to trick you out of your home. I know you're not as young as you used to be, and you keep telling me you're getting forgetful. But I have to say I was blown away about how well you played her just now."

Noreen poured a little more tea from the pot into her cup to heat it up. Then she looked at Maria straight on. "I may be getting a little forgetful, Maria, but I'm not stupid. Now, if you wouldn't mind, be an angel and pour the milk for me. Remember, I just take a splash."

Chapter Eleven
In the Deep End

Rick's dive made barely a splash. He didn't swim as much as he used to, but this evening it felt good. He did an entry dive—long and shallow, fast and sleek. A lifetime ago, when he was young, he had worked as a lifeguard in Watertown, his hometown. He was sad he had given it all up years ago, but at least he still had the form and the style of a good swimmer—he hadn't lost that. None of that mattered anymore. All that mattered now was staying preoccupied. Before the swim, he had worked out hard in the gym for over an hour, just as he had every day that week. It was Friday night, and the club was quieter than usual.

Despite his grueling session, his mind flashed to *her*. What would *she* be doing tonight? He knew he was being a fool, a total idiot, but still his mind played games with him.

The first time he had seen Jessie was like being hit by a lightning bolt. He still remembered walking into the hall when the damn dog was barking and then—whammo, there she was, the most beautiful girl he'd ever seen in his life.

It wasn't just her pretty hair or her face and a body straight from heaven. No, it was more than that—something primal. He was drawn to her on a deeper level. Could it be what people called spiritual? Rick's faith was weak, although he'd been brought up Catholic. But the thoughts and fantasies he was having for Jessie Armstrong sure weren't within the guidelines of his religion.

Of course, he had fought his feelings for her. He was a married man, a good husband to Maria and father to the kids. He'd never done anything behind her back. That wasn't his style. Rick had considered himself a good guy, until he'd seen Jessie. Why had she walked into their happy lives? If he'd just never met her, he would have been okay.

He reached the far wall of the Olympic-sized pool and did a perfect flip turn in his lane. Sure, if he were single, he'd go for her, pursuing her the way he'd once pursued Maria. And he'd get her, too. He was confident of that. Rick wasn't the kind of man who took no for an answer. That's how he'd hooked Maria back at college, and he was pretty certain he could win Jessie over with charm and charisma mixed with the right amount of romance and persuasion.

Naturally this was all hypothetical, because he wasn't going to do anything about Jessie Armstrong. She was their sitter, a child herself—but no, she was a young woman.

She wasn't really a child, was she? Maria had filled him in on Jessie's life while Rick had tried to act disinterested. But the truth was he had sucked up every word his wife dropped.

Jessie was roughly the same age Maria had been when Rick first met her, maybe older. Jessie was plenty grown up.

Stop, he said to himself and plowed harder through the water. He made another perfect flip turn at the far wall. If he could just get the girl out of his head, that would be a start.

He might have succeeded in forgetting about her if he hadn't seen her again in his damn kitchen. Perhaps if he had been better prepared. Known she was going to be there. But he hadn't, so, again, she'd caught him unawares. He rarely went home during the workday. What were the chances of her being there the one day he did? Was fate playing with him? Had they been destined to meet up that morning?

Rick had only rushed into the kitchen to say hi to his wife. His plan was to collect the document fast and get back into Boston. But there she was again. Jessie—beautiful, funny, charming, intoxicating Jessie.

He swam even harder. *Get her out of your head, you fool, you old man*, he roared at himself. *She is way too young for a guy my age. She wouldn't even be attracted to me . . . or would she?*

Rick kept himself in good shape, and he thought he still looked pretty good, but a girl like Jessie could get anybody. Then again, she'd said she didn't have a significant other yet. Maybe she preferred older guys, and that was why she hadn't found anybody at college. It made sense.

While Rick's mind raced, his body began to suffer from the grueling pace he was trying to maintain. He couldn't keep up his top speed in the water, so he slowed a little. *Adultery? Men have been doing it since time began*, he thought as he took it easier. In fact, it was pretty normal.

When women got older, they lost interest in romance and all that stuff. He had seen it happen to Maria. There was a time when he had thought she would never run out of steam. Maria had been the hottest girl in college. It wasn't just about her looks—she had an excitement and life about her that was intoxicating.

He had loved her like a drug. Darn it, he still did, but it was fair to say the fizz had gone flat. If she was his drug, he realized with regret, he'd built up immunity to her particular cocktail of charm and charisma.

Now it was all about the kids, the mortgage, what they were doing for summer vacation. It was all a bit of a pain in the ass now. The fun was done.

He wondered if maybe Maria thought he had become as dull as he believed she had. Dull. It was a strong word, but looking at Jessie, he realized Maria really had lost most of her magic. She was tired all the time, weepy a lot, too. She seemed to have no interest in her looks or sex. What was a guy to do? He hadn't changed at all. He was still running and working out. Sure, he had aged, but he was still, for the most part, the same guy. Her Ricky—fun, playful, sociable, romantic Ricky.

Maybe he should try to romance Maria a bit more. If he could focus his energies on his wife and not on some hottie who had invaded his life, that would be time better spent—smarter, too. But Rick thought about Jessie again. There was no effort required with her. It would be a pleasure to entertain her, fun to take her around Boston and show her the sights. But that was a job for another man, not him. Rick reminded himself that he was married to a terrific woman with two wonderful kids. He needed to get home and focus on his family.

Rick felt a lot better. He knew he did his best thinking when he was pushing his body hard. *Better than pushing Jessie's beautiful body . . . stop*, he commanded his rogue and rampant imagination yet again. He had get out of the pool, shower, and visit Maria's favorite flower shop, The Crimson Petal, in Newton. He would buy Maria the largest bunch of roses they had, and he would treat her like a queen. Maybe they could share a bottle of wine and have some time together when Cody went to bed. If the baby stayed asleep for the night, who knew how good the night could be?

Rick stopped at the end of his swimming lane and pulled off his goggles. He took a few deep breaths to slow his heart rate.

"Hey, buddy, are you getting out of this lane?"

Rick looked up and into the face of a younger man who was waiting for one of the racing lanes to open. He smiled and nodded. "Sure thing. I'm done for the night," he said and swam over to the steps.

It was time to stop exercising, he decided. It was time to focus on his wife. And time to stop fantasizing about his babysitter.

The younger man gave him a nod of thanks and then slipped on his goggles. That was when Rick noticed the tattoo on his forearm of a falcon in flight. It was an impressive tattoo, as was his dive. Rick couldn't help but notice the guy was well-built, too—obviously trained hard. A body that sculpted didn't come without working for it. Nothing good in life came without working for it.

"Hi, honey, I'm home," Rick called from the front door. He was in a better mood. His workout had done wonders, and he'd bought a huge bunch of blood-red roses for his wife. She always loved the deeper colors. Maria was passion personified, and he loved that about her. That was what was going through his mind when she bellowed down the stairs.

"Jeez, could you *be* any louder, Rick?" Alice started to cry. "Oh, great. It took me an hour to settle her while you were out having a fun time at the gym, and then you stomp in, yelling and waking the baby."

Rick resolved he wouldn't let this upset him. He could hear his tired and frustrated wife heading across the upstairs hall to Alice's bedroom.

"Shit," he said to himself. This was not the way he saw the night panning out, and he wasn't going to give up that easy. He bounded up the stairs two at a time, taking Maria's flowers with him. Undaunted by the screams of his daughter, he breezed into the room where Maria had scooped Alice out of the crib and was trying to soothe her again.

"Hey, hey, what's this?" he said. "Is my princess making trouble for my queen?" Alice was distracted with Rick's arrival and hiccupped.

"Typical. She stops just as soon as she sees her father walk in," Maria said. He put his arm around his wife's waist.

"Ah, I remember a time when that's all it took to put a smile on your dial." His voice was playful. "These are for you, my queen." He kissed her on the cheek. "To the most wonderful woman on the planet. I love you, and I'm sorry I woke Alice. You go downstairs and pour yourself a large glass of wine. I'll look after this little lady."

Rick could feel his wife's body relax with his words. It was perhaps more relief than relaxation, but whatever. It was good. She kissed him back and gave him a grateful smile.

"Thank you for the flowers. These are beautiful. I'll put them in water and get us a bottle of something from the pantry. Do you want red or white?"

He smiled at her. "Whatever you'd like."

Maria was relieved her husband was making such an effort to help. He took Alice in his arms and began to rock her, and then he gestured for Maria to leave them. She checked that Cody was ready for bed and gave him a five-minute countdown. Then she went to find a nice bottle of red wine.

By the time Alice had gone back to sleep and Rick was downstairs, Maria had the fire lit and two large glasses of wine on the coffee table with a bowl of potato chips.

"You did say you didn't want dinner, right?"

He nodded and sat beside her. That in itself was rare enough these days. They usually sat on different sofas hugging a child each.

"I just tucked Cody into bed, too," he said.

"Thanks, Ricky. Peace at last."

"Alone at last." He gave her a flirty grin, winked, and then raised his glass to her. "Cheers."

She touched her glass to his. "What are you up to?" Maria asked, getting more suspicious.

"Nothing. Can't a guy enjoy his wife's company?" He looked around the room. "I love the fire—nice touch."

That was when Maria understood. Rick was on a mission. He wanted sex. They had stopped having spontaneous romantic nights. Now it was always after they had been out and perhaps had a few drinks. During the week, she was always too tired or asleep before he even came to bed. Maria felt a mild sense of panic. She hadn't showered. Would he notice? She needed to shave, too. Darn it, a little warning would have been nice. Maybe she could squeeze in a quick shower—or have a bath with him. Would Cody hear them?

"Honey?" he asked her again.

"Oh, did you say something?"

Rick's mouth tightened, like he was suppressing his frustration. "I was telling you we got the Fidelity account again. That's my bonus guaranteed for this year."

"Hey, that's great news." Maria tried to sound enthusiastic, but she was distracted. Maybe five minutes in the bathroom would be enough for her to freshen up. Perhaps he didn't want sex at all and was just being nice. No, Ricky always wanted sex, and he was bringing home flowers and suggesting wine. She shouldn't have lit the fire—that would give him ideas for sure, and Alice was certain to wake up and cry which would wake Cody. And then he would find them in the bath together. The shock would scar him for life, devastate him. It might put him off sex in his adult life, render him—

"Maria, did you hear a word I said?" He was talking a little louder now.

"What? Oh, sorry, I was miles away. What's on your mind?"

He stood up and went to stoke the fire. "Wow, what does a guy have to do around here to get some attention? The flowers, the wine . . . I'm really trying to get some quality time with you, but your mind's somewhere else. Is something up?"

She shook her head. "I'm sorry. It's been another crazy, busy day with the kids. Cody had two of his friends over for a playdate, and they smashed up part of the hedge. Alice has some new teeth coming in. Orga pooped in the house today, whatever that's about. I don't know where the time goes, but I haven't had a spare minute. And now you're home, all flowers and red wine and smelling nice from the showers in the gym." Her bottom lip began to quiver. "And I—I smell of dirty diapers and dog poop."

He came back to where Maria was sitting on the sofa, wringing her hands together, feeling like she might burst out crying any second, and he wrapped his arms around her.

"Shh, baby, it's okay. It's tough being a mom with young kids. They're a handful, I know. I get it. You've a hard time here with them." He stroked her hair and kept talking. "I guess it's easier to be at the office than home with a couple of kids."

His words worked. Maria managed to stop a full breakdown. She blew her nose and mopped her eyes with a tissue. Then she stared up into her husband's eyes. "You really do understand, don't you?"

He nodded. "Yeah, I do. Don't worry. It's good for us to unwind together with a glass of wine and a nice fire."

Maria sat back on the sofa. It was okay to be strung out. This was normal. This was acceptable. Rick didn't mind. That was such a relief. Ever since she'd seen the way he looked at Jessie, she'd been worried. Over the last ten years she had changed so much, but was it possible he hadn't? Was he still the high octane, higher energy, highest libido man in the world? While she had turned into the low energy, lower self-esteem, no libido woman she was today.

They switched on the television and watched a cop show with plenty of action. Rick sat with his arm around Maria's shoulders, and she relaxed into his body even though she knew she stank.

"Do you ever wonder what it would be like to live somewhere else?" she asked him when the show ended.

Rick looked surprised. "Where else would you want to live? The Northeast is the best part of the States."

"It's just that TV show was based in Miami. The sun looks really good. They don't have any snow," Maria said. "Puerto Rico is pretty good, too."

Rick raised an eyebrow. "Seriously?"

She shrugged. "It's just as good as up here."

"Yeah, of course, it's great down there. I mean it's a great place to *visit,* but you couldn't live down there at this stage, could you? You've grown too much. Your tastes are more sophisticated."

Maria pulled away from her husband and sat up straight. "What do you mean 'sophisticated'? Puerto Rico isn't exactly in the last century, you know."

"That's not what I meant, Maria. I know you love Puerto Rico. What's not to love? It's an amazing island, but it wouldn't have the business opportunities we have up here. The schools for the kids wouldn't be as good, for a start."

"I'll have you know Puerto Rican schools are very good. I was educated there, and we've plenty of opportunities for those ambitious enough to find them."

"I'm sorry," he said and rubbed this temples. "The last thing I want is a fight, Maria. Puerto Rico is the best—better than here, if that's what you want to hear. Okay?"

She stood up and started to pace the room. "No, it's not okay. You're just saying what you think I want to hear to stop the argument."

"Is that so bad?"

"Yes, it is." She scowled. "I had no idea you felt so negative toward my home and, might I add, the home of your mother and mother's mother."

Rick stood up, too. "Maria, stop. I love Puerto Rico. I just said something dumb. I'm sorry. What more do you want? I'm too tired for this."

"Too tired for what? Don't let me keep you up. If you're that exhausted, go to bed." Maria's anger shocked even her. Why was she so hostile all of a sudden? Was she still anxious that he had wanted sex and the baby would wake?

"I think I will." He looked at her with sad, tired eyes. "Goodnight, *cariño*," he said and walked out of the room.

She watched him go. Why was he being so difficult? He'd said he understood. Why would he be so hurtful about her home? And he'd left the room without even kissing her. He always kissed her good-night. Maria wanted to run after him to say she was sorry, but sorry for what? She hadn't done anything wrong. All she was guilty of was being tired and emotional after a day watching *his* children. He had what sounded like a terrific day at the office, followed by a session in the gym.

Rick had a charmed life, while hers was crap. No, she wouldn't apologize. If anyone was going to do the apologizing, it should be him—but he would have to darn well mean it. There was no excuse for the way he was treating her.

Chapter Twelve
The Second Date

"There is no excuse for the way he is treating you, Jessie," Ely said for the umpteenth time. "I don't care what he says to explain his radio silence. If he calls you at this point, you have to tell him to shove it."

Jessie wasn't convinced. "Maybe I gave him the wrong impression. Perhaps he thought I wasn't interested. I can't remember what we agreed at the end of our last date."

"That's 'cause it was so damn long ago," Ely said, but Jessie ignored her. "Two weeks? I've had full relationships that lasted less time."

"What if I was meant to phone him?"

"That right there is horse manure and you know it," she said. "You don't even have his number, do you?"

Jessie didn't respond.

"J?" Her roomie had taken to shortening Jessie's name even more. Nobody had ever called her J before, but she liked it.

"J, are you listening to me? Do you have his number? I thought you told me you didn't save it for this very reason."

"I didn't save it, but I might have it. I'm not sure."

"Now what in the hell does that mean? Either you have it or you don't."

Jessie harrumphed and began to gather up her books. She couldn't study in their room. Ely was too talkative. It would be Thanksgiving soon, and she still had a mountain of work to do.

"He phoned me, didn't he? That means his number is in my mobile. I figure, if I really want to, I could just search back through the incoming calls. Lord knows I don't get many callers on my US phone outside of a few school friends, except Maria when she wants me to babysit."

Ely looked stern. "Jessica Armstrong, don't you dare call him. You know that's the worst thing you could do. No guy wants a woman to call him. He has to do the chasing, and if he's not chasing you, there is no chase—game over. It's that simple. I don't need a degree in psychology to teach me that."

Jessie wasn't so sure. She'd never done the chasing before. It sounded so vain, but the truth was she had never been ditched by a guy. In fact, she wondered if that was one of the reasons she found Dan so attractive. He didn't seem to be *into* her.

She got her folders together and shoved them into her bag. "I'm going to the library to do some work, and I suggest you consider doing likewise."

Ely pushed the chair back and kicked her heels up onto her study desk. "Come on, it's practically the holidays. Heck, why start now? You know they'll throw me out sooner or later."

Jessie stopped at the door of their room. She held the door open with her shoe. "After all that work I did for you last week. Darn it, Ely, if we don't get an A for that, I'll eat my thesis. I even wrote it in Ely-type talk. It was some of my best work. Now if you just focus on reading for the afternoon, maybe—just maybe—we can scrape you a pass on this term's work. Wouldn't that make a nice Thanksgiving present for your parents?"

"We don't do gifts at Thanksgiving, but I am grateful for all the help you've given me. You're a star, J."

Now it was Jessie's turn to look stern. "Maybe, but what about the warnings you got from Professor Donovan? You told me she didn't like your attitude. And Professor Spitz—didn't she suggest you attend a few more classes?"

Ely waved her hand in the air like she was swatting a fly. "Why should I have to go to the classes if I'm getting the homework done?"

Jessie shook her head in exasperation. "I won't be able to help you in your finals. You've got to put some work in."

"Do not call that boy." Ely shook her finger at Jessie. "We're going home in a few days, and you can experience a proper Southern Thanksgiving celebration. I'm gonna put you on a horse, and believe me, that'll get Dan the Fireman out of your head."

Jessie rolled her eyes, pulled her foot away from the door, and walked into the corridor. She was very grateful Ely had invited her home for the Thanksgiving holiday and was indebted to Ely's father who had bought their plane tickets. But she was also very frustrated with her roommate's attitude toward schoolwork. The only thing she focused on was her harebrained shampoo idea.

Jessie, on the other hand, needed to focus on work. Her bag was heavy and her mood even heavier. Was it really so dreadful if she phoned Dan? What was the worst that could happen? He would tell her he wasn't interested. At least then she would know and move on with her life. Besides, she didn't want a serious relationship.

Dan was only meant to be a bit of short-term fun anyway. Unfortunately, the fun hadn't materialized, and now she couldn't get the guy out of her mind. Jessie knew it was nuts. The date had been pleasant but not particularly fantastic. Sure, the picnic had been nice, but he hadn't set her on fire with scintillating conversation. Nor had there been major chemistry between them. She knew she was just in a bad mood because it was a Saturday and she didn't have plans for the weekend, again.

Ely and Josh would let her tag along, but she didn't like to intrude on the lovebirds no matter what her friends said. Even babysitting would be something, but Maria didn't seem to want her on the weekends, just weekday mornings.

"Oh well." She sighed out loud. "I can always study." But the idea of studying Dan had more appeal.

It was all so frustrating. If he had been like a normal guy and phoned her and asked for a shallow, casual relationship, she would have been happy with that. It would have been the perfect way to spend her spare time during the year, and then she could have gone back to England having really sampled *American* fare. But no, she had to fall for the one guy in New England—or perhaps the world—who didn't have an interest in casual sex.

When she walked out of her dorm, she heard him before she saw him. The guttural throb of the motorcycle's engine was hard to forget. A wave of excited panic washed through her system. Jessie kept her head down, focusing on the ground with her bag of books thrown over her shoulder. She was headed in the direction of the library, but it seemed Dan had spotted her before she could get away unnoticed.

He drove the motorbike up beside her and cruised along the road next to where she was walking. She knew he was waiting for her to turn around and notice him, but Jessie had other ideas. She wasn't going to make it that easy for him. She pretended not to notice the *ten million CCs* of power purring right next to her. He gunned the engine even louder. Her hair almost whooshed back from the noise level, but she still didn't look up.

In the end he sped ahead about fifty yards to a pedestrian walkway where he parked his bike on the sidewalk, blocking her way. Then he cut the engine, dismounted, and propped the machine up on its stand.

Dan took his helmet off and shook his hair to get the long fringe out of his eyes. Then he beamed at her. "Jessie, hi," he said as soon as she got close. She had to acknowledge him then. He still had that gorgeous, roguish grin—damn.

"Oh, hullo." She couldn't decide whether to play it frosty or ignore the two-week silence. Before she made her mind up, he did it for her. Dan walked over, wrapped his arms around her waist, and pulled her close.

"God, I missed you," he whispered and kissed her with a ferocity and hunger that shocked her. If she'd wanted to resist him—which she didn't—it would've been futile. His passion was contagious. She dropped her bag, wrapping her arms round his neck, and responded with just as much enthusiasm. Some things were beyond psychology.

They kissed like they had done it a million times before. Already she felt at home in his embrace, familiar with his touch. He wrapped his arms around her, pushing his hands inside the waistband of her jeans. Two could play that game, she decided. She pulled his shirt out of his jeans and ran her hands up the smooth skin of his exquisitely toned back. How in heaven could she have thought there was no chemistry between them? They were on fire from the moment they touched. Dan pulled her hair back and looked into her face.

"I really want to be with you. Where can we go?" he asked, his voice husky.

A nanosecond of sense flittered through Jessie's head. "Dan, this is all a bit sudden." She tried to pull back, but he tightened his arms around her waist and smiled with that bold boy grin again.

"Oh no you don't. I haven't seen you for two weeks, and you've been all I was able to think about. I'm not letting you get away from me now."

He kissed her again, and she felt her libido soar. Jessie pulled back and almost heard a vacuum pop between their mouths when she did.

"I don't understand. We've had one date—which, if I remember right, you were a perfect gent at—and since then I haven't heard a word from you. Now you're all"—she looked him up and down—"this."

"Yes, and *this*"—he thrust his pelvis into hers—"really wants to get to know *that* a whole lot better." If he had been vague and a little distant at Morses Pond over how he felt about her, there was no doubt now. This type of situation—amorous men—Jessie understood. She was back in her comfort zone. She pushed a little and broke out of his embrace.

"Well, it's nice to see you, too, Dan, but I have to ask where the heck have you been for the last couple of weeks?"

"Where have I been? I could ask you the same thing. Why didn't you reply to any of my texts or calls?"

"Pardon?"

He smirked at her. "You're cute when you say *pardon* instead of *what*— very British." Then he looked more serious. "Jessie, I texted you so many times. In the end I gave up. But I couldn't stop thinking about you, so my buddy said I should just come out here to see you and ask you what went wrong."

"Dan, I never got any texts or phone messages from you." She took another step back.

Dan looked confused for a moment, and then realization washed over his face. "I must have had the wrong number."

"But you called me before, no problem," she said.

Dan scowled and raised his hands in the air. "Yeah, but I do this all the time. I'm not very techno. I'm always calling the wrong people by mistake."

She picked her bag up again. "Well, what number did you call me on?"

He made no effort to pull out his cell phone but reached for her instead. He put his hands on her hips and drew her closer. "The wrong one, I guess, and now we have to make up for a lot of lost time. Jessie, I'm sorry," he said and pulled her even closer still. "I've been a fool. Let me make it up to you. Please? God, you're so gorgeous."

That was all she needed to hear. She dropped her bag again and melted back into his arms and let him kiss her some more. All the doubts she had about his affection were washed away in the tsunami of wanton lust that coursed through her.

"I need to be somewhere a little more private with you," he whispered into her hair.

She knew he was right. Their overt affection was morphing into lewd behavior. If the Wiswall campus police drove by, they'd be arrested—or at the very least have a bucket of cold water thrown over them.

"I could take you to my room," she heard herself saying. "You know—to talk."

"For sure." He kept kissing her. "Yeah, we need to *talk*," he said and nibbled her earlobe.

"My books," she said.

"My bike."

It took all her willpower to pull herself away from him again and gather up her stuff. He got his bike, and they walked back to her building. Jessie hadn't thought this through. She was going to have to come clean about her girl-only accommodation and the fact she had a roommate.

"You know we're not meant to have male guests up in our rooms without signing them in," she said when they got to her front door.

He winked at her and pulled out his wallet, flashing his firefighter ID. "If I get stopped, I'll say I was here on official business as a follow-up to the incident on Crystal Lake."

She laughed. "Have you done this before?"

They went into the building together and quickly made their way up to her room without getting caught. Ely was at her desk working on something, and she swung around when she heard the door open.

"Oh, Ely . . . eh . . . this is Dan." In her romantic confusion, Jessie had forgotten her friend was in their room.

Ely jumped to her feet. "Well, well, well. You're Dan." She looked the newcomer up and down.

"Hi." He gave her one of his heart-melting smiles.

"Hi, yourself. I haven't heard your name in these parts for some time," she said with a little hostility.

It embarrassed Jessie. "Oh, it was all a misunderstanding," she said, trying to smooth over Ely's overbearing attitude.

The Southerner wasn't so timid. She walked around Dan, eyeing him up and down as she might one of her horses. "A misunderstanding, you say, J?" She eyed Dan. "How exactly did that happen?"

"Ely . . ." Jessie stamped her foot hard on the floor. It made both Dan and Ely look at her.

"Oh, like that, is it?" Ely's tone changed, and she smiled. "Well, okay." She winked at Dan. "So it appears you're welcome back with open arms, and I am getting the distinct feeling I have to be somewhere else."

Now it was Ely's turn to gather up her papers. She threw everything into her satchel and grabbed her coat from behind the door. She glanced at Jessie and smirked. "Don't do anything I wouldn't do," she said and swept out the door with a flourish.

For a moment, Dan and Jessie just looked at the door. Ely was such a force of nature, but a good force. Then they looked at each other, and in a second, they were locked together again. This time there was no possibility of hanging back.

Jessie hadn't made the conscious decision she wanted to be with him, because there was simply no decision to make. She needed to be with him. She wanted to wash away the weeks of self-doubt and confusion she felt. He was gorgeous, she wanted him, and it was pretty clear he wanted her, too.

They didn't even make it to her small twin bed. Nor did they bother to lock the door. They peeled off their clothes like they had been lovers forever. When they were both naked, Dan made the supreme effort of slowing down.

"I don't want to rush this," he said in a whisper.

"I do," she said, breathless.

Dan laughed at her. "Can't I enjoy you? You're so beautiful. Your skin is so soft, so pale." He stroked her flat stomach, but that only made her more desperate for him.

"Enjoy me next time. Just be with me now," she said, pulling his head down to her so she could kiss him again. She wasn't prepared to tell him, but the truth was Jessie hadn't been with a guy for years. Not since she'd had her heart broken. Right now, all she really needed was plain old-fashioned sex, and Dan was the man for the job.

"You'll need a condom," she said.

"Do you have any?"

She shook her head in a sudden panic. "What can I say? I didn't see this coming."

He laughed at her and went to find his wallet in his jacket. "Don't worry, baby. You may not have seen this coming, but you'll certainly feel it." His tone was almost menacing, but it gave her a shiver of anticipation.

Dan knew what he was doing.

It was good he'd brought more than one condom, because they needed three before they eventually ran out of steam. At one point Jessie even remembered to lock the door. Physically drained by evening, they made their way to Jessie's twin bed and snuggled under her down comforter.

"I'm glad you came to find me when I didn't return your calls or texts," she said as she lay in the crook of his arm and rested her head on his shoulder.

"So am I," he said. "That was one hell of an afternoon. Want to do it again sometime?"

She raised up to balance herself on her elbow. "Um, yes. Like maybe tomorrow and the day after and the day after that?" Then she gave a nervous laugh.

Didn't a session like that mean they were in some sort of a relationship? She thought it, but didn't say.

Dan smiled and stroked her disheveled hair. "Whoa, baby. I'm at work for the next five days. How about I call you?"

She flopped back down onto his shoulder. "With your calling history? Maybe I should phone you, Dan," she said. She tried to sound flippant, but she could hear the bitchy tone of her voice. *Oh God, don't let me get snippy now*.

He tipped her face toward him and frowned. "Hey, Jessie, I'm real sorry about the phone confusion. I will call you. This is great. I like you." He kissed the top of her nose.

It was enough. Jessie made herself breathe. She was being dumb. Guys were goofy. They got numbers wrong all the time. They didn't count days the way women did. This was all okay. She kissed him again.

"I'm sorry. Bad joke. I'll give you my number again, and just call me when you're off work. As you said, this is good—great. Let's just enjoy each other when we can. I know you have to work, and to be honest, I have to study, too. A lot. We'll work around each other's schedules."

His hands had begun to wander as she spoke. "We can work around each other, too," he said and started to kiss her bare shoulders again.

It looked like he was ready for more action. Maybe what he lacked in phone contact, he made up for in physical contact, she thought with satisfaction.

It seemed like Dan was reading her mind. He rolled his body over so he was on top of her, pinning her down onto the mattress. "I have something I'd like to try," he said. He sounded more menacing than usual. "Tell me, baby, do you have any baby oil?"

Chapter Thirteen
Johnson's Baby Oil

"Baby oil? Who knew?" Cathi was bursting with excitement and had phoned Maria to tell her everything. "I have to admit, I've never seen the stainless steel in my kitchen gleam so bright. After you've given it a good scrub, just polish it up with baby oil and it shines as well as it did the day you bought it."

"Yeah?"

That wasn't the reaction Cathi wanted. "Seriously, that's all you can say? Maria, you could try to inject some sincerity into your voice."

"Huh? Sorry. This is important to you."

It was very important to Cathi. "Oh, don't worry, I'm just so nervous. What if my realtor was off the mark? Maybe she was overly optimistic."

"She's a professional, *chica*. If she thinks your house is worth a small lottery, who are we to argue? It's a fantastic appraisal—just go with it."

Cathi knew they'd already had this conversation, but she still needed reassuring. It was all they had talked about since she'd set foot in Noreen Palmer's house. If it was possible to move mountains with sheer willpower, Cathi Grant was going to do it.

Her husband had little say in the matter. Cathi hadn't told him about getting the realtor until the report came back with the whopping appraisal. Only then had Cathi told Michael, and he was thrilled. The house was worth way more than they'd paid for it almost a decade earlier. What he wasn't so thrilled about was her desire to move them to Crystal Lake. Michael liked their home, and he didn't want to live too close to Rick Sanchez. They already worked together. He argued that living so close might be a little too much of a good thing. Cathi had admitted all of this to Maria already. Her friend had agreed, but there was no talking Cathi down. One way or another she was going to trade up, and there was no way anybody was going tell her otherwise.

"Oh, that's the doorbell. I have to go," Cathi said.

"Good luck."

Cathi laughed. "Maria, how many times do I have to tell you? It's not a question of luck—it's all careful planning. Trust me." She hung up and headed for her front door.

As she swept through her house, she double-checked that cushions were plumped up and the throws were smoothed down. Everything was as ready as it could ever be, so Cathi opened her front door with flourish.

"Collette, how are you? Come in." She smiled her biggest, brightest, most house-proud smile and ushered the realtor in. As always, Collette was dressed immaculately in a smart black suit. Her shoulder-length blond hair was freshly blown out and looked dangerously similar to Cathi's. The realtor looked like a consummate pro. Cathi had chosen well.

Collette Bispham laughed as soon as she entered the house. "I can smell the freshly brewed coffee and homemade bread from here."

"Can you?" Cathi preened. "Good. I read it creates a welcoming environment for prospective house buyers."

Her realtor nodded. "That's true," she said. "But for a house of this value, you're dealing with a more sophisticated buyer. Things like brewed coffee and homemade bread—well, let's just say they're prudent clients."

Cathi didn't care. She shrugged away her realtor's caution, and they walked into the kitchen together.

"This place looks fantastic."

"Yes, I worked hard and used the baby oil trick on the stainless steel dishwasher and refrigerator. Don't they look like new?"

Again, Collette smiled but avoided touching the shiny appliances. "Well, you can head out now if you like. I put up the open house sign at your gate and I've already had a few phone calls, so I hope we'll get a couple of visits."

Cathi didn't look so sure. "I was thinking I might stay here. I could answer any questions that buyers have."

Collette's smile slipped. "Mrs. Grant, in my experience, buyers feel more comfortable wandering around a house alone. They like to poke and have a good look, and they're less inclined to do that if you're here. Are there any other family members still in the house?"

"No, my husband took the girls to a circus in Boston," Cathi said.

What she didn't tell Collette was that she'd avoided telling Michael about the open house altogether. He had taken the news of their high appraisal so well that she'd decided the best way to handle her husband was to tell him after the fact. If they got a good offer, she would bring it to him on a silver platter. Much better than getting him involved at this early stage. The house hunters would be in and out, without him even knowing or having to worry about it. How cool would it be to go to him with a firm offer at or even over the asking price? Then she would have to convince him to take the money and she would be halfway to Crystal Lake.

"Mrs. Grant?" Collette interrupted her daydream. "Are you leaving?"

Cathi snapped back to reality. "No, Collette. I won't. This is my house. I know everything there is to know about it. It might be a little unorthodox and I'll keep out of your way, but I'm staying."

Collette shrugged and smiled. "Suit yourself," she said and headed back out to the front door to wait for potential buyers.

Cathi lapped the ground floor of her home again to ensure everything was perfect. She had been jittery in the morning with Michael, and with the children, particularly, because she couldn't tell them why she was so uptight. Earlier, Michael had buttered some bread on the kitchen counter, and she had overreacted. She knew that now.

"I just wiped that down," she had said, exasperated. "Can't you use a plate?"

Michael pulled out the dish and dropped his buttered bread onto it. By then, of course, it didn't matter. He had managed to mess up the counter and a plate.

"Can I have permission to put some jelly on my toast?" he asked, his tone dripping with annoyance.

"Oh, Michael, I just spent the morning cleaning the kitchen. Is it such a crime that I don't want to see it messed up again?" She was doing her best to sound reasonable and hide her excitement, but then she turned on one of her girls with the anger of a banshee. "Stacy, get your feet off the footstool. I just vacuumed that. And switch off that darn television. Look, can you play outside this morning?"

Stacy looked understandably shocked. "It's a footstool—it's designed for feet. And I can't go outside. It's freezing," she said, rolling her eyes.

Cathi's shoulders fell in defeat, but Michael saw her. "Baby, what's eating you?" He left the toast and focused on her. "Is it the kids? Do you need a little mommy time? To be honest, I think you've been working around the house too much. Why don't you come to the circus with us?"

Cathi felt her shoulders tense up even more at the suggestion of her leaving the house. "I don't want to go to the circus. I want to stay here."

"Okay, so I'm guessing it *is* the kids. I'll take them into town and get lunch at Quincy Market. Then I'll take them to the circus and give you plenty of head space, but I'm doing this on the condition you rest and decompress a bit. Okay?"

She looked up into his concerned eyes and nodded, feeling grateful. He was a good husband.

"You promise you'll chill out and do nothing?" he asked again.

"I promise I'll relax, and I won't even leave the house," she said.

He smiled. "No more cleaning or home improving?"

"What's left to do?" She avoided his question. "The place is immaculate. I think that's why I'm jumpy about letting it get messy again. It took such a gargantuan effort to get it this neat and tidy, and I just don't want to see it trashed."

He nodded. "It may be a fantastic house and now even a valuable one, but it's also a home, Cathi. You have to let the kids kick their heels up, and you have to let me eat!"

She gave a guilty smile. "Sorry if I'm being a bit obsessive."

Michael had taken the girls out of the house pretty fast after that talk. She had tried not to lie to him. Technically, she wasn't going to leave the house. Nor would she clean. It was all done. All she had to do was walk in ever decreasing circles, ensuring everything was perfect for her maybe house buyers.

Having lapped the lower lever, Cathi headed upstairs to double- and triple-check the bedrooms. That's when she heard the first set of visitors. A shiver of apprehension tickled down her spine. Should she pretend to be another buyer or tell them the truth that she was, in fact, the owner and as such could answer any questions they had? She was in Katie's bedroom at the time, so she checked her reflection in the full-length mirror there.

Just like every detail in her house, Cathi gave quite a lot of thought to her own style for the day. Today she was in Parisian black wool from head to toe, and she wore a long gold chain. Cathi liked a classic style of tailoring as opposed to Maria's more flamboyant form. She knew her friend turned more heads than she did, but Cathi was stable, steady, and reliable. She didn't live life at the same high-octane level Maria did. Although today sure was frantic.

She heard another couple arrive, and her heart beat faster. Returning to her reflection, she studied herself. Cathi worried if the all-black look was a little too morbid, like she was going to a funeral, but then she reminded herself it was very chic and classy. That was what she was selling today—style and grace. She heard voices coming up the stairs. Strangers were wandering around her house with a view to buying it. How incredible was that? Then they were in the room with her.

The man nodded at Cathi when she turned to say hello.

"Isn't it a fabulous house?" She hadn't planned on saying anything. It just came out.

The woman looked at Cathi and gave a slight nod of agreement.

"Just look at the proportions of this room," she said. "And the décor? So pretty."

Not looking as convinced as Cathi sounded, the couple glanced around at the much lauded décor.

"Isn't it tasteful?" Cathi was finding her stride. "It's so charming and elegant."

The man shrugged. "We have three boys," he said and walked out.

The woman gave Cathi an apologetic smile and then followed her husband. It sure stopped Cathi in her tracks. Her tiny rosebud-print wallpaper would be of no use to them. Oh dear. She let them go and waited for the next party to arrive. Within minutes, two ladies walked in. They looked like mother and daughter—the daughter being Cathi's age. She smiled at her newest guests.

"Hello there," she said. "Isn't this a fabulous house?"

The woman her age looked nice and beamed at Cathi. "Oh yes," she said. "The downstairs is lovely, too. All the rooms work together."

Cathi's heart skipped a beat. This woman understood her vision. "Don't they? They *blend*. So much thought and money went into the house. It'll make a fabulous home for somebody."

"Oh, I agree and the location . . ." The younger woman was just as enthusiastic. Her mother hadn't spoken yet. She was busy looking around the room and opening closet doors.

"What do you think?" Cathi tried to engage her, too.

She looked at Cathi for the first time and then at her daughter. Then she sniffed. "Smells funny," she said.

"Oh, I think that's potpourri," Cathi tried to explain.

"Smells like cats to me," the older woman said. "And the wallpaper looks like somebody threw up on it." She walked out of the room.

Her daughter looked helpless. "I don't think she likes it."

"But you do?"

"Oh yes, I think it's a dream home, but I'm not the one who's buying here. It's my mother-in-law, and I don't think it's what she had in mind." She looked out the bedroom door to see which way the older woman was heading. "If you'll excuse me, I think I better keep up with her," she said and ran out of Katie's bedroom.

Cathi was disheartened. She looked at the wallpaper anew. How could anybody think it looked like vomit, cat's or otherwise. She turned her head to the side. *They are clearly rosebuds*, she thought petulantly. Was cat puke pink? Some people had no taste.

She swung around. "Oh, hi," she said looking a little startled. Distracted as she was, she hadn't notice the man entering her daughter's room. He was alone and had a quiet walk. "I didn't hear you come in."

He nodded. "I hope I didn't scare you."

"No, I was just admiring this wallpaper. Do you like it? They're rosebuds —not, not anything else."

He gave the walls a quick once-over. "Yes, very nice. I have a daughter who's just seven years old. I think she might like this room."

Cathi's heart leapt. "A daughter? There's another lovely room just next door. I, um, saw it, too. It looks like it might be for a younger girl. This is all red, while the other is all pink."

He smiled at Cathi. "Better and better. I have two daughters, so they could have a room each. Which way did you say it was?"

Cathi wasn't going to tell him when she could show him. She moved out of the room faster than she could say *sale pending* and brought him into Stacy's pink paradise.

"Wow." He laughed. "You weren't exaggerating when you said it was pink. But I guess this is what little girls like."

"Oh, it is, it is." Cathi was beside herself. Was she looking at the buyer of her home? He sure looked rich enough. She glanced out Stacy's bedroom window and saw a rather gorgeous Mercedes parked in the driveway. If that was his car, he could afford the house.

"Is it just the two girls you have?" She watched her mystery man open the closet doors to see what sort of space lay within. She'd blitzed them over the last few days, too.

"My wife is pregnant with number three. That's why I'm out looking by myself. She's due in a few weeks, and she really wants to have a bit more room. I figure it's the least I can do while she's the one with the big job making the babies."

Cathi was smitten. Was this guy for real? Rich and adorable. What a perfect match for her perfect house.

He looked at her a little more sharply. "Are you another realtor?"

"Me? Oh no. I'm not a realtor. I . . . I just live near here and thought I'd have a look." She hadn't planned on fibbing. It just happened.

He seemed to accept her answer. "Do you know if there's a bedroom that would work well as a nursery for the new arrival?"

"Yes! Yes, I do." She couldn't hide her excitement. "Well, it's a man's study now, but it could be converted back into a bedroom for the baby, no problem, and it's just next to the master suite, so that's convenient. Have you seen that room yet? It's to die for."

It didn't bother Cathi that there were no more prospective buyers after the man she now thought of as her Prince Charming. Collette didn't seem too happy with just three parties, but Cathi was walking on air.

"I'm telling you, Collette, he's our buyer. He loved everything about upstairs, and we both know the downstairs is even better than the upper level. I think he's our buyer."

Collette gave her a weak smile. "I've been in the business a long time, Cathi. They can say one thing and think another. Please don't get your hopes up just yet. We'll have more open house days, and I'm sure I could get more interest if I put a for sale sign up in your yard."

"No." Cathi's tone was harsher than she meant. "I mean, no thank you. Really, Collette, I don't want to unsettle the children. We haven't told them about the move yet, and if we have the deal done before they know, that would be a great help."

"I wish you'd reconsider. You'd sell a lot faster with a sign."

Cathi didn't care, because she was convinced she already had her buyer. That gorgeous man with the big car loved her home. He was rich, good-looking, and adored his family. What more could any woman want?

"Okay, I think I better pack up." Collette interrupted her house-selling dreams, which was a good thing because it made Cathi check her watch for the first time all afternoon.

"Oh my! I had no idea it was so late. Yes, yes, you must go. Take your open house sign and all the house brochures." She was almost pushing Collette out the door now.

"Can't I leave the brochures and the sign here for next weekend?"

"No." Cathi panicked. "Take them with you. I'll call you. Let's see if we get anywhere with today's house hunters first."

If Collette thought her client's attitude was strange, she didn't show it. She bundled the kit into the back of her car and left a rather frazzled Cathi in peace.

Alone once more, Cathi rushed around the house. She switched on the television, threw some popcorn in the microwave and did a quick tour to ensure all the rooms looked normal. Thank goodness she did, because to her horror a house brochure lay on her bed.

"Vindictive old woman," Cathi muttered, assuming it was the granny who had disliked the house so much. She pushed the brochure down to the very bottom of the trash. Then she rushed about the house making it look a bit more disheveled. She lit the gas fire and bounced on the sofa cushions so it looked like she'd been lounging there for the afternoon. When her popcorn pinged, she threw it into a big yellow plastic bowl and brought it into the living room.

Cathi found *Gone With the Wind* on cable and started watching it from the halfway point. Just as it began to look like she had everything settled, she remembered Fifi. She'd put her in the garden shed for the afternoon. It was unfortunate but necessary.

Some house buyers weren't into small dogs. Some were even cat people —who knew? She wondered which her Mr. Perfect was as she went to get the dog. Fifi was livid and barked her annoyance until Cathi picked her up.

"Hi, honey, we're home." She was in the kitchen when she heard her husband call from the living room.

Ooh, that was close, she thought.

He walked into the room and gave his wife a kiss on the cheek. "I can smell freshly baked bread in here. What a great idea—you're watching *Gone With the Wind*. Good girl. Nice afternoon?" he asked as he headed over to the fridge and opened the massive chrome doors. "Hey, what's on this door?" He winced in disgust when his hand brushed up against the outside. "Were the kids messing around with the fridge this morning? This feels gross. It's covered in some sort of oil."

Cathi reached for a tissue.

Chapter Fourteen
Mixed Blessings

Maria reached for a tissue and blew her nose loudly. She'd read so many stories and seen one too many *Oprah*s on this subject. They all said the same thing—if a woman thought her husband was having an affair, she was probably right. One thing Maria was certain about—they were having major marital problems.

She and Ricky had moved beyond the fighting stage. They hadn't had a full conversation since the stupid fight over Puerto Rico. Maria understood there was more than a simple argument going on here. They often disagreed on stuff. She knew she was quick to fly off the handle, but he used to love that about her. Some of their best makeup sex happened after those fights, but that sure wasn't happening now.

Rick had refused to look at her the morning after they'd fought. Instead he'd told her he had to work all weekend. She hadn't believed him, but he had left early both mornings and worked late. The following week, he had been up and out before she and the kids were even awake. He had maintained that grueling pace of work ever since. She didn't need to worry about Rick bumping into their sitter anymore, because he was in the house so little. This was day ten of their cold war. Was that a record?

All the previous week, he had e-mailed her and said he was going to the gym after work. She had gotten into the habit of putting his dinner in the microwave, and then she would be in bed pretending to be asleep before he got home. The second weekend, he had claimed to be still working on his new Fidelity account.

She decided it was easier when he was out of the house. Then she could push thoughts of him away—most of the time. What had happened? How had it gone so bad so fast? There was only one real plausible explanation—Rick was sleeping with somebody else. No man could be spending that much time in the gym.

Maria had all but given up her running ambitions, but now that she had childcare, she could get out for some head space. That was the best thing in her life—her few hours of freedom.

She preferred to spend the time wandering around Bloomingdale's in Chestnut Hill or heading for one of the bigger shopping malls while Jessie had Alice. With winter upon them, the shops were full of festive colors and gorgeous holiday decorations. She was never able to window-shop with the kids hanging on her, but with the sitter watching Alice, she could spend hours wandering around, enjoying the season and soaking up the atmosphere. Heaven.

Thanksgiving was looming, and they didn't have plans to go anywhere. They usually celebrated with Cathi and Michael. Cathi was the organizer and said she preferred to host the big dinner, but this year she hadn't invited them. Maria was pretty sure it was because her friend was focused on keeping the house in pristine condition, so she hadn't mentioned it.

Now, with only three days to go, she had nothing planned. She hadn't even bought a turkey. She considered inviting Cathi, Michael, and the girls to her house. That would have been the nice thing to do, but she didn't feel like being nice. The truth was Maria was fed up with Cathi, too.

Her friend had become a real pain in the ass about her big plans to trade up. She'd told Maria she was convinced she had a buyer for the house, and she was all fired up about converting their upstairs study into a nursery in order to make the house more appealing. All that—and she hadn't even told Michael what she was up to.

Maria was tempted to blow the whistle on Cathi, but she wouldn't. What sort of friend would that make her? Not a very nice one. She was already proving to be a less than perfect wife—or so Rick seemed to think. The last thing she needed to do was risk losing her friend, too.

She blew her nose again. She had just put the kids to bed. Alice was sleeping much better these days thanks to all the stimulation she was getting from that psychology major. Jessie was a mixed blessing. She was a huge help with the baby and a terrific sitter. Even Cody loved her. Then again, it was when Jessie had arrived that Maria's problems with Rick had started.

Maria knew she couldn't blame the girl for the issues in her marriage, but it was the first time she had seen her husband look at another woman. Jessie wasn't even a woman, she was a girl. She just happened to be a very beautiful one, and oblivious to all the commotion she caused in the Sanchez household.

Rick was an alpha male. He had his brood with Maria, and now he was looking for another, younger mate. She started to cry again.

Here she was, trying to get her figure back, trying to fight the hands of time, while her husband's hands were quite possibly moving all over his next conquest. What would she do? What could she do?

"Mami," she said almost to herself and looked at her watch. Seven o'clock in Boston meant six in Puerto Rico. She would call home. Maria didn't call enough. There was no real reason for it. She'd just fallen out of the habit.

Her mother's life was full with Maria's three younger sisters, all of whom had stayed on the island and married local men. They thought Maria was crazy to live in New England with all the snow. There had been no big fights—it was just life that had made them drift apart over time. Maria tried to remember the last time she'd spoken to her mom. Too long.

"Fool," she chastised herself and pulled out her cell to dial her mother.

"Maria?" Her mother, Leticia, must have recognized the incoming number and answered on the first ring.

"Mami." Maria didn't mean for it to happen, but when she heard her mother's familiar, soft loving voice on the other end of the line, she burst out crying—again.

"*Cariño*, what's the matter? Are you ill? Is it the babies?"

"No, no." She tried to compose herself. "Everybody is well. I just miss you."

Maria knew Leticia Garcia was a wise old woman, having reared four girls and buried one husband. So Maria also knew her mom would see right through her.

"Maria, you are a red-blooded and passionate Puerto Rican woman. You do not phone me in tears often. In fact, you never have."

Hearing that made Maria cry even more. "Oh, Mami."

"The last time I heard you cry was when you called to announce the arrival of Alice. Before that it was for Cody's birth, and the only other time you cried was when you called to say Rick had proposed. *Chica*, is it Rick? Maybe you are pregnant again?"

Maria let out a miserable laugh. "That's impossible, trust me."

And with those four words Maria knew her mom would understand.

"Come home, *cariño*. Come home to me and we can talk."

Leticia made it sound so simple. She could just catch a flight into San Juan. One of her sisters, or maybe a brother-in-law, would come get her and she would be back home in no time. But life wasn't that simple anymore.

"Mami, I have the children. I can't just drop everything and come home to you."

"Why not?"

"Well, there's school for Cody, and Alice has a routine now. She's even beginning to sleep better."

"Bah." Her mother gave a small sound of exasperation. "What? You don't have Thanksgiving in America anymore? I am sure Cody has a school vacation soon."

That hadn't even occurred to Maria. Of course her son would be out of school. Maybe Rick would even come with them. Would that be a way back to her husband? If he felt the warm sun and the golden sand between his toes, maybe, and maybe he would see Maria the way he used to. It had been years since they'd been to Puerto Rico. Time had whizzed by, and life in

Newton just swept her along. Without realizing it, she'd grown steadily apart from her family. How dumb was that?

"You're a genius. I would love to come home, but I'll have to ask Ricky. Can I call you tomorrow after I've spoken to him?"

"Call me anytime you like, *cariño*. I'd love to see all of you for Thanksgiving. You can fly down tomorrow or Wednesday. You know we have the room." She laughed.

Maria thought about the house she grew up in. She had been very involved in discussions over the years, when she and her sisters urged Leticia to downsize, but her mother always refused. She was determined to stay in the house she had raised her family in until her own death. It was the house her husband had built for her when they had been married only a few years, and it was in that house that she had married off her four girls. Sadly, it was also the house where she had held her husband's funeral, but Leticia was determined she would one day die in it, too. She told her daughters she didn't want to leave the big house because, if it were ever necessary, they could return—even with their children. Maria hadn't understood until that moment just how wise her mom was.

One little phone call, just a five minute chat with her mother, and Maria was feeling better. Why hadn't she thought of it herself? All she and Ricky needed was a little time away from Crystal Lake.

Naturally the kids would come with them, but even that was good. They would love the sun, the sea, and getting to know all of their cousins. Things were getting much colder in Newton. Maria shivered at the thought of another long winter. No matter how many years she lived in New England, she would never get used to the cold.

Her mind floated to the aquamarine waters of her beloved home. How she wanted to walk barefoot on the alabaster sand with Ricky by her side. He would love it. How could he not?

Maria looked at her phone. It had been so easy to call her mom, but she couldn't quite get up the nerve to dial her husband. E-mail was so much easier, although impersonal, but at least she would be making an effort. She needed to end this stupid fight.

Maria clicked open her e-mail on her cell. He said he'd be home late, but he didn't mentioned the gym. Was it possible he was still at the office? Maria forced herself to be positive. He was not with another woman. He was working late, and that was all. There was no other woman.

Would you like to go to Puerto Rico for Thanksgiving? Mami has invited us to stay with her.

She typed the message into her phone, hit send, and waited.

"Please answer, please answer." E-mail and texting had been their only means of communication for ten days now. The waiting was killing her, so she started looking at flights to pass the time. It didn't take Maria long to discover that even though flights were still available, they were the price of a small private plane. How could airlines justify such prices?

Finally, she found a few flights out of Boston. She could still put Alice on her lap, so that cut the cost a little. Maria worried when she saw there were only three seats left at the lowest price. If she didn't book them soon, they would be gone. It was an anxious time, waiting for Rick to reply.

Then she heard the welcome ping and minimized her flights page.

I told you about the Fidelity account. You know how much work that is. I can't take off now for a vacation.

Her heart sank.

I'll probably have to work right through Thanksgiving.

This last bit made her angry. What was she supposed to do while he played big business politics? Everybody took Thanksgiving off—everybody. That was when it hit her. Was he even telling the truth? Was he with somebody else?

The thought made her nauseous. How could she ignore what her gut was telling her? Only a fool did that. She had heard of women who let themselves ignore all the signs. Working late, growing apart, fighting more—that was what she and Ricky were doing.

Are you really at the office?

She clicked send before she could stop herself.

The silence was deafening. He was ignoring her on purpose—the shit.

Maria went back to her flights page. She changed the details to see the cost if she were flying out the very next day.

"Half price? That's nuts," she said and adjusted the flight details so it was just her, Cody, and the baby—no Ricky. Again the price dropped. She could do it so easily. All she had to do was hit the *book flights* button and she would be on her way.

It was a direct flight that left the next afternoon. That would give her enough time to do some last-minute errands when Jessie had Alice, and then she would pack for the kids. If Rick was going to play around, she was leaving. Even if he wasn't playing around, Maria knew she couldn't live with this constant state of tension.

She had to get away to think straight. Where better than home? Who better than her mother to help her through this? Maria barely believed it herself that she and Ricky had reached this point. She thought they were together for the long haul, but heartbreaking though it was, it appeared not. Distance and time would give her a clearer perspective.

Even as she inputted her credit card number, Maria couldn't believe what she was doing. She was running away with her babies. "Let's see how he feels about this." She hit the return button on her phone with more force than was necessary.

Her e-mail pinged with a new message.

Of course I'm in the office. What sort of a stupid question is that?

She read the next e-mail aloud. "Purchase complete."

Maria was giddy with excitement. She was going home. That she was doing it behind Ricky's back was insane. She'd never done anything like this before, but then again, Ricky had never looked at another woman before. Crazy times called for drastic measures.

Even though it felt surreal, Maria knew it was time to shake things up. She was leaving him, and he could damn well chase her like he used to. That would get them back to basics. It was the oldest game in the world.

Maria went to get ready for bed. As she stripped out of her clothes, she couldn't help but notice her baby fat. "So much for my Operation: Transformation," she said to her reflection, but then she made herself stop. So what if she was a little softer around the middle? That's what came of getting older and having kids. With a little Puerto Rican sun, she would look pretty darn good for a mother of two.

If Ricky Sanchez had any plans to have an affair or take a lover, Maria intended to change his mind and his plans entirely.

Chapter Fifteen
Maybe Baby

"There's been a change of plan," Ely announced when Jessie walked back into their room after another long day.

"I didn't even know there was a plan to begin with." Jessie dropped her bag of books to the floor.

It was late Monday evening, and she was shattered. She had spent the morning minding Alice and the rest of the day studying. Passing the entire weekend with Dan had done wonders for her libido, but it hadn't been great for studying. She knew Ely wouldn't be happy about it, but Jessie was planning to do homework over Thanksgiving in South Carolina. It was a shame, but what choice did she have? She had to make up for her playtime with Dan.

The man was insatiable. Thankfully, so was she. Another blessing was how understanding Ely was being. She all but moved in with Josh to give the new lovebirds space. Dan lived with his parents, so he couldn't do the things he wanted to do to her there. It made Jessie shiver with delight, because the man was gifted in bed. She convinced herself she would catch up on lost study time.

"What's on your mind?" Jessie asked Ely.

"Well, I'd planned on spending tomorrow night—our last night before we fly home—with Josh, but then I had a better idea. We should throw a party." Ely looked self-satisfied.

"A party? Are you mad? You know there's a strict no booze rule, not to mention the signing-in of every guest. I'm pretty sure they have a no parties policy here, too."

Ely clapped her hands together. "Ah, but that's where you're wrong. Did I tell you I did a semester of law in Miami?"

"Yes."

"Well, anyway, as far as I know there ain't no rules sayin' this is a no party zone. So I say, lawfully, we are within our rights."

Jessie flopped down onto her bed. "Yeah? Well, Ely, I've never studied law, but even I know ignorance is no defense."

"Ah, that's in England. Things are different over here, J. If I've told you once, I've said a million times—we only got one life."

Jessie joined in for the second part of her roomie's favorite slogan, and together they chanted, "You gotta live it." She covered her face with her hands. "I was hoping to spend the night with Dan."

"Invite him."

"I don't even know if he's around yet. He might be working."

Ely sat up on her bed. "He's very vague about when he's available and when he's not, ain't he?"

Jessie knew what Ely was talking about. Her roomie had made no secret of the fact she was suspicious about Dan. Ely was trying to protect her. It was endearing. Sometimes.

She pulled one of her pillows from under her head and threw it across the room at Ely. "Your new word for today is *shift work*, Ely. He doesn't know from one end of the week to the other what shifts he'll be on. It's no big deal."

Ely sat forward to avoid the incoming pillow, and that was when she saw the laminated card fly out of the pillowcase and hit the floor. She was on her feet and bending over it in a second. "What's this?" she said, sounding playful as she picked it up.

Jessie's eyes snapped open when she heard her roommate's tone. "What did you find?" She sat up.

"Well, well, well. Look at what we have here." Ely's tone was teasing.

Jessie came straight over. She knew she had nothing to hide but still felt defensive for some reason.

"What is it?"

"It's Dan 'Romeo' Walker's driver's license."

Jessie tried to grab it out of her hand, so Ely jerked it back. "Ah, ah. Back to my legal lessons—possession in nine-tenths of the law."

"Let me see it." Jessie stomped her foot and scowled.

But Ely was reading the fine print. "Well, I never thought he was that old, and now I even know where he lives." She tapped the license against her chin. "Should we send Josh and the boys around to check his place out?"

Jessie made another lunge for the card, and Ely let her have it. She took it back to the security of her bed to study it. "You know, you're right. He's thirty. I didn't think he was that old."

"What? You're sleeping with the guy and you haven't even asked him his age? J, I'd assumed you'd asked him if he's married or divorced and if he has any transmittable diseases at this point." She looked at Jessie for a reply but didn't get one.

"J?" Ely tried again, using three syllables on the letter.

This time Jessie looked up. "No, I haven't asked any of those questions. We use condoms, so I'm sure we're safe. Regarding his personal life—well, we haven't got around to that yet."

Ely groaned and threw herself back down on her bed. "J, J, J . . . how can you be so smart and so dumb at the same time? You gotta ask those questions. For all you know, he might have a wife and three kids across town. He is thirty, you know."

Jessie stood up and began pacing the floor, trying to defend herself. "No, Ely. You don't understand. We British, we're a lot more discreet. We're a very private bunch and we don't probe."

Ely let out a guffaw. "Seems to me Dan's done plenty of probing, judging by your smiles. I thought you two were getting real close, real fast. Isn't all this stuff just pillow talk?"

Jessie kept pacing but didn't feel like talking.

"Darlin'," Ely said, trying again, "you did tell me this man is just some light entertainment for you while you're on this side of the pond and nothing more. I'm wondering if you still feel that way."

"What are you getting at?"

Ely shook her head. She looked like she didn't want to go on, but Jessie was starting to feel paranoid.

"Ely, I'm serious. What are you saying?"

The other girl shrugged, still silent.

"You think I'm falling for him?"

Ely looked at Jessie, her face the picture of sincerity and her eyes worried. She sat up on her bed. "I gotta say, J, you're walkin' around here like a broodmare. Your eyes have gone all glassy. I don't see you eating much, and Lord knows you have all but stopped doing my homework for me." She was trying to make a joke out of it, but Jessie didn't laugh.

"All I'm saying is if I was your mom, I'd be concerned. I can smell trouble around that boy, and you yourself told me you're staying in the States for just one year. Don't let that guy break your heart, girl."

Jessie started to feel angry. Dan was the first bit of fun she'd had in years. She was still getting her homework done and she managed to keep the babysitting thing going, too. "Well, you're not my mother, so you don't need to be concerned." Her tone was harsh. "And I'm sorry I don't have time to do your homework anymore. Here's a novel idea—do it yourself!"

Ely waved her hands in the air. "I don't care about the damn work, Jessie. But like it or not, I do care about you."

This softened Jessie a bit. She looked at her roomie and gave a weak smile. "Thanks. You know what, ignore me. I'm just tired."

Ely nodded as if that was an end to it. "Me, too. Let's get to sleep, because tomorrow's gonna be a big night," she said, rubbing her hands together.

Jessie moaned. "For real?"

"Darn sure. Somebody has to see to it that these are the best days of our life." Ely winked at Jessie. "I know you got sittin' in the morning and classes in the afternoon, so why don't you leave all the preparations to me.

It's what I do best, anyway. Now you know where Dan lives. Why don't you go take him his license in the evening and invite him to the party. It's a good reason to check out his place, and you get to meet his folks at the same time."

Jessie was intrigued. "He shouldn't really be living at home at his age." It was the first even vaguely negative thing she had ever said about her new love.

"Maybe he just hasn't found the right woman yet." Ely shrugged.

Jessie beamed at her. "You think? Maybe?"

"Maybe, baby."

Michael Grant was ready for bed. Work was hectic at the moment, and he was looking forward to the Thanksgiving break. He rubbed his tired eyes and called the dog. He didn't much like Fifi. She was all bark and no bite. But the women in his life loved her. Michael liked Rick's dog. A Labrador was a proper family pet, not a shih tzu. But it had been Cathi's decision, and like most times, she had gotten what she wanted.

She'd had the good sense to go to bed before the movie started. Wise woman. Stupidly, he had stayed up to watch a film he had seen before, and for what? Michael walked to the back door to let the dog out.

The night was mild for the end of November. Naturally there was a chill in the air, but it was a clear sky with no sign of snow, so he wandered out into the backyard to enjoy the mild weather while he still could. Within a few weeks, the yard would be deep in snow.

It was great to just sit and let his mind drift. He had been a creative editor in the firm for fifteen years now, writing the catchiest jingles and wittiest one-liners in the business. *Don't go without your Flo* was his biggest success. Now Flo Smoothies ranked as the nation's number one smoothie chain, but what Michael really wanted to do was write a book. It was burning inside him. He knew what he was going to write about. He had his characters, the plot, location—everything was in his head. All he needed was to get it onto paper.

That was the catch. There was just no time between the day job and the girls, and of course, Cathi. He liked to take his wife out at least once on the weekend and maybe once during the week, too. Then he had basketball one night a week. Time was in short supply, and up until now, money had been, too. The biggest drain on his finances was the girls' school fees, and that wasn't going to change any time soon. It was terrific to hear the house was worth more than he thought.

Michael looked at the night sky and thought about taking some of the equity out of the house. If he refinanced the place, he could take a year's sabbatical from work and write. Twelve months would be enough to figure out if he had what it took to make it as a novelist. Then he could pack in the catchphrases and jingles altogether and focus on being a full-time writer. There would be enough money to keep the family in the style to which they were accustomed, and he would have his dream job. He needed to discuss it with Cathi, but any time he brought up writing full-time she laughed at him and changed the subject. Michael realized he needed to sit her down and explain how serious he was. He had to make her hear him.

Fifi was running back to him, so Michael hauled his tired body out of the yard chair.

He'd just about given up his dream of writing when the girls had started school and the bills had begun to mount, but when he'd heard how much the house was worth, it had seemed there might just be another option. Michael felt he owed it to himself to try.

He and the dog headed back inside. He locked up and set the alarm, but just before he went upstairs, he took a brief detour into the library. Cathi had a set of drawers where she kept her business things. He wanted to see if she had a copy of the newest appraisal for their house. With the exact figures, maybe he could do some financial calculations before he went to sleep.

As expected, the top drawer was full of pens, tape, and stamps. The second one had blank paper and envelopes.

He opened the third drawer and found it full of brochures. "Dammit, she isn't thinking of decorating again—not after the last time," he mumbled.

Michael knew she had ceremonially dumped all her decorating folders when the project was over last time, because she had done it in front of him in an effort to calm him. He remembered it well. They had been in the kitchen, and she had opened the trash bin and laughed. *"Look, Michael. These are all my interior décor files and catalogs. You're safe. We're done."*

That had been just after he'd written a bunch of checks to cover the last redecorating job—the big one that had redone the entire downstairs but not the second floor. He was certain these brochures were new. One of them had a letter from the supplier.

Before he could think about Cathi's privacy, Michael was reading the letter.

Dear Mrs. Grant, it started.

Thank you for your inquiry phone call this morning to Child Style. We offer a full decorating service for children's bedrooms and playrooms.

Michael felt his panic rising.

I understand you're interested in our nursery package. If you already know the sex of your baby or if you have a color in mind, we'd be happy to have an interior decorator come out to your home and advise you on your options. Our prices are highly competitive, and we have a strong after-sales service.

Michael was still reading, but he had stopped taking in the words. Cathi?

The sex of her baby? Jesus, was Cathi pregnant? That couldn't be right, not again, not after all these years. It would explain why she was acting so weird lately. But they'd agreed they were done.

When had they last had sex? God, was there any chance in hell Cathi was expecting? He stood up but had to sit back down again. Pregnant? No, there had to be some mistake, but why not? That was how Katie and Stacy had come into their lives.

Was it really so bad? He shook his head.

It was good. Yeah, it was great, terrific. Of course it was great, wasn't it? Why hadn't she told him? Maybe she was embarrassed at getting caught after all these years. Didn't she use an IUD as protection? Weren't those things foolproof?

Dear God, another child—more bills. He checked the date of the letter. Monday, November eighteenth, today's date.

"This letter was written this morning?" he said to himself, trying to take it all in. "She picked up the brochures today?"

That was when it hit him between the eyes. There was no way he was giving up the day job now. If there was equity in the house, great—but he would need to work harder than ever to feed, educate, and entertain a third kid.

Michael put the brochure and letter back in drawer. Typical of his wife to think about decorating the baby's room before she'd even told him. Maybe it was the nesting hormones kicking in. He wondered how far along she was. When did she plan on telling him? He should wait—let her deliver the news when she wanted and in the way she wanted. It wouldn't be fair to steal her thunder.

Michael stood back and looked at the desk. There was no sign of his intrusion. He didn't want her to discover that he already knew. Wow, a new baby. No—it was good, great. Better than being a writer. He was going to be a dad again.

Wow.

He crept up the stairs and peeped into his two sleeping daughters' rooms. They looked like perfect angels when they slept. Then he tiptoed into his own room. Cathi was out cold. That wasn't surprising. The first few weeks were always exhausting.

Memories came flooding back to him. Cathi had suffered from extreme exhaustion in that first trimester. He would need to take better care of her. He would talk to the girls tomorrow about helping out more at home, he decided as he changed into his pj's. Cathi might want a midmorning nap, and yes, they would have to investigate turning the fourth bedroom, which he now used as a home office, into a nursery. *What the heck? Life has a habit of throwing curve balls at you*, he thought, brushing his teeth as quietly as he could. *It's a heck of an adventure.*

Chapter Sixteen
Going on an Adventure

"We're going on an adventure, children," Maria said as she pulled her car into the long-term lot of Logan Airport on Tuesday afternoon.

"But how can we spend Thanksgiving in Puerto Rico without Dad? Why can't he come, too?" Cody still managed to sound miserable even though he was heading to a tropical island in the Caribbean.

"I already said. Daddy has to work Thanksgiving. If he can get away, he'll follow us," she said while looking for an elusive parking spot.

She had heard on the radio that Wednesday was the busiest air traffic day of the year, so she had hoped Tuesday wouldn't be so bad. How wrong was she. It was mayhem. Alice picked up on Maria's anxiety and started to wail in agreement.

One frazzled hour later, she was feeding Cody burgers and fries, and Alice a yogurt, having stashed the car, negotiated the bus to the right terminal, and checked in. It hadn't been easy with two uncooperative minors. Nor did Maria know how to travel light—even when she was heading to the lovely warmth of Puerto Rico. In theory, she needed a few sundresses and a bikini, but she had brought enough for a month. She hoped she was running away for just a short while and then—if things went according to plan—Rick would run after her.

But Maria was mature enough to buy a round trip ticket. She had no choice with Cody heading back to school the following Tuesday. She was beginning to understand what women meant when they said they were trapped in a marriage. It wasn't just about her and Ricky anymore. There were the children to consider. How could she move back to Puerto Rico when Cody, in particular, was so attached to his father and his home? She sent up a silent prayer, hoping her husband would come to his senses soon and they would make peace. Maria checked her phone again for a message from him. Nothing. What a crazy day it had been.

That morning, when Jessie came to babysit and Cody was in school,

Maria had made a dash to the mall. She picked up some summer gear for Cody and a cute little swimsuit for Alice, and then she got some things for herself. It was only after Jessie left and she had packed that she wondered how she would tell Rick what she was doing. It was eleven days since their fight. There had been arguments in the past, but they had never lasted so long without Rick caving.

She started by writing a note, explaining how trapped she felt and how insecure she had become about his affection. She wrote about feeling exhausted all the time and never having quality time with women her age— or with him, for that matter. It didn't take long for Maria to start crying as she wrote. She got mad with herself for going on so much, so she crumpled up her letter and threw it in the trash.

An e-mail would be easier, she decided. She could be more concise, and there was a chance, just a tiny chance, that when Ricky read it, he would get right into his car and zoom out to stop her. Maybe he'd even come with her if he realized how badly she needed to get away.

Ricky, she started.

I understand you're very busy, but you know we need to work on our marriage, too. Things between us are really shitty now. Please, please come to Puerto Rico with me and the children. I have to get away, so I'm flying back home with the children today. Please follow us out when you get this message.

Maria

She read her message a few times. There was no love, no kisses. She couldn't find the strength to insert them. Maria hurt too much. Then she hit send and waited. She gave Alice her lunch and checked her e-mails, but there was no reply. Twice, after lunch, she thought she heard his car and rushed out to the front of the house, but he wasn't there. Cody came back from school and there still was no word from Rick.

She told her son about the surprise holiday, and he was delighted until he realized his father wasn't coming. By midafternoon there were no e-mails or panicked texts from Ricky, so at last she locked up the house and left Orga in the kitchen to wait for Rick's return from the office—whenever that would be. Damn him.

They clicked on their seat belts, and the flight attendant asked them to switch off their phones over the plane's intercom system. Maria was worried. Was there a chance something was wrong? Was that why he hadn't called?

She couldn't resist. She dialed his office phone number, and Barbara, the receptionist, answered.

"Hi, Barbara." Maria tried to sound upbeat. "Is Ricky there?"

"Sure, just a minute and I'll put you through."

"No, no that's not necessary. It's just I e-mailed him earlier and I kinda thought he'd reply, but maybe he hasn't got it yet."

"It's a madhouse in here today, Maria. Do you want me to check?"

"No, don't bother. Just tell Rick I'm at Mom's with the kids and he needs to get home to Orga at some point because she's locked in the kitchen."

"Got it. You're at your mom's and Orga's in the kitchen."

"That's it, Barbara, and thanks."

"No problem. I'll see he gets it. These guys have become workaholics with this new account. They're working late every night and all weekend. I don't know how you put up with it, Maria. I hear they're working right over Thanksgiving, too. You corporate wives are very patient," she said.

"I'm sorry, but you'll have to shut your phone down now, ma'am." One of the flight attendants was standing over Maria.

"Mom, get off the phone." Cody poked her.

Maria smiled up at the stewardess. "I have to go, Barbara. Thanks for that." She switched the phone off and slipped it into the pouch of Alice's diaper bag.

So Ricky *was* working straight through the holiday. Why had she thought it was another woman? He would think she had lost it. Maybe she had. Maria looked up and watched the airplane doors being closed. The cabin crew was doing the head count. There was no turning back. Maria and the kids were on their way without Rick. What would he think?

What do you think?" Ely asked Jessie when she arrived at their room after another afternoon in the library.

"Oh my God!" She didn't know what to think.

"You like?"

Ely had cleared the room. There was no sign of their desks or chairs, and the beds were propped up on their sides. She had somehow managed to take out their center lightbulb and replace it with a rotating glitter ball, and there were red, blue, and green lights flashing along the floor where once her desk had stood.

"What have you done with our furniture?"

Ely laughed. "Why? You wanna study some more? Girl, when you ever gonna relax?"

Jessie glared at her roommate.

"It's okay. Everything you don't see is in Amy's room next door. She'll keep it safe. Josh is getting me the keg, and I just need to focus on the bar now. It's lookin' good, ain't it?"

Jessie nodded. "Yes, it's great. I just wish it was in somebody else's room. I really can't afford to get kicked out of college, Ely. I have too much invested in this course. If I don't—"

"J, it's Thanksgiving. We're simply givin' thanks. You know, we only got one life . . ."

That was usually the point where Jessie collapsed onto her bed, but that wasn't an option this evening.

"You wanna drink?" Ely said.

"Yes, please. I think I need a beer."

"That's my girl." Ely went into the bathroom and came out with two bottles, one for each of them. "I filled the tub with ice so it can be the cooler."

Jessie was torn. She sat down on the floor next to the window and took a sip from her beer bottle. The place looked fantastic, and with a bath full of beer, it was sure to pull in enough party people later.

Ely seemed to read her mind. "Before you worry yourself sick, you know my friend Brian?"

"The campus cop that buys all your booze for you?"

"I am old enough to buy my own drink, you know. It's just I like to delegate. He makes a little profit, but most of all, it makes him complicit— and my friend!" She nodded and took a swig from her beer bottle. "Anyway, he's on duty tonight and gonna cover for us."

"Terrific," Jessie said without conviction. "So now we can add bribing an official to our list of misdemeanors."

Ely laughed. "You make it all sound so damn serious. It's just a party."

"Did someone say party?" Josh pushed their bedroom door open with his shoulder and lugged in a keg of beer.

Jessie stayed sitting on the floor and watched Ely welcome her boyfriend. Then they started to argue over where the keg should be set up. It was funny.

"Behind the door is good because I can hide it quick if we get raided," Ely said.

Josh shook his head. "Next to the window is better. You can throw shit out onto the grass, and it won't stink up the room."

"I like it next to the bathroom door, because you have the sink in there and it's close to the rest of the drink in the bath," Jessie said, trying to be helpful.

"And the toilet," Ely said, looking disgusted. "I don't want the keg anywhere near the *john*. That's gross."

Jessie raised her hands in surrender and pulled out her phone to check for messages from Dan. *Nada.* Why was he so distant when there was such a good vibe between them?

"Looking forward to the party?" Josh asked as he connected pipes together for the keg.

"Eh, I think so. I have no idea where anything I own is, and I'm a little scared about getting kicked out of college. But as usual, Ely tells me I'm being too serious."

He nodded. "She's a bit of a wild child all right, but she's got a heart of gold." He winked at his girlfriend. "Tell me, is your biker boyfriend coming?"

Jessie gave him a sideways glance. Josh was obsessed with the Bugatti Dan drove. "I think he might be at work tonight."

"Can't you call him?" Ely asked, watching Josh set the keg set up behind the door. It made Jessie smile. Ely had won that argument.

"I keep getting his bloody voice mail, and I don't want to leave another message."

Ely walked over to where Jessie sat and gave her foot a gentle kick. "Go over to his house," she said. Then Ely glanced at her boyfriend. "You could drive her over, couldn't you?"

"Sure." He winked at Jessie. "Soon as I get this baby connected, I got a couple of free hours. Let's go over to say hi. You can tell him about the party, and I can have a look at this famous bike of his."

Jessie groaned. "Is that not a bit eager? I mean, wouldn't that qualify as stalking?"

Ely slapped her forehead with her hand. "You're dating the guy. How could it be stalking?"

Jessie looked at Josh. "You're a guy."

"Thanks for noticing."

"Well, do you think I'm being too forward going over to his house?"

He shook his head. "This guy has a killer bike—he's probably used to women showing up to his house unannounced. Guys, too, for that matter. What the heck, let's go."

Ely pulled Jessie up off the floor. "If you don't go, it's all we're gonna hear about for the next three hours. Don't make a big deal of it. Just say you were in the neighborhood."

"He'll never believe that." Jessie winced.

Josh laughed. "Why not? It'd be the truth." He poured the first beer from the now assembled keg and took a sip. Then he nodded in approval and looked back at Jessie. "This is ridiculous. Come on, Jessie. Let's go visit your boyfriend and his bike."

Suddenly it seemed out of her control. Her friends had made her mind up for her, and the truth was she wanted to see him before leaving for South Carolina. With only a little reluctance, Jessie got to her feet, handed the empty beer bottle to Ely, and followed Josh outside.

"Where are we going?" he asked once they were in the car and he had the GPS working.

Jessie didn't need to double-check Dan's license—she'd memorized his address and even checked it out on the Internet. Maybe she was getting close to stalking-girlfriend syndrome. This was very unlike her, but then again, Dan wasn't exactly being the perfect gent. He had sent her a sweet text after their fabulous day in bed on Saturday, and she'd saved his number then. But he hadn't contacted her on Sunday or Monday. Today was almost over and still no word. She had left one text and one message on his voice mail, but she couldn't bring herself to leave any more. That would scream of desperation.

The car pulled out into the busy traffic on Commonwealth Avenue.

She knew she'd told him about going to Ely's for Thanksgiving. She remembered the conversation well because she had asked him what he was doing. "Nothing much," had been his reply. He wasn't a man of many words. Then again, she reminded herself, she wasn't with him for his conversation skills but rather his talent in a whole other area.

"It's snowing!" Josh said with delight.

It wasn't the first time Jessie had seen snow. They had plenty of wintry weather in the UK but not like this. Huge fluffy flakes landed softly on the hood of the car and on the windshield.

"It's beautiful," she said in a whisper.

"You think?" he said. "Wait till you come back after Thanksgiving. It'll be a complete whiteout. Shit, I hope this doesn't close the airport."

The GPS interrupted them and told them to take a left onto Arapahoe Drive.

"You don't suppose there's any chance of that, do you? The airports closing, I mean?"

Josh shrugged and focused on the road. "It happens sometimes, but they're ready for big winters up here. They can clear a lot of snow."

Jessie watched the Newton neighborhood whizz by and saw the snow was beginning to stick. People were walking with purpose, their heads huddled down in their jackets. It made her shiver even though the car was warm. She was glad Josh was driving. She still couldn't get used to the traffic on the other side of the road, and she'd never driven in a snowstorm.

"You have reached your destination," the GPS said a few moments later.

"That was fast." Jessie was feeling a bit insecure now that she was outside Dan's home.

Josh stopped the car and looked at the house. "If he's here, I guess the bike's in the garage. Doubt he'll be using it in this weather . . . shoot!" Then he turned his attention to Jessie. "If he asks you in, come back out and tell me. I'm not sitting here all afternoon while you two get cozy inside."

Jessie wasn't so sure about being there at all. Something held her back. "Maybe I shouldn't be calling round unannounced."

"You tried to phone the guy, didn't you? Anyway, Ely said you had to give him back his driver's license. You know it's illegal to drive without that in the US. You're doing the guy a favor. Go on, I'll wait." He reached across her and opened the car door. A wave of icy air rushed into the warm car. "Man, that's cold. Hurry, woman."

Despite her reluctance, she got out of the car.

Jessie got Dan's driver's license out of her purse and clutched it for reassurance. She was just bringing it back—no big deal. If his mother or father answered, she'd be polite and say she was a friend of Dan's.

Jessie wasn't dressed for snow, with a pair of black boots and gray jeans. She didn't have a coat with her either. Usually, it hung on the back of the bedroom door, but Ely had cleared away all that stuff, too.

She rang the doorbell. "Maybe there'll be nobody here," she whispered. The door opened.

"Hi." Jessie smiled overenthusiastically. "I'm guessing you're Mrs. Walker. I'm Jessie, a friend of Dan's. I was just, um, in the neighborhood, and you see, I have Dan's driver's license. That is to say, he dropped it." She held it out as proof that she wasn't a crazy stalker. "Um, is he here?" She was sure she sounded like an idiot.

Mrs. Walker's face was impassive for a second, but then she smiled. "What a nice thing to do." She took the license and read the name on it. "Yes, this is Dan's. He's not here just at the moment. He's at work, but I'll see he gets it."

"Who's that, Mom?" Jessie heard a younger woman say from somewhere in the house.

"It's okay, Sadie. I've got it. You go put your feet up." Mrs. Walker spoke over her shoulder. But Sadie, it appeared, had other plans. She came up to the front door and pushed past Mrs. Walker to have a look at Jessie.

"Hullo," Jessie said, still flashing her bright British grin.

"I'm Sadie Walker. What can we do for you?" She was a small blonde, maybe in her late twenties, Jessie thought, and very pregnant.

"I was just telling your mother here that I was in the neighborhood. I'm a friend of Dan's. He dropped his driver's license, so I thought I'd bring it back."

"Did he drop his license or his pants?" the blonde asked, her voice rising by the second. "He said he was done with this, Mom. He said that was all behind him."

Sadie wasn't talking to Jessie anymore. She grabbed the license from Mrs. Walker and started to cry.

"He is, he is. This is just a friend. Nothing more," Mrs. Walker said. "Don't get yourself upset. You're too far along." She looked at Jessie. "Thank you for this, but I think you better go now."

Jessie watched. She knew what was happening, but she didn't want to believe it.

"I'm sorry. Did I say something wrong?"

Mrs. Walker was closing the door on her now, but Sadie pushed it open. "That depends. Are you screwing Dan Walker, my husband and the father of my child?" she shouted through her tears just as Mrs. Walker pulled her back inside and clicked the door shut.

The snow was falling heavier now, but Jessie didn't feel it. She turned from the door and walked back to the car.

"I'm guessing he wasn't there," Josh said. His voice sounded normal and friendly like nothing had changed.

Jessie got into the car.

"Hey, you're covered in snow. Will you wipe that shit off? You'll catch a cold." He looked at her face. "Hey, you okay? You look kinda—I dunno—dazed."

"Is that what you call it?" she said, but her eyes remained glazed over as she stared, unblinking, out the front window of the car.

The engine was running and the car was warm, but she didn't notice. Josh had the wiper blades on full speed to keep the window from freezing up. She didn't care. What did it matter? If they got buried in a blizzard, she couldn't have cared less. The blades whizzed over and back, over and back —*stu-pid, stu-pid.* Was that what they were saying to her?

Josh started to move the car. "Was that his mom I saw you talking to?"

Jessie kept watching the wipers. *Stu-pid.* "Yes."

"And the other woman? His sister?"

"Um, no. That was his mom with his wife."

Chapter Seventeen
At the End of the Day

"Your wife is with her mom." Barbara delivered the news as she delivered their millionth round of double espressos to Rick and his brainstorming team.

At first he thought it was a joke. He laughed at the receptionist, but she gave him a blank look. "Orga is locked in the kitchen, so don't be too late this evening."

The other men jeered Rick when they heard that. Rick knew that all of the wives had been complaining about the late work nights, and now his team could see he was getting the same grief. What these guys didn't know was Rick's mother-in-law lived in Puerto Rico. It wasn't like Maria had hopped over to Watertown. It had to be a joke. Just to be sure, he checked his phone. There were no new texts or e-mails, but he did see a missed call from Maria. He tried to call her back but got her voice mail and didn't have time to leave a message. There were seven men sitting around the table watching at him.

They wrapped up the meeting at nine o'clock, and then he called the house phone. When he got the answering service, he assumed Maria was in the bath or in bed already. She had started going to bed earlier and earlier. He was pretty sure it was to avoid him, but then again, the kids exhausted her.

This fight they were having was a bitch. The only way he handled it was by working himself into the ground. The gym helped, too. Thinking about Jessie didn't help. The less he thought about her, the better.

Somebody had mentioned it was snowing when they were working, but he didn't realize how heavy it was until he whisked his red sports car out of the underground parking lot in Post Office Square. The snowfall was heavy, and he knew only too well the slick roads would make traffic worse. He tried the house phone again. Still no luck. Why would Orga be locked in the kitchen? Was Maria joking? Maybe she was trying to reconnect. Jeez, that would be a relief. He was done fighting. In fact, he couldn't even recall what the fight was over. Rick tried to remember. It had been the night he brought flowers home.

"Aw, shit," he said to the empty car. "Puerto Rico." That was what they'd fought about.

She had said how great it was, and he had dissed it a little too much. Driving through the snow now, he could sure see its appeal. All he could do was crawl along in the fast lane of the Mass Pike, and that was where Rick got his first jolt of panic. Was it possible Maria hadn't been joking? Could she actually have gone to Puerto Rico with the kids?

"No way," he mumbled. "Not possible."

He slipped into the middle lane of the jam-packed road, because it seemed to be moving a bit faster. A car honked at him. "Screw you," he yelled and shook his fist at the SUV behind him, not even sure it was the same driver. "Jesus!"

He turned down the heat in the car because the noise of the fan had started to annoy him. "Work's hard enough these days without the added bonus of a nagging wife." If she'd gone AWOL with the kids for Thanksgiving—well, he wasn't sure what he would do. Rick was getting angrier. He tried her cell again. The traffic began to move, and he slipped back into the fast lane.

It wasn't smart to drive fast in heavy snow. The roads were slippery—even with the sand that had been put down—but Rick didn't care. He had to get home. He kept telling himself it wasn't anything serious because otherwise Maria would have texted or e-mailed. She wasn't that mad at him —or was she?

The houses on Crystal Lake Lane were lit up with holiday lights, twinkling a warm welcome home. The snow that had settled on the ground in a soft blanket was the perfect backdrop for Thanksgiving. Any other day, Rick might have slowed to enjoy the picture postcard beauty of it. The novelty of the first snowfall always drew the kids out to make snowmen and snow angels.

It would be Alice's first time to really see it. He wanted to hold her and help her catch a snowflake, just like he had with Cody when he was little. Rick knew he had to work the next day, but maybe he could go in late. He wanted to see the kids' reaction to the winter wonderland they would wake up to in the morning.

He pressed the opener for the garage door and waited for it to rise. It was just a few feet up when he saw Maria's car was gone. "What the— seriously?"

Rick called Cathi. "Is Maria at your house?"

Cathi sounded as annoyed as he. "What? Of course not. It's almost ten, Rick. Are you at home?"

"No. Sorry I called so late. Forget it. I'm not at home. I'm sure she's there." It was a half lie. Technically he wasn't in the house yet.

He wasted no time getting into the kitchen where, just as Barbara had said, Orga was locked inside. The dog was thrilled to see him and needed to get out into the backyard. Rick let her out and then ran through the house. Everything looked normal. The furniture was just as it had been that morning. He bounded up the stairs—first to Alice's room, then Cody's, and last his own. There were no bodies in beds.

"Maria!" he bellowed into the silence. Then he ran back down the stairs again and scanned the surfaces of the kitchen. There were no notes—nothing on the fridge or the family notice board. Rick went into every room in the house and switched on all the lights. He hoped, prayed he was mistaken, but he knew he wasn't. His wife and kids were gone.

Michael thought he heard his wife's voice. He tiptoed into the bedroom where Cathi was settling back down to sleep.

"Were you talking to yourself?"

"No, it was Rick on the phone. Very strange. He was looking for Maria. I assume she's in bed if she has any sense. Why was he calling us?" She pulled her down comforter under her chin and closed her eyes.

"Well, don't let it bother you, honey. Just get back to sleep. You need your rest."

Cathi still hadn't told him about the pregnancy, and he had been bursting to discuss it with her for over twenty-four hours. Michael wasn't sure how long he could hold out.

"Mmm." She sounded like she was drifting off.

All day at work, Michael's thoughts had kept drifting back to his wife. He was still getting used to the news of the new baby, but he wanted to talk to her about it—soon. What was she waiting for? He snuck out of the room and checked on his sleeping daughters.

Michael headed back downstairs. Thanksgiving was only two days away—perhaps Cathi was waiting until then and wanted to give him the news as a Thanksgiving Day surprise.

He had been thinking about how he should play it. Would he say he had already guessed, or should he feign surprise? His wife knew him well. It would be hard to convince her it was a shock.

He was looking forward to Thanksgiving. It was going to be the four of them—or should that be five? Cathi had said she was tired of asking Maria and her family and never getting a reciprocal invite back. It was time the Sanchez family stepped up their game. He looked at his watch and thought about calling Rick back to make sure he was okay but decided against it. If there was a problem, he would call.

Michael thought about the wine for Thanksgiving. If Cathi was going to tell him the big news, it would be smart to have some champagne. Of course she wouldn't be drinking, but she could sip on a glass. A baby was a cause for celebration. Definitely champagne.

Ely was worried about her roommate. "Are you sure you want another drink?" she asked. She'd never seen her friend in such a state.

"Oh yeah . . ." Jessie said, slurring her words as she handed her glass over to the guy working the keg.

"You know, you're not supposed to mix the grape and the grain," Ely said.

Jessie had already drunk at least a bottle of cheap white wine and then a glass or two of something pink and fizzy. They'd run out of wine, so Jessie had moved on to beer. This wasn't going to end well.

She hadn't been too shocked when Josh and Jessie were gone for so long. She'd assumed they had met up with Dan the Fireman—as she liked to call him—and he had invited them in for a drink or maybe even a bite to eat. But she had been surprised and a little annoyed when they weren't back by the time the party started.

Things had been well under way when her friend walked in. Josh had been by her side, with Jessie already looking a little the worse for wear. He'd filled Ely in on the situation, and somebody gave Jessie yet another glass of wine. Josh said he had taken her to a bar called The Local in Newton as soon as he heard about the pregnant wife, and he'd warned Ely that Jessie had already had a lot of wine. That worried her because Jessie wasn't a big drinker.

"J, too much of a good thing is not as good as it sounds. I love you, honey, but I think it's time you had some water and maybe even some fresh air," she yelled over the music. The party showed no signs of slowing down, which Ely was happy about, but Jessie was more important.

"I'm purrrrfectly fine." Jessie was working hard to sound coherent.

It was funny, but Ely knew Jessie was anything but fine. Her roomie had fallen for the firefighter in a big way. He was a great-looking guy, but there had been something about him that always made Ely nervous. Now she knew what it was—he was a two-timing bastard.

Men! They were just like horses, and she could tell a good one from a bad one on instinct alone. Some people called it karma or a sixth sense. Whatever it was, she'd always sensed trouble with Dan.

Damn him, she thought while watching Jessie try to keep it together. Why would he do something like that? With a pregnant wife? What an ass. Somebody needed to teach that jerk a lesson and, Ely decided, that somebody would be her!

Ely looked around the crowded bedroom. The disco ball was working great, and light bounced off all the walls as Taylor Swift sang about breaking up.

Not the best thing for Jessie to be listening to.

"Come on," she said to her friend, coaxing the plastic disposable cup out of her hand. "We don't need this anymore. Let's head outside and go for a walk." She maneuvered Jessie toward the door and out of the party. She gave a quick glance behind her. The party was rocking. Nobody would even notice them gone.

Outside, the snow had stopped, but it was bitterly cold. Even Jessie in her drunken state noticed. "We can't stay out here. It's bloody freezing." She folded her arms across her chest in a futile attempt to stay warm.

"Well, at least that means your senses are still functioning," Ely said with a laugh. "Come on. Josh never locks his car, and I know where he hides his spare key. We can sit inside and turn on the engine for warmth."

Sure enough, his car was in the lot just next to their building, and as usual it was unlocked with a spare key in the glove compartment. Ely started up the engine so the two girls were able to sit in the front seats and stay warm.

"What are we doing out here when the party is in there?" Jessie asked, like she was just figuring out what was going on.

"I thought you could do with a little quiet time." Ely looked up at their bedroom window. They'd tried to black out the glass, but it was pretty obvious with the flashing lights and muffled music that there was a party going on up there.

"Might be a good idea to wrap it up soon. The last thing we need is trouble with the Wiswall cops," Ely said in a rare moment of maturity. "Then again, maybe my man on the inside has managed to keep the cops away from this madness."

"The madness isn't here—it's over the other side of Newton," Jessie said, her voice hollow.

"J, I'm so sorry. I still can't believe it. What a lowlife."

Jessie looked at her roommate. "He is, isn't he?" Her eyes were watery, like she might cry.

Ely had never seen Jessie emotional before. Ely was the hothead in their partnership, and it broke her heart to see Jessie so upset.

"If I could get my hands on him . . . do you want me to have the guys rough him up?" she asked, but Jessie shook her head.

"Wuzza point?" She slurred a little. "He's just a sicko, and he's going to be a father! Can you believe it?"

If it hadn't been so sad, Ely might have laughed. Jessie looked so animated, with her big eyes even bigger than usual and her eyebrows in a high arch of indignation.

"You mushn't hurt him. That baby needs him, no matter what an arse he is." She was working hard to sound sober.

Ely nodded like she agreed, but already her mind was working the possibilities.

A single tear slipped down Jessie's cheek. Ely reached over from the driver's seat and gave her friend a hug. "I know this sucks, sunshine, but I swear that jerk just ain't worth your tears, J. Do not let him get to you like this!" She slapped the steering wheel. "I say we take the douche bag down."

Jessie pulled back. "Jesus, Ely. Do I have sucker written across my forehead? I mean, I must be a right idiot to attract these men. You know this isn't the first time, right? I seem to be a bastard-magnet. Or are all men bastards?" She seemed more angry than upset.

"There's a few good guys, honey. You just gotta keep your eyes open. There's a lot of idiots out there, too."

"You knew!" It sounded like an accusation, especially with Jessie's alcohol-fueled, drunken gestures. "You did! From the vurrry beginning you were warning me off Dan. Why is that? What did you see that I didn't? Christ, I'm meant to be the psychologist, and I can't even spot a total bastard when he's right in front of me." She slapped her forehead with the heel of her hand.

Ely winced, then reached over and took her friend's hand so she couldn't do herself any more damage. "You were infatuated. That clouds judgment. Believe me, I've had my share of assholes, too."

"Not as bad as me."

Ely persevered. "You were only in it for the fun, remember? You told me you just wanted a few months of romance. That's what you said. Don't let him ruin your time in the States, okay?"

Jessie didn't reply, but a few more tears trickled down her face. Ely hugged her again. She said soothing words and rubbed Jessie's back, but suddenly her buddy pulled away and lunged for the door. She made it just in time to get out of the car and deposit most of what she'd drunk onto the clean white snow. Ely hopped out of her side and rushed over to help.

"Atta girl," she said when she realized her friend needed to be sick. "Better out than in. That's the fresh air hittin' your system."

"Wahghh." Jessie made an unintelligible sound.

"Don't talk. Just get it all up so we can get you a drink of water and maybe even a bed somewhere."

Ely was used to this. She'd had her first drink at age twelve and knew all about overindulgence. Jessie, it seemed, did not.

She was focusing on trying to keep her friend's long hair out of everything, so she didn't see the cop cars drive up. There were no sirens or flashing lights. Maybe they were trying to arrive unannounced, because it was quite by chance that Ely looked up and saw the men in full uniform walking into her building and up to her party.

"Ah crap," she said as Jessie retched again. "I think the party's over."

"Good." Jessie moaned, still doubled over. "This is hell, and I need my bed."

Chapter Eighteen
Home Sweet Home

This is heaven. I love my bed, Maria thought. She rolled over and kept her eyes closed because she wanted to get back into her dream of birds, lush trees, and warm, bright sunshine. Despite her best efforts, though, she blinked and opened her eyes. That's when she remembered. She wasn't dreaming. She was really home, and home was the closest thing to heaven.

Maria was in her old bedroom in her mother's house and the noises, sights, and sounds permeating her skull weren't from some dreamland but wonderful, fabulous Puerto Rico. It was such a relief to be back.

The night before, as soon as their plane touched down, the tropical island had begun to work its magic. Cody, who had sulked about the absence of his father for almost the entire trip, perked up as soon as he felt the heat. Her mother had been waiting for them at the airport.

"I thought you'd be too busy to come get us. I would have caught a cab, Mami," Maria had said, but her mother, Leticia, clearly didn't agree.

"My firstborn flies home with her beautiful children to spend Thanksgiving with me. I will not let you catch a taxi!" Then she attacked her grandchildren with hugs and kisses.

Everybody got a second burst of energy when they got to Leticia's big family home. Cody wanted to swim in the pool right away. Even little Alice got caught up in the atmosphere and gurgled for everyone who fussed over her. Maria's overriding feeling was relief. Seeing her mother was like turning back the clock, and now she was the daughter again—not a wife and mother.

Of course, Leticia had organized a feast for them, and over the evening, each of her three sisters visited to say hi and play with the kids. Paloma, the sister she was closest to, came with her husband and two children. They stayed for dinner, as well.

Maria felt strange doing all the family stuff without Ricky by her side, but nobody said a word. Instead, they acted like it was the most natural thing in the world. Bernardo, Paloma's husband, asked about Rick and his business. Paloma lamented he was so busy and sent her love, but nobody judged.

They ate outside at a long wooden table that overlooked the swimming pool. It was the same furniture the family had used since Maria had been young. Paloma reminded her big sister that her name was still engraved into the wood from what felt like a million years before. Way back then, Maria had got into big trouble for damaging the table with her school compass, but now her mother smiled when her two grown daughters giggled over the old autograph.

Alice spent most of the night on Paloma's lap, while Leticia served up mountains of Maria's favorite childhood dishes. They had taquitos first, which Cody thought were like his mom's tortillas. Then they had *arroz con pollo,* which was one of Maria's favorite.

"Mine never tastes as good as yours does, Mami. What's with that?"

Leticia smiled. "Local ingredients."

"What is it anyway?" Cody pinched up his nose in distrust and pushed the plate around to see it from another angle.

"Chicken and rice. Eat it and be polite," she told her little boy, because she knew her mother had gone to a lot of effort. There were olives and capers peppered through the dish, and Maria knew she cooked it in beer. Leticia was pulling out all the stops, and it wasn't even Thanksgiving yet.

"Mami, you must let me help you tomorrow. There'll be a lot more to do because we've come at the last minute," Maria said.

Paloma laughed. "You? You won't do a thing, girl! You're the prodigal daughter. We'll all have to work while you put your feet up." She nudged her sister's shoulder, so Maria knew there was no jealousy.

But Maria also knew Paloma was right—Mami wouldn't let her lift a finger. It had been a long time since she had been able to put her feet up. Heaven.

As always in Puerto Rico, she stayed up too late and ate too much. *Carnes guisada,* a beef stew dish, came out after the chicken and rice, and then—after all that—Leticia produced *budin de pan,* a bread pudding, and *mantecaditos,* a traditional Puerto Rican cookie that Maria loved. Her tummy ached by the time they were done, but she didn't care. It was worth the discomfort.

Both her children loved the magic of eating outside under a clear sky of stars by candlelight. She didn't feel the need to rush them off to bed, because they were having such fun. Cody went midnight swimming with Paloma's two boys, who were just a little older.

The perfume of night jasmine floated on the warm air while the crickets started up their night chorus. It was all so reassuring and familiar to Maria. There were several times when Ricky slipped into her mind, lingering in her guilty conscience. She wondered what he was doing and why he hadn't called. Was he furious or winging his way to her on the next flight? She prayed he was on a plane.

When they cleared dinner away, Leticia wouldn't let her do anything to help, so Maria settled for getting her own kids off to bed while Paloma cleaned. Then her sister, brother-in-law, and two nephews went home, promising Maria they would come back the next day.

Finally Maria was alone with her mother. Leticia offered her a nightcap, but she turned it down. It was the first day of what would be a busy holiday. Leticia was not an old lady at sixty-two, but even so, Maria didn't want to overtax her.

That night she slept with the windows open in her old bedroom. The Puerto Rican night evoked so many memories, and it lulled her into a deep sleep. She slept better than she had in months, but all too soon it was the morning of a new day.

"Time to get up," she told herself and slipped out of the deliciously soft, old bed sheets.

She had the good sense to bring her summer sleepwear—a short little night dress with spaghetti straps. It was ample enough with the heat they enjoyed at this time of year. Before dressing, she went to check on her children but found both bed and crib empty. Panicked, Maria went straight to the kitchen and sighed in relief when she found them there. Having a pool at the house was wonderful, but it terrified her, too. For her kids to get to Crystal Lake, they had to climb the hedge at the bottom of their yard, but here, Alice could crawl across the patio and fall in.

This morning, thankfully her fears were unfounded. Alice was perched on her grandmother's hip, listening to the finer points of Puerto Rican cuisine regaled to her in fast-flowing Spanish.

"Mami, I'm sorry. I didn't hear Alice wake. I would have gotten her up."

Leticia swung around. "Good morning, *guapa*. Alice didn't make a sound this morning. I just happened to put my head around her door when she was waking, and she was happy to come with me. We have been having fine conversations since."

Maria kissed her mother and daughter then made some coffee.

"Cody's in the pool already. He hasn't even had breakfast yet."

Maria laughed. "He loves the water. He's just like his dad." She said it before remembering Rick was a taboo subject.

"How are things?" Her mother let the question hang in the bright morning sunlight.

"The same as they were last night—fine." Maria refused to be drawn into anything deeper than her coffee.

The back door to the kitchen opened out into the courtyard, and she could see her boy practicing his dives. The long table where they had dined the night before had been reset. Now it was draped in a multicolored tablecloth, and Leticia had put a vase of sunflowers in the center. It was very pretty, but she wondered how long it would last with Cody's ability to destroy anything in sight and Alice's curious little hands. Alice would have that tablecloth off in seconds. Nevertheless, Maria took her mug of fresh brewed coffee and a large orange out to the courtyard to eat *al fresco*.

"Hey, Mom, check this out," Cody called as soon as he saw her, and then without any more warning, he did a backward flip into the pool.

"Please, be careful." Maria frowned and drank some coffee. Leticia and Alice joined her.

"You know, even the coffee tastes better here," Maria said as she peeled her orange.

Leticia looked pleased. "Of course it does. It's local."

"I buy Puerto Rican coffee in Newton. I think it's being able to enjoy it outside under a sunny sky, watching Cody in the pool—that's what makes the difference." She caressed one of the sunflowers.

Leticia fed Alice her bottle as they watched Cody's water antics. "Is there anything you would like to do today, *chica?*"

Maria shrugged. "I don't know. I guess it depends on whether Ricky arrives or not."

"Do you think he will?"

Maria shrugged again.

"Have you spoken with him?"

Maria shook her head.

"You need to talk, *cariño*," Leticia said.

Maria began to feel defensive. "I e-mailed him," she said but knew that wouldn't be enough for her mother.

"You look good." Leticia reached over and stroked her cheek. "Tired, but good. Even one night here, and I see you're looking less stressed. Maybe you just needed a little rest?"

"Maybe." Maria drank more of the strong coffee. It was nice to be home. Why was Rick so wrapped up with work he couldn't see there was a life outside Newton and his job? She pushed thoughts of her husband out of her mind and focused on the moment at hand.

"You know, I think I want to go into San Juan today," she said just as the thought entered her mind.

"No problem. Leave Alice here. Cody can help me with her. You go and have some quiet time. It'll be good for you."

"I can take them with me," Maria said, but Leticia closed her eyes and shook her head—something she did when there was no room for negotiation. It made Maria smile.

"I have so little time with these gorgeous grandchildren of mine. You go and let me play with them. Enjoy." It was like the matter was already settled, so Maria caved.

"*Gracias*, Mami," she said and finished her delicious coffee.

Rick knew what he needed was a strong coffee, but there was no time to get it now. He would have to hit Starbucks on the way into town. He had already missed three phone messages from the office, and he hadn't even bothered to open his e-mails. He was the one who had called the seven a.m. meeting, and undoubtedly he was the only person to do the no-show. That was so damn unprofessional, and on the day before Thanksgiving, too.

"Shit," he said as he stepped out of the shower. He thought he had set the alarm on his phone to wake him at six but perhaps not. He had been very drunk by the time he'd fallen into bed the night before.

It was a heck of a shock to come home and find his family gone. He had left several messages on Maria's phone. The first was a lighthearted one, but when he called again several more times, his messages were more frantic. He had been close to calling the police at one point, but then he had double-checked his phone and incoming e-mails. Finally he had thought to check his junk mail folder. Sure enough, there had been her message.

Anything with bad language got dumped into that file, and he didn't check it enough. When Maria had written about her life being "shit", the software had taken over and trashed the mail. He cursed the efficiency of his smart phone now.

If he had known, maybe he could have convinced her to stay. *What would I have done?* he wondered as he hurriedly dressed and slapped on some aftershave. He didn't know.

At first he had been relieved she was okay and hadn't been kidnapped with the kids. Then he'd been furious and frustrated she had taken such a drastic step. His voice mail messages reflected these myriad emotions. Having found the e-mail, he had called back with a soft, encouraging message. But then he'd called again and pleaded with her to pick up and have some degree of maturity about the situation.

He was working his ass off for her and the kids. Every cent he earned came into the house. Was it his fault work was so damn busy at the moment? Then he'd begun to drink. After that, he was a little vague about how many times he'd called and what exactly he had said. What did it matter? She wasn't returning his calls. He knew he could phone his mother-in-law's, but he so didn't want to talk to her before he spoke with his wife.

"Hullo, Maria?" A female voice came from downstairs.

Rick froze, startled, but he knew who owned that sweet English accent. Then he quickly moved into action, double-checking himself in the mirror. He looked fine—clean and fresh, anyway. His eyes were a little bloodshot, but that was to be expected after a bottle of whiskey.

"Jessie, is that you?" He came down the stairs and into the kitchen.

"Hi, Mr. San—er, Rick. How are you?"

"Yeah, good, great." She was still gorgeous. Even hungover, he couldn't help but notice the tight jeans that covered her long, skinny legs. Her white blouse was tucked in, but the top two buttons were open. Her bra was white, too.

Rick! he yelled inside his head.

"Okay, um, bit of a change of plans." He glanced around, looking helpless, and combed his hand through his hair. "Maria has taken the kids to her mom's in Puerto Rico. I'm working right through the holiday, so it made sense." The lie came easy.

"Oh." Jessie looked nonplussed.

Orga fought for her attention, and Rick remembered he hadn't fed the dog.

"I know this isn't what you came for, but is there any way you would dog-sit instead of babysit? I have to get to work, and I haven't even given Orga her breakfast. If you could take her for a walk so she can get out for a while, we'd pay you the same rate."

She smiled.

Jeez, she's pretty, he thought but then pushed the idea from his mind.

"I'd be glad to. I'm sorry, I had no idea Maria was going. She didn't mention it yesterday, or I wouldn't have come."

"Why are you apologizing?" He laughed. "We're the ones who forgot to mention it. This is great. You'll walk Orga, then? Maria can deal with the finances when she comes back, because I'm rushing today."

"Sure, but I'm flying out to South Carolina this afternoon for Thanksgiving, and I won't be back till Saturday night, so I can't help for the next few days."

"Ah. Too bad. Who are you going to South Carolina with?" Had she finally been snatched up by some guy?

"My college roommate has invited me to her place. I couldn't get home for a short break like this, but I hope to get back to England for Christmas."

"Sure, I guess London would be fantastic around then."

Jessie laughed. "Maybe, but to be honest, I'll be at home in Dorking. We have a low-key family celebration, but it's fun, too."

She was so stunning when she laughed. Rick mentally reminded himself he was a married man, but then again, his wife had just run off. And for what? No, he was the wronged party. Maria was the bad guy here. He wasn't doing anything wrong—was he?

"Okay." He slapped his thighs with the palms of his hands. "I better get going. I'm late."

"Um, I'm afraid your drive is still covered in snow. I'm not sure you'll be able to get your car out."

"What?"

"The snow's stopped, and they've cleared the main roads and sidewalks, so I was able to walk no problem, but your driveway's still blocked."

Rick was furious. "I pay a guy to clear my driveway at the first sign of snow. He should have been here hours ago. How the hell will I get to work?" He headed out of the kitchen. "Damn snow," he said when he opened the front door.

It was glorious. The sun was out and bouncing off the fresh blanket of white, making him squint. Orga rushed past him and into the light powder. Jessie chased after the dog but stopped at the door behind Rick.

"It's okay. She's just going out to pee. She'll be back in a moment," Rick said.

"Can I make you a cup of coffee?" she asked. "Just while you're looking for the snow guy's number."

He turned and looked at the gorgeous babysitter. He was snowed in, his wife and kids were away, and she was offering to make him coffee. Where was the harm in that? Rick's hangover started to fade, and his mood began to improve. He smiled at her and nodded.

They walked back into the kitchen together, Jessie going for the coffee machine and Rick for the milk in the fridge, but they arrived at the cupboard for mugs together. It was an innocent mistake. They both reached up for the handle at the exact same time, and his hand landed on hers. She turned to look at him, and their eyes met and locked. Her skin was so soft, so warm. He jerked back his hand and stepped aside.

"You know your way around this kitchen better than I do." He forced a laugh, but it sounded weird to him.

She backed away then and bit her bottom lip. "Sorry."

"Don't be sorry. Everything's great." He brought the mugs over to the coffee machine. "Don't suppose you know if we have any cookies?"

She walked around him and over to a cupboard beside the fridge.

"So that's where she keeps them."

Jessie nodded. "Alice has a sweet tooth, but I don't give her more than one a day."

Rick grinned. "She's a tough little nut—gives her mom a real hard time, but she seems to like you." He didn't mean it as a suggestive comment, but Jessie looked at him with a kind of guilty-as-charged expression and kept biting that damn bottom lip. God, she was cute. He wondered if she was doing it on purpose.

The percolator clicked. "Coffee's ready," she said a little too brightly but didn't move. It would have meant getting very close to Rick. He took the hint and turned his attention to the machine.

"How do you like it?"

"Excuse me?"

"Your coffee? How do you like it?" Rick couldn't tell if it was his imagination or not, but she seemed to be acting differently. There was something between them today. Was it chemistry? That would mean the attraction wasn't one-sided. He didn't know whether to feel relief or panic, but his heart rate was sure up.

"You know, I should really go walk Orga." She gestured toward the door with her head.

Damn, she wanted distance. Hell, she was right, but damn all the same.

"You gonna be able to get out before they clear the drive?"

"Absolutely. I got in, didn't I?" Again with the overbright smile.

"You sure did." He looked at her square on. He didn't mean to do it, but somehow they were looking straight into each other's eyes. The tension between them was palpable. The time for games was over. They were locked together for a second, drawn in. Now he knew it wasn't just his imagination. This was real. It would be to be easier to cross the room and take her in his arms than to break away from those magnetic blue eyes.

"Okay, I'll go get my coat." She broke the spell and looked away.

"You sure?" His voice was lower than he intended.

"What?" She looked a little dazed now.

He felt the electricity between them dissipate. There was no tension in the air now. They were back to being Rick and Jessie. He shook himself and coughed to clear his already clear throat. He became aware of Orga sniffing around the floor. A helicopter flew overhead. Normal life had returned to the kitchen.

"Sorry, yes, go," he said and looked back down at his coffee mug.

Jessie headed for the door.

"Jessie?"

She turned back to look at him.

"Thanks," he said.

She gave a half nod, whistled for the dog, and left the kitchen.

Rick wasn't even sure what he was thanking her for. What in the hell was he doing? He took a few deep breaths to calm himself. Damn it, that girl had almost got him going—like really going. He was aroused and closed his eyes tight to bring himself back under control. God, she was gorgeous and his wife had just walked out on him, but he wasn't the type of man to have an affair—or was he? Rick hit his head with his fist.

He heard the front door bang closed. Orga and Jessie had left the building.

"Get it together, man." His mind tried to make sense of things. Okay, it was a damn mess that Maria had taken off to her mom's. It was fair to say they were going through choppy waters, but there was an ocean of difference between Maria running away to her mother's house and him hooking up with a younger woman. That would be a game changer. "You're an idiot," he said angrily under his breath.

Outside, he heard the familiar *bing bing bing* of the snowplow reversing down his driveway. The snow clearers had arrived. "About time, too." He put the untouched cookies away.

So what if Jessie was a lovely girl who seemed to even maybe have feelings for him. So what? He was a married man and a damn fine husband, and he was determined to remain that way. The coffee machine pinged that it was good to go again. He drained the contents of his mug and switched off the machine. The last thing he needed in his life was an affair with

Jessie Armstrong—or any more coffee.

Chapter Nineteen
Daydream Believer

After Maria's lovely coffee with her mother, she was quick to shower, dress, and get out of the house. She drove her mother's car into town and started her day in Old San Juan. Maria wandered around the maze of cobblestone streets that twisted and turned like a spider's web. It had been years since she'd admired the beautiful white-washed, low-rise buildings of her hometown. Growing up there had made her immune to the incredible colonial architecture and historic fortresses. Now she saw them with new eyes. They were heart-stoppingly pretty, especially the Plaza de Armas, in the central square. That had been the meeting point for her teenage school friends a long time ago. As she walked through the streets of her youth watching a new generation of teenagers flirting, she wondered what life would have been like if she'd stayed, like her sisters. Paloma had told her the evening before that Carlos, her high school sweetheart, was single again.

There were no secrets in San Juan. Everybody knew everybody's business. Poor Carlos. Maria knew he'd gone to Florida to study pharmacology and then come home to take over his father's pharmacy. It had to be tough now that CVS was in town, but Paloma said his business was still good. During her walk, she narrowly avoided his street. The last thing she needed was to bump into an old boyfriend. Life was confusing enough without that added into the mix.

She found a lovely little coffee house along one of the side streets and stopped there around midmorning. That was when she got up the nerve to check her phone for messages from Rick. There were seven. The first was a little confusing. Rick was joking and laughing. Then he was anxious, and listening to it, Maria thought her heart would break with guilt. The next message was after he'd found her e-mail. He explained how it landed in his junk folder, and she could hear the annoyance in his voice. Her guilt evaporated, and then she felt as angry as his tone suggested he was.

Maria listened to the last messages—where it was pretty obvious he'd gotten very drunk. He vacillated from apologies to anger, but there was no suggestion of him leaving his blessed job to come get her. There was a new message from Cathi, too, asking her where she was and why was Ricky calling them in the middle of the night.

Sitting in the bustling little coffee shop, with the sound of Puerto Rican music in the air and people chatting in Spanish, Maria felt lonelier than she ever had before.

She threw the phone into her purse and, refueled with another stiff shot of local coffee, started to walk again. At least things were easier without the kids. She loved them, but Cody demanded so much attention. Of course, it was her job to listen to every word and admire every school project, but it was exhausting, too. Then there was her darling daughter. She loved Alice, naturally, but the baby cried so much and never seemed happy with her. It was breaking Maria's heart and wearing her down.

She upped her pace. Parts of the Old Town had been founded in the sixteenth century, but as she walked now, she wondered how could she have forgotten that it was so darn picturesque? Eventually, she headed for the sea views and ended up at El Morro.

It was the jewel in the crown of San Juan—the largest fortification in the Caribbean. El Morro held a special place in Maria's heart, too, because it was where Ricky had proposed to her. She hadn't meant to walk back to the exact place, but her feet had decided for her. It was a round tower with a tall, thin vertical slit for a window. Maria wandered in to look out at the sea through the window, just as she'd done twelve years before.

She wrapped her arms around her body like she were cold, even though it was in the eighties. The last time she had been there, things were very different. When she'd walked into the lookout tower, Rick had walked in behind her. Instead of her own arms around her body, they had been Rick's strong swimmer's arms.

"This is where we watch out for invaders," he whispered into her ear.
His touch was so thrilling.

"These mighty fortresses with their lookout towers are how we protect our womenfolk from marauding Caribbean pirates." Rick squeezed her tighter. "I want to protect you forever, Maria Belen Garcia." Then he turned her around to face him. In that ancient lookout tower, Ricky got down on one knee and asked her to marry him.

She burst out crying, pulled him up, and said, "Yes, Ricky, yes, yes, I will marry you."

The memory made her cry all over again, and she had to move on fast. Her next stop was a beautiful hotel she knew nearby. She only planned on heading in to use the restroom, but as she was walking out, the courtyard looked so inviting that she paused and sat for a while to admire the dappled shadows dance on the tables and cobblestone ground.

It wasn't long before a waiter glided to her table and offered her coffee or perhaps wine.

"What the heck," she said with a smile. "It's the holidays, so I'll have a glass of pinot grigio, please." When he took his leave, her smile faded. First off, she'd had all the coffee she could manage in one day, and secondly, maybe a glass of wine would help her calm down. The morning had been emotional.

Her wine was served in a long-stemmed glass that glistened with moisture. The waiter laid a thick white napkin on the glass table and placed her drink on top of it. To the side, he settled a bowl of cashew nuts. The man moved with the grace of a dancer, and the surroundings were pure opulence, too. After her active morning, it was good to relax, and the Hotel El Convento was one of her favorite places in Puerto Rico. It carried a charm and elegance that only old buildings could, and it was sure old enough.

"Leave it to the nuns," she said as she raised her glass to her lips and tasted the wine. It was perfect. She knew the history of the convent well. It had been built for the Carmelite nuns back in the sixteen hundreds, thanks to King Philip IV of Spain, and the women had only moved out in the early nineteen hundreds. After that, it had been turned into a luxury hotel.

Maria knew every square inch of the 350-year-old building. The courtyard, where she now sat, was the same one she'd married Ricky Sanchez in only eleven short years ago. Seemed like she didn't have the staying power of the nuns, she thought sadly now. It was impossible to sit there and not think of Ricky. She took another sip of wine and forced her husband out of her mind just as the waiter reappeared.

"Is everything to your satisfaction, *señora*?" he asked with all the serenity of a Carmelite nun.

Maria nodded. "This is perfect. Just perfect."

"Would you like to see our lunch menu?"

She hadn't thought of food, but hearing the suggestion made her realize she was quite hungry. She glanced at her watch. "Oh, I didn't realize it was that time. Yes, please," she said and watched him glide off to fetch a menu.

After he took her order, he gave her time to relax and enjoy the peace, but when he returned to dress the table for lunch, she watched him with fascination. He used the same finesse he had for her wine—like he was performing a ritual. Setting the table was serious business at this hotel. When she did that job back in Boston, she threw the knives and forks down any old way. Her family was lucky if they even got a glass of water. Maria felt guilt begin to swell. Had she stopped trying with Rick and the kids?

"Are you enjoying San Juan, *señora*?" he asked as he finished up.

"Oh, yes. It's a great city." She was going to say she was a local, but somehow it seemed too late. When she first came in, he'd spoken to her in English, so she answered in kind. Maybe he assumed she was on vacation. Was that what she was at this stage—a tourist in her hometown? That seemed wrong, and yet she had seen the city from a whole new perspective this time.

He took her order and then took his leave.

She closed her eyes and enjoyed the peace. That was when it hit her. The entire tour she'd taken that morning had followed a distinct path. Without meaning to, she had started in the place of her youth, her teen years, in the Old Town. From there she'd gone pretty close to the pharmacy of her ex-boyfriend and then to the tower where Rick had proposed. Now she was in the hotel where they had married. It was in this ancient and holy courtyard that they'd pledged themselves to each other, sworn undying love and been so very happy, certain in the knowledge that theirs was the forever kind of love.

"Is everything all right, *señora*?" The graceful waiter was back. Maria realized there were tears trickling down her face. She dashed them away.

"Oh, yes. I'm sorry. I was remembering," she said.

He nodded. "Your snapper," he said and placed the large, fine bone china plate in front of her.

"Black pepper?"

"Hmm . . ." Maria couldn't focus on pepper, black or otherwise, when she was so focused on her marriage and husband.

"Please." She waved her hand with indifference.

Her subconscious was certainly hard at work. The big question was where would she go next? Was she moving forward with Rick or without him?

She took a mouthful of snapper. It was delicious. Before she could analyze what she should do next, her phone rang and she got to it fast, hoping it was her husband.

"Hello?"

"Maria, *guapa*. It's Mami. I'm just wondering how you are. I will need the car this afternoon because I still have some errands to run for tomorrow's Thanksgiving party."

Maria swallowed hard. How could she have been so thoughtless? "*Si*, Mami. I'll come straight home. I got so absorbed in town, I didn't think." She kept the phone call short and caught the server's attention.

Funny, she thought, before the phone call she'd been wondering where she should go next. "There's my answer," she said to no one in particular, and then she paid her bill, adding a generous tip for her lovely waiter. "Real life beckons. My children need me," she told herself, getting her car keys out of her bag. "Enough daydreaming."

"That's some daydream, you're having." Ely elbowed her travel companion.

"Hmm?" Jessie snapped out of it. "Oh, sorry. What were you saying?"

Ely looked at her roomie with concern. "How's the head? Are you sure you don't want my famous hangover remedy? It's a surefire cure. I'm telling you, it works."

She had already pushed Jessie to have a drink when she'd woken up first thing in the morning. Then she'd tried again when Jessie got back from the Sanchez house, but Jessie had turned her down. Now they were at thirty-thousand feet, flying to South Carolina to meet up with the Briskin family, but Jessie still didn't want to drink.

She shook her head and winced. "If I drink, I'll ralph."

"Ralph? I like that. Is that another English colloquialism? I'm gonna ralph!" Ely tried the word out, but Jessie looked pained.

"I'm thinking of never drinking again."

"Look on the bright side—at least the airport was still open and our plane got out. Those Bostonians aren't scared of a little snowfall."

Jessie didn't respond.

Ely felt for her. It was a real mess. Her best friend had a broken heart, and she'd been given their notice of eviction for throwing a party with alcohol and narcotics on the premises. Ely was pretty mad about the narcotics. Pot? Who knew? She hadn't seen it, but evidently when she had gone out to the car with Jessie, some of Josh's friends had lit up.

Needless to say, the Wiswall police hadn't been too thrilled. The party had been broken up, and she'd been tracked down pretty fast. At least she hadn't been arrested, which could have happened. But the powers-that-be had arrived and told them on the spot they were to vacate the premises within a week.

Oh joy.

Jessie didn't even know they had lost their college accommodation yet. The night before, Ely had left her friend in the car while she sorted everything out. She'd gotten their beds back in, and then Josh had carried Jessie from his car to her bed. Ely hoped she could figure out a solution over Thanksgiving. Maybe she could talk her father into bankrolling an apartment for them. Ely was racked with guilt. She knew Jessie needed this postgrad, and now her stupid party might have blown that. And she had to fix it—fast.

"So what were you dreaming about?" Ely sounded more upbeat than she felt. "Please don't tell me you were thinking about *Dan the Pan*?"

"The Pan?"

"Yeah, it means toilet. It's all I could come up that rhymes with Dan." Ely smiled.

Jessie nodded but didn't look happy. "I'm doing my best not to think about him. God, I feel rotten."

"You weren't this bad this morning when you went to the Sanchez house."

"Maybe I was still a bit drunk then?"

Ely pulled a small bottle from her bag. "Here, take a mouthful of this. It'll make you feel a whole lot better." She thrust it toward Jessie.

Jessie looked worried. "Is it alcohol?"

"It's medicine."

Jessie sniffed it. "Doesn't smell like booze."

"Drink!"

Jessie looked like she was all out of fight and took a large gulp, and then she winced and shivered. "Oh, Ely, what was that?"

"You're gonna feel better soon. Now, tell me about this morning again."

Jessie wiped her mouth with the airline napkin. "It's so odd. Maria never mentioned leaving town, but she was gone this morning with the kids. Rick seemed cool with it. He's going to work all across Thanksgiving while she has fun in the sun."

Ely shrugged. "Sounds like a smart woman to me. Why stay in all that snow if he's out workin' when she can be on a beach in the Caribbean?" Then she looked out the airplane window. "I wonder if they have any good colleges in Puerto Rico."

"Rick couldn't get out to work after all that. He was snowed in."

Ely gave her friend a sideways glance. "You like that guy? You've been talking about him for a long time now."

"He's too old and he's married."

"Maybe not." Ely smiled. "Darn it, his wife is a couple of thousand miles away. I reckon you need a cure to *Dan the Pan*."

"Can you please stop calling him that?"

Ely held her hands up. "Sorry, just sayin'."

"You're saying I should have an affair with a married man, after I've just experienced firsthand the pain that can cause. Seriously?" Jessie looked mad.

"Aw, shucks, J. I'm just trying to find you some happy. Sorry."

"Well, thanks, but leave me out of your plans. Yes, Rick is nice, but I happen to like Maria and I wouldn't dream of doing that to her."

"But I can see a glint in your eye. You *fancy* him."

Jessie rolled her eyes. "You know it's possible to *fancy* a guy and do nothing about it."

"Is it?" Ely arched an eyebrow.

"Changing the subject, I met Mrs. Palmer again this morning."

"Who's she? Remind me," Ely said.

"The old lady who lives next door. She's going a bit senile, but I love her. We were both out with the dogs in the snow."

Ely nodded and tried to look interested—which she really wasn't.

"Remember I told you, she's the one who had Mick Wolf at her parties in the sixties?"

"Jeez, how old is she?"

"Very. Anyway, she seems so nice. I like her, and I told her we got into trouble last night with our party because the school has a no parties rule. She was horrified and said we could throw our parties at her house in the future."

"For real?" Ely felt a tiny flicker of hope, but Jessie looked impatient.

"We're not taking her up on the offer, Elyse Briskin. She's a very nice old lady. We're not going to ransack her house. But she did also say if we ever need a place to stay, we could have a room in her house. Wasn't that nice?"

Ely's heart stopped. "She'd let us live with her? Are you serious?" Had Jessie solved their housing problem, all the while oblivious to the situation?

Jessie laughed. "Well, clearly we're not going to take her up on the offer, but that's just the kind of woman she is. Isn't she kind to offer us accommodation? I like her so much, so—to answer your question, Ely—that's what I was daydreaming about."

Ely smiled. "Well, as daydreams go, Jessie, that's a pretty good one." She stared out the window and sent up a quick prayer of thanks. "It really doesn't get better than this."

Chapter Twenty
Thanksgiving

"Could it be any better than this?" Cathi gushed when she showed her husband the Thanksgiving table. She thought it was a work of art. Five place settings were furnished, each with three different glasses—fifteen glasses in all—just as *Festive Living*, her new favorite magazine, suggested. It was insane, but it looked wonderful. There was a dazzling array of knives and forks at each placemat, too, and the napkins were folded to stand upright. They looked like bishops' hats.

"Cathi, you went to a serious amount of work this year. Should you be pushing yourself so hard?" Michael's eyes were soft with concern.

It made Cathi feel good. He was such a caring husband.

"I like to do this, Michael. You know how much a pretty home means to me." She adjusted one of the glasses by a quarter inch, so it was aligned with the others.

He came over and wrapped his arms around her from behind. "I know, honey, and I know you love a pretty house, full of kids and laughter."

She snorted a laugh. "Well, everybody loves laughter, but the kids? They can be trouble."

He pulled back and looked at her. "Oh, everything okay?"

Cathi didn't know what he was talking about. She shrugged and nodded. "Yes, of course. Now, tell me about Rick. Did you get any more news from him?"

Michael sighed and shook his head. He pulled out one of the dining room chairs and sat while he talked. It irked Cathi, but she let it slip in the interest of keeping him in a good mood. She needed him happy. Things were moving much faster than she'd expected. She had to tell him about the offer on the house soon.

"I had no idea there was any trouble between them. They looked great together at that party last month, didn't they?"

"Yes. I don't think they're breaking up or anything like that, Michael.

Maria's just at the end of her rope with the kids. He's working too hard, and she can't keep it all together. She needed to get away and he wouldn't go, so she took off with the kids. If you ask me, she's crying out for help. He should be following her down there, not coming here for dinner."

"Are you kidding?" He looked surprised. "What the hell has he done wrong? The guy is heading up one of the biggest marketing campaigns in the US this year, and she expects him to head to the sun? Hello. It's a miracle he gets home at all."

"Michael, you know I've spoken with her. She hasn't gone off with another guy. She's taken the kids to her mother's. It's not a party for her either."

Michael shook his head and looked frustrated. "All she has to do is keep the house together like you do. It's not that big of a deal, is it? I mean, they have a great house in a nice neighborhood. Cody's even at school all day, for God's sake. What's her problem?"

Cathi was stunned at her husband's insensitivity. Michael tended to be empathetic and understood women needed love and room to grow. They needed support—and not just financial—because kids could drain the lifeblood out of their mothers. It was up to men to nurture their wives. That was possibly even more important than bringing home the bucks. How was she going to convince him they needed to move house if he was in such a chauvinistic frame of mind? She felt her eyes water. The last thing she wanted to do was fight with him. Not after all this work. She had achieved so much without bothering him. Now all she needed was his approval for the next part of her plan and they could move up and on—together.

"Ah hell, I've upset you, baby." He rose from the chair and came over to hug her again.

"I'm sorry," she said, sounding shaky. "I don't want anything to happen to Maria and Rick. I love those guys."

"I'm sure they'll be fine." He stroked her hair. "Don't worry about them. Maybe a little time apart is just what they need. But, please, promise me you won't stress yourself about them." He studied her face, his own the picture of concern.

She couldn't help but smile. "You're a perfect husband."

"And don't you forget it." He kissed the tip of her nose.

Just then the doorbell rang. "That'll be him now. I hope he's okay—crazy that he was even working today. Working on Thanksgiving? That's just not American!" Michael headed out to the front door to greet Rick.

Cathi turned her attention back to the table. It was probably her best Thanksgiving setting ever. She had spent a small fortune on new decorations, but wasn't it worth it? She headed to the kitchen to check on her turkey. The roast potatoes were coming along well. They would be crispy and brown in another half hour.

Cathi referred to her timetable, which was stuck to the fridge door with a magnet. She checked the time on her nautical kitchen clock. Everything was synchronized to absolute precision. That was what made such an ambitious meal possible. Nothing was left to chance. She could hear her kids laughing and playing with Rick in the hall. For a moment her mind moved from the job at hand to her friend in Puerto Rico. It had been a heck of a shock when Maria returned her call. All cool, calm, and collected, she had informed Cathi she had gone home to her mother with the kids.

At first, Cathi had thought her friend was joking. Maria had never done anything like that before. Sure, she was a hotheaded woman and life was never dull when Maria was around, but she'd never actually run away before. Over the last decade, Cathi's best friend had been quite levelheaded. This was a new development.

Maria had explained she needed to get away and Rick couldn't take the time off, so she had gone by herself with the kids. She'd expressed a hope her husband might follow, but Cathi didn't have the nerve to say she doubted that would happen.

"Cathi." Rick arrived into the kitchen with Michael right behind. "So this is where it's all happening. Everything smells so good." He kissed her on the cheek, and she stopped her fussing for a moment to give him a little extra attention.

"Rick, how are you?"

He shrugged and glanced around the kitchen rather than at her. "Oh, you know, same ol', same ol'. Hey, thanks for asking me over. It would have been a microwave dinner otherwise."

Michael poured the wine. "You won't believe the amount of work this girl has gone to." He nodded toward Cathi. "Wait till you see the dining room table. You must be one special guest, Rick. I never get this kind of treatment."

Cathi snapped her head up, mouth open, ready to defend herself, but then Michael winked at her and she knew he was playing with her. "It's Thanksgiving," she said instead. "We have to make it special."

Stacy, the youngest in the family, followed the men into the kitchen. "Where's Cody and Alice?"

Cathi kicked herself for not warning her nine-year-old not to mention the missing family, but Rick seemed fine with it. "They've gone with Maria to visit their cousins in Puerto Rico. It's sunny there and a nice place to be right now." He looked out of the kitchen window at the snow-covered ground. "I think it was a good idea," he said, sounding a little glum.

Michael walked over and gave him a glass of red wine. "Maybe next year we'll all go down there for Thanksgiving."

Rick's smile was tinged by his sad eyes.

"Hey, cool." Stacy's eyes lit up at the suggestion and skipped out of the room.

"Don't I get a glass of wine?" Cathi tapped the base of her empty wine glass with a French-manicured nail.

"Oh, sorry, honey. Do you want one?"

"Of course I do." What was he thinking? He knew she liked her wine as much as he did. She studied Rick again while Michael got her a glass of red.

"So you're okay with Maria and the kids being in Puerto Rico?" she asked.

He was back to looking out the window. "Hey, what can I say? She's gone. I was—no, I *am* mad as hell with her for being so damn impetuous. We hadn't even discussed it. I called her Tuesday night and left a ton of messages, and she hasn't even called back. I'm not calling again. She can come home when she wants to."

Cathi shivered. The tone in his voice was so different from the one he had just used with Stacy. How good he was at acting cool when he wasn't. He was furious. She felt for Maria. This was a big deal. Michael gave her a glass of red wine. She looked at it and then at him. Why was he only giving her half a glass? She didn't say anything because Rick was talking again.

"Did you know about this, Cathi?"

"Me? Heck, no. I knew she was finding it hard that you were working so hard, but to be honest, I think she was a bit depressed, too."

Rick's head snapped around. "What?"

"Um, yeah. I haven't seen her for a few weeks, but you know we talk all the time on the phone. Now that I think about it, perhaps she wasn't her usual happy self. Damn it, I should've been there for her."

"Hey, it's not your fault," Rick said in a soft tone.

"When did you last see her?" Michael asked.

Cathi didn't want to tell the men about her visit to the house for sale on Crystal Lake Lane so she was vague. "We had a coffee together one morning a few weeks ago. She'd been out running. I think she was trying to lose a few pounds before her big birthday in the spring."

"Maria? Running?" Rick looked surprised. "She's not into running. She's never gone for a run in her life."

"Oh yes she did. She was just coming back on that day I stopped by."

Rick looked upset. "I had no idea." He took a big drink of wine. "And you think she's trying to get in shape before her fortieth?"

"I guess. Look, Rick, I don't know. Why don't you go visit her and talk all of this out?"

His demeanor changed. "No way. She's the one who left me. I made a million calls. She can damn well come back to me. I've done enough chasing."

It wasn't the response Cathi had been hoping for. She finished her tiny glass of red wine and checked the clock. It was time to take the turkey out so it could rest for thirty minutes.

"Michael, any chance of some more wine?" She gave him a flirty grin and opened the oven door.

"You sure?" His face was drenched with concern.

"Uh, yeah," she said. "That first glass was mouthwash sized. What's wrong? Are we on rations?" She pouted and arched her eyebrows to tease him. Then she poked at the massive bird in the hot oven.

"Cathi, this is crazy. You have to tell me." He glanced at Rick and then to the door. "The girls are out of earshot. We have to talk about this, and here, give me that." He sounded impatient and pulled the oven mitts from her. "You shouldn't be carrying heavy things anymore." Michael nudged her out of the way and took over the job of moving the turkey.

She gave a confused laugh. "What are you talking about, Michael? What am I supposed to tell you? I can't drink? I can't lift heavy things? What is it?"

"You're pregnant!" he said in exasperation, sounding like he was, at last, releasing a secret that had been bursting to get out. *Or was it the exertion of carrying an enormous stuffed turkey*, she wondered fleetingly. Her mind raced, but she didn't speak. He thought she was pregnant? Where in the world did he get that crazy notion?

With the bird settled safe on the countertop, Michael faced his wife. "Cathi, I'm sorry I stole your thunder, and I'm sorry I was snooping, but I found all the information about decorating a baby nursery. I've seen how tired you've been in the last few weeks. Isn't that always the case?" He gave a soft smile like he was remembering the last time she'd been pregnant. "So yes, I already know. I'm sure it must be a heck of a shock for you because we'd agreed we were finished. But I think, heck, it's a miracle —a God-given miracle. I'm thrilled." He glanced at Rick, who was watching the whole situation unfold with his mouth wide open in shock.

"You think I'm pregnant?" she whispered the words while her mind tried to catch up. She looked to Rick.

Michael remained focused on his wife. "Am I wrong?" He gave her a lopsided grin and held his arms out to embrace her.

She looked at him and smiled. He looked so happy. Then she remembered something her mother used to say: *A new baby means a new house.*

This could be the miracle she had been praying for. Was this the way she'd get her wish? Cathi made a monumental decision in a microsecond. She shook her head and beamed at her husband. "No, Michael, you're not wrong," she said and rushed into his arms.

His red wine was set aside, and Rick opened the champagne Michael had been hiding in the fridge. Of course, she just sipped a tiny amount of champagne. She had to watch her health now. More importantly, she had to stay sober to focus on what the hell she had just done. How in the heck had she ended up here?

Cathi wasn't allowed to serve her fabulous Thanksgiving meal—the men took over with the help of the girls. Michael suggested it was too soon to tell the children and they should keep it quiet for a few more weeks. Cathi absolutely agreed. It would be a mistake for the children to hear about it.

While everybody else fussed over getting the food to the table, Cathi was sent to the living room to sit down with her feet up. It was her first chance to think about her predicament. She hadn't meant to lie. It just slipped out. Michael seemed to want it so much, and even Rick looked like he wanted good news. She sipped a glass of ice water and thought about what she had accidently agreed to.

It wasn't all her fault. What the heck had Michael been doing snooping through her stuff, and why had he dropped it on her like that? She hadn't planned on this massive deception. Damn it, her highest aspiration for the afternoon was a nice Thanksgiving meal, but everything had gone way out of control. She should have said he was mistaken, but something in her mind had skipped ahead.

If he thought she was pregnant, maybe he would be easier to manipulate on the whole buying a new house thing. Yes, it was a big lie, but she would just pretend to miscarry in a few weeks. At first he would be upset, but he would get over it. Women had miscarriages all the time. They were a fact of life. It just might be a factor to help her convince him to move.

The meal was everything she had hoped it would be. Rick seemed to be able to compartmentalize his problems. Her friend's husband talked and laughed with the family like he didn't have a care in the world. Michael, on the other hand, kept giving her furtive glances and beaming like the Cheshire cat. It was obvious he was walking on air. She was in shock. Another baby hadn't occurred to her in nine years. They were so done on that front.

"Can I propose a toast?" Michael said after they had cleared away the dinner plates.

Everybody looked at him. "Here's to my wonderful, growing family and my best friend. May we all be thankful for the last twelve months, and here's to the next twelve." He raised his glass high. Rick and Cathi did the same, and the girls lifted their glasses of soda to join in. "Let's all meet here this time next year and give thanks again."

Cathi's heart skipped a beat. She didn't want to be here in a year's time.

"Actually." She cut into his toast. "What if we were to meet somewhere else in twelve months' time?" Michael looked confused. She knew he hadn't expected to be heckled.

"Like Puerto Rico?" Stacy asked.

Cathi shot her a warning look. "Well, I have a bit of a surprise for you also."

"It's too early," Michael said, clearly thinking she was going to talk about the baby, but nothing was further from her mind.

"No, darling, not that. It's another surprise. The thing is, we've had an offer on our beautiful home. It came out of the blue, but there's a family that, um, drove by the house and decided the location was perfect. I think the dad got a job somewhere around here. They approached me through an agent. She called me yesterday and made a very generous offer. Put it this way—it's well over the estimate we got." She said this last part to Michael and then continued. "You see, I was thinking if we took it"—she looked pleading at him—"that is to say, if we accepted their offer, we could buy a bigger house . . . which now seems like a great idea."

"I like this house," Katie, her ten-year-old, said.

Cathi ignored the child and locked eyes with her husband. It was a decision for the two of them, but he already knew how she felt. Cathi saw the confusion in his eyes, but then she recognized the same expression he wore when he was talking about the pregnancy.

"What a day for surprises." His face broke into a smile. "Is this what you want, Cathi?"

"Oh yes, Michael, more than anything." She thought she would burst with happiness. This was turning out perfect.

He nodded and raised his glass again. "Okay, then—to moving up and on." He changed the toast. Cathi was beyond ecstatic. How fate helped her along today.

But then she spotted Rick studying his glass as he repeated the toast. "To moving up and on."

It had a very different connotation for him. She knew he wasn't in a good place, no matter how well he hid it. Oh well, she couldn't think about that now. Cathi got up and went over to her husband's chair. He stood and they kissed.

"Thank you, Michael. Thank you so much for this."

"No, thank you," he said, and then he glanced down at her still-flat tummy and whispered so his daughters couldn't hear him. "After all, we're going to need more room."

A brief jolt of panic hit her, but she suppressed it and kept her smile in place.

"Now," she asked everybody, "who's for homemade pumpkin pie?"

Chapter Twenty-One
A Family Affair

"That was your tastiest pumpkin pie ever." Ely patted her stomach.

Jessie knew her friend was on her best behavior, and she could see why. The Ely she knew back in Newton was a wild child and a bit of a hell-raiser. At home she was a lot calmer. And with a father like Mr. Briskin, she had to be.

He was a giant of a man, both in stature and personality. Ely had introduced him as William Briskin, but he had immediately corrected his daughter and told Jessie to call him Bull because everybody did.

Bull, it seemed, ran the household with an iron fist. He was pure power, and it was no surprise Margaret, Ely's mother, was a consummate Southern lady. She was soft-spoken, when she spoke at all—which wasn't very much.

The Briskins had a full house for Thanksgiving, and what a big house it was, too. Jessie was accustomed to large families, but she had never been a guest in such an enormous home before. Everything about the house was super-sized, starting with the front door. It was about fourteen feet high, like a hotel. She wondered why anybody would need a door that tall. The front hall that they first walked into was huge, too—two stories high, with a massive marble fireplace and a big curving staircase. Jessie would have been very inhibited if she weren't with her best friend, Ely, and the family —whom, she soon discovered, were all friendly, open people, too. The dining room was like the rest of the house. Even the dining table was enormous.

Ely never talked about the house. For her it was all about the horses, and for that, just next to the house was the ranch. Bull had rebuilt the house a decade earlier, doubling it in size as his business empire doubled. Everything about the Briskins was larger than life.

Ely's aunt Mona was there with her husband John and their two teenage daughters, Becky and Kaitlin. They lived in Charleston, too. Margaret also had a single sister, Marybeth, who had come to stay. Jessie thought she was achingly shy and quiet. Then there was Ely's older brother, John Jr. Jessie smiled.

Her roommate had told her countless times she should hook up with John Jr. Ely hadn't been exaggerating, because he was a good-looking guy and full of fun. John was quite like a male version of Ely, just a little older. Jessie had asked how he came to be John Jr. when his father was in fact a William, but Ely explained it was because she had an Uncle John, so John Jr. just made sense. He was the same age as Jessie, but despite her roomie's encouragement, Jessie knew there was no chemistry between them. How could anyone follow an act like Dan? Well, that act was over.

"What about it, Jessie?" Bull interrupted her daydream. She had been given the seat on his right side which she knew was an honor. Ely sat opposite her on Bull's left hand.

"Sorry, what did you say?" She smiled at her host, annoyed with herself for wasting time dreaming about bloody Dan Walker.

"Ely here says you're practically a genius. Photographic memory? Is that true?"

"She's just saying that to make me sound good, Mr. . . . um . . . Bull."

Bull laughed and raised his glass of red wine to salute Jessie. "Her mom and I are just happy she ended up with such a nice girl like you as a roommate. I figure you're a steady influence on my little girl."

Ely rolled her eyes. "Daddy, I'm not a geeky teenager anymore." She looked down the table at sixteen-year-old Kaitlin. "Sorry, Kaitlin, no offense."

Kaitlin shrugged in a show of sublime teenage indifference.

"But you're going back to London when you finish the school year at Wiswall in June? Is that right, Jessie?" Margaret was the one speaking, in a tone that was softer than the rest of the family.

Jessie nodded at her hostess. "Yes, but I hope Ely will come to visit me there."

"Hey, maybe she can go to college there next," John Jr. said and laughed. Jessie noted both parents scowled. They didn't approve of Ely's irregular academic path.

"That's rich coming from you." Ely took a sip of water. "You didn't even finish freshman year."

Her brother raised his hands in defeat. "Hey, I had a vocation. What can I say?"

Jessie knew all about John's wild past. Ely had explained that the father and son clashed too much, so her brother had taken off to California as soon as he had finished high school. He'd surfed for a few years and then set up a surf shop. Rumor had it that his shop was doing well. John was starting to make a go of it, but it was still a sore point in the Briskin family. Ely shouldn't have brought it up.

"Becky is a senior next year. Would you recommend Wiswall for liberal arts for my little girl?" Mona asked Jessie.

"Certainly. It's a great campus."

"If you don't like parties, boys, or any kind of life." Ely rolled her eyes.

Bull took his daughter's hand. "You don't like it up north, baby?"

"No, Daddy, I don't. And don't ask me what I'd do if J wasn't there." She glanced across the table to her roommate. "She's kept me sane." Ely gave her dad the best big round eyes Jessie had ever seen. "Can I transfer down south next year when Jessie's gone?"

"What about Josh?" Margaret asked.

"You want to change colleges again?" John Jr. said. "How many is that? Six? Seven?"

"I was in London once." Marybeth spoke just above a whisper. If Jessie hadn't been sitting right beside her, she wouldn't have heard.

"Were you? Where did you visit?" Jessie asked Margaret's sister.

"I have a business idea!" Ely suddenly commanded the entire table's attention again.

Jessie looked over at her roomie. "Maybe now isn't the time?" she said, but Bull thought otherwise.

"Hell, we love new business ideas in this house, Jessie. It's the lifeblood of America." He looked at his little girl. "Shoot."

"This one's good, Daddy. I can feel it in my bones, and it's even in the shampoo line."

Jessie shook her head. She didn't know Ely's family that well, but she was pretty sure that Thanksgiving dinner wasn't the time to go "down under."

"I think the shampoo industry's pretty full," Margaret said with a look of concern on her face.

"I don't think so, and it would appeal to both men and women—definite adult market."

Jessie squirmed, but Ely kept going.

"It's a totally new product—revolutionary." She was getting more animated.

"Them's fighting words." Uncle John smiled at his niece. "I'm intrigued."

"Ely, maybe later? After the meal?" Jessie asked.

"Nonsense. In this house, business is a family affair. All the best business plans come up at the dinner table. Isaac Newton, Alexander Graham Bell— they all made their inventions at the family table," Bull said.

"The last supper," Jessie mumbled, which made Bull guffaw and Marybeth titter.

"If it's bad, we'll be the first to tell her," he said.

Ely's smile broadened. "And if you like it, you'll back me and let me quit college?"

"Just show us your business plan," Margaret said.

Ely was up and out of the dining room in a flash. She returned with two little bottles of shampoo Jessie hadn't seen before. The labels were obviously homemade, but it gave the general idea, the first being pink and the second blue—his and hers. She stood up, the same way she had when she performed for Jessie and Josh a few weeks earlier.

Jessie couldn't watch, so she closed her eyes and listened.

"Straight hair, curly hair, dry hair . . ."

First, Jessie heard Marybeth gasp. Then she heard Uncle John snigger. To her left, there was a total silence from normally loud Bull.

Jessie risked looking up as Ely continued on with conviction.

"This ain't no different just 'cause it's there."

Becky, the seventeen-year-old cousin, was holding her nose to keep from laughing. Mona, Becky's mother, was gawking, and John Jr. was wearing a broad smile. He liked it! Did he get where she was going with this?

"For those delicate curls." Ely finished up with a flourish. Jessie noticed Ely seemed more fluent with the little song since the last time she had heard it. Maybe her roomie had been practicing in secret.

John Jr. applauded. "Go, sis. What a whacked-out idea. It's so crazy, I think it might work," he said with enthusiasm. "I'll stock it in my shop."

Jessie glanced at Ely's mother—the emotional barometer of the family. She was staring toward her husband, so Jessie's eyes went that way, too. Everybody was looking to Bull for his reaction.

The room went quiet. If he got mad, Thanksgiving would be ruined. He was studying his empty pie plate, like he was deciding which way to go with this. For the first time since Jessie had met him, his face was totally without expression.

This is bad, Jessie thought in a panic. She had never seen one man with such power. So this was what a true Alpha looked like—scary.

Then Bull began to laugh. It started as a small snort, and then another. Jessie now knew how he got his name. He opened his broad mouth into a great big laugh, and he clapped his hands together. Jessie saw Margaret was smiling as well. How odd.

Everybody took Bull's lead and laughed—except of course John Jr. who had already approved. That's when Jessie realized she was smiling along with them. She was mirroring everybody else's behavior. This was textbook group dynamics. It was amazing.

"So you approve?" Ely was still standing in the middle of the floor with the two bottles of homemade Down Under.

"Do I approve?" He laughed some more. "I think it's brilliant, baby, but it has no chance of ever getting off the ground. There's no network in the world that'd take an ad like that. Supermarkets wouldn't stock it, but I love your balls, Ely."

If this was meant to make his little girl happy, it didn't. Jessie saw her friend's face fall when she understood her father was rejecting her.

Bull clapped the table and all the plates jumped. He shook his head. "Delicate curls—I love it." He laughed again.

Ely's mother rose to clear some plates, and so did every other woman at the table. It was time for a change of scenery. The teenage cousins were still tittering as they helped. The aunties were shocked and silent. Uncle John excused himself, but John Jr. came over to hug his sister.

"I would back you if I had the money, sis," he said. Ely looked grateful.

Jessie fled the room with a load of dirty plates behind Margaret. She missed what Bull said to his daughter, but she reckoned it wouldn't be good. Ely had said that her parents were conservative people—traditionalists and active in the church. They didn't seem like the kind of people to hit the world with the first ever pubic hair product! She worried about her friend. Ely was a maverick, and college didn't suit her. There was very little chance she would even do her exams in June. Her parents were going to have to face up to it sooner or later.

While Mona and Marybeth loaded the two dishwashers and the cousins started to wash pots, Ely's mom broke away and began to surf the web on her laptop at the kitchen side counter.

"I wonder if such a product already exists," Margaret said when Jessie walked by. It surprised her. Maybe the older woman wasn't as compliant or submissive as she seemed.

"Good thinking," Jessie said and offloaded her dirty plates on the counter. She hovered for a while beside Margaret. "Find anything?"

"Doesn't seem to be any such product available," she said, her eyes glued to the monitor. "This might be worth investigating. It's an unorthodox product, I'll give her that, but do you have any idea how long it's been since we've had an exciting new product in the hair care business?"

Jessie shrugged. "I thought the height of sophistication was using separate shampoos and conditioners instead of the all-in-one bottles," she said with a laugh, but Margaret blanched.

Jessie made a mental note not to joke about shampoos. It was a serious business in this house. Margaret's computer pinged, demanding her attention again.

She headed back into the dining room to see if she could help clear away anything else. Ely and Bull were sitting now and deep in conversation. Her roommate seemed sad and beaten down, and Bull looked like he was lecturing her. It didn't take a genius to figure he was telling her she had to stay in college and forget about Down Under.

Margaret marched into the room behind Jessie, carrying her laptop. "What's this about a party?" She sounded furious and had gone a bit pale.

It was enough to make Jessie sit back down. *Here it comes*, she thought.

"We had one last Tuesday night." Ely sounded meek.

John Jr. poured himself another glass of red wine. "This sounds good."

"I know you had a party. You just got an e-mail saying you've been kicked out."

Jessie's head snapped up. "What? That's impossible."

"Of college?" Ely asked, looking just as surprised.

"I can't be kicked out," Jessie said, feeling her panic rising.

"What in the hell is going on?" Bull raised his voice and stood up, a thunderous look on his face. "You got an e-mail just now, Margaret?"

"Well, it must have been sent yesterday, but I was a little preoccupied with Thanksgiving. I'm assuming it was meant for Ely, but you gave them my e-mail for all your residential correspondence. Remember?" She looked at her daughter.

"Oh, I guess that was a mistake." Ely studied the floor.

"Does it mention me?" Jessie asked.

For a moment Margaret's eyes softened. "No, honey. You'll have to check your own e-mails for that." She turned back to Bull. "I didn't have any time to check my mail last night. It's a letter from the housing department and it's addressed to Ely. It basically says—oh, I don't know, some rule or college ethics—Ely, you've lost your accommodation privileges."

"So we haven't been kicked out of our actual classes, just our rooms? Is that right?" Jessie clutched the back of the dining chair she was sitting on.

"Maybe you're not in trouble, Jessie." Margaret gave her a weak smile.

"You knew you'd been kicked out and didn't tell me? When did you find out?" Jessie stood up angrily and balled her fists into her sides. "Jesus, Ely, my entire future is riding on this." Her eyes were huge with worry.

John Jr. stood. "Actually, I think I'll retire to the kitchen," he said and left them.

Ely persevered. "I was gonna tell you, but I thought it could wait till after Thanksgiving or maybe I could deal with it all myself."

"I don't believe it. You? Handle it? The same way you handled the party? Or your last three attempts at college? You're a walking disaster, Ely! You're sabotaging your own life, and now you're taking me down with you. Fuck this!" She ran her hands through her hair. "I have to find out if I've lost my digs. Margaret, can I log in to my e-mails on your computer? My cell phone is dead, and I didn't get the chance to recharge it today. I haven't seen an e-mail since the party."

Margaret handed the laptop to her guest, and it only took Jessie a moment to log in.

"Jesus Christ, I've lost my digs, too. And to add insult to injury you knew and didn't tell me? Will this affect my grant? Or my scholarship? Ever think about that? Does this mean I have to go home? Oh, Ely, what have you done?"

"I didn't know about you—well, not for sure. I did have my doubts, but I thought I might figure something out before you found out. It'll be okay." Ely took a step toward her friend.

"No, it won't be okay. What else are you not telling me? I don't have the support of a rich family to back me up. This was my big chance, my one shot to make something of myself, and you threw it away for a stupid party." She shook her head in disbelief. "This isn't happening. Tell me it's just a nightmare and I'll wake up in a minute. God, what will I do now?" She looked around the room like maybe the answer was there somewhere.

Bull Briskin was standing, silent and still watching his guest, but Margaret's expression softened as she spoke. "Oh, Jessie, I'm so sorry, honey. We'll sort this out. Bull and I will help. Go back to the laptop and read your e-mails. Call if you want, but I doubt you'll get anybody today. As I read it, Ely's lost her room, but I don't think she's out of school. You'll be the same."

She snapped back around to her daughter. "You, on the other hand, missy, are in more trouble than ever. Come to the study right now with your father and me."

Ely glanced at Jessie with an expression of poor misery in her eyes, but Jessie was in no mood to feel sorry for her.

"Don't you dare look at me like that. You made this mess. It's your mess. I'm sorry I ever met you." Jessie ran from the room close to tears.

Ely came looking for her a while later. Jessie had been too furious to make conversation with anyone, so she took refuge in her guest room. She knew Ely was nervous, because she knocked before entering—very out of character. She usually barged through doors, life, friends.

"Can I come in?" Ely asked from the other side of the closed door.

"It's your house. Do what you bloody well want." Jessie was sitting on her bed, attempting to study but failing miserably. She had her back propped up by some incredibly luxuriant feather pillows.

Ely opened the door slowly and stuck her head around. "So, I guess you hate me?" she said in a small voice.

"Yes." Jessie didn't look up from the psych journal she was reading.

"I'm sorry."

"That's not good enough."

"I drafted a letter with my parents before I came to find you. My dad is gonna e-mail it to the housing department first thing in the morning. I take full responsibility and liability for the party. I said you were in no way involved. They might move you to a different room, and if they don't, Dad says he'll pay for other accommodation for you while you finish out your year in the US."

"What about you?" Jessie looked up. Her friend's eyes were red-rimmed and her cheeks were tear-stained. She'd never seen Ely cry before. Good.

Ely slumped into one of two large yellow armchairs, keeping her distance from Jessie. She shrugged. "I'm grounded for life. They tell me I have to finish my degree or they'll cut me off. I have no choice. He who holds the wallet, holds the power."

"Listen to yourself. Do you have any idea how spoilt you sound? Christ, Ely, you've had everything in life handed to you on a silver platter, and yet you manage to sound like you're getting the raw deal. I never realized before just how overindulged you are!" Jessie got off the bed and began to pace the floor. "You tell your daddy I don't need his money. Clearing my name would be nice, but I'm pretty sure Mrs. Palmer was serious when she offered me a place to stay. I guess I can pay her with the money I make minding the Sanchez kids. It'll be tight, but if you think I'm taking your charity after you landed me in this mess, you can . . . you can . . . oh God, can you just leave me alone?"

Ely looked stunned. Jessie had never been so angry with her before.

"I'm sorry. I never meant to bring all this shit on you." Ely studied the floor.

"You sure?" Jessie stopped and looked at the girl she'd thought was her one friend in the US.

Ely snapped her head up. "What does that mean? You know you're my best friend and I'd never intentionally set out to hurt you."

"Hurt me? Ha!" Jessie threw her head back in a fake laugh. "You haven't just hurt me. You've utterly sabotaged my entire life. Jesus, Ely. You have no idea what havoc you've wreaked."

Ely wrung her hands. "I can fix this."

"Stop! You say we're good friends, but I don't think you know what true friendship even is. You just take while I do all the giving with us. I do your homework, I leave as soon as you want a quickie with Josh, and God help me, I let you walk all over me."

"Now, just one damn minute," Ely seemed to have found some fight still in her. "I disappeared pretty damn fast when you wanted space with Dan. I think you're being unfair here."

"Oh puh-lease. I said no to this party, but did you even listen? Not a chance!" Jessie knew she was shouting, but she didn't care who else in the house heard. "Wake up and smell the horse shit, Ely. You do what you like, and the only reason we're friends is because I go along with your harebrained ideas. Well, not any more. We are done." She stopped, a little out of breath.

Ely looked beaten back into submission. "J, you're my best friend. Really, you are. I love you. Please give me another chance," she said. "I'll leave you alone if that's what you want, but you gotta believe me. I'll do whatever you want if you'll forgive me."

"Get out. Just get out, Ely!"

Chapter Twenty-Two
Feelings Change

"Come in, come in," Leticia Garcia said when she opened the door.

Maria had just finished loading the dishwasher when she glanced at her watch. It was ten p.m. and still people were arriving. She smiled. How different Puerto Rican life was to her New England one. At home, her little family would have been well tucked up in bed by now. When Alice had finally started to yawn, Maria had put her down, but it was still warm enough for Cody to be night-swimming with his cousins and several neighborhood kids who had joined up with the Garcia Thanksgiving celebrations. Now more guests were arriving at this late hour. She walked into the hall to greet the new guests.

"Maria, you remember Carlos Alvarez and his mother, Lola?" Leticia said.

"Of course I do. *Hola*." She smiled.

She had known it was only a matter of time before she bumped into her ex-boyfriend Carlos, but in her own home? Lola was one of Leticia's best friends, so she should have guessed. The two had once harbored dreams of Carlos and Maria getting married. When Maria had gone off to college and Ricky entered her life, Carlos had become part of her history. She had been as honest as she could back then. Maria had flown home and broken up with him before she and Ricky got too close, but there was a bit of an overlap when she had been dating both men.

In due course, she had heard from her sisters that Carlos had met someone new and married. His divorce was new information to her, though. She felt for his loss. Much to her discomfort, Lola and Leticia linked arms and headed out to the courtyard, leaving Maria and Carlos alone in the hall.

"It's good to see you, Maria." He gave her a hesitant smile, making no effort to kiss her cheek.

Funny, every other person who had come into the house had covered her in kisses. Carlos was different, of course. Damn, she felt uncomfortable.

Inside, she cursed her husband for not being there.

"Come in," she said. "How have you been? It's been—how long?" She studied the ground, avoiding eye contact. They hadn't spoken since the breakup.

"Yes, it's been a while." His voice was soft.

They walked out into the courtyard. Festive strings of Christmas lights trailed their way through the night-blooming jasmine along the walls of the courtyard. As the night darkened, the tiny bulbs seemed to shine brighter. The underwater lights around the edges of the pool had been switched on, too, and gave the water a magical glow. Best of all were her mother's old-style lanterns. She had hung about twenty of them, no bigger than coffee mugs, from the orange trees on either side of dining table. Their natural candlelight attracted Maria as much as it did the magenta dragonflies.

Carlos was showered with *hellos* and *where-have-you-beens* by her brothers-in-law. The entire family was dining at Leticia's house. That meant Maria's three sisters, their husbands, and all the nephews and nieces—ten children and eight adults—were there. Then, after the meal, the neighbors had started to arrive to socialize and Maria had lost count. It was a full house—crazy but fabulous.

Maria felt a bit like a stranger. Carlos seemed to be more at home there than she was. When had that happened? He hadn't been at any of their weddings. She would have remembered. But San Juan wasn't a big town, and no doubt they all supported the local *pharmacia* over the new international one. Bernardo brought Carlos a beer, and Maria saw her chance to escape quietly. She wandered over to the pool and tried to look busy watching Cody. *Maybe I should creep off to bed*, she thought. Things felt awkward.

"I hear your husband is working over Thanksgiving and you brought the kids down alone." Carlos had come up beside her. Maybe he didn't feel as uncomfortable. "Which ones are yours?"

"Him." She pointed to Cody, who was climbing on top of one of his cousins' shoulders.

"He looks strong." Carlos's voice was still so familiar, even after all the years. His accent was deep and warm. It was a comfort.

She turned to face him. "Carlos, I'm sorry to hear about your marriage."

He gave a shrug. "So am I. What can I say? We tried to save it, but we failed. At least there were no children involved." He watched the kids in the pool. The splashing and games had reached a fever pitch, but there was no sign of them running out of steam.

"And you?"

"Me?" Maria didn't want to speak about Rick.

"Have you had a nice day?"

"Oh, the day? Right, the day. Yes, it's been marvelous. Mami made me and the kids come to church with her this morning. It was so busy."

"I know, I saw you."

"You did?"

"Yes, I would have said hello, but as you say, it was a full house and you were gone before I got the chance."

"I didn't see you."

"No. I think you had your hands full with a baby."

"That's my little girl, Alice. She'll be one next month, and she's beginning to become hard to handle."

This time he smiled at her. "Ah, a son and a daughter? You're lucky."

"Yeah, but they're a handful, too. We spent most of the afternoon eating a fabulous meal. I loved it, but my all-American son was not so impressed when the *guineos en escabeche* were served up as a starter."

"You don't cook them in your home?"

"No." She laughed. "He didn't trust bananas combined with garlic, but Alice loved them and couldn't get enough."

"You should start cooking them in the future," he said. "What about the rest of the meal?"

She could feel herself relaxing. It was easy to talk to Carlos. She had forgotten he was so nice. "The turkey was pretty much as I fix it—only the stuffing was different—and, of course, everybody adores Mami's special *dulce de leche* custard."

He nodded in agreement.

"I've never seen my daughter put away so much food, but then again they were outside for most of the day. The fresh air must have made her hungry."

"Carlos!" Bernardo gestured for him to join in.

Carlos raised his beer bottle to say he was coming, but then he whispered, "It's been really good to see you, Maria. You look good. I'm happy things have turned out so well for you."

This time he did reach over and kiss her on the cheek. His cologne, she realized, was the same he had always worn. Such a sudden jolt to her memory startled her, and he sensed her change.

"*Esta bien?*"

"*Si, si.*" She lied. Maria wasn't really okay.

This was all lies. She was acting like she had a fabulous life back in Newton, when in fact she hadn't even spoken to her husband for almost two weeks. Maria felt like an outsider. Why had she thought this would work? Coming home like this? Yes, she still loved Puerto Rico, but it wasn't her home anymore. She had been gone too long.

Maria folded her arms tight as if she were cold and looked around the courtyard with new eyes. She'd grown up inside these walls, been born in this house, learned to walk, talk, and swim here. She had even fallen in love with Carlos when she'd lived in this house, but she had fallen out of love with him somewhere else.

Carlos and Puerto Rico were part of her past. Ricky, Newton, and her children were her present. Like it or not, that was where her home was now.

She folded her arms even tighter despite the heat of the night.

Carlos was chatting with her sisters and their husbands who were all sitting together, laughing and talking. At the other end of the table were the older neighbors with Leticia. Maria wanted to sit at the table with her siblings, but something held her back.

Was she all of a sudden shy with Carlos, or was it more than that? Was it disloyal to her husband to talk to her ex? And why hadn't he called her for Thanksgiving? Moreover, why hadn't he joined them?

Maria had enough. She was exhausted and had a strong need for her bed. Seeing Carlos didn't help. After a quick word with her son, who swore he would go to bed when his cousins did, she left the party without saying good-bye to anyone else.

As always, though, one person noticed.

Maria had just climbed into bed when she heard a soft knock on her bedroom door. "Maria, are you in there?"

"Yes. Come in, Mami," Maria called through the door.

Leticia opened the door. "I thought you might be here," her mother said and smiled as she came into her room. "But I couldn't let my firstborn go to bed on Thanksgiving without a good-night kiss." She sat on her daughter's bed.

"I'm sorry. I didn't want to make a big fuss and risk breaking up the party. Cody promised he'll go to bed when his cousins do."

Leticia shrugged. "He's a good boy and growing up so fast." She studied Maria's face. "What about you, *cariño*. I worry about you."

Maria focused on the beautiful white bedspread that covered her body. It was hardly necessary with the heat outside. She didn't know what to say, so she shook her head.

"How many years have you been married now?"

"Eleven."

"That many? Eleven? It feels like three, but Cody is ten, so it makes sense."

"Sometimes I feel like I've been married for a thousand years." She gave a weak smile. "How can I find two children so overwhelming when you had four and managed so easily?"

Leticia stroked her daughter's hair. "Your memory is playing tricks on you. I screamed a lot and cried, too. But I do think women today seem to have more pressure. Always rushing with the children, trying to do everything. Things were simpler before."

Maria studied her mother's face but didn't speak.

"And then there is my most beautiful youngest granddaughter, Alice— almost one." Leticia stroked Maria's cheek. "That is one strong lady, much more work than Cody. I saw that yesterday. I'm sure she'll grow out of it but, *Dios mío*, she was a handful when you were in town. It's not easy when the babies come, *cariño*. It puts huge pressure on the parents."

"It's not that." Maria dropped her gaze and shook her head. "Between Ricky and me, I mean."

"Is there another woman?"

Another head shake.

"Another man?"

Maria's head shot up. "You mean me? Am I having an affair?"

Her mother shrugged. "I'm not suggesting anything. I am just wondering why your heart is so heavy. I know how much you love Rick, and now you have these two fabulous children, but I see you're so sad, too. How can I help if I don't know what the problem is?"

"Oh, Mami, it's everything. He works so hard, and I never see him. Then when I do, he's looking at younger women. I did think he was having an affair, but now I believe I was wrong. It was work. He's in that damn office all the time. I'm at home with the children, and sometimes I think I'm just going crazy. I'm getting fatter every day—and older. Did I mention that Ricky is still running and looks the same as he did eleven years ago while I've aged decades? We're growing apart, and he doesn't even chase me anymore when I run away." She felt her eyes fill with tears. "I think Ricky has fallen out of love with me. I think that's the bottom line. He doesn't love me anymore."

Leticia hugged her tight like she had when Maria was a little girl. "Shh, cariño. You don't know any of this. It's not certain."

"I do. I feel it." Maria cried into her mother's shoulder.

"Sometimes our feelings get things wrong," Leticia said. "And even if you're right, feelings can change. You can fix this situation if you want to, baby." Leticia pulled back and wiped Maria's eyes with her hankie.

"You think?"

"I know."

"How?"

"You think your father and I didn't have our problems? Everybody has problems, Maria. Anybody who says otherwise is lying." She sat back on the bed now, giving Maria a little more room. "You have two children. I had four, and believe me, you girls were quite a handful. Your father and I didn't always agree, but we got through it. It takes effort, my girl. Is he really working in the office over the holiday?"

Maria nodded.

"He needs to work less, but you must support his career more."

"I already do."

Leticia cocked an eyebrow as if to say she didn't believe her.

"Well, I did until it took over his life. I mean, who works over Thanksgiving?"

"Doctors, nurses, pilots, businessmen—many people. Rick seems to be one of them. Did you have an argument?"

She looked at her mother and knew she couldn't lie to her at this point. "We had a big fight almost two weeks ago and stopped talking. That's why

I had to get away. The atmosphere in the house was killing me."

"Two weeks?" Leticia blessed herself. "You haven't spoken for two weeks? That's even more than your father and me. Oh, you are so hotheaded, Maria. You have to break this fight."

"Why can't he?"

"I don't know, but it's clear somebody has to, so it may as well be you." Her mother was looking a lot less sympathetic now.

She cupped Maria's face in her hands. "Do you want to stay married to the father of your children, *mija*?"

"Yes."

"Then fight for your marriage. Don't let it slip away." She was so earnest. "You have to cherish it like you do your children. Your love needs time and nurturing just like your babies. You and Rick need time alone to rediscover each other. Your sisters and I can take the children."

Maria shook her head. "Cody has to go back to school, and if I asked Ricky, he would say he couldn't get the time off from his blessed work."

"He must." Leticia slapped the bed cover. "Your marriage is more important than any work he is doing. Just a weekend away together. Surely he can do that . . ."

"You're talking about a man who couldn't even give me Thanksgiving."

Leticia shook her head. "I know Rick. He's a good man. You have to end this argument, *chica*. Somehow you have to make peace with your husband and fight for your marriage."

Maria pulled her knees up to her body so she could hug them. "I know. I just don't know how."

Then Leticia smiled. "Oh, I think you do."

"Oh God, you're not suggesting I seduce him like the old days."

"Is that so bad?"

"I'm too tired and fat."

"You're not fat!" Leticia snapped her head up with a look of indignation, like it was an insult against her. "You're beautiful. Did you see the way Carlos Alvarez looked at you? If you were living here and single, I think you could be his wife easy."

"But I don't live here and I'm not single."

"*Correcto.* So you must go home to your husband, and I'm not saying you have to seduce him. But you could start with a simple apology."

Maria knew her mother was right. Until now Maria really hadn't wanted to apologize to her husband. She was too mad at him for working so hard. But she knew it wasn't all his fault. She couldn't blame him for her getting older. It wasn't his fault she had a weak spot for baby crackers, and deep down, she knew it was maybe just a little immature to have run away.

"I have to go home, don't I?" she said, just above a whisper.

Leticia didn't speak, only nodded.

"This house—I thought it would feel like home, but it's different now."

"Of course it is. It will always be a home for you, Maria, but you have another home now. It's pulling you more than you know."

"I want to stay here—it's safe."

"No, you don't." Leticia stroked her daughter's hair again. "You always hated safe."

It made Maria smile. "It's looking kinda nice right now."

"You can come back anytime. I'm always here."

"Thanks." They hugged again.

Leticia stood and kissed the top of her head. "The most important thing for you to remember is that all of this is very normal in a marriage." She walked back over to the bedroom door. "But what you do next is critical." She took a deep breath and then spoke with a stronger tone than before. "Go home to Rick, Maria. Fight to save your marriage." Her mother's eyes were bright, and she was speaking from the heart. "I know what it's like to be alone. You don't want that. Fight for your love."

"I will, Mami. I'll go home Sunday," Maria said, feeling a little better. "I know what I have to do."

Chapter Twenty-Three
One Lump or Two?

"So you're sure you know what you have to do?" Jessie used her sternest voice.

The girls were being driven by Josh to their new home. Ely was in the front, next to her boyfriend, and Jessie was in the back. Ely sank down in her car seat and folded her arms defensively.

"Yeah. Stop treating me like a kid. I know—no drinkin', no parties, no late nights. I get it. Basically, I have to act like a nun for the next six months, or you'll never speak to me again."

Jessie smiled. "Yes, that's it in a nutshell. You just be a regular little Girl Scout. Go to all your classes, do all your own homework. You can see Josh at the weekends but not during the week. This is your very last chance. Do you hear me?"

Ely scowled. "How has it come to this?"

Jessie knew her friend would behave.

She had been so mad with her roommate on the night of Thanksgiving, she really thought perhaps their friendship was over, but one of Ely's greatest talents was charming people. Jessie was no exception.

Ely had cried and begged. She'd promised the sun, moon, and stars if only Jessie would forgive her. Ely's parents had even tried. Margaret, Ely's mother, was so upset about the girls getting kicked out of their rooms, and while she was furious with her daughter, she had pleaded with Jessie not to desert Ely. Margaret had insisted Jessie was the grounding influence on her wild child. Bull had agreed. He'd pushed Jessie to take an apartment he would pay for, but she couldn't accept that. It would have made her feel cheap. And Dan had cheapened her enough.

Ely had called Noreen Palmer on the morning after Thanksgiving. The old woman listened to Ely's sorry tale and was determined they should both come and stay with her for the remainder of the academic year. Mrs. Palmer had explained she wanted company, so it was a win-win situation, and if they paid for their food and utilities, she would be delighted for them to move in as soon as they could. That was when Jessie had begun to soften.

Living with Mrs. Palmer was a good solution, but the truth was Jessie didn't want to lose Ely—her only real friend in America. Adorable as their new landlady was, Ely was Jessie's emotional support—even if she had gotten them into so much trouble.

The atmosphere in the Briskin house on the day after Thanksgiving had been cooler than November in Newton. The extended family had all returned to their own homes, and Ely had kept a very low profile, avoiding her father for the entire day. It was Ely's mother who had driven them to the airport on Saturday morning.

The only one who had seemed immune to the suddenly hostile atmosphere in the house was Ely's brother, John. He'd told Jessie during a private moment that big family fights were common enough in their home. More often, however, it was him and Bull. John said it was a relief for once that Ely was the one in the doghouse. He'd told her not to worry about it, because his little sister was the apple of her father's eye and the argument would blow over soon enough.

It was all so strange for Jessie. They didn't have "family fights" at her house back in Dorking. Yes, there were arguments, but nothing on this scale or with such drama. But by the time they'd arrived at the airport, Margaret was hugging her daughter, and it had been clear she was going to miss her baby. They'd promised to stay in touch, and Jessie had felt a sharp pang for England and her mother.

Now Noreen Palmer was expecting them, and Jessie was making sure Ely was on her best behavior. Josh had landed back into Boston earlier that day and had been roped into getting them from the airport. No surprise, he already knew all about his girlfriend's Thanksgiving family fight and was extra affectionate as a result.

"You guys are going to have to control yourselves. You can't take him up to your room in Mrs. Palmer's house," Jessie said when she saw them holding hands as he drove.

"I really don't like the rule about not being able to see her during the week. That's too much." He scowled at Jessie in his rearview mirror.

"Ely has a mountain of studying to catch up on," Jessie said. "She's been slacking off since the start of term and has promised she'll put her heart and soul into her studies if we're going to keep living together."

Josh harrumphed, but Ely didn't argue.

"And you have to walk Rusty sometimes, too," she said as an afterthought.

Ely smiled and nodded. "I love dogs."

Jessie almost laughed. She could have asked for the crown jewels, and her roommate would have agreed just to keep things calm. "He's a bulldog, so he's ugly as hell but full of personality."

"Sounds like my first boyfriend," Ely said, and Josh gave her a playful poke.

Crystal Lake Lane looked beautiful on that first Saturday just after Thanksgiving. There had been a fresh fall of powdery snow, so the yards were blanketed in white. Some families who had stayed in the neighborhood over the holiday had snowmen in their gardens, which gave a definite holiday spirit to the street.

"Decorating your house for the holiday is taken much more seriously over here than it is in England," Jessie said when they were turning into Noreen's drive.

"Yeah? Why's that?" Josh asked, putting the car in park.

"I don't know." She got out of the back of the car. "We just don't do it."

"We think you're all too uptight," he said as they got out of his car and opened the trunk.

Jessie was shocked. "Who? Us? The British? We're not at all uptight."

"No? When was the last time your queen did something crazy?"

Ely giggled and started unloading the car, but Jessie wasn't impressed. "She's the queen—she doesn't *do crazy*." Jessie tried to say *do crazy* with an American accent but failed.

It made Josh and Ely snort with laughter. "Okay then—when was she last in a bikini? That's not crazy. That's just swimmin'."

"She's a great-grandmother." Jessie defended her queen. "And royalty."

Josh shrugged and pulled one of the enormous cases out of the trunk. "Just sayin'."

Noreen opened her front door, and the argument was closed.

"Welcome," she said with Rusty at her feet. The last time she'd visited, Jessie had used the side door, but today Noreen was at the main entrance, which opened out onto the sun deck. There were a couple of deck chairs and a double swing, but they had been covered for the winter. Now the whole thing was dusted with snow.

"Oh, Mrs. Palmer, thank you for taking us in," Jessie said, going straight for a hug.

"Yeah, that was real decent of you, Mrs. Palmer." Ely said, adding to the conversation.

The old woman chuckled and hugged them both like they were her grandchildren. "Nonsense. You're the ones doing me the favor. I need the company and you can remind me what day of the week it is, because they tell me I'm very forgetful."

Josh lumbered up the slippery steps, lugging two of the girls' suitcases.

"My, you have a heavy load there, son. Come with me and I'll show you to the rooms." He followed her into the house while the girls made fast work getting the rest of their gear out of the car. The air was too cold to linger outside, and it was getting dark fast.

Ely, in particular, hated the cold New England winter, having complained about it enough. Jessie was a little hardier, being accustomed to the cold

English winter back home, so she was the one who double-checked they had everything out of the car.

Just before Jessie went inside, she took a moment to stop and savor the incredible stillness of the night. It was a new kind of silence for her. An absolute quiet, because the snow absorbed all the normal night noises. Nature truly went to sleep when it got this cold. She stood on the sun deck, loving the atmosphere and admiring the house decorations across the street. Jessie remembered it was Todd's house, Noreen's grandson. *Nice to have family so near*, she thought. They had an enormous snowman and lights around every window frame.

"Hullo," somebody said and startled her.

"Oh, hullo," she said, trying to mask her surprise when she saw a lone man walking along the lane. This was a dead-end street, so pedestrians were rare—plus it wasn't really walking weather. Jessie didn't want to encourage the man, so she turned and walked into her new home. She closed the door and wondered if it had been her imagination or had the man in the flat cap had an English accent? It would be nice to have a countryman nearby. They weren't uptight. Were they? *Who ever heard of the queen in a bikini? Such a notion.*

"Ely?" Jessie called from inside the large front hall. She had been in the house before and knew it was pretty, in a faded elegance sort of way, but this was her first time to view it as her new home.

"We're upstairs, J. Come up."

Jessie could hear the excitement in her friend's voice, so she bounded up the steps two at a time. Noreen, Josh, and Ely were in a large bedroom at the back of the house.

"This one's yours." Ely grinned at her. It was a large room with a king-size bed. Jessie looked at her roommate with worried eyes, but Ely seemed to know what she was thinking. "We're not sharing a room. This is your room. Isn't it great? So big. I have one across the hall, and check out your view."

They looked out the back window to where the yard was covered in snow and the lake beyond was just visible in the fading light.

"The lake's frozen solid. Wow, that was fast," Jessie said. "I saw it just a few weeks ago from the Sanchez house and it was still water."

"Darn, it's clouded over. You should have seen it a few minutes ago. The moon was shining on the ice of the lake. It was awesome," Ely said.

"I'm glad you like it. This used to be my room," Noreen said.

"Oh, please don't say you moved on my account, Mrs. Palmer."

Noreen smiled. "Not at all, Jessie. I prefer to sleep downstairs now. It's easier for my knees, you see. This room has been empty for years."

Josh wandered into the room across the hall and let out a low whistle. The girls followed.

"And this is my room." Ely gave a victorious grin. It wasn't a big room, but it was more modern and the carpet looked new. It also had a king-size bed.

"Who decided who got which room?" Jessie asked with suspicion.

"Noreen told me to choose, so I did," Ely said.

Jessie rolled her shoulders with indifference. "I prefer my lake view, so I'm happy," she said and wandered over to Ely's window which overlooked Crystal Lake Lane. "Did you see a man walking along the road a minute ago?" she asked.

Ely joined her. "No. Did you?"

"Yes. He was wearing a flat cap, and I think he might have had an English accent, but it could have been my imagination."

"It must have been Bruce. He lives in number three. Miserable old soul. Never talks to anybody," Noreen said. It was the first time Jessie had heard the old lady say anything negative about anyone.

"That's funny. He didn't seem miserable, but rather quite nice."

Noreen shook her head. "Then it wasn't Bruce. We tried to be friendly to him when we moved in here, Joe and me, but he was so fractious. You'd do well to avoid him."

Jessie nodded, but she didn't think Bruce, if that's who he was, seemed too nasty.

When Josh had moved all the suitcases into the right rooms, they went downstairs and had a glass of wine with Mrs. Palmer. Then Josh said his good-byes. He was reluctant to go, and Ely wanted him to stay, but she was stoic and pushed him out the door. "I'll see you tomorrow at your place," Jessie heard her friend whisper to Josh.

"The rest of our stuff will be coming from our dorm tomorrow, Mrs. Palmer. I can't thank you enough for taking us in on such short notice," Jessie said when the two lovebirds were out of earshot.

"Enough of that talk now. We both need each other—it's a perfect fit. I'd been thinking of taking in lodgers for years, so I'm happy to give it a go at last. It was either this or move in with my son across the road, and I'm not sure I want to do that."

They were sitting in the same room where they had enjoyed the milk and cookies on Jessie's last visit. This time the fire was lit, and the place was warm and welcoming.

"I'll give you both keys. You can come and go as you please. Just let me know if you want me to cook some supper for you."

Jessie was overwhelmed. It was like coming home. Noreen was such a maternal sort. "This is fantastic, Mrs. Palmer. Thanks so much, and I'll help keep the place clean and dishes washed."

Noreen gave that light chuckle again. "Oh, I might not let you go if you're that good to me. But please stop calling me Mrs. Palmer. It makes me feel like an old woman! Call me Noreen."

Jessie nodded, and then Ely came in, looking a little lost.

"You're still here?" Noreen looked surprised.

"Eh, yeah. Sure."

Jessie knew her friend didn't want to state the obvious. It was their first night in their new home. She couldn't very well gallivant off with her boyfriend already.

Noreen shook her head and eyed Ely with a smirk. "If I had a hunky boyfriend like that, I wouldn't be sitting around here with us looking at the fire and drinking house red. Why don't you go with him, dear?"

Ely glanced from Noreen to her friend. Jessie knew she was waiting for her blessing after all the trouble she had caused. But how could she turn down a face like that?

She laughed at Ely.

"Go on. Git," she said, using her friend's lingo.

Ely kissed them both on the cheek. "Oh, thank you, thank you, thank you. I've missed him so much. It's been ages."

She headed for the door but was texting already.

"Just be careful, and I'm not talking about the slippery roads," Noreen said.

"It hasn't been ages. It's been three days. We went away on Wednesday." Jessie laughed.

" 'Absence makes the heart grow fonder'," Noreen said. "Shakespeare."

Jessie sipped her wine. Her new landlady didn't seem too forgetful this evening. Josh's car roared back up the driveway. "Bye!" Ely yelled as she banged the door behind her.

"I'm surprised you don't have your own handsome man delighted to see you back in Newton," Noreen said.

Jessie focused on the dancing flames in the fire. "I thought there was somebody, but he turned out to be someone else's property."

"Oh dear. But there's plenty of fish in the sea. And you're such a pretty girl I'm sure you'll find somebody else very soon."

Rusty began to bark. "What's got into you?" Jessie tried to calm him, but Noreen was on her feet.

"It means somebody's coming to the back door of the house. He can hear the snow crunching. It's quite convenient," Noreen said as she headed out of the room.

Jessie wasn't sure whether to stay put or to follow, so she trailed after Noreen. She heard the conversation before she saw him. It was Rick Sanchez, and he sounded stressed.

"Jeez, Noreen, what'll I do?"

Jessie felt like she was eavesdropping, so she walked over to let him know she was there.

"Jessie." His expression changed.

"Hi, Rick." They hadn't seen each other since the "coffee offer." Jessie had done her best to forget about that morning. There was enough going on in her life, between two-timing boyfriends and almost getting kicked out of college. Now Rick was standing in front of her again—a little more difficult to ignore. She didn't want to think there was anything between them, because there wasn't, was there? He was way too old and way too married. No, she convinced herself again. There was absolutely nothing between her and Rick Sanchez, her very attractive, new next-door neighbor.

"You know each other?" Noreen sounded surprised.

"I mind Rick's kids sometimes. That's how I met you, remember?" Jessie said, but she was looking at Rick.

"It's Orga," he said. "She's run off in the snow and I can't find her. I was hoping she came over here."

"No, I'm afraid not. Jessie and her friend Ely have moved in with me, so we've had a lot of commotion, but we haven't seen Orga, have we, dear?"

Jessie shook her head. "No sign."

"I'm sure Jessie could help you search for the dog. Wouldn't you?" Noreen looked at her.

"Sure." Jessie forced a smile.

"That would be great." Rick's eyes moved from his neighbor to Jessie. "If it's okay with you?"

"No problem."

"I'll just go and get you a flashlight, Jessie." Noreen shuffled off, leaving them alone.

"How are you?" His tone was soft, more intimate than usual.

"I've had a tough couple of days, actually." She raked her hand through her hair.

"Tell me about it." He smiled and reached out to squeeze her arm.

Jessie felt herself being drawn in. It was wrong, she knew that, but then again, they were just being friends—good friends. It didn't have to be anything more. She wouldn't do that to Maria. Would she?

Chapter Twenty-Four
New Neighbors

"What more could I do?" Ricky sounded helpless, and that made Maria even madder.

"I don't know, but I'm sure you could have done something," she said with exasperation. "Five nights. That's all you had to watch the damn dog for, and you lose her. Ricky? Hello?"

Her husband was holding Alice and watching her pace the kitchen floor. "I did a big search last night as soon as I noticed Orga missing, and then again this morning. I called the cops and I even nailed signs up all over the neighborhood."

Cody was quiet. Even though he'd told Maria he loved the time in Puerto Rico, he had been excited to be coming home. He had told her he missed his dad and Orga, and now the dog was missing. This was a disaster.

"Cody, honey, do you want to go over to Todd's and the two of you can search?"

"I guess." He didn't sound too convinced.

"You don't have to if you don't want to. Your dad will find her." She threw a filthy look in Ricky's direction. Cody didn't move.

Traveling home from the Caribbean, she had spent all her time trying to think of ways to fire up her marriage. She had played with the idea of getting some more kinky toys, but the last time she'd done that, Alice had arrived nine months later. Next she'd considered buying some expensive lingerie, but that was so not happening now.

Maria walked to the sink and took a cloth to wipe the already clean countertops. "Did you leave her in the house all day?"

"No. I even took her to work on Thanksgiving morning. Okay, I left the dog here for a few hours when I went over to Michael's and Cathi's for dinner, but that's only because they have that shitty thing."

"Shih tzu. Fifi is a shih tzu."

"Whatever. I took care of Orga just fine—which is more than I can say for you," he said.

That was the comment she had been waiting for. She knew he was mad as hell with her. She'd hoped he would miss her and appreciate her all the more after her absence, but the opposite had happened.

"Me?" She threw the cloth back into the sink.

Alice started to cry.

"Now look what you've done." Maria took the baby back.

"I did this? Maria, you're the one shrieking." He stopped talking. Cody was staring at them.

Maria forced herself to sound more composed. "Honey, can you bring your suitcase upstairs and get your clothes out of it?" she said. Cody groaned. She knew there was little chance of him even opening the case, but if he left the room, at least he wouldn't hear his parents argue.

As soon as he was gone, Maria continued her rant in a loud whisper. "I wouldn't have gone if you were around this place a bit more, Ricky. You're more interested in your damn job than you are in your family. You were gone so much I even wondered if you were maybe having an affair."

"Ha!" He started to walk toward the door to the hall.

"You think it's funny? That a woman would see so little of her husband she thinks he has a mistress?"

He walked back to her and stopped short, ominously close. "All I do is work my ass off, and you should know that because you sure know how to spend it!"

She could feel his breath on her face, smell his cologne. Maria had never seen him so steamed up. He was staring into her eyes, but the look was utter contempt. How could they have come to this? She looked away.

"Just find the damn dog, Ricky," she said, the anger gone from her voice and sad resignation in its place.

"Jesus!" He balled his fists and raised them in the air like he couldn't contain his frustration. Then he stormed out.

Maria sat heavily down on a kitchen chair and tried to sooth Alice. She hugged her daughter close and rocked her. "Shh, baby. Mommy's here. Why don't we get you a bottle?" She spoke softly to help calm the baby. "I'm not a big spender, am I? Lord, if he thinks I'm bad, he should see how Cathi cuts through cash."

Alice's mood improved when she heard the mention of milk.

The little girl began to chant. "Ba, ba, ba . . ."

Maria put her down on the floor to play with some toys while she started to make the bottle. She heard the front door bang shut. Judging by the force, she thought it had to have been Ricky.

Cody didn't look like he was that interested in heading out into the snow. She didn't blame him. Returning from Puerto Rico had only highlighted how cold it was in Newton. Inside, the house was nice and warm, but the snow had built up outside. There had to be at least three feet of the stuff at this stage. What a difference between her mother's courtyard and her own backyard, she mused while bringing the bottles over to the sink and looking out her kitchen window. In the space of a week, one little week, the entire lake had frozen over.

"A bit like my marriage," she said and filled three bottles with water.

The lake never ceased to amaze her. During the summer days, it was inky black and shimmered when the sun caught ripples on its surface. On the brightest days, it could look blue.

But in winter, things were different. If the low solstice sun bounced off the surface, it was blindingly bright. During the winter, it really lived up to its name—Crystal Lake. Looking out, she couldn't help but wonder how thick the ice was.

Maria recalled the old wives' tale—blue hue, drive on through. Translated, that meant if the ice looked blue, it was thick enough to drive a horse and carriage over. Nobody had been dumb enough to try in the last few decades. She sometimes saw skaters out there, but she wouldn't let Cody do it. Everybody knew about global warming. What if it wasn't thick enough? She had never let him skate on the lake. Never.

Despite the warmth of the kitchen, Maria felt a chill. She hugged herself. "What am I going to do?" she said to Alice, who was using the kitchen chair to pull herself up into a standing position. "I came home fully intending to make peace, and within minutes we're at each other's throats again."

Maria started to scoop the powdered formula into the bottles. "Maybe Mami was wrong. Maybe this marriage can't be saved." The idea shook her to the core. Was this really happening to her and Ricky? Sure, she had friends who had broken up, but her? Jesus. Maria's vision blurred as her eyes filled with tears. Some of the formula fell outside one of the bottles.

"Damn and double damn," she said, knocking them all over and pushing them into the sink. She would have to start again—washing, sterilizing, boiling up more water and mixing new formula. She couldn't even make a baby bottle right anymore. Was it her? Had she fallen apart? Maybe Ricky was right. All she did now was complain, spend money, and make life hell. What if she was the problem? Maria wiped her eyes and put the unused baby bottles into the dishwasher. She went over to the mirror in the kitchen to check her reflection. Her eyes were bloodshot.

"Da," Alice said behind her.

"Da," Maria said without turning around. She looked like hell. Crying didn't do her any favors, but she wasn't wearing makeup either. Their flight out of Puerto Rico had been early. There hadn't been time to clean up before coming home to Newton.

"Make time," she said to her reflection. "You need to make the effort."

"Da," Alice said again. This time Maria turned to look at her daughter.

"Oh my God, you're standing!" Maria froze, scared that if she rushed to the baby, she'd fall. Alice smiled and tried to clap which was enough to unbalance her. She fell back down onto her diaper-cushioned bottom and gave a self-satisfied grin. Maria rushed over to her now. "You are so clever —standing up and not even one. I'm so proud of you, Alice." She snuggled her daughter and inhaled her sweet baby smell.

" 'Sup?" Cody walked into the kitchen.

"Alice just stood by herself without holding on to anything. Isn't she smart?"

The boy shrugged and gave his mom a half nod.

"Come on, Cody. That's a big deal. She can stand."

Cody opened the fridge and studied the lack of contents.

"I think I'll have to go grocery shopping this evening. Do you want to come with me?"

Another shrug. Maria felt a stab of guilt. She knew he had seen and heard her argument with Rick. Damn it, why hadn't they been more discreet? She put Alice down next to the kitchen chair again so she could work on her standing. Then Maria walked over to her boy.

"Look, Cody, I'm sorry Orga is missing, but she's microchipped. We'll get her back, and I'm sorry you had to hear Dad and I fight like that."

"Are you guys going to get a divorce?"

The question was so sudden it stunned her for a moment. "What? Cody, how could you think such a thing? No, we're not getting a divorce. We were just arguing about Orga."

"Yeah, and we just spent Thanksgiving away from him, and you were fighting before we went away."

"How did—" Of course he had known. He wasn't stupid. Even Alice got upset when her parents fought. Cody would be a lot more perceptive.

This was a mess. It wasn't about her and Ricky anymore. It was about the kids, too. What was she thinking? She had to find a way back to her husband. She had to fix this—somehow.

She took Cody in her arms. "Honey, your dad and I are arguing a lot these days, but he's working very hard. He's under a lot of pressure. But we're not talking divorce. We'll get through this, I promise."

Cody wrapped his arms around her, which was pretty unusual these days. He let her hug him on occasion but never returned the gesture. She understood that mom-hugs weren't high on a ten-year-old's agenda. For him to hug her back spoke volumes. He was feeling the pain. It broke her heart. She couldn't hurt her babies like this. It wasn't fair.

"I know. Let's order pizza tonight. We can go food shopping tomorrow."

He pulled back from her and smiled. "Score," he said with a smile. Then he looked over to Alice. "Hey, she's doing it again."

They both turned around and looked at the baby.

"Good girl." Maria clapped.

"You go, little sis. Look at you standing on your own."

That struck a chord with Maria. Her own daughter was standing on her own two feet. She had found a way. Couldn't Maria do the same? Had she become so unbalanced in the last few years? Maria needed to be strong for the sake of her children and her marriage. She would get through this mess with Ricky and find a way to save her marriage for her sake, his, and her two adorable kids. And she would damn well learn to stand on her own two feet again—just like Alice.

"Be careful, it's icy out here." He spoke from behind her, which surprised Jessie, and she almost lost her balance. She turned around and saw miserable Bruce. He didn't look too glum to her, but she trusted Noreen Palmer.

"I didn't hear you coming up behind me," she said. "I've just never seen the lake iced over before. I had to come out and have a look."

"Spectacular, isn't it?" he said. Bruce inhaled a barrelful of air, as if to savor the moment. He smiled at her. "Hullo, I'm Bruce Wiswall."

"Jessie Armstrong." They shook hands. He wasn't a large man—tall, yes, but thin. His legs were long, because he was taller than Jessie. His arms seemed lanky, too, but it was difficult to tell because he was well wrapped up.

"You're the lady I waved to last night?"

"I think so. You had a flat cap on?"

He smiled. It was a nice smile. "Yes, should have worn it this morning. I keep forgetting how bloody cold it is over here."

"You're English?"

"Yup. You, too? You sound it."

She nodded and smiled. "It's nice to meet a countryman. Do you live around here?" She already knew he did but asked to be polite.

"Number three." He pointed down along the lakeshore toward the back of his house.

They were standing on the edge of the ice just behind Noreen's house. Like Maria, Noreen had a long garden that was walled off with a small hedge, but Noreen had a fence with a gate in hers.

"I'm in here." Jessie pointed to the house behind them. "We're lodgers of Noreen Palmer's for the next few months."

"Noreen?" He raised a dark brown eyebrow. Bruce Wiswall looked a lot younger than she'd expected by the way her landlady had talked. His face was thin and angular, with nice cheekbones—he couldn't have been more than thirty years old. Jessie quickly appraised the wide apart eyes, long nose, handsome mouth. Then she was distracted by a dog bounding up to them.

"Orga!" Jessie bent down and hugged her.

"You know this dog?"

"Yes, and her family is freaking out. You had her? She belongs to the Sanchez family." She pointed to the house next door.

"I found her outside my front door last night." Bruce crouched down and petted the dog. "Poor girl, she was freezing, so I took her in and we had supper together."

"I was out looking for her last night. Why didn't you call the number on her tag?"

"What tag?" Bruce raised his eyebrow again. *Cute.*

"Wow, she's not wearing her collar. That's weird."

"I figured I'd take her to a dog shelter tomorrow and have her scanned for a chip, but if you're sure she belongs to those people . . ."

"Let's go," she said. "Come with me—I'm sure they'll want to say thanks to you."

Bruce fell into step with her. "What did you call her?"

"Orga."

"New one on me. Does it mean something?"

"It's the Irish for gold."

"Oh, I'd never have guessed. Are the owners Irish?"

"No, Puerto Rican and American—go figure."

The dog bounded ahead once they got into the Sanchez yard and headed straight for the back door with Bruce and Jessie a few steps behind. Jessie rang the doorbell, and Cody came out.

"Orga! You found Orga," he said and wrapped his arms around the dog. Maria appeared next with Alice in her arms.

"Jessie, hi." She glanced at Bruce. "Great to see you, and you found Orga. Come in."

"This is Bruce Wiswall, Maria. He's from number three."

"Nice to meet you, Bruce. This is my daughter Alice, and that's Cody. He's the one who owns Orga." She looked at Jessie again. "How'd she end up with you? Did she wander onto campus?"

"Um, no. It was Bruce who found her last night, but she's lost her collar, so he didn't know who to phone."

"What the heck?" Cody moaned. "I bet it was Dad. He always takes it off when he gives her a bath and forgets to put it back on."

"A bath at this time of year? Chilly." Bruce smirked. Again, Jessie was struck by how pleasant he seemed. Why did Noreen say he was miserable?

The front door of the house banged closed, and Orga tore off to see who had just arrived. "Orga!" Rick shouted in delight.

"How did you find the dog?" Rick said as he walked into the kitchen. "Oh! Hi, Jessie." He looked at Bruce. "Hey."

Jessie thought Maria looked mutinous. "Yes, Orga's back." Her tone was icier than the air outside.

The tension shimmered between Rick and his wife, and Jessie felt her stomach start to form knots. Was she adding to their problems? She tried to break the tense atmosphere by introducing Bruce to Rick. "He's the one who found the dog."

Maria was in no mood to be cheered up. "Orga didn't have on his collar.

Know anything about that?" She glared at her husband.

"No collar? Damn it. I took it off her on Friday, I think. It was soaking wet after she was rolling in the snow, and I wanted it to dry off. I must've forgotten to put it back on."

"Understandable," Bruce said.

Jessie knew he was siding with Rick to help him out, but Maria looked like she was going to skewer him with her nasty glares.

"Cody, can you take Orga into the living room and put her collar back on? I'm pretty sure I left it on the mantelpiece." The boy ran out of the room with the dog in hot pursuit.

"Honey, has Jessie told you she's moved in next door with Noreen Palmer?"

Maria's attention swooped around to Jessie now.

"You live next door now?"

Jessie heard the manic tone in Maria's voice.

Was she that awful a neighbor? Jessie felt even more uncomfortable.

"Um, yes. We got kicked out of our college accommodation for throwing a party, but Noreen took us in. Don't worry, there won't be any more parties. We're lying low and studying hard for the next few months."

Just then, and to Jessie's enormous relief, the doorbell rang. Orga started to bark, and Maria shook her head with a look of bewilderment. "This house it too damn busy." Alice was gurgling in her mother's arms but smiling at Jessie.

"It's the Grants," Cody said when he walked back into the kitchen.

Michael and Cathi entered the already busy kitchen. Cathi smiled at everybody in the room, but then she came over to her friend.

"I have the best possible news, Maria. You'll never guess."

"Surprise me." She couldn't have sounded less interested.

Cathi, on the other hand was bursting with excitement. "We've made an offer on number sixteen, and they've accepted! We're going to be neighbors."

Chapter Twenty-Five
Bells and Balls

For Jessie, time seemed to speed up after Thanksgiving. Living with Noreen was great. She was a good-humored woman, who was full of stories from the old days. She liked to cook for the girls, and they in turn cleaned the house—well, Jessie did. Ely was more of a hindrance than a help, but she kept everybody laughing, so the others were happy to have her around.

It also meant Jessie could throw all her energy into her studies, because the end of year exams were looming. If she worked very hard, she didn't have to think about Dan. It was better not to dwell on what a fool she had been—again. Would she ever learn?

Ely seemed to have learned her lesson. Jessie still thought her friend spent too much time with Josh, but she had started to study. Life seemed calmer on Crystal Lake than it had been when they'd lived on campus. Perhaps it was Noreen's influence, or maybe it was the peace that seemed to surround the lake.

There was one area that troubled Jessie, however, and that was her new next-door neighbor. Maria Sanchez had cooled toward her. The babysitting had all but stopped after she'd found Orga, and Jessie had a pretty good idea why. She had recognized the look in Maria's eye. Maria didn't trust Rick Sanchez, and to a certain extent, Jessie felt responsible.

The disturbing truth was that there was something between Jessie and Rick. They hadn't done anything, but she knew the chemistry had changed. To deny it would be naive. They had become overly friendly between coffees and looking for the damn dog together. She didn't like to think about it, because she felt a bit guilty. That was the surest sign that her relationship with Rick had veered in the wrong direction.

Jessie was sitting at her desk in Noreen's house, trying to focus on external influences on the stability of a marriage under strain. That was what had made her mind wander in the first place. How could she study that and not think of Rick and Maria?

She hoped they would be okay. Rick was nice, and Jessie didn't want to hurt their marriage—even if it meant losing her job as their sitter. Jessie threw the pen down on the desk and pushed her chair back. It was time for a break.

She wandered downstairs and found Noreen and Ely in the kitchen. Noreen greeted her with her usual smile. "Hello, love. It's good to see you taking a rest."

"Hi, Noreen," Jessie said, and then she addressed her friend. "How's the studying going?"

Ely groaned and buried her head in her arms at the kitchen table with ample melodrama.

It made Jessie laugh. She tousled Ely's long hair. "Come on, it can't be that bad. It's only your first year, and all of your written papers are excellent. I should know."

"It's not that." Ely brought her head back up. "I feel rotten, and I didn't even stay out late last night."

"Didn't you? I thought I heard your rendition of 'Santa Baby' at around three this morning in the upstairs hall, or maybe that was Noreen?"

The older woman laughed. "Oh, I hope I was tucked up safe at three o'clock this morning, but there was one Christmas party here—in the early seventies. I remember some of the boys trying to ski off the roof. Crazy, now that I think about it."

Ely's eyes brightened. "Why don't we have parties like that anymore?"

But then Jessie saw her wince in pain. "You really are in trouble, aren't you? Do you want a tablet or a doctor?"

Ely shook her head. "No, I just need my bed. I don't think eggnog agrees with me."

Noreen shuffled over to her great big range and turned on one of the back rings. "I'll get to work and we can all have hot chocolate."

Jessie got the milk from the fridge and gave it to Noreen. "You make the best drinking chocolate I've ever tasted." She had grown very fond of Noreen in the three weeks since they had moved in.

"Greg brought over a Christmas tree this afternoon. It's not a big one, but I thought you girls could help me decorate it this evening?"

Ely flopped her head back down onto her arms again and groaned, while Jessie thought about the mountain of work on her desk, but she also saw the hopeful look on Noreen's face.

"We'd love to," she said.

Noreen hadn't been exaggerating when she'd said it was a small tree. It was three feet tall. Jessie thought about Greg choosing the tree for his mom.

Why would she want an enormous tree anymore? Big trees were for big families. This was perfect for them—three feet for three people.

"I'm afraid I have far too many decorations," she said when Jessie came up from the basement with yet another box.

"You do seem to have more than Macy's." Ely was lying on the sofa watching them do all the work. She had said she wasn't able to help and they believed her. She was as white as the snow outside.

"Well, there was a time when we had a huge tree. One year I think we even had two. I don't want a big thing anymore, but I still have all these decorations."

"You could give some away," Jessie said. "Maybe your son across the road would like a few."

Noreen remained silent but nodded like she was mulling it over. Rusty started to run in circles.

"Jessie, be a dear and let the dog out," Noreen said, keeping her eyes on the little tree. "Ely, do we have enough lights?"

Ely groaned, which made Jessie laugh. "Girl, you're a terrible patient."

She opened the front door to let Rusty out, but the air was so still and the night so peaceful, Jessie decided to step out for a moment. It was great to breathe the chilled air after so much time cooped up in her room studying. Snow clearers had shoveled the excess powder off the stoop and walkway, so it was safe to venture down the path now. Jessie folded her arms around herself to keep warm and stared up at the night sky. It was the blackest Jessie had ever seen, and there were tiny stars scattered everywhere. *Funny,* she thought, *it really does look different to the night skies in England.*

"Pretty, isn't it?"

Jessie spun around. "Holy crack, you scared me!"

Bruce laughed. "I seem to be good at that. Did you say 'holy crack'?"

"Yes, it's a family expression. When one of the boys was small, they used to say 'holy crack.' I think he meant to say 'holy crap' but got it wrong. Anyway, we kind of adopted it as a family phrase."

He smiled. "Nice, and sorry I keep scaring you. This is just like the time down by the lake."

"It is a bit creepy," she said in jest. Then she brightened. "Tell you what —let's start again. Hi, Bruce."

"Hullo, Jessie. Out with the dog?"

"Just letting him do his business. What are you up to?"

"I have a dog back in London, and I miss our evening walks." He grinned and looked a little bashful. It was cute. "So now that I'm here, I still take the walks, only without the dog."

"I thought you lived here."

"Just for a couple of months. I'm getting some business straightened out."

Jessie was intrigued. He still didn't seem too miserable. "I'm sure Noreen would let you walk Rusty if you wanted to borrow her dog. None of us really walk him, and he's getting a bit chunky. It would do him good."

Bruce laughed and called the bulldog over with a very good whistle. He hunkered down and tickled Rusty's ears. "Hey, boy, how are you? You're not chunky—that's just your build."

She could see that Rusty liked him. "Look, why don't you come in and meet Noreen. I'm sure she'd let you take the dog for your evening walks."

He stood up again. "Noreen Palmer? Wow, she's still alive and well? I haven't seen her in years. I'd love to say hi."

They headed back in with Rusty running ahead and barking to announce their arrival.

The blast of heat welcomed Jessie after the chill of the New England night. "Noreen, I've brought one of your neighbors in. You remember Bruce Wiswall, don't you?"

Noreen looked up from where she was kneeling beside her Christmas tree. "You're not Bruce," she said with indignation. "Are you trying to confuse me?"

He smiled as if he was used to this accusation. "Um, I am actually, but I think you might know my grandfather better."

"Miserable Bruce was your grandfather? How is the old man?"

"He passed away in October."

"Oh, I'm sorry to hear that." Noreen stood up. "He was a good man, even if he was an old curmudgeon."

Jessie was uncomfortable with Noreen's comments, but it didn't seem to bother Bruce.

"Yep, that seems to be the general consensus. He was a good man, but a bloody miserable one."

Ely sat up, clasping her stomach. "I think I'm gonna hurl," she said and ran for the bathroom.

"Have you met Ely?" Noreen asked.

"I have now," he said and grimaced at her discomfort.

"You're not at all like your grandfather, are you?" Noreen came closer to study his face. "Although you do look very like him."

"So I've been told. If I wear his flat cap, I gather I'm his double. You know, I met you years ago, but I doubt you'd remember. I was a nipper, just a kid."

"How do you remember that long ago?"

He shrugged. "You know the way some childhood memories just get locked in. I think Crystal Lake Lane must have made an impact on me."

"I forget everything these days. I wouldn't take it personally, son, and in my defense, I'm sure you've changed quite a bit since we last met."

He smiled and nodded, so Noreen continued. "You've moved into the house. Isn't it a bit large for you? Hasn't your grandfather been away for years?"

Bruce glanced to Jessie. "Yes, my grandfather was in a nursing home for the last few years. The house is going to be sold, but the family sent me over to go through it and sort out the legal work."

"You're a lawyer?"

"Yes."

"What a nice boy you are. Jessie here is single, you know."

"Is she now?" Bruce grinned.

She felt herself blush. "Noreen! I'm not single."

"Oh?"

"Well, I mean." She didn't know what she meant. "You can't just say things like that."

"Yes, I can. I'm old. I don't beat about the bush." She shrugged and then turned her attention back to her male guest. "Would you like a glass of wine?"

"Thank you, Noreen. I think that would be very nice."

Jessie could tell he was enjoying Noreen's old-fashioned interrogation. Perhaps having Miserable Bruce as a grandfather had toughened him up a bit.

Not her. Jessie was still too easily embarrassed. "I'm going to check on Ely," she said and fled the room.

When Jessie found her, Ely was in a bad way. She had made it to the bathroom just in time, so Jessie stood behind and pulled her friend's hair back from her face. Then she took out her own clasp and clipped back Ely's hair.

"Looks like you've got a bad stomach virus." Jessie crouched down beside her.

Ely gave her a miserable look.

"Should I ring Josh? I know he's no doctor, but he might make you feel better."

"You think?" Ely said.

Before Jessie could respond, Ely retched again, so she put her arm around her friend's shoulders.

"Ely, poor honey. There's no chance you're pregnant, is there?" Jessie said with a laugh. She didn't think it was a possibility. Her friend had more sense.

"There's every chance."

"What?"

Ely sat on the floor next to the toilet basin.

"I don't believe it," Jessie said, pulling back from her friend in shock.

"Believe."

"Ely, we have to get a test. You have to find out for sure."

"I've done the test. I do know for sure."

"What? When? Why didn't you tell me?"

"I'm telling you now. I did it last night, and then I went out and got drunker than I think I've ever been in my life." She rested her cheek on her hand, on the rim of the toilet basin. Jessie winced and made a mental note to clean the bathrooms even more thoroughly as soon as she got a chance.

"Oh my God, Ely, you're pregnant! You have to stop drinking. Does Josh know?" Jessie sat back against the other wall.

"Who do you think got me into this mess?"

"Yes, but that doesn't mean he knows. Have you told him?"

"He suspected last week. He said he could see it in my eyes even before I did the test. He says it's the same with mares. He can tell."

"Jesus, he compared you to one of his horses? Smooth talker," Jessie said. "How many weeks pregnant are you?"

"I remember having a period around Halloween, so I guess I'm about seven weeks along. I haven't gone to a doctor yet."

Ely had stopped retching.

"Can I help you up to bed?" Jessica asked.

She shook her head. "I'm not tired. I slept all morning." She pushed back from the toilet rim, which made Jessie a bit more comfortable. "It's just all this damn nausea. I think I'm gonna puke almost all the time."

"You poor pet. But hey, congratulations—I think. Have you thought about what you're going to do?"

Ely covered her face with her hands. "Before or after my father kills me?"

Jessie scooched along the floor and took her friend in her arms. "Shh, I know it's scary, but you know it's going to be okay. At least you and Josh love each other. This will work out."

Ely pulled back. "Yeah, I love him, but I hadn't settled on spending my life with him. Okay, it was a possibility, but jeez, I'm twenty-three. I'm too young to be thinking about settling down."

There was a knock on the bathroom door.

"Is everything okay in there?" Noreen said from the other side. "Bruce and I have decided to have a glass of mulled wine to welcome my little Christmas tree into the house. Will you join us?"

Ely gave a panicky look and covered her mouth, like she was going to be ill again, so Jessie spoke. "That sounds great. I'll be there in just a moment, but I think I'll get Ely to bed first."

Despite the protests she wasn't tired, Ely was content to hide in her room, saying she didn't want to see a glass of red wine—much less mulled with herbs and oranges. Jessie gave her own hair a quick brush because she had lost her clasp and headed back down to Bruce and Noreen.

It was a relief to know he wasn't Miserable Bruce after all, even if it meant Mr. Miserable had gone to his great reward. He seemed so nice, but she was still embarrassed by Noreen's blundering attempts at matchmaking. Bruce could be married, for all anyone knew. Once bitten, twice shy. She was off men for the foreseeable future.

"Sorry about that," she said with a forced smile when she got back to them.

Bruce and Noreen were standing in front of a rekindled fire and drinking mulled wine, admiring the little Christmas tree. Its twinkling lights flickered rhythmically.

"Oh, this is nice," Jessie said. "Very festive."

Bruce handed her a warm glass and gave her a warmer smile.

"Tell me, Jessie, is there a town called Epsom anywhere near your mother's home?" Noreen asked.

"Yes, I know it well. It's quite close to where I live." She took a sip. It had been years since she'd had mulled wine. It was warm and sweet—very pleasant, even more so with the snow piled high outside. All they needed now was George Michael's "Last Christmas" crooning in the background. Jessie smiled to herself. Noreen's taste for music and musicians was a little older than George.

"I work in Epsom," Bruce said.

"Oh, I live in Dorking. Funny that we meet all the way over here."

"Funny, indeed." Noreen looked from one to the other. At that moment her eyes were Crystal Lake clear, and Jessie knew she wasn't missing a thing. Rusty started to bark again and headed for the door.

"Do you think he needs another visit to the great outdoors?" Jessie said, eager to move the conversation along, but then the doorbell rang.

"Clever dog." Bruce crouched down, and Rusty came running back to him.

"I think my dog likes you," Noreen said.

"That's why I brought Bruce in to meet you. He'll walk Rusty if you want," Jessie said, but her landlady had left the room to answer the door and was out of earshot.

"She's quite a force of nature," Bruce whispered when it looked like Noreen couldn't hear them.

"I'm sorry if she embarrassed you. She's a bit eccentric."

He looked surprised. "Me? I'm all right, gov." He used a London Town-East End accent. "I thought it was you who was feeling the heat."

"Me? Why should I?"

They stopped talking because Noreen was back, with Cathi Grant in tow. Jessie had only met her twice, once in this very room and once in Maria's kitchen, but already she didn't like the woman.

Noreen did the introductions. Bruce smiled and gave her a slight nod.

"Hello." Cathi was polite, but her focus was Jessie. "It's you I came to see. Well, you and your friend who lives here. I was wondering if you girls could help me with a holiday party I want to throw. The thing is, it's a bit rushed now with the holidays coming in so fast, and all the caterers I've called are booked. I need people to serve drinks and small plates of food. Would you be interested?"

Jessie was thrilled. With all of her sitter's work disappearing, she needed extra cash. "Yes, I'd love to." Then she thought of her friend in bed upstairs. "But I don't think Ely can. She's not well."

"Oh dear." Cathi looked disappointed for a moment, but then she eyed up Bruce. "What about you? Would you help Jessie? You look like you could work behind a bar, no problem."

Jessie watched Bruce suppress his smile. She guessed it had been a while since he'd done bar work, although he still looked young enough.

"I'd be delighted to help," he said.

Cathi's eyes brightened. "Your accent—are you British, too?"

He smiled warmly. "Yup."

Cathi looked smitten. "This is neat—very international. It won't be a big party. I'm just doing a sort of get-to-know-your-neighbors thing because we've only just moved in. I haven't even come up with a theme yet, and it's next Saturday."

"You could do the ever popular bells and balls party?" Noreen said.

Cathi looked at her. "What?"

"You know, festive holiday bells and decorative balls you hang on your tree?" Jessie said.

"Oh, I see. Yes, well, I'll have to think about that. See you both next Saturday, then, around six?"

Noreen walked Cathi back out to the door. "I didn't mean festive bells and balls at all," she said when she returned. "I was talking about Southern belles, and balls referred to the men in the room." She said it with such an angelic smile it was impossible not to laugh.

"Your reputation for wild parties is legendary, Mrs. Palmer," Bruce said. "My grandfather told me all about them."

"Did he now?" Her eyes twinkled. "Well, I get the feeling Cathi Grant's holiday party will be a much more sophisticated affair."

Chapter Twenty-Six
The Same Only Different

"It's going to be a sophisticated affair." Cathi gushed when she called at Maria's house just after Noreen's.

"But of course." Maria didn't even try to feign enthusiasm. She was too tired, and she was fed up hearing about Cathi's fabulous life. Maria set a mug of coffee down in front of her friend.

"Coffee? They're having mulled wine next door."

"You wanna go back there?"

"No. Sorry. Coffee's great. So put my party in your diary for next week—big night at my house."

"Your house? You bought it now?"

"No, Maria, what's wrong with you? I haven't bought it, but I'm renting, so it's mine for now."

"Whatever you say. Want me to bring something?"

"Just yourself and your fabulous husband," Cathi said and smiled.

Maria collapsed onto one of the kitchen chairs at her table. "Believe me, he's not so fabulous."

"Oh, honey, are you two still arguing? Can't you get past it? Have you thought about counseling?"

"You need to be talking to each other to manage counseling. All we're doing is screaming at each other."

Cathi sat down next to her friend. "Maria, this is nuts. You guys were so good together. You have to talk."

Maria looked down to her kitchen floor. It needed to be mopped again. "We've tried. Every time we talk, we end up fighting. It's exhausting. Even Cody knows about it at this stage. I can see it's wearing him down. Alice has probably picked up on it, too. You know, there comes a time when I think it's better to just walk away while there's still some civility there."

Cathi put her hand to her mouth. "Oh, Maria. I had no idea you were in this much trouble. Can I help? Can I do anything?"

Maria wrapped her hands around her big mug of coffee. "You? You should be resting, *chica*. You know you shouldn't be throwing this crazy party. No disrespect, but we're not as young as we used to be. Having a baby at forty-one means you should be taking it easy."

"Oh, don't worry about that." Cathi waved her hand in the air.

Maria looked at her friend. She was acting strangely for a woman in her condition.

"How come you're so calm about this baby? Why aren't you freaking out?"

Cathi squirmed in the seat and looked around. "It's a long story, but don't worry, everything's fine."

"Are you in denial? What's up?"

Again Cathi looked around. "Where's Rick?"

"He took Cody and Todd to the movies, and Alice is in bed. It's just you and me. Spill."

Cathi studied her mug like she was trying to weigh up the situation. Then she spoke. "Well, here's the thing. I'm not pregnant." She smiled. "I don't know how this crazy misunderstanding came about." She shook her head and looked bewildered. "Michael somehow decided I was pregnant, and then he blurted it out over Thanksgiving dinner in front of Rick. Well, I was stunned, and I don't even know why—I just told him he was right."

Maria stood up. "You what? You're not pregnant? Are you stark raving mad? You have to tell him."

Cathi stood up then. "I will, I will. He just seems so happy. I didn't want to disappoint him. I don't even know how I got into this insane situation."

"I do. You admitted to being pregnant when you weren't. You do know that's certifiably insane, right? How are you going to tell Michael now? He'll be crushed. He was so happy about it, Cathi."

She came over and took Maria's hands in hers. "It's not that bad. I'll have to fake a miscarriage—probably at my next period."

Maria pulled her hands back. "What? Now you're going to fake a miscarriage? Cathi, you should hear yourself. You can't go around faking everything."

"Why not?" Cathi grinned. "You and I have laughed about faking orgasms in the past. We've sure faked interest in our husbands' business lives for years. Anything we've done has always been with the best intent. This is the same—only different."

Maria went over and switched on the coffee machine again, just to have something to do. "There's a huge difference between pretending to be interested in a corporate publicity campaign and pretending to miscarry a baby—and don't get me started on the pretending to be pregnant in the first place. *Chica*, you've so abused Michael's trust. Do you hear me?"

Cathi raised her hands in the air. "Honey, you're way overreacting. First off, I didn't start this ball in motion. He did. He was snooping through my stuff and came up with this crazy idea. I just went along with it, and I have to tell you, it made him very happy. Now I'm afraid the game will have to end, because I can't just produce a baby out of thin air. I know he'll be sad for a while, but after, he'll be himself again. Look, I managed to convince him to sell our old house, and I'm living on Crystal Lake Lane, just like I always wanted."

Maria felt sick. Was her friend that delusional? "But at what cost, Cathi? You've manipulated Michael so badly—all to your own ends. He made this house move in good faith. You have to tell him."

Cathi stomped her foot. "Oh my God, will you lighten up? I'll tell him. It's not that big of a deal. Women have miscarriages all the time. If anything, he's been more attentive to me over the last month than over the last year. I will tell him and we'll get over it together."

"Together? Get over what? Cathi, there is no baby! You're not pregnant!"

Cathi looked around her nervously. "Can you keep your voice down? Let me handle it. I shouldn't have told you."

"No you shouldn't have, because I have to tell you, I feel obliged to tell Michael."

"What?"

"You heard me. If you don't tell Michael, I will."

"You wouldn't."

"I would, and I swear I'll do it if you don't. This is so wrong."

"Wrong? Where do you get off talking to me about wrong?"

Cathi balled her hands into fists, and for a moment Maria thought her friend would punch her.

"You deserted your husband for Thanksgiving. You ran off with the kids with no note or warning. You just took off while he was working all those hours. That man tries so hard to give you all the best things in life and what do you do?" She raised her voice. "You run away to the sun and to Mommy. You're so ungrateful." Cathi looked around her like she was looking for answers.

"And you have the nerve to talk to me about good communication? At least Michael and I are happy together. We have a good marriage. Okay, I have this one little situation—not of my making, I might add—but our marriage is good. You, on the other hand? You're sabotaging yours, and why? What has Rick done wrong? He works!"

Cathi stopped at this point and took a few deep breaths.

Maria was dead calm when she spoke. "I think you better go now, Cathi."

"Yes, I think I'll leave. But don't you dare come anywhere near my husband. This is none of your business."

"Maybe not, but it sure is his. Tell him."

"I will, but in my way."

Cathi ran out of the house. Maria sat down again, drained from the interaction.

"What a mess," she said to herself. Okay, she was having problems, real problems with her marriage, but at least they were honest with each other—

as far as she knew, anyway. Had Cathi really lost all sense of decency? Didn't she see how wrong this was?

But Maria wondered if she was overreacting. Maybe sticking her nose into Cathi's marriage was a step too far, but somebody had to tell Michael. He was making all of their life decisions with the understanding there was another little Grant on the way, and in reality there wasn't. How horrible was that?

There was one thing she was pretty sure about—she wasn't going to make the invite list to Cathi's party.

Maria took a sip of her coffee, but it was cold. She really wanted wine anyway. Coffee wasn't as good at dulling the edges of the day, and her problems didn't seem so bad when she'd had a glass or two. Maria hauled her sorry self out of the chair and washed out the two mugs of coffee into the sink. She put them in the dishwasher and got herself a large glass of white wine instead. Just as she was leaving the kitchen, she caught sight of her reflection in the window.

"What the hell?" She was speaking to an empty room. How had a glass of wine ended up in her hand? Again?

The night before, she had single-handedly drunk a full bottle of wine, and so when she had woken with a hangover that morning, she'd promised herself no more drink for a while. Yet here she was holding a glass of wine —again. She rushed to the sink before she could stop herself and poured it down after the coffee.

"No," she said aloud. "I don't need this." She was shaking a little. What the hell was going on? Was she going to have to add alcoholism to her list of problems?

"Michael, I think I have a problem," Cathi said as soon as she got back into the house. "I have the most terrible cramps." She didn't think about what she was saying. She just had to get through this fast.

Michael was up and on his feet. "Do you think it's serious? Do you want me to take you to the hospital?" He wrapped a loving arm around her.

"Oh no, I just need to go to bed. Can you make sure the girls are ready for school tomorrow? It's finals this week. Don't let them stay up too late."

"They're my children, too, you know. I can manage them. It's you I'm worried about. Should I call the doctor?"

That made her more nervous than anything. She could fake a miscarriage with Michael, but not in a hospital environment. Without proper management, this could be trickier than she'd first thought.

"Please stop fussing," she said. "I just need to rest. Put Fifi out before you come to bed."

"Sure," he said as he walked with her to the stairs. "Did you get that young girl to help us next weekend?"

Cathi's face brightened. "Oh yes, and she has a nice male friend. He's going to work the bar. Her college friend can't help. She's ill or something."

"I hope you weren't exposed to some virus in their house."

"No, I don't think so. I didn't even see her. Anyway, we know why my stomach is upset. I very much doubt that young girl has the same problem," she said with a smile and started to mount the stairs of her new house.

"Did you visit Maria and Rick?"

Cathi stopped. "You know, I'm worried about those two. Maria was there, but she seemed so depressed. I think their marriage might really be in trouble."

"No way."

"Way. It might be a good idea if we give them space, just while they figure things out." She tried to look concerned. "Okay, I'm off to bed. See you soon."

"Watch that tummy for me. It's very precious," he said as she reached the top of the stairs.

Cathi felt a real stab in her stomach, and she clutched it. She looked back at her husband and smiled. She knew the pain she felt was guilt—pure, unadulterated guilt. Cathi went into her new bedroom and lay down on her bed.

Maria had said some nasty things to her, and Cathi was pretty shook-up. The frustration was that those same things had been lingering at the back of her mind since Thanksgiving, but Cathi had been very good at suppressing them up until now. Ignoring her conscience was difficult but countered by Michael's adorable affection. It had gotten easier to lie to him because he was so wrapped up in the pregnancy. Who knew he wanted another baby? They were done, as far as she was concerned, but when he'd asked her that day—with such hope in his eyes—it had been easier to say yes than no.

Then, of course, there were all the fringe benefits. She had managed to talk him into selling their old house and even renting this one. She had no idea how they were going to afford to buy it, but the market was still very shaky. Maybe she would get lucky.

Her conversation with Maria, though annoying, had served to remind her how imperative it was she end this little white lie with her husband. Okay, it was true she had manipulated her husband, but what woman didn't? Everything in marriage was a manipulation, whether it was deciding who put the trash out or where they were going to live. Cathi's situation was a little more complex than most. She wasn't going to hurt anybody. Yes, Michael was working under the illusion the family was growing, but it could be true. Just because she hadn't got pregnant didn't mean she couldn't.

More and more women were getting pregnant in their forties. Michael had brought up that delicate subject just the week before. Cathi had her story straight, though. She'd lied and said her IUD had to be taken out because it was due to be changed. Then she had to wait a month before the new one could be inserted. That was when she'd gotten pregnant. She'd read in a magazine about that happening to a woman, so she knew it was plausible.

He had accepted the lie, but now she was going to have to pull off the biggest fib of her marriage. She was going to have to fake a miscarriage during her next period. She hadn't thought about him dragging her to the hospital. That would never work. The doctors would know the difference between a miscarriage and a period—wouldn't they?

Cathi had to find a way to get him out of the house—preferably away from Newton for a few days. Then she could say it happened while he was gone. That would be much safer. She pulled her knees up and curled into the fetal position. If she couldn't get him away, maybe she would leave. She could visit New York for a shopping weekend and pretend she miscarried while she was there.

There was a soft knock on the door. "I brought you a glass of milk," Michael said when he walked in. "And a cookie. I figured you might need the sugar." He looked so anxious. "You sure you're feeling all right? Who's your doctor? I should know these things."

Cathi sat up in the bed. "Oh, you're fussing." She smiled. "I'm feeling better already. I'm just tired. It's all normal, so stop worrying. Really, I've never been healthier." Well, at least that part wasn't a lie. She was healthy. *Darn,* she thought, was she going to have to fake a doctor, too?

When Rick got home from the movies with Cody and Todd, he was glad to go to his neighbor's house for a beer. Anything was better than being at home and trying to avoid his wife. Todd's parents, Greg and Michelle Palmer, were nice people. They were a little older than Rick and Maria, so for some reason they had never really gotten too close, but beer was beer.

"How's your mom doing with her two new tenants?" Rick asked Greg.

Greg laughed. "Funny, I've been asking her for years to get tenants, and she's ignored me. Then this little English gal saunters in and it's a done deal. Do you know her well? Cody told me that she's Alice's sitter."

Rick took a swig of beer from the bottle and nodded. "I think that's how she met Noreen. It was the night of the toasting. Then they met a few more times. Jessie seems like a nice kid. She'll be good to your mom."

Greg looked relieved. "Just in the nick of time. I gotta tell you, Rick— Mom is getting more and more forgetful. It's really concerning. I'm thrilled the girls are there. Don't know what I'll do when they've finished college."

"I think they're here until the summer. You'll have to find new students after that."

"Darn. I'd hoped we might have them for a couple of years."

"I wouldn't worry too much. Things are changing all the time. I bet somebody else will turn up. Have you met the new neighbors yet? The Grants? I know Michael pretty well. We're friends."

"Did they buy number sixteen?"

Rick shook his head. "Nah, they're renting. I think that price is too high."

"Hey, I'm not complaining if it's expensive. That's great news for us. If I got Mom to sell, she could have her pick of retirement homes or assisted living places."

Rick winced. "I'm not sure she's ready for the long jump just yet, buddy. She seems so independent."

Michelle, Greg's wife, walked into the room. "And therein is the problem. Good to see you, neighbor," she said with a smile. "So no more toasting emergencies lately?"

He smiled. "No more of those, thank you very much."

"Did I hear you talking about the new neighbors? I met her this afternoon, and she invited me to a party there next Saturday."

"Cathi?"

Greg nodded. "That's it—Cathi. She knocked on the front door, introduced herself, and invited us over next Saturday."

"Oh, that'd be Cathi all right. She's a real doer. I hadn't heard about the party yet."

Greg gave him a lopsided grin. "Maybe you haven't been invited."

Ricky took another swig of beer. "Ha, see that's where you're wrong. I know Cathi, and I can tell you now, she'll invite everybody on the street. That's how she rolls—a supreme networker. I'm telling you, before the end of the year she'll know everybody on this road better than you and me."

"Did you see there's a guy living in the old Wiswall place?"

"Yeah, he found our dog for us a few weeks ago. It's old man Wiswall's grandson. Did you hear the old man died?"

Greg shook his head. "He was a private sort of guy. Never really knew him."

"The grandson seems a lot friendlier."

"Good. We need some new blood in the neighborhood," Michelle said. "Rick, would you like to stay for something to eat?"

He wanted to, but shook his head. "Thanks, Michelle, but Cody has school in the morning. I better get him home and into bed."

"Maria will be worrying," Greg said.

If only, Rick thought. *If only.*

Chapter Twenty-Seven
Botox and Bollinger

Another week whizzed by, and with only a few days to Christmas, Rick's workload seemed to be diminishing. He looked around his office at three o'clock and was stunned to see he was the only one left. Okay, it was a Saturday and nobody should have been in anyway, but the agency had ramped up to a seven-days-a-week workplace months ago with no sign of abatement until today.

"Bah humbug," he said to himself as he left the office.

He hadn't given any thought to buying Maria a present. What was the point? They weren't even speaking, so a present was way down on his list of priorities. Then for some reason he thought about his mother. If she were alive, she'd smack him. It was Christmas. He should buy his wife the biggest, brightest thing he could afford and maybe manage to end this stupid fight. Rick was driving out of Boston on Route 9 when an ad came on the radio for Bloomingdale's in Chestnut Hill. It claimed to have one of the finest fur vaults in New England. It was right on his path home. Rick could get something very nice in there that would melt even the coldest heart.

It didn't take him long to get talked into a magnificent full-length chestnut brown fur. He had no idea what animal it came from, but he felt skinned alive when his credit card was processed for the purchase. Who knew a garment could cost so much? Rick didn't let himself think about the cost. He was working damn hard, and his year-end bonus was one of the benefits. Maybe if he blew the whole thing on Maria, she would forgive him for the hours he worked.

"I know it's a little early, but Merry Christmas," he said to her as soon as he got home. It was the first full sentence between them in weeks.

She looked stunned. "Ricky? It's not even Christmas yet."

He smiled. "I know, but open it anyway. If you don't like it you can exchange it."

She didn't need to be asked twice. He knew she'd already spotted the big Bloomingdale's bag. That was enough to brighten any woman's day.

"Oh, Ricky." She stared at him, wide-eyed with excitement, as she unfolded the white tissue paper inside the box.

"You like?"

"I love."

"I love, too," he said looking into her eyes.

Maria put the fur down and reached for her husband. He hugged her tight and wouldn't let her go. It felt like coming home, and he thought he might cry. The fight had been bad, their worst ever. Six weeks of fighting was insane.

"Oh, God, I've missed you," he whispered into her ear.

"I've missed you, too. What the hell went wrong?"

"I don't know, but I don't want it to happen again, please, Maria. I love you. I don't want to lose you."

She squeezed him just as tight. "Nor I you."

Just then Cody ran into the room and saw his parents wrapped around each other. He slapped his forehead. "Aw man, get a room," he said, making them laugh.

"Sounds like an idea." Rick said it too quietly for his son to hear, but Maria did.

She winked at him and mouthed one word. "Later."

They agreed to order pizzas, and Ricky insisted they open a bottle of champagne because it was the weekend before Christmas. Cody was on Christmas break from school, and Alice was in great form because she had already opened her first present—a plastic school bus with lights and buttons that spun and flashed.

"What more could a girl want?" Rick said.

"A full-length fur?" Maria winked.

That evening, Rick was snuggled on the sofa with Maria as they watched television with Cody and Alice. It was pretty obvious they didn't want to go to Cathi's housewarming party. The invitation had arrived a few days before and was sitting on the mantelpiece staring at both of them. Ricky said that Michael had begged him to come early.

"I'm not sure I'm even invited," Maria said.

He pulled back from her and looked at his wife. "Why would you say that? You're Cathi's best friend."

"Not anymore. We had an argument last week." She sounded unsure of herself.

"Whoa, you were fighting with her, too?" Ricky was teasing, but he saw the look of impatience flash across Maria's face. They were still on shaky ground—it wasn't a good idea to stir things up.

Maria sat upright on the sofa. "Look, it's a long story, and I don't think I should tell you but she's . . . she's being very unfair to Michael."

Cody looked at his parents. It was obvious he was listening, and Maria stopped talking. Rick put his arm around his wife and pulled her back onto the sofa again.

"Don't worry about it. She's been moving house, getting ready for a big party—all of this on top of being pregnant. It's too much. Forget about your argument. It'll all blow over. But we have to go to the party, babe. Not going would be rude. We don't have to stay long."

She sank deeper into the sofa and into him, and he didn't want to move either.

"Here, drink some more champagne and you'll feel better. Who's sitting for the kids?"

"Ely, from next door. Noreen is going to the party, and Jessie has been roped in to help with the catering. That's another thing I'm fed up with. She stole my sitter."

Ricky laughed. "You don't own Jessie, and Ely is a lovely girl, too. Cody will be old enough in a few more years. Hey, how about that?"

Cody thumped his fist in the air. He was still listening to them. Ricky felt a jolt of guilt. His son was watching every move they made, maybe scared they would fight again.

Maria pulled away and stood up. "Okay, in that case, I better go freshen up and call to confirm with Ely. I told her it was a provisional booking because I didn't know if I was going to go, but I think you're right. We should make the effort—but not for long, okay?"

"Okay." He looked at his wife and gave a little smirk. He liked the idea of getting home early with his wife, and they both knew why.

Cathi was putting the finishing touches to her makeup when her daughter shouted up the stairs at her. "Mom, the salon lady is here."

Cathi called down from the bedroom door. "Bring her into the study to set up. I'll be down in a minute." One of the disadvantages of a larger house was the need to shout just to be heard, and then of course, annoyingly, everybody else heard, too.

Michael walked into their bedroom. "A stylist? Aren't you leaving it a bit late to get pampered, honey? People will be arriving any minute." He winked at her playfully.

"I told you about this, Michael. She's here as entertainment for the party. It's Botox at all the best parties these days."

"She's dishing out Botox? You can't be serious!" He put his hands to his head in horror.

"Only to those who want it, dear. She's a registered aesthetician. It's all above board and legal—more than I can say for the cocaine years of the nineties."

"We never went to one of those parties." He held himself a little higher, indignant.

She was facing the mirror but glanced back to him. "Didn't you?"

"Cathi, this is insane. We agreed that this was just a get-together for a few Newton neighbors to celebrate the holidays. But Botox? Come on!"

She stomped her foot and glared at him in annoyance. "No, Michael, we talked about it. You approved it. Remember? I said it would nice if we presented the neighbors with some sort of festive gift."

"Yes, and I suggested mistletoe."

"That's right, and then I laughed and said, 'How about a Botox and Bollinger party?' "

Michael's face looked blank. "Did you say that? Well, if you did, I didn't hear you. We're certainly not serving Bollinger are we?"

She didn't answer but gave him a guilty look.

"Oh God, you've got to be kidding me. We're serving Bollinger champagne? Do you know how much that stuff costs? It's the most expensive champagne there is!"

"I got it at Costco."

Michael ran his hands through his hair, something he only did when he was very stressed. Cathi noted it was getting grayer. She would have to deal with that in the New Year. He stormed out of the room, and she heard him bounding down the stairs—maybe heading to where Jessie and Bruce were setting up.

Cathi checked her reflection in her full-length mirror again. She knew her Botox and Bollinger conversation with Michael earlier in the week had gone too well. She'd thought he understood what she wanted to do, but it was pretty clear this evening he hadn't. Perhaps he had thought she was joking. Well, now he knew otherwise. This was going to be the biggest and best party of the holiday season on the best road in Newton.

She had done it. She made it to the top of the Boston social totem pole. Now that she was here, all she had to do was throw a fabulous party and her name would be in society columns before she could say *VIP*. She knew she could do it. She had never doubted it. The problem was finding the budget and convincing her husband to live the high life with her. Michael was a bit more discreet than she was—silly old man. She would show him. Once they got a reputation as big players, he would suddenly start to get invitations to big-ticket events. Next would come top-tier networking. Who knew where it might end? He could get asked to be on various boards of directors, and they would end up rubbing shoulders with sports celebrities. The sky was the limit, and she was getting them there. Everybody knew Boston was where the big business deals went down in America.

She studied her reflection. Her hair had been highlighted just a little more than usual. She wore a black sheath dress that was very flattering on her slim form. She had bought it new for the party, and it was the most expensive dress she had ever bought, but what choice did she have? If she wanted to play with the big boys, she had to dress the part. Pity she couldn't convince Michael to revamp his wardrobe. That would come, she assured herself, as soon as he began to see the fruits of her labor.

"Cathi," Michael called from downstairs.

"Damn," she said. He sounded angry, but she didn't know which he was more annoyed about—the Botox or the Bollinger. A quick visit to the toilet and then she would find him, to calm him down. Cathi glanced at her watch and wondered if she could manage a quick romantic interlude before the guests arrived. That always worked when he was mad. Before she found him, however, she found out her period had arrived.

"Of all the times," she said to herself in the bathroom. "Now where did I hide all the tampons?"

Ely was still feeling pretty rotten. The nausea was gone, which was a huge relief, but she couldn't believe how exhausted she was. There was no way she would have accepted a babysitting job if it hadn't been for Jessie. Jessie had begged her to say yes. She said if Maria got a new sitter she would lose her future jobs in the Sanchez household, and that was why Ely was trekking her way through the snow to the next-door neighbor's house to babysit two little brats. Could life be any worse?

Cody, the boy, answered the door.

"You're not Jessie," he said.

"Go you, but no prize."

"Ely. Hi, come on in." Rick Sanchez was a bit more welcoming. "Do you play Xbox?"

"No, but maybe Cody can show me." Ely tried to make a bit of an effort, even though all she wanted to do was sleep.

Maria arrived next, looking amazing. She was wearing a figure-hugging, scarlet-red dress. The plunging V-neck highlighted her stunning hourglass figure, and her hair bounced around her shoulders in big soft curls. "Wow, Mrs. Sanchez, you look terrific."

"Thanks." Maria did a twirl and winked at her husband. There was serious chemistry between the two of them. It was hard not to think about herself and Josh. Not a lot going on there these days.

"Jessie tells me you're good with babies." Maria needed reassurance, and Ely nodded just like Jessie told her. In fact, Jessie had said to call if there were any problems and she would run over. She was just down the road, and Jessie swore Alice was an easy baby.

"I have young cousins," Ely said with great authority. "I kept them amused for the entire Thanksgiving holiday." That much was true-*ish*.

Maria nodded. "It shouldn't be a problem. I put Alice down. She'll probably sleep all night. Just watch this guy for me, but he's promised to be on his best behavior."

Cody gave his mother a *you're embarrassing me* look.

"We'll be just dandy," Ely said.

Cody focused on Ely then. "You talk funny."

"So do you." She was in no mood for kids.

He switched on the television. "Can we rent a movie? We have pay-per-view."

"If it's age appropriate. Ely, make sure he doesn't rent anything unsuitable."

She nodded.

"Okay, we gotta go. You have our numbers if there's any problem, and you know we're at number sixteen," Rick said.

She nodded again. "Go have fun. We'll be fine."

Once they had left, Ely pulled out her phone. No new messages from Josh. *Damn*.

"How about *The Hangover 3*?" Cody said.

"What's the rating on it?"

He raised his hands to say he didn't know.

"What the heck? Just don't tell your folks. If they ask, you watched *The Smurfs*—deal?"

He gave her a fabulous smile. "Deal! I think you and me are gonna get along just fine." He spoke with an excellent put-on Southern drawl, which made Ely giggle. It felt good—she hadn't done much laughing in a while.

"Are you okay watching this for a bit? I need to make a call. I can do it in the kitchen."

"Sure." He was already pressing the necessary buttons to get the movie up and running.

Ely sat at the kitchen table and speed-dialed Josh's number.

He answered it on the first ring. "I got nothing to say to you."

She tried to humor him. "That's something."

"Ely, I don't want you even calling me. Not unless you've changed your mind. Have you?"

She couldn't answer. She so needed his support at this time, but he wouldn't help. He had all but left her.

"Please, Josh, don't be like this. We can get through it and come out the other side together."

"No way. What you're doin' is wrong—plain and simple. That's our baby you got in your belly. Yours and mine. I have every bit as much right to see him or her as you do. You can't just get rid of it."

Even though she was alone in the kitchen, she looked around to make sure nobody could hear. "But you have to understand my side of this. I'm the woman. It would finish my life. I'll end up working some deadbeat job with some kid I didn't want."

"I want it. I'll take it."

"You say that now, but we're too young, Josh. This is all too soon."

"I'm hanging up, Ely. I can't talk to you. If you change your mind, I can be there in three minutes, but I'm not standing by you if you're gonna have an abortion."

Tears rolled down Ely's cheeks. "I'm so alone. I need you."

"No, you don't. Seems like you don't need anybody. You're an ice queen, Ely. I told you I love you, and God help me I still do, and now you're carrying my baby . . . I agree it was a lot earlier than we planned, but damn it, we're not teenagers either. I'll be out of college in a few years. I'd even quit if you wanted me to—just to make money for us. But you? You got other plans that don't include our child. I can't be part of those plans."

She had heard it all before. This was where he asked her one more time to reconsider.

"Well?" he said right on cue.

"I can't," she said.

"Then we got nothing more to say." He hung up.

Ely listened to the dead line and let herself feel miserable. It hadn't been an easy decision. She abhorred the idea of an abortion. Who the heck wanted one? She had gone through hell deciding what to do but ultimately concluded she had no choice. Her life was over if a baby arrived. Of course it was a terrible thing to do, but she simply had no options. She hated herself for it, and now it looked like Josh did, too.

She didn't dare tell Jessie. They hadn't discussed it, but Ely knew Jessie would be dead against her plans. She'd never felt so alone or lost. The sooner she went through with it the better. Sometimes, just sometimes, she could pretend it wasn't happening or it was all a dream, but most of the time she was living in terror. If she had an abortion, she could put it behind her. She would lose Josh, but that was a price she had to pay.

Cody appeared in front of her. "You okay?"

She sniffed hard and rubbed her eyes with her sleeve. "Yeah, I'm fine. Allergies."

He didn't look convinced but accepted it. "Movie's started."

Ely tried to smile. "Great, I'll be right in. Just gotta make one more quick call. You start without me, okay?"

He studied her face and then nodded again, leaving her alone.

Ely pulled herself together. She knew she had no choice about calling her mother. Getting her on the cell instead of the house phone was smart, because Ely was still avoiding her father after the Thanksgiving speed bump. Her mom answered almost immediately. She always knew when it was her daughter phoning because of the caller ID.

"Honey, it's lovely to hear from you. I'm looking forward to seeing you tomorrow." Her mother sounded so good, so warm and reassuring—like hot chocolate.

"Oh, Mama, that's why I'm calling. I'm afraid I'm going to have to stay here a few more days. One of my tutors is giving me grief. He's not happy with my paper but says if I do it again, he'll grade the new one higher."

"Elyse, that's shameful. Can't you bring it home, write it here, and e-mail it back to him?"

Ely's mind moved fast. She thought one thing but said another. "All the reference books (*abortion clinics*) are here. I need the library (*doctor*). Don't worry (*I'm worried enough for two of us*), I'll fly home on Tuesday (*I'll desperately need you on Tuesday*)."

Her mother wasn't happy. "That's Christmas Eve. Must you stay so late?"

"Yep." She tried to sound like her normal self. "That's me—a regular little Santa Claus landing into your living room on Christmas Eve."

It worked. Margaret Briskin laughed. "You're all the present I want this holiday, darlin'."

Ely thought she might lose it again if she heard too much affection from her mom.

"Okay, gotta go. See you in a few days."

"I'll be at the airport to welcome you. Just text me your flight details."

Page 200

Chapter Twenty-Eight
Bring on the Fireworks

"You're so welcome," Cathi said, but Maria knew she didn't mean it. Her eyes always glazed over when she was being insincere, and right now they were as frosty as the sidewalk outside.

"Oh my God, is that mink? I haven't seen this before." She pawed one of the soft arms of Maria's new coat. "It's darling." Her eyes were pierced with clarity now but she sounded ridiculously pretentious.

"Just a little Christmas present from Rick," Maria said and slid her arms out of the coat. "Darling." Maria dropped the word at Cathi's feet like a snowball.

Rick stepped in to kiss the hostess on the cheek. "This is my first time in your new house, Cathi. Congrats. It looks amazing." Maria knew he was trying to smooth things over between the women. He was good at that.

"Thanks, Rick. I must say we're very happy here. There's so much space, the location is fabulous, as you know, and the views of the lake? Well, they just take my breath away."

Maria tried to suppress the annoyance she felt toward her friend. She sounded so fake, like she was playing a role. What the hell was she doing? This wasn't the Cathi that Maria knew and once loved.

"Katie and Stacy are doing tours if you're interested."

Ricky laughed. "Are they? Wow, you've thought of everything. I think I'll go find the bar first." Then he turned to Maria. "Honey, can I get you a drink?"

The doorbell chimed again, and Cathi moved on to her next performance.

Ricky slipped his hand into his wife's. "Sheesh, what's got into her?"

Maria was relieved he felt the same way. "I know, right? It's like she's swallowed a bowl of bullshit. She's pretending she's above the rest of us. What's with that?"

They walked through the house and into the enormous kitchen. Rick was scanning the place for familiar faces. "See anybody we know?"

"Not a one. Who are all these people?" Maria asked, looking around. Party music pulsed throughout the entire house.

Rick whispered into her ear. "These, honey, are what I'd call the *beautiful people*."

Maria kept looking. "Ah, that explains why everybody here is tanned and in perfect shape."

Rick nodded. "And that's just the guys."

Maria laughed. "It's like she rented a crowd from some Hollywood red carpet event."

"We should have known when we saw the Porsches and Ferraris parked along the street."

"This is so weird." Maria looked about. "We left the perfectly ordinary world of number seven, Crystal Lake Lane where everything felt normal—grumpy kid, messy kitchen—but now I feel like we've entered some sort of parallel universe. On this side of the road, everything is *darling*," Maria said, exaggerating the word.

Rick wrapped his arm around Maria's waist and guided her toward the bar. "Come on, let's get us some *darling* drinks."

The barman smiled at them. "Maria and Rick, am I right?"

"Impressive," Rick said, looking a little confused, but Maria recognized him.

"You're our new neighbor in number three—Bruce, isn't it?"

He nodded and offered them both a glass of champagne.

"Ah yeah, you're the guy who found Orga. Thanks again for that." Rick looked at the glasses of champagne. "You don't have any beer, by any chance?"

"Sorry about that. It's champagne or nothing. That's all she's serving."

"What?" Maria felt cheated. "I wanted a vodka and orange juice."

"You're not alone. Noreen Palmer was complaining about the lack of strong martinis. She told me a weak martini is even worse than a weak dollar," Bruce said.

"Is this meant to be cool or something?" Maria asked.

Bruce leaned toward them so he could whisper. "Haven't you heard? It's a Botox and Bollinger party. The Botox is in the front room. They have a certified lady doing the job, and I'm the Bollinger boy."

"Ah man, gimme that drink," Rick said. He took the glass and swallowed half of it in one gulp. "I think I'm going to need a few of these." Then he downed the rest of it.

Jessie walked by with a large silver tray balanced on her hand, up over head. It was full of glasses of champagne.

"Jessie," Maria said upon seeing another familiar face. The waitress swung around, but the champagne in the glasses didn't move.

Maria glanced up. "Whoa, how do you do that?"

"Years of practice. I worked in a pizza restaurant in Dorking all through my teens."

"Neat." Rick smiled. "Don't suppose you have anything other than champagne? This stuff doesn't agree with me."

Jessie shook her head. "Sorry, guys it's Botox and Bollinger or sparkly water."

"Jeez, even the water sparkles?" Maria was getting fed up and chose to drink the champagne. "Isn't anything dull around here? I like dull."

Jessie laughed. "Not at a Cathi Grant party," she said and headed back into the crowd.

"I'm going to find Michael. He's got to have a beer stash somewhere," Rick said. "Want to come?"

Maria shook her head. "I think I'll wander around. You said Greg and Michelle Palmer would be here. Some of these people have to be nice. They can't all be as shallow as they look. I'm going to find some fun."

He smiled at her. "That's my girl. Call me when you find the fun people." He kissed her on the cheek and headed off in search of his friend.

Maria wandered back out into the hall.

"Is that you, sweetie?" Noreen Palmer came up beside her.

"Hi." Maria kissed her next-door neighbor on the cheek. "Crazy party, isn't it?"

"Wonderful. Have you seen the champagne pyramid in the dining room? Reminds me of something similar we had back in the day. Don't know how you can call it a party without a good strong martini, though."

There was an attractive gentleman hovering beside Noreen. "Oh, where are my manners? Maria, this is Hugo Hendrix, a very dear old friend of mine."

He had nice olive-toned skin and was well-dressed. Even at his mature years, the man had class. They made a cute couple, too.

"How do you two know each other?" Maria asked.

"I've known Noreen and her late husband Joe for decades." Hugo smiled indulgently at Noreen. "We've stayed in touch ever since. I was in Boston on business, and she agreed to meet me."

Bruce was walking by and replenished their glasses without interrupting.

"Have you had a look at the Botox room yet? Hugo and I are thinking of getting some bits done," Noreen said.

"You're not!"

"We are! We've only got one life, we gotta live it. That's what my lovely lodger, Ely, always says. Now come with us." She took Hugo in one hand and Maria in the other.

They made their way into the study where a very beautiful young woman was dressed in a white coat. Her hair was pulled back tight into a high ponytail, and she wore red patent leather stilettos. Maria thought she looked more like a James Bond spy than a regular aesthetician. She had three ladies sitting on the sofa, their faces covered in a thick white cream.

"What's that?" Maria whispered to Noreen.

"It's the topical," one of the sofa ladies answered.

"Looks like diaper cream to me," Maria whispered, but Noreen nudged her to hush.

"It kills the pain," another lady on the sofa said, and pointed to the study desk where a row of syringes were lined up and ready for use.

The woman in the lab coat spoke with a strong Russian accent. "I am Svetlana. I am registered aesthetician. My qualifications are on the table."

Definitely a spy, Maria thought but decided not to mention it. "Hi, Svetlana. My friends and I just wanted to watch for a while," she said, grateful for Bruce's recent refill.

"Let's do it." Noreen's eyes twinkled with mischief, and she winked at Hugo. Then she turned to Svetlana again. "I'd prefer something stronger than a topical. What have you got?"

The Russian beauty clicked her heels and nodded. She seemed happy with the request for stronger drugs. From her metal case, she pulled out another set of vials. "With this, you will feel absolutely nothing."

"I'm in," Hugo said. "At my age, it's great to feel nothing, and if I look more handsome after, so much the better."

"I'm not so sure," Maria said.

"You don't need it." Noreen smiled at her next-door neighbor. "You're still beautiful, angel." She stroked Maria's cheek with her hand. "Your life is perfect right now."

For that split second, time seemed to stand still. Maria felt the warm soft skin of Noreen's hand on her face. It was like a mother-daughter connection, but just as quickly, the feeling slipped away. Maria felt bereft.

"I have to go. I have to find Ricky." Maria fled the room, leaving Noreen and her new friend in the capable hands of the Russian spy.

"Maria, there you are." Cathi was gliding through her hallway with the grace and stealth of an F-22 fighter jet. "Have you seen Michael? I need him to speak with the pyrotechnics people."

Maria knew this was all part of the show. Her friend wasn't even looking at her. She just needed somebody to talk at. *What the heck? It's her party. If this is the way she wants to play,* Maria thought, *I won't spoil it.*

"No idea where he is, but I think Ricky's with him. Can I help?"

This time Cathi did look at her. "Oh, you are a *darling*, aren't you?" Cathi gave one of her frosty smiles. "No, no, everything's under control. It's just the fireworks men are here, and they're worried about hitting some of the rather gorgeous cars out front. I think we should move the show out back, but they think it's too tight on space. Can you imagine? That backyard is so large it's crazy. I'm sure there's enough room."

Who are you and what have you done with my friend? Maria thought but said nothing while forcing a smile.

Cathi flapped her arms a few more times and huffed a little bit more, and then she swooped off to find a new place to complain.

Bruce reappeared and filled her glass again. "Having fun yet?"

"The more visits I get from you the better the party seems to get." She raised her glass to toast him. "Don't suppose you've seen Ricky anywhere."

"Yup, he and Michael are in the laundry room feeding Fifi eggnog. I think they found something else to drink for themselves, too."

She gave Bruce a suspicious glare. "Please tell me it's beer. What did they find?"

"Um, I'm not sure."

"You're stalling. You know exactly what they're doing. Are you going to tell me, or do I have to find them myself?"

"I think it might have been a wee bottle of tequila, but you didn't hear it from me."

"Aw jeez, this party just got a whole lot messier."

"It's a mess." Michael sounded miserable.

Jessie overheard her employer talking when she came into the laundry room to get more kitchen paper. Michael and Rick were sitting on the top step of the stairs that led to the basement. They had their backs turned to Jessie, so they didn't see her. Next to them, Fifi was drinking what looked like a bowl of milk.

"It'll work out." Rick wrapped his arm around his friend's shoulders. "Maria and I? We've just come through the biggest fight of our lives. I mean huge, but now I think we're back on track. Just take one day at a time, bro." He slapped Michael on the shoulder.

Jessie stepped back to the doorway for the kitchen, so it would look like she was just walking in if they turned around. She watched Rick refill their shot glasses. He laughed. "Oops, we finished a full bottle between us."

"It's this pregnancy, Rick. It's changed her—like she's possessed."

Jessie froze. Cathi Grant was pregnant? It had to be very early days, because she sure didn't look it. Michael was still talking. "I don't know any of the people here tonight."

"Where'd she find 'em?"

"The girls' school. They're private-school types—cliquey." He tapped the side of his nose as if to say they were snobs, but even that was enough to make him sway a little. Rick wrapped an arm round his shoulders and steadied his friend, and then they clinked their glasses. She knew they were getting really drunk, really fast. Cathi wouldn't be happy.

Michael scooped up the dog and kept talking. "I mean what was she thinking? Botox and Bollinger?"

"Bullshit and Bollinger more like." Rick banged his shoulder into his friend in agreement.

"Yeah." Michael sounded vindicated.

Jessie thought it would have been comical if it wasn't so sad.

"I don't even know how much it's going to cost!"

"Michael, you gotta explain to her that money doesn't grow on trees."

"She won't listen. Even this house." He pushed the empty tequila bottle down the basement stairs. Jessie winced as she listened to it *plop, plop, plop* down the carpeted steps. Thankfully, it didn't break.

"This is way out of our price range. What the hell are we doing here? And now a baby?"

Jessie had heard enough. She backed out of the laundry room and returned to the noise and bustle of the kitchen. The music was loud and the people even louder at this stage.

"You okay?" Bruce was by her side again. He was good at that, but she had stopped jumping every time it happened.

"Yeah, the host and Rick are sitting on the stairs to the basement getting absolutely steamed."

Bruce smiled. "Do you blame them? Have you ever seen such a shower of pretentious people?"

"Cathi's pregnant."

"The boss?"

"Yeah, her husband sounds a bit overwhelmed."

"Over the hill more like. How old are they?"

She laughed. "Far side of forty."

Bruce made a hissing sound and shook his head. "No, no, no. Too late. You have to be young having babies."

She laughed at him. "I don't see you rushing out to Babies 'R' Us, Mr. Wiswall."

He looked at her straight in the eye. "Maybe I haven't found the right girl yet."

Jessie looked away. What was he doing? What was *she* doing? No, there would be no new men in her life. Not now—not ever. Dan the fireman had reminded her once and for all that men were horrible—at least the ones she always ended up with.

"Gotta go," she said, scooping up the tray of glasses and heading back into the crowd.

"Jessie, there you are. Where have you been?" Cathi sounded annoyed.

"Just restocking my tray."

"Do you know where Michael is? He has to speak with the pyrotechnician."

"Um, I think I saw him around. Shall I find him for you?" She didn't want her boss to overhear the men or see what they were up to.

Cathi's face softened. "Would you? Thanks, Jessie. You're a good girl."

Her condescension annoyed Jessie, but she let it go. She was getting paid. Jessie left the tray on the hall table and went back in search of Michael. He hadn't moved. Neither had Rick or Fifi.

"Michael, Cathi needs your help," she said as soon as she came into the laundry room.

Michael let the dog down and tried to jump to his feet. That was when she noticed the bottle of eggnog beside the dog's bowl. Fifi, at least, had four legs and was lower to the ground. She seemed better at holding her liquor than Michael.

"Jessie, sorry," he said. "I'm just catching up with my good buddy here."

Rick pulled himself up to a standing position with the help of the banister rail.

"Where is she?"

"In the hall. I think she needs you to talk with the fireworks guys."

"We have fireworks?" Michael walked out of the room doing his best impression of a sober man with Fifi trotting behind.

Rick didn't seem too bothered. "You're a great girl, Jessie," he said. "Did I ever tell you that?" He was making his way over to her, but he was swaying a little.

"Um, I think you did." She backed toward the door to the kitchen, not wanting to get stuck in a conversation with a drunk Rick Sanchez.

Rick seemed to have no such reservations. "You know." He raised his hand and pointed to her. "If I was a younger guy, I'd have chased you, girl. I mean really chased you."

Jessie faked a laugh.

"Where have you been?" Maria walked into the laundry room.

Rick gave a tequila-soaked smile. "I was just talking to this little delight here."

Jessie knew it was the wrong thing to say, because Maria wasn't too sober either. She tried to help. "I was getting Michael for Cathi. He was talking with Ricky."

"*Ricky?*"

"Rick. Sorry, I mean Rick. I know you're the only one who calls him Ricky."

"Seriously, Ricky. She knows not to call you Ricky—not in front of me. You told her that was my name for you? Or is she able to use it when I'm out of earshot? Is that it?"

"No!" Jessie shouted. "No, he wasn't . . . we weren't . . . that is . . . I mean Rick was here, with Michael all this time."

An enormous explosion went off outside the house, making all the windows and even the walls shake.

"Christ, that was a bit close," Bruce said, coming into the laundry room to grab another bottle of champagne.

Cathi was on his heels. "Have the fireworks begun?"

You could say that, Jessie thought, but she didn't dare speak.

"Is it you or him?" Maria was shouting now. "Which of you is doing this? Because every time I see the two of you together, I feel it. I know there's something going on. Tell me!"

Jessie squirmed, but Cathi looked horrified. "What's wrong?" she said.

"Nothing to concern yourself about," Maria said a little too sharply. "It's between Ricky and me." She glared at her husband, and Jessie could see he was squaring up for a fight, too.

"Jeez, Maria. Are we going to do this here? Now?"

There was another dangerously loud explosion from outside.

"Those fireworks are too near the house," Bruce said.

Cathi Grant was more concerned about the action inside, however. "You two," she said. "Can you take your dirty laundry somewhere else? I don't want you fighting here."

Maria glared at her. "God forbid we tarnish your fabulous new life, Cathi. What's the matter? We not good enough for you now?"

Cathi shook her head and closed her eyes. Jessie stayed silent, terrified she would make the situation worse if she spoke. Michael walked back in at this point.

"Cathi, you ordered fireworks?" He looked perplexed.

Another massive explosion shook the house.

"I think you should leave," Cathi said to Maria. There was a scream from the kitchen. Bruce ran out to see what happened, but everybody else ignored it.

"Honey, what's going on? You can't get stressed in your state."

"You still haven't told him?"

"Get out."

"Get real."

"Told me what?"

Maria looked at Michael. "Cathi's not pregnant."

Jessie was confused.

Michael tilted his head. "What? Yes she is."

"No, she's not," Maria said. Then she stormed out of the laundry room and out of the house.

That was when they heard the sirens. "Cops are here," somebody said, but Michael didn't move.

Bruce came back into the laundry room. "Michael, a firework just came in through the kitchen window. I think you need to get in here. It's fizzled out, but the whole room is filling up with smoke."

"I deactivated the smoke alarms. The pyro guy told me to earlier," Cathi said, looking proud of herself.

Michael didn't respond. He was frozen solid—his face a combination of confusion and hurt.

Jessie watched the saga unravel when Fifi came yelping into the laundry room, dragging her back left leg behind her. Hugo was chasing after her, as fast as the old guy could. "She sat on a syringe. Fifi got a Botoxed backside!"

Hugo was the only one laughing, so he scooped up the dog and they escaped to the kitchen. The sirens were growing louder now, and there was banging on the front door.

"Maybe I should get that," Bruce said, glancing to where Michael and

Cathi were standing motionless—he looking at her and she looking at her festive fiasco.

Jessie tried to get out of the room unnoticed, but at that moment, the automated sprinkler system swished into life. Jessie, like everyone else, screamed at the sudden soaking. She had seen sprinklers in the ceilings of hotels but never in a private house.

Noreen appeared, her face shiny and a little puffy. "This reminds me of Woodstock. Hugo, it's raining inside!" She laughed, but her eyebrows didn't move.

Chapter Twenty-Nine
After the Party

Cathi didn't even know the house had been fitted with sprinklers. Thankfully, they were smoke sensitive and so only sprang to life in the hall and kitchen. The rest of the house was spared and they stopped pretty quickly, but it was still enough to put an end to her glorious party.

The police moved in and the guests moved out, but Cathi didn't go anywhere because she didn't know where to go. She stood on the slippery floor in her lovely new hall bidding guests good night. Her furniture there was ruined. Even worse, many of her guests had been in the wrong place when the sprinklers attacked, so thousands of dollars of damage had been done to couture cocktail dresses.

Cathi had stored the coats upstairs, so they were all still dry when her daughters handed them out, but the party was a complete disaster. All her wonderful new friends were slipping away faster than she could say country club candidate. How was she going to fix this?

"Cathi, is it true?" Michael was touching her arm now. The guests were all gone, and she had sent her daughters to bed. "Cathi? Can you hear me?" His voice was quavering with emotion. "What Maria said, is it true? You're not pregnant?"

She looked at him—poor confused Michael. He looked wretched with sprinkler water dripping down his hair. In a way, this was all his fault, she realized. If he hadn't dropped his suspicions on her like that at Thanksgiving . . .

"Yes, it's true Michael. I'm not pregnant. I never was, at least not this decade. You sprang it on me so fast and in front of Rick. I was stunned, I was confused. I didn't know how to say I wasn't. You seemed so excited and happy when you thought I was."

He covered his ears and backed away. "I don't believe this. What the hell were you thinking? Why didn't you just say no?"

"Mr. Grant?" A police officer was calling him out to the backyard. Cathi watched her husband pretend to be sober. It was the fireworks that had caused the trouble. One of her neighbors must have called the cops, which was odd because all of the residents from Crystal Lake Lane were at the party.

Cathi wandered into her flooded kitchen. Jessie and Bruce were busy mopping, clearing away glasses, and trying to salvage what food was left.

"Shall I just put all of this in the fridge?" Jessie asked, but Cathi had lost interest. What did any of it matter now? She had made herself the laughing stock of Newton. The police, she could have handled. It was her friend—no, her ex-friend, Maria. Too many people would have heard her saying Cathi wasn't pregnant.

She wandered aimlessly back into the sodden hall and noticed that even the walls were drenched.

"I will go now, Mrs. Grant?" Svetlana was standing there in her sterile white coat and stilettos holding the silver, metallic case. She was perfectly dry.

"Oh, yes. Thanks, Svetlana. You'll send me a bill?"

"I have it here. Better to settle now, please."

Cathi took the little invoice and glanced at the bottom line. "This is enormous. It can't be real? Is this a joke?"

Svetlana looked like she might have been expecting such a reaction. "You did say to give them whatever they wanted. I have breakdown of the bill here with a list of all medications used."

"Oh God." Cathi checked to see if her husband was within earshot just as there was another pounding on the door.

"Fire department." A man lumbered into her front hall with big heavy boots. Cathi winced. If the water hadn't wrecked her bleached hardwoods, those boots sure would.

She pointed through the hall and out through the kitchen. "There's no fire. It was just a few fireworks. My husband's out there with the police and the pyrotechnics man." She looked at her aesthetician. "You come with me."

They went into the study where Cathi pulled out a check book from her personal drawer in the desk. "Please don't cash this for a few days. I'd expected your bill to be a quarter of that."

Svetlana raised her still functioning eyebrows with a look of utter indifference. "Quality work costs."

"But what a lovely job you do." Noreen Palmer was sitting on the sofa in the semidarkness with Hugo Hendrix. Fifi was on her lap.

"Hugo, Noreen, I didn't see you there."

"No, we were enjoying the privacy," he said, sounding annoyed.

"Oh my." Cathi understood. They'd been making out—too gross. "What happened to Fifi?"

"She was acting very strange. If I didn't know any better, I'd say she was drunk," Noreen said. "She was walking in reverse and backed onto a needle."

Hugo stroked the little mutt. "I'd say it's raised her rump by a good half inch, but she's none too pleased."

Cathi looked accusingly at Svetlana. "Did you charge me for that shot?"

"The syringe was almost empty. No charge for dog. Fifi will have no problem."

"Yes, well, I think we should go." Noreen got to her feet.

"Let me drive you home," Hugo said. "My driver is just outside."

Noreen laughed. "A driver? Oh, this is just like the old days. Hugo, you know I live about thirty yards up the lane?"

"I'm sure we'll think of something we can do to pass the time." He winked at Svetlana. "Night, Cathi. Thanks for a great party." Hugo walked out with his arm around Noreen Palmer's waist.

Svetlana left after them, and Cathi was alone for the first time all night. She glanced at her watch. It was after three a.m. Maybe the night hadn't been a total disaster. She wanted a reputation for throwing wild and crazy parties, and surely this one was wet and wild enough for anyone. She was starting to see the angle already.

Her only real issue now was Michael and the bogus baby. *How to play that?* she wondered. She could either get mad and blame him, or she could do the weak, confused woman routine. Which would work better?

"Dan!" Jessie saw him before he saw her. It was a bit difficult to miss a big burly firefighter clomping through the kitchen.

"Jessie." He stopped and looked at her. "It's good to see you."

Jessie was standing at the sink but had turned around to face him. She followed his gaze and looked down at her chest.

"Shit," she mumbled, realizing the water sprinklers had given her a good splash and her white blouse was now semitransparent.

Jessie crossed her arms over her chest and sent up a silent prayer for Bruce to reappear. "Yes, well, I'm not so thrilled to see you. Perhaps it's better if we just ignore each other."

He didn't move for a moment, and she matched his gaze, refusing to drop eye contact. Then Bruce walked into the kitchen and the spell was broken. Dan sized him up, nodded, and moved out into the garden. As soon as he was gone, Jessie turned back to the soapy water, grabbing the side of the sink for support. Dan was in the house, *this very house*. How could she think straight? Dan the Pan? He had just walked through the room like he'd walked into her life before. He had slept with her while his wife was pregnant!

Bruce came over to her. "Are you okay?"

She didn't look up but nodded. "Just a ghost from the past."

"Muhahahaha." Bruce did a Count Dracula impersonation, which made her smile.

"Thanks." His humor helped her calm down.

"Hey, we all have skeletons in the closet. Some are just larger than others." Bruce glanced out the window to where Michael looked like he was listening with interest to what the police and firemen had to say. There was a lot of pointing and gesturing around the garden.

"Do you think Michael Grant is in trouble?" Bruce asked.

"Hey, you're the lawyer. How would I know? But I do feel sorry for him. Did you hear all that madness with his wife?"

Bruce shook his head and picked up a hand towel to start drying Jessie's plates.

She continued. "I heard him talking to Rick earlier about her being pregnant, and this evening Maria announced that Cathi wasn't. So it sounds like she was faking a pregnancy. How weird is that?"

"Maybe she miscarried?"

Jessie shrugged. "It didn't sound like that. All very strange."

Bruce folded his dish cloth and put it down beside the sink. "Look, Jessie, we're almost finished here. Do you fancy coming back to my place to watch a movie and maybe have a glass of wine—just to unwind?"

She shook her head. "Not tonight, I'm afraid. The truth is—well, I've been trying to hide it, but I'm afraid I look like a loser from a wet T-shirt competition just now." She turned to face him.

He smirked. "To be honest, you look like a winner to me."

Jessie gave him a friendly thump. "Bruce, I'm getting cold and I'm a bit tired, too, so I think I'll skip this one. But thanks." She tried to sound normal, and in control even, although she was still a bit shook-up having seen Dan.

"No problem. It was just a thought—nothing serious, you understand."

"Yeah, of course."

He disappeared from the kitchen for a moment and returned with the navy jacket he had worn earlier. Bruce put it over her shoulders as she stood at the sink. She gave him a grateful nod, and he smiled down at her. He was a good friend—Jessie needed those.

Bruce clapped his hands. "I'm going to find Cathi and tell her we're done."

The police were the first to leave. Before the firefighters left, Dan tried to talk to her again, but Jessie was stronger this time. "Just go," she said with a lot more conviction than she felt. There was nothing to say. Better to avoid him altogether—even if he did look gorgeous.

By the time Bruce and Jessie were finished, the house was back in pretty good shape. The floors were still wet and so were the walls, but everything else had been cleaned and put away. They had worked hard for Cathi, not that she seemed to notice. She paid them, thanked them, and then showed them the door, so they walked down Crystal Lake Lane together. Bruce counted his money as they walked.

"Eighty bucks? Is that all we're worth?"

"Really? We were there for more than nine hours," Jessie said. "Miserable old bat. That's the last time I'm working for her."

"Too right."

She glanced at Bruce. "Why did you even do it? I mean, she has no idea you're a lawyer. If she'd known, she probably would have asked you to the party."

He stopped and looked at her. "But then I would have missed all the fun. Ely wasn't up to it. I think you might have been carrying the load by yourself if I hadn't helped out."

"That was very kind of you, but I am a big girl." Her tone was defensive.

"God, you are prickly, aren't you? I was just trying to be a nice neighbor." They'd reached Noreen's house. "Hey, who owns the Rolls Royce?"

"There's a driver in it, too. It must be Hugo's car. I guess he's still here."

"You sure I can't talk you into an old movie and bottle of cheap red wine? Sorry, but it's all I've got. Granddad wasn't a big supporter of fine wines."

"Smooth talker." Jessie laughed. Even though she had said no just a half hour earlier, she was now considering it. It was so nice to meet a regular guy who understood her. Bruce didn't have those movie star good looks like Dan, but he was warm and sweet, like a favorite sweater, comfortable. If Dan were a garment, he would have been an Armani suit.

"Not tonight," she said, suddenly realizing Bruce was waiting for an answer while she daydreamed about her wearing her ex. "Think I need to be asleep. Hey, tomorrow I fly home."

"Do you? That's funny, so do I. What airline are you with? What time?"

"British Airways, nine o'clock tomorrow morning."

Bruce looked surprised. "Wow. I'm pretty sure that's the one I'm on, too. At least I think it is."

"Well, it may not be the same plane, but if our flights are near the same time, do you want to share a cab?"

"Great idea." He hovered with her on the sidewalk for a moment.

Jessie took the initiative and kissed him on the cheek. "Thanks for all your help tonight, Bruce. Even if you did it just to be a nice Newton neighbor."

He put on a goofy expression to make her laugh. "Ah shucks," he said and turned to walked away.

"Oh, your jacket." Jessie shrugged out of it.

"Keep it until tomorrow."

She watched him walk away and then turned into her driveway. Jessie was going to smile at Hugo's driver, but it looked like he'd nodded off in the car with the engine running. Perhaps he was used to sitting out on

December nights while his employer paid visits to old lady friends. Jessie smiled to herself. Noreen was an interesting person, regardless of her years.

She was at the side door of the house when someone moved behind her. "Jessie."

She screamed and swung around. "Dan?"

He stepped forward and laughed. "Hi. I came back to the party to talk to you, but then I saw you walking here. You live here now?"

She nodded, her eyes a little wider, and took a step back.

"Look, I didn't mean to scare you. I just felt so bad seeing you tonight. We never got to talk after—you know, after you met my mom."

"You mean your wife—your *pregnant* wife?"

Dan took another step forward. "Yeah, that's one of the reasons I wanted to see you. That was a mess. She and I, we got together for all the wrong reasons. That's why I was so slow with you in the beginning. I didn't know what to do. I'm so into you, Jessie, but now there's this situation."

"Situation?" Jessie stepped forward. "That situation is called Sadie and she's carrying your baby, and you slept with me, Dan. What the hell was that about? You don't think you should have maybe mentioned it?"

"I know, but it isn't that simple."

Jessie held up her hands. "You know what? Save your breath. There's nothing you can say to fix this. I should have a medal for picking the wrong guy, honest. You're not the first. I seem to hone in on the wrong man time and time again, so just go away, okay? Forget it ever happened. I'm doing my best to."

"No, wait." Dan sounded desperate now. He held his head like he was trying to think faster. "I don't want to. You and me? We could still make a go of it. I really like you, and I have a pretty good idea you still like me. The chemistry is off the wall. Maybe we can work around this?"

"No, Dan. You and I are over. I don't want to work around a wife."

"I don't accept that." He stepped closer and tried to take her in his arms, but she pushed him away.

"I said no!" she shouted.

"Yes." He pulled her closer.

"She said *no*." Bruce spoke loud and clear from behind them, startling Dan.

"Hey, nice timing," Jessie said.

"Who the hell are you?" Dan released his hold of her when he heard the new voice.

"He's my neighbor and friend, you ass. Now go." Jessie was more furious than scared now.

Dan folded his arms over his chest. "Yeah, right." His aggression was palpable—Bruce's was not.

"I don't want any trouble, man. I just think you need to leave the lady alone." Bruce was trying to sound friendly, more peacemaker than troublemaker.

It appeared, however, Dan *did* want trouble. He took a lunge and punched Bruce hard on the left jaw. Bruce fell back onto the snowy verge of the path, and Jessie screamed for help.

Hugo's driver jumped out of his car and was pulling Dan off Bruce within seconds, which was just as well, because Dan was breathing hard and had murder in his eyes.

"Go," Jessie said when Dan looked at her.

"This isn't over," Dan said.

"Yes, it is. If you don't leave me alone, I'll get a restraining order." Dan looked torn, glancing from her to the driver and to Bruce who was still on the ground. Jessie knew he was considering taking them all on. His face was red, and it was obvious that his blood was boiling. "I'm serious, Dan. I'll call 911 right now and you'll be arrested. So go!"

His shoulders fell, defeated. He spat on the ground in one last act of defiance. Then he turned and jogged away, off into the night.

"Ex-boyfriend?" the driver asked Jessie as he helped Bruce up. "Who are you, then?"

"I'm just the bloody neighbor." Bruce wiped his bleeding lip with the back of his hand.

"Oh, Bruce. Thank you." She stroked his face. "Thank you for saving me. Come inside, we need to get you cleaned up."

Cathi was waiting in bed for Michael because she knew they had to settle this before they slept. She had chosen her sexiest nightgown and even decided to keep her makeup on. Tonight Cathi was going to have to pull off the best act of her life.

"You want to tell me why I thought you were pregnant and Maria Sanchez didn't?"

"It was all just a huge misunderstanding, Michael. You have to believe me."

"One that most couples seem to escape. I don't get it. I asked you were you pregnant—why didn't you just say no?"

"I wanted to—more than you can imagine—and every day since, but the lie just got bigger and bigger."

"You realize it's the only reason I agreed to sell our house and rent this place." He glanced about the bedroom with a look of distaste. "Jesus, was that all part of your plan?"

"No." Cathi tried to sound desperate. She wrung her hands and then reached out to him. "Come to bed. It's like I told you already. You seemed so pumped when you asked me, so I just went along with it. I see now it was really stupid, but I don't really know how it happened. I was going to tell you—of course, I was. Well, we could still try to have a baby if you want." She tried to look as alluring as she could. She saw the confusion wash over her husband's face. Then it turned to annoyance.

"What? You're suggesting we try for a baby now?"

"Well, we can't tonight—I just got my period. But I know I could show you a good time."

"You got your period? My pregnant wife got her period and still didn't think to tell me she wasn't pregnant."

"That only happened this evening. I was going to tell you as soon as I could. Damn it, Michael, do you want a baby or not?"

"Yes, no. Damn, Cathi, it wasn't on my agenda. Then you threw it at me."

"No." She kneeled on the bed. "You, Michael—you threw it at me! It was the last thing on my mind, and all of a sudden you're talking about a third child. Where in the hell did that come from?"

"I saw your letter about decorating a nursery."

"That?" She shook her head. "You know I'm always looking at interior design ideas. I was just goofing around."

"A baby's nursery is goofing round? Hello, Cathi, you told me you were pregnant. You let me live with that belief for over a month."

She sat back down on her heels. "I'm sorry."

Michael looked at her then, and she saw something different in his eyes. Was it resignation?

"You think that's enough after all this? 'Sorry.' Jesus, do I even know you anymore?" He shook his head and headed for the door.

"Where are you going?" Cathi felt real panic rising. Michael had never been this mad at her before. She was always able to sweet-talk him.

He looked back at her from the bedroom door. "I don't know. But I can't sleep here tonight."

Chapter Thirty
The Morning After

"Where did you sleep last night?" Rick asked as soon as his wife walked into the kitchen. He was sitting at their table, drinking coffee and eating some toast.

Maria hadn't slept, not really, but there was no point in discussing that with him this morning. "I stayed in Alice's room. She's still out cold."

"You want to talk about it?"

"She'll be one tomorrow."

"No way. She's one year old already? Where did that time go?" This seemed to quiet him for a moment, though not for long. "Do you want to talk about us, I mean."

She shook her head slowly. "What's left to discuss?" She sat down at the table across from him.

"We have to talk."

She closed her eyes and rubbed her temples with her fingers. Then she took a deep breath and opened her eyes to face her husband straight on. "Here's the thing, Ricky. The fur was a lovely gesture. I mean it and I don't want to fight, but I have to tell you I saw the way you looked at Jessie last night."

"Jesus." Rick slammed the palm of his hand down on the table, making the breakfast things and Maria jump.

"Where's Cody?" she asked, anxious their son would overhear them fighting—again.

"He's inside watching TV. Maria, you know this is all in your mind."

"You think?" His reaction annoyed her. She stood and headed to the coffee machine. "I'm not the one who downed a bottle of tequila. Ask Jessie, if you don't believe me. You were making a pass at her, Ricky. You're not the man I married. God help me, I wish you were. I loved him. I remember Vermont and all those love letters your wrote me. Do remember writing those?"

Rick didn't respond, but she saw the recollection in his eyes.

She flicked the coffee machine on and came back to the table, sitting across from him. "Where is that man, Ricky? I miss him so much, but I can't live like this. I can't go to every party with you wondering if you're going to hit on the help, and that's when you even come home. You've become a workaholic. I haven't seen you for the last four months. You live in that office. We do nothing together anymore, and the kids never see you. This isn't a marriage. I don't know what it is, but I've been trying to survive in it, and I've come to the conclusion I can't go on like this."

Rick didn't seem angry now—he looked worried. "What are you saying?"

She studied the leg of the table, unable to face her husband. "I'm saying I think we need to do a trial separation and step back for a while."

"You're not serious?"

"I've never been more serious in my life. It's been more of a slow realization than a sudden heartbreak. But it seems to me you have everything you want—a fabulous career, your time in the gym, a good social life with the wife and kids at home." Maria made herself look into his eyes so he would know she was talking from the heart. "Me? I'm lost. I don't have you. The kids are draining me, and I have no family support. I want to go home."

He pushed his breakfast things away. "You can't take the kids to live in Puerto Rico."

"Is that a challenge? Are you saying you'd fight me in court? Are we talking custody battles already? Wow." She rose again to get herself a mug.

Rick kneaded his hands together. "I didn't mean that. I just meant you can't seriously be thinking about moving there for good while I'm up here. I thought you just wanted a trial separation."

"I have family there—support. I don't have that here. Plus the kids love it."

"I don't want to break up."

She thought she heard his voice break and turned to look at him. He met her eyes. She realized his were full of tears.

Maria turned back to the machine and pressed the big-mug button. "I don't want to either, but staying together like this isn't working. It's killing us."

"Look, maybe you just need a vacation," he said. "Why don't you go with the kids down to your mom's for Christmas and New Year's? That would be a two-week break. I'll stay here and work. See how you feel. Maybe then you'll be ready to come home. We can pick things up and move forward together in the New Year. Just come back."

"You're telling me to go with the kids?" Maria felt her body go cold as the steam started to rise from her mug.

"I'm not telling you to go. I don't want you to go. I want you to stay here and for us to be together, but you're saying you want space, so take it and then come home."

Maria felt her own eyes welling up. "So this is really happening. We're breaking up." She came back and sat at the table with her coffee.

Rick got up, came over to her side of the table, and took the seat next to hers. He gently removed the mug from her grasp and took her hands in his. "No, we're not. You just want a bit of a rest to figure things out, that's all. We're still married. We can save this. We just need some time apart."

Maria nodded at him because she didn't want to fight, but deep down, she knew this was the beginning of the end.

Despite her own problems, Ely was glad to see Jessie so happy. "I've never seen you excited like this before. Girl, you sure like your kin."

Jessie laughed. "You know we're a close-knit family, and we've never been apart for this long before. I can't wait to see them. I don't know who'll be at Heathrow, but I'm sure it'll be more than just Mum, and the whole place will be decorated for Christmas. I can't wait."

"What, the airport?"

Jessie grinned like a five-year-old. "You'll have to come see it at Christmas next year. The whole place—cities, the airport, houses, of course —everybody gets into the holiday cheer. The airport will have giant snowmen and Santa Clauses. Even the planes sometimes have red noses painted on them for the fun."

Ely harrumphed. "I'd be just as happy to hang around here. I don't much want to go home."

"Is Josh on his way over?"

Ely watched her best friend cramming the last things into her suitcase. Jessie had no idea she and Josh were at war, because she didn't know about Ely's plans to terminate the pregnancy. She forced a smile. "Yep, he'll be over when he wakes, the big lug. We'll spend the day together, and then we both fly home to our respective families."

"Oh." Jessie stopped rushing around for a moment and sat down on the bed. "I thought he might fly home with you to talk to your parents."

"No, not yet. We can do that after the holidays."

Jessie looked torn—like she was trying to decide whether or not she should speak. Ely prayed she wouldn't. The last thing Ely needed now was more kind words or encouragement. By the time they were all back to school, everything would be sorted. Her daddy had once taught her it was sometimes wiser to seek forgiveness than permission. This was one of those times.

"When is your flight?" She tried to distract Jessie.

"Ely, there's something I've been trying to get up the nerve to tell you."

"Hey, some things are better left unsaid." Ely forced a laugh.

"Not this. I think I should tell you."

Ely knew she was beaten. She sat down on the bed beside Jessie. "Aw, heck, get it over with, then."

"Well, it's about Tristan."

"Your little brother?"

"That's just it. He's not my brother. He's my son."

Ely stood again. "What? Bull. Shit!"

Jessie winced at her friend's reaction but persevered. "No, I'm for real. He's my son. I was so young at the time that my parents decided to bring him up as one of their own. I was fifteen."

"Crap." Ely sat back down beside Jessie and put her arm around her shoulders.

"Yes, you could say that." Jessie looked like she might cry. "It was my fifteenth birthday, and I was out with friends. I thought I was grown-up and mature. I started to drink, and well, it doesn't take a rocket scientist to figure out what happened next."

"What about the father?"

"I don't even know his name. We went to a pub."

"Jesus."

"In his defense, I said I was seventeen. It was around the back of the bar in an alleyway." She started to cry. "I thought it was a rite of passage. I was growing up."

"Shh, J. You don't have to tell me all of this."

"I think I do, Ely. I know what you're going through. That's the point. I was so young and stupid. I didn't even know I was pregnant for a few months—my periods were irregular back then. What are the chances of getting pregnant the same night you lose your virginity? Anyway, by the time I found out, I was eighteen weeks. My parents decided to bring the baby up as one of their children. Now Tristan is kind of like my kid brother."

"Does he know?"

"Yes. Most people around our neighborhood do, but the scandalmongers and gossipers ran out of steam years ago. The point is you're twenty-three, Josh loves you, and you're way ahead of where I was. You'll be okay, Ely. Honest. And I love Tristan more than I love my own life. I'd do anything for him. That's why I'm so driven to succeed. My mum's been carrying the load for all these years. Now it's time for me to step up and face my responsibilities. You need to, too."

Ely felt like she was going to cry. If her friend only knew what her plans were.

"This is the darkest hour, Ely. Things will get better. You'll look back on these days as being tough, but you know, it might just be the best thing that ever happened to you. Josh has already told you he loves you. You're so wild, I don't know if he'd ever have managed to tame you, but this baby will. Just go with it, Ely. Believe me."

She wanted to. Elyse Briskin wanted to be another one of those bad stories turned good, but she knew her life didn't work that way. Her parents would disown her. She would be cut off financially. Josh was too young to be tied down. As heartwarming as Jessie's story was, it was her story—not Ely's.

Ely made a supreme effort to smile and pretend this was all making an impact on her. "I hear you, J. I do believe it'll all work out. I know it will." She kissed Jessie on the cheek. "Thank you for telling me. I know it took a lot, and give Tristan an extra special hug for me. He's one lucky little man."

"I think I'm the lucky one," Jessie said and started to pack again.

Not long after Jessie and Ely's talk, Bruce came to pick her up.

"I didn't know he was bringing you to the airport." Ely nudged her friend's shoulder as they headed downstairs and into the kitchen to look for Noreen.

"Our planes are leaving Logan around the same time. It's just a coincidence."

"What was it Freud said about coincidences? 'There's no such thing.' "

"Ha, you have been studying!" They both laughed, and Ely gave her best friend one last hug. Jessie held her very tight. After a moment, she pulled back and looked deep into Ely's eyes. "You mind yourself, and I'll see you in the New Year. Okay?"

"Don't worry, I'll keep a close eye on her." Noreen joined in and wrapped her arms around both girls.

Ely was the first to break up the group hug. "I'll be fine. Don't worry about me."

Noreen and Ely waved Bruce and Jessie off together. The landlady was old, but it seemed like she was still perceptive, because when they came back inside, the questions started.

"Ely, why is Jessie fussing over you so much?" They walked into the front room of the house together where the fire was already ablaze.

"Oh, you know her. She's a worrywart—a heart of gold but a worrywart, just the same."

"So you're okay?"

"Me? Never better. Jessie was just fussin'."

"Yes, she's a very responsible young lady. Works hard—too hard, I think. Like you always say, you only got one life."

It made Ely smile. "I get the feeling you live a fairly full life, Mrs. Palmer."

The old lady chuckled. "How many times have I told you to call me Noreen? Mrs. Palmer sounds so old."

Fifi, the Grants' dog, trotted into the room with Rusty.

"Hey, what's she doing here?"

Noreen patted the sofa, and both dogs jumped up and settled themselves next to her. "I think Fifi has moved in with us. I opened the door this morning and she was sitting on the front step."

"Is it my imagination or does she look slightly bigger on one side than the other?"

"Funny you should say that. Fifi got a shot of Botox in her hindquarter last night. I think it's perked her up a bit on one side."

"No way!"

"Oh, don't worry. She was well sedated at the time. Jessie told me she'd been drinking eggnog in the kitchen. Poor Fifi was plastered."

"That can't be good for her."

"Oh, I don't know. We always give Rusty a little whiskey at Christmas, but the Botox is a new one, even for me." She looked at the two dogs. "You know, I think she's taken a shine to Rusty." Noreen rubbed her bulldog's head.

"Hey, Rusty's a boy and Fifi's a girl. If they get together . . ."

Noreen chuckled. "Yes, we'll have little bull-shits! Wouldn't that be fun? If Cathi Grant keeps them, I can tell her in all honesty, once and for all, that I really am allergic to her bullshit."

Ely exploded into laughter, which made the dogs start to yap. "Oh wow, I do hope Rusty gets his way with her."

"I'm sure he'll give it a good shot, if you'll pardon the pun."

"Poor Fifi." Ely waved her finger at the small dog. "You stay away from that big bad boy."

The landlady focused on the fire. "Life would be very dull if we all stayed away from the bad boys."

"Is Hugo a bad boy? I heard him come in last night."

Noreen glanced at Ely. "I wasn't going to tell you this until after the holidays, but now that you mention him—I'd like to clear something with you." Noreen petted the dogs while she talked. "You see, Hugo has asked me to go on a Valentine's cruise with him in February, and I think I'll say yes. Would you girls be okay here on your own? I checked and I'll be able to take Rusty with me, but I'm worried about you two. Would that be all right?"

"Sure. We won't do anything wild. We've learned our lesson. You have my word."

Noreen stood up and went over to fuss with the fire, even though it didn't need it. "I'm not in the slightest bit worried. It's an utter pleasure having you stay here. If you want to throw a party, knock yourselves out. This house was made for parties. The one thing I ask is that my room be locked. I don't want any young people getting down in my boudoir."

"Mrs. Palmer!"

"Noreen."

"Sorry. So are you and Hugo dating seriously?" It felt odd to say the words to an old lady, but Noreen didn't seem to think so.

"Well, dating might be too strong a word for it, but we're having fun together. There are so many wonderful new drugs on the market these days. Who knew?" Her eyes were bright.

Ely's mind whirred. Was Noreen talking about Viagra or Ecstasy?

"I turned eighty last July and I didn't celebrate it in any sort of remarkable way. Of course, my son took me out for dinner with his wife and kids and that was all very nice, but Hugo was thinking of something a little more exciting. He wants to take me to Tuscany next summer, but in February he wants to go on a cruise around the Caribbean, and then head down to his place in Jamaica. I gather it's more of a complex than just one house. It used to belong to his big brother Jimi."

"Oh my God, you're dating Jimi Hendrix's little brother, Hugo Hendrix? I never made the connection."

Noreen nodded like it wasn't anything big. "Hugo was telling me Mick Wolf is eager to celebrate his seventieth from a few months back. If memory serves, he's a July baby, too. We're twins, only I'm a decade older. Then again, Mick always did prefer older women."

Her eyes took on a glazed look, and Ely wondered if any of this was for real. Greg had warned her and Jessie about Noreen's overactive imagination and her lapses into senility. This had to be one of them. She wondered what she should do.

Noreen continued, oblivious. "Anyway, we might all get together down in Jamaica."

Ely decided to play along and check in with Greg after the holidays. "You're going to party with Wolf? You know, they say he's slept with four thousand women over his life."

"Do they now? Better make that four thousand . . . and one." She gave Ely a dazzling smile.

"Mrs. Palmer, you didn't!"

Noreen gave a guilty nod and then changed the subject. "Now, tell me more about your shampoo idea. I think it's terrific. Hugo is a friend of Richard Worthington, that billionaire entrepreneur, you know. Imagine if he bought it from you. It's just the kind of thing he'd go for, I believe."

"I don't know what to believe anymore. That's the problem, Cathi." Michael didn't sound angry. He looked tired and sad. He was sitting at the table in their kitchen, and she was pacing the floor.

"You have to believe this. Fifi was here a few hours ago and now she's gone. I searched everywhere."

"Maybe it was the fireworks."

"She didn't run away last night. It was this morning." Cathi tried not to sound annoyed, but how could she help it? "That dog is like a baby to me." The words were out before she could stop herself. Michael gave her a nasty look.

"Yeah? Well, you know—easy come, easy go," he said with contempt.

"Oh, Michael, how many times can I say it? How many ways? I'm sorry I hurt you. That wasn't my intent. I got carried away in the moment."

"I want to move."

"What?" She sat down on the chair next to him at their kitchen table. It wasn't a great match with her new kitchen, but that didn't matter just now. Michael was what mattered.

He didn't sound happy. "You heard me. I want to move. I don't want to live in this pretentious house. You knew I didn't want it. And what the hell are we going to do about the smoke and water damage?" Michael glanced around the kitchen. "Have you even thought about that?"

Cathi followed his gaze, but the kitchen was unharmed. "Oh, it's not that bad, and I'm sure it's covered by insurance."

He ran his hands through his hair. "That's not the point. The point, Cathi, is you've been on your own little personal crusade for I don't know how long. You haven't given a thought to the girls' or my needs. It's all been about you and your manic ambition to live on this dumb road. Do you have any idea the hurt you've caused me? The embarrassment? But I don't even care about that. It's the fact that you've lied so easily. God, do I even know you anymore?"

Cathi reached across the table and tried to take his hands. "Michael, it wasn't just for me. It was for you and the girls, too."

He pulled back and stood up. "No. No more mind games. Listen to yourself. Hello? I never wanted this. You've been on your own agenda for a long time. Jesus, Cathi—you faked a pregnancy!"

Michael swore under his breath. She had never seen him this furious.

"Cathi. You're still in complete denial of all the damage you've done and, quite frankly, you're still doing. I know we had something real—*had*. We both still love the kids, but you and me? I really am lost about what the hell is going on here. First the house, then the baby. When did you shut me out?"

"No, I never." She stood up alongside her husband. "Please, Michael. I never meant to do that."

"You know the money we got from our own house? That would have been enough to buy a nice place in a less expensive town. I could've taken a year off to write that book I've been promising myself I'd do someday."

Cathi panicked inside but tried to stay composed on the surface. "What about the girls? They're already settled in school, and it's a great school."

"You're not gonna change are you? You're not even sorry. You're just sorry you got caught—not that I have any idea how you were going to fake a birth. I have to get away. I'm sorry. I just need some space to figure out what the heck is going on with us."

"You don't mean that."

"What do you think?" Michael looked at her with tired, miserable eyes.

She tried to hide her panic. "For God's sake, it's the twenty-second of December, Michael. Be realistic."

"Realistic? Ha! What the heck do you know about reality? You're delusional, Cathi. I'm packing my things. I'm sorry. Jesus, why am I apologizing? I just can't go on like this. Life is gonna have to change around here. So you better buckle up, because it's gonna be a bumpy ride."

Chapter Thirty-One
Up, Up, and Away

"Are you buckled in? It's getting a little bumpy." Bruce leaned over and checked Jessie's seat belt.

"Tell me about it," Jessie said.

"Oh? Everything okay?"

She'd been thinking of Ely and worrying over leaving her back in Boston. Telling her about Tristan had been emotional but worth it. She snapped back to reality now. It had been a happy coincidence to discover that Bruce was on the same plane as her, regardless of what Ely had said. He was fast becoming one of her best friends in Newton.

"I'm sorry, Tristan. It's been a manic few days with schoolwork, late nights, and I have a lot on my mind at the moment. I'm distracted."

"So it would seem." Bruce brushed imaginary dust off his shoulder lapel. "My name's not Tristan. I'm Bruce—nice to meet you."

She slapped her hand over her mouth, horrified. "Oh God, I called you Tristan? I'm so sorry, Bruce."

"Was it Tristan who gave me that right hook last night?"

"Um, no. That was Dan."

"Ah."

"Dan and I were together for a while but he—well, it appears he's married, actually."

Bruce raised an eyebrow at her and pretended to be shocked.

"I didn't know. I assumed he was single. He sure acted single. So that's it. Now you know why I don't want to have anything to do with him ever again."

This time Bruce looked more sympathetic. "That must have been hard."

"To be honest, it hurt like hell at the time, but I'm a strong girl. I'll get over it."

"I'll help you," Bruce said and pressed the call button. "Best way to get over anything is with champagne. What do you say? We served enough of it last night—I think we need to celebrate Christmas. Yeah?"

Jessie didn't have that kind of money, but it appeared Bruce did. "That sounds like heaven," she said. *Why can't I find a nice guy like this one?* she wondered and looked out at the darkening sky.

"What time do we land?" she asked when he'd placed the order.

"About two a.m. Boston time, seven a.m. in London town."

"Will somebody be meeting you?"

"No. I'll catch a cab. Can I offer you a ride anywhere?"

"Bruce, you're so kind. My mum will be there and maybe a few brothers and sisters, too. I've never been away from home before. I really hope Tristan comes out."

"Tristan? So I'm guessing he's the man in your life now."

She decided to have some fun. "Yes he is, Bruce. I love him with all my heart, and I hope we'll be together forever."

"Lucky guy." Bruce drained his champagne glass and refilled it from his little bottle.

"I'm joking." She nudged him gently with her elbow. "He's my kid brother. Tristan is only eight, and he's the love of my life. I've missed him so much."

Bruce nodded that he understood. "Ah, your little brother? I thought he was your boyfriend."

"Has anyone ever said you look like Jude Law?" Jessie asked, feeling more relaxed as the champagne moved into her system.

"Yes—and no, we're not related, nor can I get you an introduction. Now tell me, do you want pasta or chicken?"

"Chicken. Let's get more champagne, too."

They laughed their way through the night sky and had quite a few more drinks before Jessie finally fell asleep on Bruce's shoulder. In a very short time, the lights were flicking back on while the stewardesses handed out prepacked orange juices.

"I feel like I slept for five minutes. It can't be the morning already."

"It's not if you're in Boston, but we're in London, my girl."

"Oh, it'll be good to be home for a while." She stretched. "Did you know I go to Wiswall College? Is it spelt the same as your last name?"

"Um, it should be."

"I know you're not related to Jude, but I don't suppose you're connected to my college."

"As a matter of fact, I am. Well, not *I* per se, but way back in the family my great-great-lots-of-greats-grandfather Thomas Wiswall set up your college."

"Shit!"

"No, ice actually."

"Excuse me?"

"Crystal Lake. The one behind our houses? It was just one of the ways he made his money. Old man Thomas used to own the lot, all thirty-three acres of it. It was called Wiswall's Pond way back then. When it froze in the winters, he'd sell the ice. In the summers it was used for baptisms. They changed the name to Baptist Pond, but I don't think that did the ice trade any favors, so they changed it to Crystal Lake. People like the idea of drinking ice from a crystal lake, I guess."

"Well, I never." Jessie gave him a wide-eyed look like she was seeing him for the first time. "So you're kind of royalty in Newton."

Bruce laughed and shook his head. "All the money's gone now, more or less. The house is the end of it, and I've been commissioned by the family back in England to sell it. There's no more family left in Newton."

"That's kind of sad. The end of an era."

"Life is ever onward, no?"

"Yeah." Then Jessie said something that really surprised her. "I lied to you earlier."

"What about? When?"

"Before I fell asleep. Tristan isn't my brother—he's my son. I had him when I was fifteen."

Bruce let out a low whistle. "That was young. It must have been tough."

She shrugged. "It's all good now. I don't even know why I'm telling you. It's just we seem to be becoming good friends, and I don't want to start on a lie. I told Ely earlier today, too, so maybe that's what has it so much on my mind. Normally it doesn't enter my head. I kind of think of him as a kid brother, but living so far away has given me a different perspective. I miss him so much."

Jessie flopped her head down on Bruce's shoulder, and he stroked her hair. "I understand—really I do. Now is your seat belt fastened? We're about to land."

Maria checked Cody's seat belt and managed to keep Alice asleep as the plane commenced its descent into San Juan. The entire day had passed her by in a sort of haze.

Since agreeing with Ricky they should take a temporary break, all the anger had left her. Now she just felt a dull pain. He had been so civil—a true gentleman about the entire thing. In a strange way, the fighting and shouting was easier. Ricky had even suggested they tell the kids together. Alice wouldn't understand much, but Cody sure would.

Maria glanced over to Cody then looked out the airplane window beyond him. The street lights of San Juan winked up at them, and her son was trying to recognize the places he knew. She was relieved to see him happy. The welfare of her kids was her main concern. That, at least, was something she and Ricky could agree about. Looking back, Maria thought he'd been fantastic with Cody earlier that day when it was time to discuss it with their son.

"Look, buddy," Rick had said as they were having lunch. "You know how hard I've been working these last few weeks, don't you?"

The boy nodded at his dad, his big brown eyes open wide with trust.

"Cody, the thing is, I'm afraid I'm going to have to work right through the holidays again. I won't be here at all, so your mom and I . . ." He glanced up at her, and Maria almost asked him to stop. Were they really doing this? But she said nothing and he kept talking. Maria busied herself feeding Alice lunch.

"Your mom and I were wondering if it wouldn't be more fun for you guys to spend the holidays in Puerto Rico."

"Score." Cody punched the air. "I love Grandma's house. We have our own pool there, and there's no snow. It's like the summer."

Rick tried to mask his disappointment, but Maria could see it. "Yeah, buddy," he said. "San Juan is an amazing place. Did you know they even have schools there?"

"Yeah?"

"Yeah. Who knows, it might even be cool to stay a few months there and even go to school, too. It could end up being a one or two month holiday. How cool would that be?"

Maria was shocked when she heard Ricky talking longer term, but maybe he was right to leave the door open for any eventuality.

"What about Todd? He's my best friend." Cody was focused on the immediate.

"Maybe he'd come visit in a few weeks, and you could show him the pool."

"Well, at least I'd get away from Mr. Travers and his extra math class," Cody said.

"And you could swim every day," Ricky said.

"Can Orga come with us?"

"Not just yet. If you wanted to stay longer, I could send her down, but I think she should stay here with me for now." Rick looked to Maria for backup. "Right, Maria?"

She nodded, unable to speak.

"Are we talking about moving house?" Cody was wide-eyed, and there was excitement in his voice.

Rick sat up straight. "No, no, nothing that drastic. We're just talking about getting out of the New England winter. It's too darn cold here, and I'm never around to help your mom. So it might be fun. This house will still be ours." Rick looked straight at Maria. "It's just for a short while. We'll be back together soon."

At that moment, Maria would have given up the whole plan. She would have stayed and rushed into his arms if he gave her the slightest indication it was what he wanted, but he didn't. Instead, Ricky stood up and patted himself down like he wanted to shake the family off.

"Right, well, I guess you guys have a lot to get done if you're going to get on the evening flight tonight."

Cody jumped to his feet, too. "When will you come down, Dad?"

Ricky gave him a big bear hug. "Soon, buddy. As soon as I can. Now, finish your lunch and then go up to your room to make a list of the toys you want to bring with you, because this is a long holiday. You can fill two suitcases."

"Aw, no—how will Santa know we've moved?"

Maria thought her heart would break, but Rick was on top of it. "I'll leave a note in the fireplace. Don't worry, I got your back."

Cody seemed satisfied. He shoved another slice of pizza into his mouth and tore out of the kitchen with bigger things to do.

"Thanks for doing that," Maria said to her husband.

Ricky threw her a small smile and tried to look indifferent, but she could see how tense he was. He reached out to take Alice in his arms. "Can I?"

"Of course." She handed over their daughter.

"Hey, you're growing up, little lady." His tone softened, and he walked around the kitchen with her. "Tomorrow you're gonna be one year old. Wow. How fast did that year go by? I remember this time last year like it was yesterday."

Maria looked away to stop herself from crying. She focused on clearing the lunch things from the table.

Rick concentrated on his daughter. "You be a good girl for your mama. No crying, and play nice with your cousins. I'll see you as soon as I can, *cosa guapa*."

To hear him call Alice *pretty thing* in Spanish was the straw that broke the camel's back. Maria's tears started to flow while she filled the sink with water.

Rick's tone changed to a colder, more businesslike one. "Do you want me to book the flights or will you?"

She bit her lip and looked out the window at Crystal Lake. "I can do it."

"Fine." She heard him kiss his daughter and say good-bye and then put her down on the floor. "I'll get out of here and make it easier for you. Text or e-mail me if you need anything."

She bit her lip and wiped her eyes. When she turned around to say good-bye, he was already gone. Alice sat on the floor grinning up at her.

Rick didn't say good-bye or even attempt a kiss or a hug. That hurt so much. Even if they were breaking up, she wanted to kiss him good-bye. The rules, it seemed, had changed, and Maria didn't know how to play this new game.

When the kitchen was clean, Maria called her mother to say she was coming home, and then she booked their flights—one way. That would have made her cry again, but Cody was in and out all afternoon discussing the merits of various toys, and Maria wanted to keep it together for his sake. Later on, Alice took a big nap in the afternoon, so they were in good shape for the flight back to Puerto Rico that evening.

"We're almost there," Cody said, looking very excited as he gazed out the airplane window.

"We are. It's going to be amazing." Maria tried to keep him enthused.

"Yeah, I'm excited about coming to live here for a while."

Maria smiled but inside she was anxious. What if a while turned out to be forever? Would her darling boy be okay with that? Would Ricky fight her for custody? He would never win, because he was married to his job and didn't have the freedom to care for his kids full time. Rick had no idea how much work was involved.

Maria was miserable. Was all of this her fault? How did other women do it? Did they lock away their own hopes and needs for the sake of their kids and husbands? Was she a selfish bitch?

She thought about her fight with Cathi the night before. It was a horrendous thing Maria had done, blowing her friend's cover like that. She wanted to call and apologize, but she couldn't bring herself to do it. Maria was still too mad at Cathi. The woman had lost touch with reality. *Or was it me?* she wondered now. Maybe she was the one who had lost touch, while Cathi was playing it just right, keeping her man in line by manipulating and telling little white lies—or in her case, big, huge lies.

All Maria knew for sure was she was miserable and, for the time being anyway, separated. Ricky wasn't there for her anymore, and she had to stay on the functioning side of sanity in order to raise her two kids. San Juan seemed to afford an anchor, something she could cling to. Her mother was a huge help and so were her sisters.

The wheels touched down on the runway.

"Score, we're here," Cody said, excitement winning over fatigue for the moment.

Alice woke up and looked around, but Maria was ready with a pacifier and plugged the little girl in before she erupted.

"Score." Maria echoed her son's words. "We're home."

Things will get better, she promised herself. Puerto Rico would make her strong again, whether or not Rick was part of her future.

Maria switched on her phone as the plane taxied to the terminal, and it pinged with a new text message. It was from her husband.

Please kiss Alice Happy Birthday from me.

Maria kissed the soft baby hair on the crown of her daughter's head. "That's from your daddy," she whispered. "He says happy birthday, baby." Maria cuddled Alice a little tighter.

Chapter Thirty-Two
An Early Christmas Present

Early Monday morning, Ely hugged Noreen tight and kissed her good-bye. She caught her plane and picked up a car rental easy enough, and she used the GPS from there.

Ely was beyond nervous. It was still difficult to believe she was pregnant at all. The morning sickness was a nightmare, but her figure still looked the same. It was impossible to think that unless she did something about it, she would be a mom in about seven months. She would turn twenty-four before the baby was born. Insane.

It broke her heart that Josh was so mad at her, but it was easy for him to be noble. He was the guy. His work, life, and studies could chug along without much intrusion. She was the one who would have to change everything. She would never be able to go out and party or take off for a weekend at the last minute.

No, there was no doubt. Her life as she knew it would be over if she continued on this path.

Ely brushed her hair to stall getting out of the car. The shame and disappointment from her parents was the worst part. She was already the wild child who was incapable of getting a simple degree, but pregnancy? Ely studied her face in the rearview mirror as she pulled the paddle brush through her long, dark hair. That was one stupid mistake she should have been able to avoid. She knew all about the birds and the bees, damn it. Her father would be so mad and her mother . . . that was even worse. She would give Ely the silent treatment.

She could make this all go away, and nobody need ever know. Well, other than Josh, who hated her already, and Jessie, who had no idea she was even thinking about an abortion.

Ely used a scrunchie she found in her purse and scooped her hair up into a ponytail. Learning about Tristan had shaken her to the core. How had Jessie been that brave? She was so young. Her parents made the decision for her. Ely didn't have that luxury. She was too old for her folks to take charge and too young to be able to handle a baby herself. It was the worst age possible. She threw her hairbrush back in her overnight bag.

Maybe she could lie to Jessie. Would that be kinder? She would pretend she miscarried—even tell Josh that. Then they wouldn't judge her. She could carry the burden and shame alone—for life.

Ely wondered about heaven. Did it exist? If it did, would she meet her baby there? Or would she go to straight to hell for having the abortion in the first place? Perhaps her baby would be really mad because she lost the chance to live, or would the baby be happy because it was dropkicked straight back up to heaven? Her eyes glassed up again. Ely didn't even know if she was carrying a boy or a girl. Was it a little Josh or little Ely? Did they make miniature cowboy boots for babies?

Ely looked at the building and stroked her stomach. Was this the smartest thing she had ever done, or the dumbest? Only time would tell. She got out of the car and started for the front door, but then her phone began to ring.

"Saved by the bell," she said and answered the call.

"Hullo, is this Elyse Briskin?" The man's voice was a rich English one.

"Yeah, who wants to know?"

"Oh, good. My name is Richard Worthington. I've been talking with your friend, Hugo Hendrix."

Ely thought it was a joke. "Oh, yeah?"

"Yes. Well, he's been telling me all about your fabulous shampoo line. I think it's a bloody marvelous idea, and I'd like to discuss it with you, if you're interested."

"Who is this really?" Ely said, backing up and sitting on the hood of her rental.

"I'm Richard Worthington. You know Worth Airways?"

"Come on. I know who Richard Worthington is. I just don't think you're him."

"Didn't he tell you I'd be calling?"

"Nope." But then she remembered Noreen talking about it. Was it possible? "You're really Richard Worthington?"

"Yes, last time I checked."

"And you wanna buy my Down Under Shampoo?"

He laughed. "I love the name. Look, could we meet in early January? Perhaps you might like to visit me at my getaway—Necker Island. You could bring a friend if that would make you more comfortable. I'll send a jet to collect you."

"A private jet?"

"Well, I do own an airline, Miss Briskin."

"Mr. Worthington, I think you can call me Ely."

"Okay, Ely. Will you visit me to talk about your shampoo line? Come to Necker Island in January. It's very nice at that time of year. I think you'll like it."

"Mr. Worthington, I think I might like that very much." Ely smiled into the phone. "Just to be clear about this. Do you want to buy my idea? Or do you want to go into business together?"

"I'm open to suggestions, Ely."

"Gee, I feel like I'm on one of those reality shows."

He laughed. "Look I've got your phone number, so I'll get my assistant to call early in the New Year and we can figure out times and dates to suit both our schedules. Hugo tells me you're in college."

"Yes, sir, but I'll be finishing that up this spring because I'm pregnant."

"Oh? Congratulations. Maybe you need to think about a range of baby shampoos, too?"

"Now, there's an idea, Mr. Worthington." She glanced up at the house she was parked outside and saw the curtains twitch. She'd been spotted. Josh came out to the front door of his North Carolina home and searched her face, his own pale with concern.

"I gotta go now, Mr. Worthington. We'll talk soon." She hit the end button on her phone and ran up the path to where Josh was waiting, her ponytail swinging from side to side like a little girl.

"I couldn't do it, baby. I couldn't go through with it, so I hope you meant it when you said you loved me and you wanted this baby."

Josh's face lit up, and he threw his arms open. "For real? You're still pregnant with our baby?"

Ely ran into his embrace and hugged him tight. "Yes. You're gonna be a daddy. I'm gonna quit school and set up my own business. It might not be the way we saw our lives going, but, heck, you only got one life."

Josh cradled her face in his hands and stared into her eyes. "We'll be young parents. That's cool. Best of all, though, I got the most wonderful, exciting, dynamic, stubborn as a mule woman in the world."

Ely stood on her tiptoes to kiss him on the lips. "You're not so bad yourself."

Josh draped his arm over her shoulders and guided her up the steps to his family home.

"I guess this is a good time for you to meet the folks."

"Okay, this is gonna be a bit awkward."

"Nah. I already told my mama all about you. It's gonna be just fine."

She put her arm around his waist and squeezed tight.

"By the way, I got an early Christmas present. Richard Worthington wants to buy my shampoo line."

"What?"

"Told you it was a good idea."

"You know what? This was a great idea." Michael held up the tumbler of whiskey.

Rick wasn't so sure. "I know it's almost Christmas, but we can't drink all day and all night. Plus I'm going in to work tomorrow morning."

"What? It'll be Christmas Eve. Don't you have any last-minute shopping to do?" Michael brought his glass down to rest on the arm of the chair. "Or not?"

Rick had never seen Michael looking so miserable. It had been just over twenty-four hours since he had moved in, but his friend was going downhill fast. He hadn't showered, shaved, or even changed clothes since his arrival. "Did you talk to Cathi today?"

Michael shook his head. "I only moved out yesterday. I can't call her already, but God, I miss the girls."

"Tell them to come visit."

Michael tried to read the time on his watch, but he seemed to be having trouble focusing. "It's late, but they're on vacation from school tomorrow. I'll call in the morning."

"You better clean yourself up and change before that."

His friend lifted a hand up and sniffed his underarm. "Bad?"

It made Rick smile. "Not yet, but you look like shit."

"Ha! Thanks! What about you, Mr. Happy? Any word from Maria?"

"Nah, I thought the kids would be tired today after the late night flight last night. Things run much later over there. I'm sure they stayed up and had a big meal when they arrived. They'll be exhausted by now. Alice turns one today."

"Ah, shit."

Rick agreed but didn't speak.

"You seriously going in to work tomorrow?" Michael's eyes were drooping now. "I think you're crazy. At least you have a gorgeous wife and two great kids who adore you. Maria just wanted to see more of you. I think Cathi would have traded me in for a richer model if she got the chance. You're one lucky bastard."

Rick drained his whiskey glass. He didn't normally drink this heavily, but nothing was normal anymore. He had plowed through the day with work like he always did, but it had been the least productive day of his life. He kept wondering what Maria and the kids were doing. Was Cody swimming? Was Alice being difficult for her mom? Was Maria crying, or was she happy in the Puerto Rican sun, surrounded by family—all except him.

"What you wanna do for Christmas Day? We can order pizza or go out to a movie?"

Rick stood up. "I need another drink—you want one?"

"Sure, why the hell not? I'm not going into the office tomorrow." Michael drained his glass and handed it to Rick.

"Jesus, Michael, it's not that big a deal. Lots of people work Christmas Eve, and I might even work Christmas Day, too. I've got a lot going on now."

"What's the point?"

"The point is . . . well, it's what I do. I'm damn good at it, and I make a lot of money. That's the way it's always been."

"Yeah? You work Christmas Day every year?" Michael's eyes seemed sharper now. He was drunk, but he was still talking smart.

"Lay off."

Rick walked out to the dining room, heading toward the cupboard where they kept the whiskey. The lake caught his eye. It had been a long time since he had admired it. The night was clear, and the moonlight bounced off the ice like lights at a Disney stage show. Rick would have to call Maria to see if she had arrived safely. He poured two huge glasses of whiskey and capped the bottle. He turned to leave the room and spotted the vase of flowers he'd given his wife on the sideboard. The roses were dead now, which annoyed him. Why hadn't she thrown them in the trash? They were weeks old.

It made him think of when he used to bring her flowers every Friday after work. When had he stopped doing that? Life had just gotten too full. He was always rushing. He tried to remember when he had bought the dead roses—early November, almost two months. Wow . . . that long.

Rick had never felt more frustrated, miserable, or alone. He headed back to Michael. "Got you another whiskey."

But his friend was asleep in the oversized armchair. Rick nudged his shoulder gently, unsure whether to wake him or let him sleep it off.

"Hey, you want this?"

Michael moved a little but didn't open his eyes. "What's the point?" he said in his sleep.

Rick didn't know if his guest was dreaming about Cathi or saying no to another drink.

He sat back down. "I believe the point was to get drunk, Michael." He raised his glass to his unconscious friend. "Here's to getting real, real drunk. I think it's a great idea."

"This was a great idea," Jessie said to her mother as they walked out of church together on Christmas Eve. It was a special family service, full of carol singing and festive cheer. The exit was flanked by enormous urns, crammed with shiny green holly and festooned in bright red berries. Ivy cascaded down the sides, and Jessie touched it as she walked by. She hadn't been to a service in all the time she'd lived in Boston. It wasn't high on her agenda, but it was for Elizabeth Armstrong.

Dorking's main street was buzzing with last-minute shoppers, and the pubs were doing a brisk trade, too. The night was very dark, but twinkling Christmas lights shone bright overhead, arching across the street along the full length of the road. It was a magical atmosphere. There was a huge town tree on the sidewalk at the top of the street where normally people parked bikes. Folks had tied cards onto the branches for friends and family who were no longer with them. Jessie wondered if her mum had done one for her dad but didn't ask.

Tristan started counting the number of plankers who were wearing Santa hats.

"So I'm guessing *planker* is your new word for *loser*. Are they all plankers just because they're wearing Santa hats?" Jessie nudged him as they walked along the sidewalk.

He shoved her back harder. "Yes."

Their house was a five-minute walk from the main street. It was a pleasant stroll because of the friendly atmosphere and the fact it was nowhere near as cold as Newton. Jessie looked up at the familiar night sky. It was good to be home. Dan was a million miles away from her and out of her life for good. She wondered about Ely. Her roommate had said she would phone when she got home. Teatime in England meant lunchtime on the east coast. Maybe she hadn't gotten there yet. She decided she would e-mail her friend to nudge her into telling her parents sooner rather than later.

As per tradition, the family was allowed to open one Christmas present each on Christmas Eve. Elizabeth Armstrong served homemade mince pies and strong tea while the younger ones ripped open the most promising looking parcels. Nobody expected the doorbell to ring.

"I'll get it!" Tristan yelled, having already opened his gift. A moment later, he walked back into the room. "It's someone for you," he said.

Surprised, Jessie jumped to her feet. "I'm not expecting anybody. I haven't spoken to a soul since I got home."

"Maybe an old school friend saw you at church," Elizabeth said as Jessie walked out into the hall.

She gasped. "Bruce! I wasn't—I mean, how did you know where I live?"

He was smiling, maybe laughing at her newfound shyness. "Hullo, Jessie."

"Um, welcome. Come in." She stood back to let him enter. The house was very modest and Jessie was embarrassed that he saw her small, terraced home. He had said his family wasn't rich anymore, but she knew they had been, once upon a time. Bruce sounded upper class. She knew a private school accent when she heard one. The hall was so narrow she had to press her back against the wall to invite him in.

"The kitchen's straight ahead," she said.

He looked just as uncomfortable as she felt and stopped in the hall to talk. "I hope it's okay, just arriving unannounced like this."

"Of course." She lied. Even with both of them standing against opposing walls, there was very little room between them. That was when she saw the young boy hiding shyly behind Bruce.

"It's just, well—Tom and I were in the neighborhood, so I phoned Noreen and got your address from her. It seemed crazy to be in Dorking and not call in to say hello and wish you a Merry Christmas."

Jessie tilted her head and raised a single eyebrow. "You just happened to be in Dorking?" This was no coincidence.

"Well, yes." Bruce smiled. "We heard Dorking was very pretty at this time of year." He looked straight at her. He was flirting with her.

Jessie turned to the young boy, Tom, and smiled. "You're very welcome here, Tom. How do you know this guy?"

"Tom's my son, Jessie. He's eight years old. I thought he might like to say hullo to Tristan."

Elizabeth Armstrong picked that very minute to come into the hall to see who her daughter's guest was. "Jessica, where are your manners? And you're letting all the heat out."

"Hullo, Mrs. Armstrong. I'm Bruce Wiswall, a friend of your daughter's, and this is my son, Tom."

"Very nice to meet you, Bruce, but can you all move along into the kitchen so I can close the front door? There's an arctic chill coming through. I have more mince pies in there." She was waving her hands trying to get everyone to move. Elizabeth was no fool either, and Jessie wasn't surprised when her mother took control. "Why don't you come into the front room with me, child?" She addressed Tom with a warm smile. "You look the same age as our Tristan. We have Cadbury's Roses chocolate in here, and the new James Bond movie is about to start."

Bruce gave her a grateful look and nudged his son toward the front room along with Elizabeth. Then he followed Jessie into the kitchen.

She was still trying to compose herself. She knew she was blushing by the heat of her cheeks, because despite her best efforts not to be, Jessie was embarrassed by her modest home compared to the mansions on Crystal Lake Lane. Mentally, she kicked herself to cop on.

"You have a son," she whispered. "Why didn't you tell me?"

He tilted his head. "I'm telling you now. I almost told you in Newton. Do you remember talking about skeletons in the closet? I told you we all have them. It's true. Everybody has a past, Jessie, but we all have a future, too."

"Where was Tom when you were in America?"

"He lives with his mother most of the time, but I get to see him often."

"Shared custody? That's hard."

"We make it work. I have a pretty demanding job, so I couldn't keep him full time even if I wanted."

Jessie watched him as he spoke. He looked bigger in her tiny kitchen. His dark charcoal coat squared up his shoulders, and he was wearing the flat cap. His eyes looked grayer than usual, and his mouth was wide— attractive.

"Jessie?"

"Hmm . . . sorry, what were you saying?"

"I was saying I very much wanted to see you."

"Oh yes?"

"Yes." He looked at the chair pushed into the kitchen table. "Can we sit?"

"Oh God, yes. Sorry, I'm not being a very good hostess, am I? Can I get you a cup of tea or a coffee and maybe a mince pie?"

Bruce looked exasperated. He glanced at the pastries, then at the chair, then at her. He shook his head, took a step toward her, and kissed her. He didn't stop kissing her either. Bruce wrapped his arms around her while Jessie's mind tried to catch up with her lips. This was unexpected but very nice. She slipped her arms around his waist and kissed him back.

"That, Jessie Armstrong, is something I've wanted to do to you since the first day I saw you on Crystal Lake Lane. You're gorgeous, you are." He said this with a London-boy accent, and it made her laugh.

"I had no idea."

"No. You were too busy swooning over that loser, Dan."

"He's a planker," Jessie said.

"You—what?"

"Tristan's new favorite word—*planker*. It means loser."

"Oh, you mean a tosser?"

Jessie laughed and started to feel very comfortable, chatting to him in his arms.

"Jessie, will you do me the honor of going out for dinner with me in the very near future?"

She smiled at him. "Yes, Bruce, I will, but I do have one question."

"Shoot."

"Were you really on my flight home or did you rig that?"

Bruce laughed. She liked his laugh. "You have no idea. I was meant to fly out a few hours later. We were both on British Airways, but I had to pay a small mortgage to change to your earlier flight." He tightened his arms around her waist. "But it was worth every penny."

Bruce leaned in to kiss her again just as there was a knock on the kitchen door, and Jessie knew it was her mother. Nobody else would be so polite. Elizabeth popped her head around the door.

"It's your phone, love. It's ringing." She handed the mobile to Jessie.

Bruce made no attempt to pull back but let her free up an arm to take the phone. It was like he wanted Elizabeth to see. He smiled at Jessie's mother. "I bet you make the best mince pies in the world, Mrs. Armstrong."

"Oh, Bruce, call me Lizzy."

Jessie recognized the number.

"Hullo, Ely. I've been worried sick about you. How are you?"

"Hey, baby. How's the Queen?" Ely tried to sound upper-class British and did it as terribly as Jessie did a South Carolina accent.

"We're all fine." She glanced up at Bruce and winked at him. She was still wrapped in his arms. "How are you?"

"I'm great. I flew down to Josh's and met his family yesterday, and then we both landed into Charleston today. We've told everybody they're gonna be grandparents."

Jessie winked at Bruce. "How did that go?"

"Way better than we thought. Josh's parents were a bit anxious, but his mom's cool. My dad was fine with it. Just goes to show—you never know how these things are gonna turn out. The Bull is bullin' 'cause I told him I'm going into business with Richard Worthington for my Down Under shampoo line."

"You what?"

"Yeah, Richard Worthington called me in the middle of everything to make an offer on Down Under. I'm not sure I'm gonna take it, though. Dad's working on a counteroffer right now. You gotta laugh."

Jessie did just that. She burst out laughing and shook her head in disbelief. "Why am I not surprised, Ely Briskin?"

"What about you? All well with Tristan and your mom?"

"And the rest of them. We're having a smashing time with mince pies, and we're opening presents. Bruce just called round." Jessie let it hang in the air.

"Say what? Bruce Wiswall?"

"Yes, he wanted to give me an early Christmas present." She wrapped her free arm around his waist tighter, and he kissed her forehead.

"Girl, that boy is into you. I can tell."

"You think?" Jessie looked at him like she was assessing him, and Bruce raised his eyebrows, as if trying to second-guess the conversation.

"I know these things," Ely said. "I can sense 'em. That man likes you, make no mistake. It's gonna be the best Christmas ever."

Chapter Thirty-Three
Feliz Navidad

"Best Christmas ever!" Cody shouted as he ran and jumped into the pool to make the biggest splash he could.

It made Maria laugh, and she applauded him. The sun was setting, and even though she was warm, she felt the need for her pashmina. She asked Paloma to keep an eye on her kids, and then Maria walked into her mother's house.

When she opened the door and entered her old bedroom, the silence enveloped her. It was lovely, quiet and peaceful. Even though it had been a great day, it had been a busy, loud one, too, so she couldn't stop herself lying down on the bed for just a moment to rest and recharge. For the first time that day, she let her mind relax and reflect.

The time since her arrival had simply flown by. On her first day back in Puerto Rico, Maria whizzed into town to do some shopping. It had only been a month since their last visit, but this time she was starting to feel more at home. She spoke Spanish now when she was in the shops, and one of her brothers-in-law had even spotted her in traffic and given her a friendly beep. That had never happened in Newton. Her mother had even commented on it when she'd swept back into the kitchen that first day with Alice's birthday cake.

"You seem good."

"I feel good." Maria had answered with a smile. "Tell me again why I went away?"

Leticia had given an empathetic nod. "I always worried about you leaving Puerto Rico, *cariño*. I knew you had to spread your wings, but I thought you'd come home. Now, of course, it's much more complicated. What about the father of your children?"

Since their talk, those thoughts had lingered, but there had been no time to feel depressed, because Leticia kept her busy. Preparing the house for Christmas Day involved doing lots of errands for her mom, which Maria was happy about because she'd forgotten how magical the island became around this time. It was the biggest event of the year, and the streets were full of music and colored lights. Christmas trees had been erected all over San Juan, the shops were decorated, and children were out of school. The mood was infectious, she thought now, lying on her bed and closing her eyes. But today—the Christmas Day party at her mom's house—that was the high point.

Bernardo, Paloma's husband, had arrived early Christmas morning with his two boys. Of course, Maria remembered e*l lechon*—the pig on the spit —and the massive meal that lasted all day. The boys and Cody helped Bernardo set it up. They were inducted into the ritual of *el lechon*, learning how to baste the beast and get it set up properly. They were entrusted with the matches while Bernardo supervised. Then a timetable was made up, whereby one of the boys had to sit with the pig all day. It couldn't be left unattended even for a moment.

She laughed, because as soon as Bernardo was gone, having made the boys promise they'd stick to their times, they lost interest. No surprise, Leticia let her grandsons off, saying she was happy to slice and dice her vegetables outside on the picnic table where she could watch the pig, too.

By early afternoon, the entire family had assembled in Leticia's house, and the smell of roast pig hung tantalizingly in the air. Drinks were poured and the feast commenced. There were traditions Cody had heard about but never witnessed. For example—just for fun—everybody wore *pava*s, straw hats they would use later for the *parranda*.

"It's a bit like your ghosting," Maria explained to her son. "We'll have a good old sing-along here after dinner, and then we'll go surprise a few of the neighbors."

"Give them candy?"

Leticia hugged him. "No, we'll surprise them by arriving on their door and having a sing-along—a bit like caroling but with Puerto Rican songs. When we're done, we'll move on to the next house."

The boy nodded and smiled, like it was all very normal to him, and Maria marveled at how adaptable kids were.

Now it was getting dark. She pulled herself up off the bed, knowing that if she didn't move soon, she'd fall asleep. Her kids would be up till three or four in the morning singing and dancing with the adults. She was out of practice, she mused as she fetched her aquamarine wrap and headed back outside to the party.

The noise level had risen since she'd left them. Everybody was full of food and needed to burn some energy, and all the kids were back in the pool. Maria smiled because it was so nice to be somewhere warm enough to swim outside in December. The dads dove in next and played rough with all the boys. It was remarkable that, between Maria and her sisters, there were nine boys. Alice was the only girl, and she was passed around like a doll. Alice loved all the attention, but it exhausted her and she soon nodded off in her stroller.

The noise level was high, so when the doorbell rang, Maria didn't even hear it. Lola and Carlos arrived to cheers of *Feliz Navidad*, and the boys tried to get Carlos into the pool. He looked like he was prepared for the midnight swim, because he didn't take much convincing and he had a swimsuit on under his clothes. She didn't mean to look when he stripped down, but Maria couldn't help noticing what great shape Carlos was in. He looked as good now as he had back when they'd dated.

"Bring back memories, *la memoria?*" Sara, Maria's younger sister, teased her.

Maria shook her head and snapped back to reality. "No, not at all."

Leticia got up to answer the door again.

"It's a letter for you, *cosa guapa.*" She handed the envelope to Maria.

"What? Where did this come from?"

"Fed Ex. Just now. I didn't know they worked Christmas Day." Leticia sat back down at the long table to watch the action in the pool.

Maria turned it over. She recognized the handwriting immediately. She glanced up to see if her mother was curious, but everyone was focusing on the water fun. Alice was still asleep in her stroller.

She nudged Sara who sat next to her. "Can you keep an eye out for a moment?" Maria pointed to the baby, and her little sister nodded.

Maria tightened the shawl around her and went into the house to read the letter. She ripped open the envelope and was surprised to see a handwritten note from Ricky. It had been a long, long time since he had done that. Everything was e-mail or text these days.

She headed for her mother's living room at the front of the house. From there, the noise of the pool was barely audible, and she could hear herself think. Maria switched on the lamp next to the brown leather sofa and sat down to read what her husband had to say.

> *Dearest Maria,*
> *Feliz Navidad. I guess that's a good place to start. I hope Cody and Alice were happy with their presents and they've had a good day. What about you? How have the last few days been?*
> *I've been in hell, Maria. I can't do this. I can't live without you and the kids. How did we get here? Was it me? Did you really think I was serious about that sitter? I swear nothing happened. I'm sorry if I looked at her the wrong way.*
> *Yes, she was attractive, but Maria, I adore you. You're the light of my life. I remember the first day I saw you in college and that quarterback was making moves on you. I didn't think I had a chance but I tried anyway, and I kept trying until you agreed to go out with me. I always thought you were the single greatest*

treasure in my life. Then, as if all of that wasn't enough, you gave me two more treasures. My life was complete, but now, somehow, I let you slip away. How did I do that? How stupid could I be?

Maria, I'll give it all up. I'll come with you to Puerto Rico. If that's what you want, I'll move. I'm sure I can get a job there. If it means this much to you, I'll move. Just don't leave me.

I love you always and forever.

Ricky

By the time she reached the last line, Maria was crying. What was she doing, so far away from her husband?

"*Hola*, Maria." He was standing in the doorway.

"Jesus, I didn't know you were here!" She grasped the arm of the sofa.

"Sorry, I didn't mean to scare you, but your mom let me in. I explained to her that I wanted to write you a letter because—well, you know why. I want to do things different this time. I'll do it your way."

"Oh, Ricky." She stood and stared at him. He was wearing light blue jeans, a white shirt, and his brown suede jacket. He looked so familiar, and she started to walk across the room, but then she faltered. "Ricky, I need you to understand—Alice. I love her so much, but she doesn't seem to want me. You and Cody can make her laugh so easy, but she just screams at me. There's no letup. I've been getting more depressed, and then I saw my weight skyrocket. I could just about cope with all of that, but the day I saw you look at Jessie, I knew I'd reached a breaking point. I didn't mean to push you away. Damn it, I wanted you to save me, even from myself, but you were either working or in that damned gym or flirting with her." She folded the letter and put it in her pocket.

He stood where he was, looking nervous to move. "I'm sorry. I know the kids really changed things, especially Alice, but she'll grow out of it. You know she will, and she loves you." He took a single step toward her but stopped again. "I love you, too." He stared at his wife. "I see now how obsessed I've become with work. You're not the only one getting older, and I think work made me feel like I was making a difference. It sounds dumb, but it made me feel young."

"What about Jessie?" She pulled the pashmina around her shoulders.

"Yes, flirting with her at Cathi's party was not my smartest move, especially since we were just getting over a rough patch, but before you get too mad at me, I swear to you, nothing actually happened."

"Nothing?"

"Well, I offered her a coffee one morning. It was the first time you came down here. She turned up to watch Alice, and I was so damned furious with you, I offered her a coffee."

Maria covered her mouth with one of her hands. "What happened?"

"She blew me off. She knew I was a stupid married man and way too old for her." Rick risked another step forward. "Honest. If you can forgive me, Maria, you need to know, I really have learned my lesson. I know you're the only woman I want, and I'm so close to losing you." His voice broke, and he began to weep.

Maria rushed over to him. "Oh, Ricky, don't cry. I'm sorry, too."

She wrapped her arms around him. "If I hadn't run away, you wouldn't have ended up in that position with her. I blame myself for this mess, too. I'm sorry I couldn't just talk all of this out without running away like a schoolgirl."

He lifted his tear-filled eyes and gave a miserable laugh. "Please, no more talk of schoolgirls. God, I love you." He hugged her. The pashmina fell to the floor, and Maria kissed him like she hadn't kissed him in years.

"Ricardo, *cariño*, I love you, too. Let's not get this crazy ever, ever again." She peppered his face with kisses. "And thank you for coming, for saving me, again."

Rick laughed through his tears and kissed her back, but then Maria remembered something. "There's an ex of mine out in the pool tonight, and I see how easy it is to appear suspicious, even if it means nothing."

"An ex of yours here? Should I worry?" But he was smiling and wiping his tears away.

"No, his mother and mine are best friends. That would be a recipe for disaster."

Maria hugged him tighter. He smelled great, too—familiar.

"I'm just glad to have you in my arms again." He nuzzled his nose into her neck and breathed her in like she was his oxygen. "And what's all this craziness about you putting on weight? How many times did I tell you in college that you were too thin?" Maria was about to disagree, but Rick continued. "You were! Now you're just perfect. Babe, you're still my very own weapon of mass seduction."

At that moment, Maria didn't feel fat or old. She felt like she had a decade earlier—treasured.

He was still talking. "I love you more than life itself. I'll do anything, and I mean anything, to keep us together."

He pulled out an envelope from his inside jacket pocket and handed it to Maria.

"What's this?"

"It's what I've been doing for the last two days. Michael Grant has moved into our house because he and Cathi are going through some stuff at the moment."

Maria rolled her eyes. "What? Are they breaking up?"

"No, I don't think so. He told me he believed in the whole for-better-for-worse thing. She's just going through one of her 'worse' phases at the moment. Looking at him, I got to say he still loves her, but who knows? I offered him the house, and he's thinking about it. He wants to take a year off to write, so he might end up renting it. It would be a heck of a lot cheaper than the one they're in now."

"Rent our house? But what about us? What about your work?"

"That's what I'm telling you. I'm staying."

Maria's heart leapt. "You'd move here?"

"This is a copy of my letter of resignation. I handed it in yesterday. So I'm here, if you'll have me."

"But, Ricky, that job is your life."

"No, *cariño*, you are. You and the kids. It's time for a change. It's time to put us first."

"Shouldn't we at least talk about this?"

"What's there to discuss? You want to live here and I want to live with you. Business is booming in Puerto Rico. I know I'll get a job. Are you having second thoughts about leaving Newton?"

"No! I want to live here!"

"Then so do I."

Maria slipped her hands down and inside the denim pockets on his backside and smiled. "Hubba-hubba," she said and kissed him.

"Daddy!" Cody climbed out of the pool and ran to Rick, hurling himself at his father.

"Hey, buddy. Merry Christmas. Looks like I managed to get here after all."

"Come on, get your clothes off. All the dads are in the pool." Cody started to pull Rick toward the water fully dressed, but Maria watched as Rick managed to sidestep the water for the few moments it took to thank his mother-in-law and greet the rest of the family. There were nephews whom Rick had never met, so it took some time, and he said wanted to see his baby girl, too. Alice slept through the reunion.

Rick excused himself and went into the house for a moment to change. When he came out, Maria couldn't care less if Carlos had a good body—Ricky's was better. He was hers, he was the father of her children, and he adored her—what a Christmas present.

Her mother came over and sat next to her. "*Esta bien, chica?*"

"Never better. I think things are going to be okay. Ricky says he'll move here."

Leticia's eyes lit up, and she clapped with delight.

"Oh, that is the best news ever. You can all stay here until you find a good house."

"Thanks, Mami."

"No, thank you. I have my four daughters living here in Puerto Rico, all married to good men. I have to tell you, Maria, that is as good as it gets. This really has been the best Christmas ever."

Chapter Thirty-Four
Cathi's Christmas

Cathi Grant wasn't having such a good Christmas. Her husband hated her, the girls were still furious about the move to a new house, and now the water-damaged floors were starting to smell. Her dream life had turned into a nightmare.

She knew where Michael was staying. As soon as he'd heard Maria was back down in Puerto Rico, he had asked Rick if he could move in with him. Cathi had tried to stop him, using every argument possible, but Michael was a changed man. She had never seen him so furious or disappointed with her.

After a rather dull Christmas dinner with her daughters, the girls went over to watch a movie with their dad. She sat, all alone in her massive house. Even Fifi, her dear little dog, seemed to have fallen out of love with her. The dog kept running away to Noreen Palmer's home, whatever that was about.

Cathi walked around number sixteen, Crystal Lake Lane. The hall rugs still squelched underfoot, and a large water stain was forming on her hardwood floors. The landlord wasn't going to like that. None of this would have happened if she had stayed in her old place. She would still have Michael and the girls. She would even still have that blasted dog. Cathi's mind wandered back to her lovely galley kitchen and the antique library. What she would give to be lounging on her sectional right now with Michael, the girls, and the dog. How had it all gone so wrong?

There was only one way to find out, she decided. Cathi grabbed her winter coat and swept out the door of her rental. She thought it would be dumb to ring the front door of Maria's house, so she let herself in the back, like always. Cathi knew the house well, so she walked into the television room and there on the sofa was Michael, with an arm around each daughter. They were tucked snugly in on either side of him. A box of Christmas candy lay open on the table, with wrappers strewn everywhere. If she were part of their day, she'd have made them clean it up, but she wasn't. He saw her come in, and in the past, he would have always smiled at her, but not today. His expression remained impassive.

Cathi felt a searing jolt of pain at not being part of this festive, familial scene. "I, um, just wanted to say Merry Christmas."

He got up without enthusiasm. "Hello. Merry Christmas to you, too." He looked back at his daughters, who hadn't moved. "Girls?"

"What? We had dinner with her," Katie said, eyes fixed on the television.

Cathi could feel the animosity bounce off her daughters. They hated her.

She addressed her husband. "Can we talk?"

He shrugged but gestured for her to move back out to the kitchen.

"Want a drink? Or a coffee?"

"I'm sorry." Her tone was final. She wasn't talking about coffee.

He sighed and headed over to the coffee maker.

"Really. I mean it this time. I'm very, very sorry. I shouldn't have tried to manipulate you like that."

"Tried?" He raised his eyebrows and jutted his chin. "I think you did more than try."

"Yes, you're right, of course. I did manipulate you and the girls. I didn't know what I was doing at the time. Strike that, I did know, but I didn't think about what it was. I sure didn't think about your side of things, Michael. Look, I know you hate me, but I really thought I was doing it for the family, not just me. I thought I was bringing you and the girls up in the world. I don't know how I got that damn idea."

He stared at the coffee maker and grimaced, as if coffee was suddenly a bad idea. "I'm having a glass of wine. You want one?"

She nodded. "Can I sit?"

"Whatever."

She sat. "I'm scared, really scared, Michael. You sound like you hate me. I'd rather you shouted at me and called me a bitch."

He glanced toward the door. "Can you keep your voice down? I don't want the kids hearing you talk like that."

"Sorry." She dropped her eyes to the table while he got a bottle of red and poured two large glasses.

"Merry damn Christmas, kiddo." He pushed a glass across the table to her and sat down opposite. "Okay, say what you gotta say and then leave."

She snapped her head up. "You mean it? Leave? You have crossed a line, haven't you? You've given up on us?"

Michael closed his eyes for a moment. "What *us*, Cathi? Seriously. What us? I did love you, with all my heart. I've loved your crazy, harebrained plans since the day I met you. You've always had your own way of doing things. I think you've done a great job with the girls, too, but you've turned into this woman I don't even know anymore. It's like I'm living with a stranger. You sold that house from right under my ass, didn't you?"

Cathi started to cry. "Yes. I thought I was saving you from the stress. I wanted to present it all as a done deal."

"I'm the damn done deal. You just run rings around me. That's not how I want to live, Cathi. That's not how we started."

She pushed her wine aside and reached across the table for his hands.

"Then for the love of God, let us start again. I'll do it your way. I'll really try. I'll move to the country. I'll go back to work so you can write your novel. I'll even change the girls to the school of your choice."

He pulled his hands back and stood up.

"You still don't get it? I don't want to move the girls. I just want us to be a team like we used to be." He paced the kitchen as he spoke. "Can we start by talking stuff through and not second-guessing the solution, like you're doing right now?"

"Oh, shit. Am I?"

This time he laughed and stopped walking. "Cathi, you don't swear. I've never heard you say *shit* before."

"Is that bad?" Cathi looked up anxiously.

Michael shook his head. "No, I think it's good. It shows you're changing, but don't start using bad language. It doesn't suit you. Can we just take one step at a time?" His expression grew softer. "But I do think we should get professional help. Would you be up for that?"

"If it means getting you back, Michael, I'll do anything."

"Come here," he said, reaching out a hand.

Cathi didn't need to be asked twice. She was in his arms in a second. "Thank you, my love. I'm so sorry I made such a mess of everything. I'll talk and listen in future."

Michael kissed her on the mouth to stop her talking. It was a real kiss—a romantic kiss, a manly kiss. He hadn't done that for quite a while. Cathi felt a frisson of that old passion.

"Oh my, Mr. Grant."

"Mom, Dad—seriously? " Stacy walked into the kitchen. "Can we rent another movie? That one's over, and Katie wants to know if we can make some popcorn."

Michael grinned at his younger daughter. "Yes, to both your requests." He sat down in one of the kitchen chairs and pulled Cathi onto his lap. "Your mother and I will be in here drinking champagne if you're looking for us."

Epilogue
A Valentine's Day Visit

Jessie and Ely were sitting in Noreen's kitchen.

"I can't believe how much stuff we've moved. This was not how I planned spending my Valentine's Day." Jessie rolled her shoulders, trying to get them to relax. "I'm exhausted."

"You're exhausted? Try doing it pregnant," Ely said.

"Doing what? You supervised!"

"And I made the tea. Is Noreen almost finished packing yet? How many cases is she taking?" Ely reached over from where she was sitting and rubbed Jessie's back. "You needed the break from studying anyway. You work too hard."

Noreen walked into the kitchen. "That was a lot more work than I realized. Sorry about that, girls, but I needed a good spring clean."

Ely looked up. "Well, you sure did that. Spring cleaning on steroids, I'd say. You're only going on a vacation, Noreen. You'll be back in what? Six weeks? From the blitz you did, it looks like you'll be gone for years."

Jessie was watching Noreen's face. The woman had grown so much stronger and more vibrant in the last few months. The change was remarkable. The change was Hugo Hendrix. Sure, having young people around helped, but he was the magic ingredient in the older woman's life. He had given her a reason to live again. She had even started taking her medication because Hugo supervised it, and now her mind was a lot clearer and she seemed so much happier.

"It's the middle of February and we're still two feet deep in snow. I'm thinking I might stay away for longer than planned," she said, looking at her two lodgers.

"I told you." Jessie gave Ely gentle nudge. "She's deserting us."

Ely whined like a baby. "Waghh, I need you, Noreen. You're like the mother I never had."

Noreen laughed. "Such melodrama. I'm well acquainted with your mother from talking to her on the phone, and you know as well as I do she's aching for you to move home."

Ely shook her head. "I may be moving back to South Carolina this summer, but I'm sure not moving home."

"Any progress on the house hunting?" Jessie stood up. "Who wants a coffee?"

Noreen shook her head and so did Ely. "No thanks to the coffee, J, and we won't worry about a house until Josh is out of school. I got a few months before this little monster arrives, but as soon as Josh finishes his last exam, we'll head south and find something nice for the three of us in Charleston—somewhere near the university, I guess."

Noreen sat. "How is his college transfer going?"

"All very smooth, thanks. He's going to slip into South Carolina life real easy while I run my new little business and little family from home. It's gonna be fine."

"It'll be hard, too, love. Don't kid yourself." Noreen's tone was gentle.

"Not as hard as sticking around here could be," Jessie said, taking out the tin of treats and putting them on the table.

Ely opened the tin and started on a cookie. "Are you still worried about the fire department coming after my man and his friends? J, if I told you once, I told you a million times—they were happy to see Dan the Pan gettin' his hide whipped."

Noreen nodded. "I'm delighted Josh and his football friends gave that brute a good going over. He needed to be taught a lesson, but I do feel sorry for his wife."

Jessie shook her head and took a cookie. "Actually, I bumped into her in Babies 'R' Us recently. I couldn't believe it was her, but she recognized me so I had to stop and talk. I apologized and explained that I didn't know Dan was married. She was surprisingly calm about the whole thing. In fact, she had quite a bit of news. Turns out she has a new man in her life and she's moved in with him. You won't believe this, but it's another firefighter! What is it with women and boys in uniform? She also told me Dan got caught in bed with his boss's wife. He's probably going to have to leave Newton."

Ely's eyes widened. "You never told me that."

"You never asked!"

"What were you doing in Babies 'R' Us anyway?"

This time Jessie smiled. "Can't a godmother window-shop?"

Ely seemed happy with this and put the lid back on the treat tin. "Take these bad boys away from me." She stood up and stretched. "I am looking forward to moving down south again. I'll have Josh nearby and Mom and Aunt Marybeth. You'd think she's having the baby she's so excited. They can watch Josh Jr. while I'm fighting with Bull over what way to take the business."

Jessie laughed. "I still can't believe you went to Necker Island with Josh, enjoyed all that hospitality, and then turned Richard Worthington down in favor of your father."

Ely winked at her friend "You know for us Briskins, at the end of the day, business is a family affair." She smirked. "Besides, I know I can handle Daddy. I'm not sure I could bend Mr. Worthington to my will so easy."

Noreen focused on Jessie. "And you? Will you be okay without me?"

Jessie knew her landlady was being sincere. The older woman had come into their lives at a time they had very much needed her. She sat down again, reached out across the table, and took Noreen's hands.

"I'll miss you more than you know, but I'm so happy for you and Hugo. I'll just bury myself in my books anyway. May is coming in so fast—I can't believe how quick the year flew by."

"And they only get faster," Noreen said with resignation. "Like Ely here always says, you only got one life."

They all joined in for the chorus. "You gotta live it!"

Jessie went back to making the coffee.

"I don't want you to go home, Jessie." Ely pouted.

"Bruce Wiswall sure does." Noreen winked at Jessie.

She couldn't hide her smile. "He does, and I miss him, too." She brought her mug to the table.

"Life moves on, Ely. Jessie needs to be in London. You need to get yourself and Josh settled in Charleston before that baby arrives, and I need to have some fun down in the Caribbean."

"Do you think Rusty's gonna like it down there?"

Noreen chuckled. "He'll love it. Hugo tells me he has a lovely little terrier. She's a Tibetan zye."

"I never heard of them."

"No, I think she's a new breed, but if Rusty gets his way with her, you know what will happen?"

"We'll have Tibetan bulls?" Ely asked.

"No." Noreen laughed. "He'll have a bullzye, get it? A bull's-eye!"

They all laughed.

"Has Cathi forgiven you yet?" Jessie asked, but Noreen raised her hands in the air.

"It wasn't my fault if she let her little shih tzu run wild with Rusty. He's an old dog and a smooth operator. Those little pups will be landing any day now. It takes about two months for a shih tzu to carry their litter."

"Lucky bitch," Ely said, rubbing her growing stomach.

A car horn beeped outside. "That'll be Hugo." Noreen sprang to her feet, and the girls followed her out to the hall. She had her suitcases ready to go, along with her purse and jacket. "Right, girls, I'm off. I have my passport and money, tablets and Rusty. Yes, I think that's everything." She ticked off her holiday list of essentials, and then she turned to the girls. "Take care of each other. I'll be back before you both head your separate ways, but just in case I stay down in the Caribbean, give me an extra special hug."

Jessie and Ely were sad to see Hugo whisk their landlady and Rusty away to sunnier places. They stood on the front porch and waved as the car drove out of sight.

"I'll really miss her," Ely said.

"Are you crying?" Jessie wrapped her arm around Ely's shoulders. "You can phone her anytime, and she'll be back in a few months. She's already agreed to visit you when you're settled."

"I know, it's just my hormones. Don't mind me."

"Who is that?" Jessie was distracted by a taxi pulling up outside the Sanchez house. She hadn't spoken to Michael or Cathi Grant since they'd moved in.

Ely swung around to look at the car. "Hey, it's the Sanchez family. Look, it's Rick, Maria, and the kids." She waved at them as they got out of the car. "That'll make a nice Valentine's Day visit."

Maria was anxious as hell, which she knew was nuts. This was her house, but another family lived there. Maybe Cathi had changed it to her tastes. She felt like a stranger on Crystal Lake Lane, but she had agreed to come. They had to finish up the move and sort things out.

"You okay?" Ricky asked.

She forced a smile. "Yeah, just a little nervous."

All of the Grants were at the front door of number seven to greet them. Michael bear-hugged Rick. Cody barely acknowledged the girls before tearing off to visit Todd. Katie and Stacy wanted to take Alice up to play in her old room. Then Cathi and Maria were left alone—standing, staring at each other.

"I really have to start with I'm sorry," Cathi said as soon as the men had moved into the house and out of earshot.

Maria was relieved to hear that. "I let you down, too."

"Come in. I feel weird saying that to you. This is your house."

They walked into the living room together.

"Can I get you anything?"

Maria looked at the woman who was once her best friend. The only thing she really wanted was to resolve this damn mess. It was time to talk.

"What happened to us, Cathi?"

That was enough to make Cathi sit. She looked close to tears instantly. "I don't know. I'm sorry. I was so wrapped up in my own troubles I didn't see how much pain you and Rick were in. I was jealous of you."

Maria sat on the sofa, creating a little distance from herself and her old friend. "Me? You're the one with the perfect kids, husband, and life."

Cathi looked around the room. "It was this damn house, this road. I just wanted what you had, and your life looked so amazing from the outside.

You're still so sexy, Maria, and you don't even see it."

"I'm about thirty pounds heavier than you."

"Yeah, fifteen on each breast." Cathi crossed her arms over her small chest.

Maria laughed and relaxed a bit more. She looked down at the sofa she was sitting on. It was hers. Funny how that didn't seem to matter anymore. "I'm sorry I wasn't there when you were going through whatever that was at Christmastime."

"Faking the pregnancy?" Cathi closed her eyes tight for a second. "What the hell was I thinking?"

"What happened with the other house anyway?"

"The damage was covered by insurance, but the landlord kicked us out. We—that is, *I*—was a bad tenant. Maria, are you sure you're good with us —that is, me—living here?"

Maria thought about lying but decided against it. She forced herself to look at Cathi. "I'll be honest. I was fine with Michael being here, but I freaked when I heard you wanted to move in with the kids. But then Rick pointed out that if you guys rented it, we could get something nice in Puerto Rico. Plus, if you didn't take it, there was a good chance we'd be stuck with an empty house for months. It made sense, so I cooled down."

"Thanks, Maria, but I have to tell you, the neighborhood isn't half as much fun now that you're gone."

Maria sat back in the sofa. "Rick told me you had a pretty bad flood in January."

Cathi mirrored her friend's action in the armchair, sitting right back, too. "Oh, wow. There was just so much rain, and water began to gather on top of the ice. Then it started to move up the yard toward the house. It wasn't dangerous, like we didn't have to evacuate, but I was terrified for everything on the ground level."

"It didn't come in?"

"No, but it was close."

"How many times did I tell you Crystal Lake Lane has terrible flooding? You wouldn't listen to me."

Cathi sat forward again. "I know. I've been quite the fool. Look, please let me get you a cup of coffee."

"In a minute, Cathi. It's great that we're clearing the air. First tell me about you and Michael. Are you guys getting through it?"

Cathi fiddled with the arm of the chair. "We're in counseling. I'm seeing a therapist to help me work out what my whole social-climbing thing was about. My shrink says it's pandemic—who knew?" She wiped the leather as if she'd fixed the problem. "Michael and I have agreed he's going to take a year off to write his book. We're going to rent this house from you guys, if that's okay. Then we'll see how his book goes. If he's a success, we can buy something around here, and if it doesn't succeed, we'll move. Whatever he wants."

Maria was surprised. "Hey, you've gone from one extreme to the other, Cathi. What you want matters, too."

She looked unsure. "No, I think I'll do it his way for a few years and see where that takes us. I think I owe him."

"Okay, now you're making me feel bad. I made Ricky give up everything he loves to come live in Puerto Rico."

Cathi shook her head. "You're all he loves, Maria. Michael tells me Rick told him it's the best decision he's ever made. He loves the pace of life down there. He sees more of you and the kids, I hear, and all that sun."

Maria sat forward now, too. They were almost done. "I think life is better down there, but I don't think it would suit you."

"Oh, you never know. You look better than ever. What's your secret?"

Maria thought of what her mother always said to her about the magic of Puerto Rico. "Local ingredients," she said, understanding it now for the first time.

Fifi waddled into the room, her swollen belly almost touching the floor.

Maria gaped at Cathi, mouth open and wide-eyed.

"Yes, she's pregnant, but Orga has been watching over her like an old aunt. I love that dog. We'd be happy to keep her if you wanted. The girls and Michael adore Orga. She has so much more personality than this prima donna."

Maria stood. "It's the one issue Cody's had with the move. He misses that darn dog so much. We have to take her with us."

Cathi got up, too. "It was Rusty, Noreen's bulldog, that got to Fifi. Now we think she's gonna have a litter of bull-shits."

Both women guffawed, and Maria knew they were heading back to being friends.

"Funny thing is, everyone in Katie's class wants one. Bull-shits are the new must-have!"

Maria bent down to tickle Fifi's swollen tummy. "Oh, I still see some of the old irrepressible Cathi in there just begging to get out."

Cathi winked. "What can I say? You can't teach an old dog new tricks. Anyway, Rusty has gone off with Noreen on a fabulous cruise in the Caribbean and then down to her new boyfriend's house in Jamaica."

Maria stood again and opened her arms. "Come here and give me a hug, *chica*. I'm so glad to see you again."

With peace restored, the women worked their way through the house to figure what was moving to Puerto Rico and what was going to charity. All of Cathi's belongings were in storage and would be moved into number seven once the Sanchez family had completed their move. Ricky was taking his red sports car, and Maria wanted her fur.

"It's going to be far too warm where you're going for a fur." Ricky sounded surprised.

"I have an idea. I gotta go out somewhere, but I'll be back soon," Maria said and walked out of the house.

She was nervous all over again, but Maria felt sure she had to do this. It was still so cold in Newton. There was a thick blanket of snow on the yard. The paths were cleared, so she walked up to Noreen Palmer's front door with the fur draped around her shoulders. When she rang the doorbell, Jessie answered.

"Mrs. Sanchez, I mean, Maria! Hi, it's nice to see you. Won't you come in?"

Maria entered the hall and followed Jessie to the front room where she had sat with Noreen the day Cathi had tried to talk the old lady out of her house.

"I came come to apologize, Jessie," Maria said. "The last time I saw you, at Cathi's party, I accused my husband of fooling around with you. I know now that wasn't the case."

Jessie looked uncomfortable. "Don't mention it. Please, sit down."

Maria did as she was told but kept talking. "No, I feel I must. You did nothing wrong. You've always been an absolute professional with me. You cared for my children and never let me down, but I didn't afford you the same courtesy. I was very rude and I'm sorry. The truth is I was going through my own stuff, and you just landed in my path around the same time."

Jessie looked straight at Maria now. She raised her hands in the air.

"Hey, we all make mistakes. Really, it's no biggie." She sat in Noreen's favorite chair. "You're living in Puerto Rico now? Noreen told me."

Maria laughed. "It's where I belong. What about you? Still plan to go back to the UK or have your plans changed?"

Jessie's smile widened, and she blushed a little. "Um, I'm going home. I've met somebody. It's still early, but we've a lot in common."

"That's a good place to start." She rose to her feet again. "So I'm forgiven?"

"Sure."

Maria took off her coat and handed it to Jessie. "Here, take this. It's a lot colder in England than it is in Puerto Rico."

Jessie looked stunned. "I can't take this."

"Please do. It would make me feel a lot better. I know that money is tight at home. I don't need it. To be honest, it represents everything I'm leaving behind, but it's still a beautiful coat. Sell it, if you like. Or take it and remember your good times in Newton, not the crazy neighbors you had."

"Oh, come on!" Jessie smiled. "The Newton neighbors are what made the adventure such fun. I'll really miss you guys."

Maria draped the fur coat over Jessie's shoulders. "Suits you." She gave a self-satisfied nod.

Jessie was wide-eyed admiring it. "Are you sure about this? It feels very heavy. I'm guessing it cost quite a lot."

Maria swatted the idea way and headed out into the hall again.

"I still have the same e-mail. Come visit us in Puerto Rico anytime."

"I think I'd like that," Jessie said, and Maria knew she meant it.

Maria left Noreen's house feeling like a weight had been lifted from her shoulders, and it wasn't just the fur. She walked down the snow-cleared path of number nine and along the sidewalk of Crystal Lake Lane. Just as she was about to head into her old house, Cathi opened her front door. Maybe she had seen Maria coming, or perhaps she saw the large black Mercedes that pulled up next to the house. A man got out and stopped Maria to ask for directions.

"Hullo. I wonder, can you tell me which of these houses is Noreen Palmer's?"

Maria studied his face—he looked familiar, but she couldn't place him. He wasn't very tall, and his frame was small. He had to be an old friend of Noreen's.

She pointed toward Noreen's. "That's it, but you've just missed her. She's gone on vacation—a cruise in the Caribbean, I think, and then she's going to one of the islands."

"Oh? You don't know which island, do you?"

"No, but I think my friend here, Cathi, does. Are you a friend of Noreen's?"

Cathi was coming up the pathway with the determination of a snowdrop in springtime.

"You could say that." He smiled, and then Maria recognized him. "I was in town, and I just thought I'd surprise her with a Valentine's Day visit."

"Oh my God," she said. "You're Mick Wolf!"

The End (for now)

Preview of *Lincoln Ladies,* Book 3 in the *New England* Trilogy Coming in 2014

Kate Kavanagh was happy raising her daughter and focusing on work, but when the girl moves to New York for a job and ends up moving in with her philandering father, Kate wonders if her time was well spent.

Kate's best friend, **Madeline Stein**, has been a career girl all her life. As a single mom, her job defined her, so when she loses it, Maddy needs a total rethink.

Portia Kavanagh hits New York with a bang. She's so hungry for adventure, she bites off more of the Big Apple than she intended. Portia retreats to what she thinks is the sanctuary of her father's home only to find she's not the only one in the family with an overactive appetite.

Kate and Maddy find themselves leaving their lovely hometown for the lush and very romantic hills of Tuscany, Italy. However, blue skies, rich wine, and charming Italians bring on a whole new world that the ladies must maneuver with the grace and style of a Lincoln Lady. Portia's high-octane life in Manhattan comes at a price, too. Out of the millions of men she could have, she chooses the only one she's meant to avoid. Her quandary: has she made a mistake of epic proportions or found the one in a million?

This is a story of three fantastic women on a journey of self-discovery. With more ups and downs than a Florentine fairground, the ladies survive love, loss, and fresh pasta by laughing at life and using a doggy bag. There are lots of thrills and spills along the way, but in the end it's all about friendship, attitude, and walking off all that fabulous food. Come on the adventure and enjoy the ride with the lovely **Lincoln Ladies**.

Dear Book Club friends,

I really hope you enjoy reading *Newton Neighbors* as much as I did writing it. As with my last book, *Wellesley Wives*, my aim was to entertain you and make you laugh at life. Did I succeed?

I was conscious of the possible discussions and debate it could spark. So, again for your entertainment (and to get you chatting!), I've included ten book club questions. Of course, there are no right or wrong answers, because all points of view are valid, but I'll post my own personal answers to the questions on my website, www.suzyduffybooks.com. It might be interesting to check out if we have the same opinions or not. Either way, it's just for fun.

Happy reading,

Lots of love, Suzy

Book Club Questions—Warning PLOT SPOILERS lurk here.
1.   What was the theme/essence of Newton Neighbors?
2.   Is there such thing as a babysitter who is just too darn good-looking?
3.   Out of Maria, Cathi, Ely, Jessie, and Noreen: Which character can you best relate to? How would you have handled her predicament? Have you or anyone you know gone through some of these situations? Which ones? How did they deal with it?
4.   Do you think Jessie and Josh were right to tell Ely what they thought of her business idea? (They thought it would fail.) Should they have kept their negative opinions to themselves? Have you been in a similar position?
5.   Maria gradually became complicit in all of Cathi's crazy plans. At what point do you think she should have stood up to her? When Cathi first approached Noreen in her house? When she started to sell her own house behind Michael's back? When she faked the pregnancy? Never?
6.   Should Jessie have told Dan's wife, Sadie, what he was up to?
7.   Would you go to a Botox and Bollinger party? Would you like a bull-shit dog?
8.   Should Ely have gone with Richard Worthington or her dad?
9.   Was Maria right to take Ricky back and was Michael right to take Cathi back? Do they remind you of someone you know? How and why?
10.   Do you think Noreen's behavior was appropriate or, at eighty years, should she be slowing down, living life at a slower pace?

Acknowledgments

I love this bit because there are so many people involved in getting a book up and out and even more who help bring that book to a larger audience, so brace yourself. Here are movers and shakers of the moment! At No. 1, I want to say . . . Dianne O'Sullivan-Gard, thank you!

Thanks also to my Literary Agent, David Forrer in Inkwell Management, NY, and the blessing in my life—Lyndsey Blessing in Foreign Rights! At TWCS, thanks to Amanda Hayward, Cindy Bidwell, Lea Dimovski. Thanks to Elyse Evans, an amazing editor, and Jen Matera (my Sandy sister!). Thanks to the incredibly patient Jenn McGuire, who guides me through all things techno, and a BIG thank you to my dear friend and mentor, Jenny Pedroza. Thanks to Christa Beebe and DJ Gann (my Sydney sister!). In New Zealand, thank you Andrea McKay and the rest of the team. What a team. In Canada, thanks to super Sarah Miniaci at Smith Publicity and my new friends at Cappelen Damm Publishing—Norway.

Of course, I want to thank the fabulous women of Wellesley and beyond, who were such a support launching *Wellesley Wives*. I expect no less for *Newton Neighbors*! Special mention to The Wellesley Book Shop and Wellesley Library—thank you. Hi, if you follow me on Twitter and Facebook. I love our cyber community. Thanks for your "likes," RTs, and "shares." If you're not already here, join the party on www.facebook.com/Suzyduffybooks1.

Thank YOU for buying my book. 10% of my royalties goes to The Friends of Boston's Homeless, so we're doing good, here—romantic comedy with a cause! Check out www.fobh.org for more.

Thanks to my dearest Michael, Alannah, Saskia, Lily, Zola, Hugo, all the Duffys and Higgins—for letting me do what I do. I love you.

About the Author

Suzy Duffy is an international and #1 bestselling author of romantic comedy (rom com). She's Irish but lives in Boston with her husband, five children and their dog (Hogan). She's writing a New England Trilogy—**Wellesley Wives, Newton Neighbors, and Lincoln Ladies**—and 10% of her royalties goes to www.fobh.org.

Other than this, Suzy was a national radio DJ and TV presenter (& had great fun!) in Ireland before she started writing. She's also been an interpreter in the United Nations, Geneva (yawn), a water ski instructor in Crete, Greece (yes!), and a corn cutter in the south of France (until she was fired).

Her ambition is to lose seven pounds (not realistic) and write a book a year for the next forty years (more realistic). Then she'll have a rethink.

Connect with her on www.suzyduffybooks.com.

Like her on www.facebook.com/Suzyduffybooks1.

Follow her on twitter.com/suzyduffybooks.

Follow her on pinterest.com/suzyduffybooks.

Also by Suzy Duffy

 Wellesley Wives - Popsy Power is pretty, popular, and insanely rich. Her husband adores her, and her two daughters are busy producing babies and romping up the corporate ladder—like good little Wellesley Wives. However, what Popsy doesn't know is that her husband and worldly wealth will soon be gone, and as for her daughters... Well, Lily's romping is not restricted to the boardroom, and Rosie finds her pilot-husband flying more than his jet.

Sandra is Popsy's best friend. She has the perfect body, bank balance, and palatial penthouse. As a second wife herself, she should know how husbands wander, but even she is shocked when she discovers where Jack has found his fun . . . When Lily's nasty, little secrets suddenly go public and Rosie finds her husband flying a little too high, it's time to escape.

Popsy and Sandra flee to beautiful, peaceful Ireland. Rosie heads to Mexico, and Lily seeks refuge in the arms of her man. The adventure continues for Popsy and Sandra. Within days, they're almost arrested and killed before finding themselves in a boathouse in Banagher—with jobs! Meanwhile Rosie is diving off the back of a catamaran into the azure-blue of the Caribbean, but she's not sure what's worse—the sharks in the sea or the ones on the beach. Back in Boston, Lily discovers that getting what she wanted was not what she wanted, but unlike her scuba diving sister, surely she's in too deep...

From Banagher to Boston and down to the Caribbean Sea, these four ladies are on a rollercoaster ride through life. Rich, poor, happy, sad, in or out of love—only one thing is certain. Things are is never dull when you're with the Wellesley Wives.